Tipp

Dinuka McKenzie is an Australian writer. She is the winner of the 2020 Banjo Prize, and her writing has been longlisted for the Richell Prize and highly commended in the Australian Crime Writers Association Louie Award. Her short fiction has appeared in the *Dark Deeds Down Under Crime and Thriller Anthology*. Before turning to writing full time, Dinuka worked in the environmental sector. She now volunteers as part of the team behind the Writers Unleashed Festival and lives in Southern Sydney on Dharawal country with her husband, two kids and their pet chicken.

Also by Dinuka McKenzie

Detective Kate Miles

The Torrent
Taken
Tipping Point

TIPPING POINT

DINUKA McKENZIE

First published in Australia in 2024 by HarperCollins*Publishers*

This edition published in the United Kingdom in 2024 by

Canelo
Unit 9, 5th Floor
Cargo Works, 1-2 Hatfields
London SE1 9PG
United Kingdom

A CIP catalogue record for this book is available from the British Library.

Print ISBN 978 1 80436 638 7
Ebook ISBN 978 1 80436 637 0

Look for more great books at www.canelo.co

Printed and bound in Great Britain by Clays Ltd, Elcograf S.p.A.

1

To Scott, Harvey and Edie for seeing all of me

and loving me anyway.

A tiny, furry creature scurries across the forest floor, its eyes attuned to the dark, its body pausing, quivering, testing the air for the scent of predators. There is no moon, and the trees knit together in an inky tangle of branches, leaves and roots. The night air is heavy with an endless summer heat. A thick, suffocating torpor that seems to be waiting for a flame to spark and engulf the whole lot.

The bushland breathes and waits. The cracks that rang through the night air a minute ago have faded, the reverberation of sound absorbed into the atmosphere like it had never been. The cacophony of insects and night-time critters has resumed, indifferent to the momentary interruption of humans and their unfathomable deeds.

On the ground several metres away, a shape lies sprawled across the parched grass, slowly cooling and leaking. A new liquid joining the earth. Iron-red seeping into chocolate-brown. Blood and bone coming home.

1

Tuesday – three weeks to Christmas

Luke Grayling focused his gaze a centimetre to the left of the HR woman's face so it seemed as though he was looking straight at her, but actually he could avoid her expression. The barely supressed contempt and something akin to... excitement, was it?

He concentrated instead on the sweeping cityscape visible through the glass panels that took up an entire wall of the level-22 meeting room. The azure blue of a boutique hotel rooftop pool visible in the distance, along with Hyde Park beyond, surrounded by craning skyscrapers full of their own importance. Sydney, all shiny and bright, living up to its hype in the December heat. He was surprised that this was the meeting room they had chosen. But maybe it was a calculated decision; they had done this before, and the view had proved to be a helpful distraction, something to focus on other than the face of your executioner.

She was speaking again. He had forgotten her name, already. It had slipped in and out of his memory like a fleck of dust, unnoticed. Kylie... Karen... Keira... perhaps? Or maybe something entirely different. Julianne? Edith? Selina? A smile hovered against his cheek muscles. His eyes flickered across to Will, his boss. No, his *former* boss, he reminded himself, and the urge to smile shrivelled and died.

His former manager's expression was glassy. The jovial, *consider me a friend rather than a superior* schtick was a distant memory. He imagined that Will had tried his best, defended him as far as he could. Or maybe he hadn't; Luke would never know. After all, Will's own survival was at stake. In the circumstances, there would be no reference. The company was in full crisis-management mode, and Luke was being dealt with. Expunged and deleted. Before his behaviour could publicly taint or sully the good name of Hull-Hayward Financial. Or worse, for news of the scandal to somehow reach the waiting arms of social media. For now, it had been contained within the auspices of an internal investigation and sealed by a non-disclosure agreement.

The stab of pain in his chest spiked.

Karen-Edith-Selina was laying out the terms of his termination package. His entitlements would be paid, which was something, at least. He would not be allowed to return to his desk; the NDA clauses coming into immediate effect. Following the surrender of his security pass, work mobile and laptop, he would be shown out of the building. Just like in the movies. If he hadn't seen it played out previously during rounds of redundancies, he would have laughed. But now, it was his turn. And he didn't have the excuse of a company downsize. Everyone here knew what this was.

He was being fired.

Afterwards, he ended up in a Surry Hills bar, where he knew his self-pity would go unnoticed and uncommented on. A solid session of trying to drown the acid in his stomach with alcohol had helped little. He needed something stronger; something to make him forget, to take away the incessant heat of anxiety. The eccys were a mistake. Cut with God only knew what, they hardly gave him a buzz, leading to a wholly unsatisfactory encounter in a darkened corridor in a club in Darlinghurst. She'd made a right meal of it. Fucking teeth and all. The eccys had made him as hard as a horse, but coming quickly was another matter. And the sound of her choking, lock-jawed gurgling was distracting as fuck.

On the train ride home, he checked his messages, ignoring the handful of texts from his now ex-colleagues; the rumour mill was gaining momentum. One WhatsApp message he hesitated over, reading it a couple of times before deleting it. Two missed calls from Kate. He raised his phone to his ear to listen to his sister's voicemail.

'Hey, Luke, not sure if you've heard… the funeral is this Thursday.'

Something stirred within him as he listened to Kate's words. A memory of himself as a young boy, with his two best friends. Riding their bikes to school, playing endless rounds of handball at lunchtime, hanging out on the weekends doing nothing at all. Grabbing each other in headlocks and laughing like drains. Detention and wagging school. Sneaking beers, and nights spent around a bonfire on the beach sharing a spliff. Best mates all the way from primary school and into their teenage years. They had been inseparable. Friends for life, until they weren't.

Two of them had ventured as far away from Esserton as they could: Brisbane and Sydney. One had stayed on in Esserton, though not by choice.

'…I know it's late notice and everything, but I think his dad would like to see you, if you can make it. Also, if you do want to stay on for a couple of days, I can maybe organise a meal with Dad and Caleb on the weekend? No pressure. Only if you have the time. Anyway, hope everything's okay with y—'

The voicemail had finally cut off his sister's long-winded message.

Luke leaned his head against the train carriage, the suburbs of Sydney flashing past outside the darkened window. Did he want to go back and poke around in the sediment of his past? For a moment, the locked drawer in his mind, where he had shoved all Esserton-related memories, his childhood, his mother, his schoolmates, had cracked open, the mess slipping out. Things he hadn't thought of in years. Things he had tried to forget.

He focused on the second part of his sister's message. An awkward attempt at a family reunion. He really should make some effort there. *Fuck it.* It wasn't like he would be tied up at work. His diary was entirely clear.

2

Thursday

The congregation fidgeted and rustled softly, as the two pedestal fans up the front did little to cool the damp skin and heated brows of the gathered mourners. The chapel was stifling in the summer heat; the first week of December in the Northern Rivers. A broken air conditioner, the apologetic usher had informed them earlier. At the lectern, the funeral celebrant soldiered on, speaking both to the congregation and the phone-tripod setup, which was livestreaming the service to interstate and overseas mourners who had not been able to attend in person.

A photo slideshow was running on repeat on the flat screen TV behind the celebrant, cataloguing half a life, as if someone had forgotten to stitch the second half of the video together. Images flashed. A chubby baby asleep in the crook of his father's arms, a fair-haired child blowing the candles on his birthday cake, slightly older versions of the same child pictured next to different homemade cakes decorated to look like a car, a farm-yard, a football. The child posing with an oversized backpack on his first day of school, a series of school photos and pictures of sports carnivals. A grungy teenager in a garage band, multiple photos of the young man now an adult with work colleagues, friends and on holiday, the years depicted by changes to hair-style, long and shaggy then shorter and more sculpted. And then back to the baby photos.

It was the absences that gave it away. There were no pictures of the man as a groom on his wedding day, or as a dad holding his firstborn, the multitude of anniversaries and years, the real grist of life that would never be photographed or documented.

'We are here to celebrate the life of Anthony Reed, beloved son, nephew and grandson… Taken too early from his friends and family at just thirty-five.'

Kate's eyes slid to a framed image of the laughing, sandy-haired man, balanced on top of the closed casket, draped in floral bouquets. The head of the casket was covered with the maroon, blue and gold flag of his favourite footy team. The cheeky schoolboy who had been one of her younger brother's best friends was traceable in the lopsided grin fixed forever to the image.

Ant Reed, Marcus Rowntree and her brother, Luke. Their Milo-streaked faces at her mother's kitchen table after school, their lanky teenage bodies taking over the TV room, and their nervous excitement posing for Year Twelve formal photos. She had seen the three boys grow up together, but she had barely a clue about how their lives had fared in the past few years, least of all her own brother's. Only surface news. Nothing that mattered. A yearning for a version of the past that she could never get back settled on her.

Her eyes moved to the far corner of the chapel, where she knew Luke was holed up. Kate had seen him sneaking in wearing a rumpled long-sleeved shirt and dress pants, just before the service had begun. He looked like he hadn't slept for days. He needed a shave, and had obviously hand-combed his dark hair into place. For all that, knowing Luke, he would probably end up with a date by the end of the service.

A new speaker was now at the lectern. One of Ant's friends, a fellow welfare worker from Brisbane, where Ant had lived and worked for the past decade, and where he had ultimately died. The man was red-faced and overdressed in a suit that was too hot for the room.

'Ant was a big softy at heart. He believed in people. He saw the good in them no matter what. He never, ever gave up on his friends. Whatever mistakes or whatever pain they were in, he made a point of standing by them. He was just so bloody good at looking after everyone else, he didn't leave enough in the tank for himself.' His voice cracked. 'I'm so sorry, mate. I should have seen that you were hurting. I should have realised.' He crumpled his notes and stumbled from the podium, tears streaming and mingling with sweat.

In the front row, Kate could hear the muffled sobs of Frank, Ant's father, cowed and bewildered by grief, being comforted by a family member – a broad, kindly woman with short, utilitarian hair. The women in the family, Ant's many aunts, had descended to help Frank with the funeral arrangements and generally take charge of the beleaguered widower.

Suicides were the worst. There was very rarely any closure for the family and those left behind ended up mired in survivor's guilt, feeling like they should have known, should have noticed something. With endless questions left unanswered, it was a no-win situation for all involved.

The death of one of their own had galvanised the town. So many of Ant's old schoolmates were here. She was glad that Luke had made the effort. In this crowd, his absence would have been noticed, despite Kate making an appearance on behalf of their family. Surveying the congregation, she placed some of the faces; others were only brief flashes of almost-recognition. A strange game of trying to discern the ghostly outlines of childhood acquaintances in unfamiliar adult bodies.

Another funeral packed with mourners rose in her mind. She had hoped to keep the memories at bay, giving them a wide berth as if from a chained feral dog. But the chapel brought them all back. They were in the same space that Kate and her family had farewelled her own mother some six years ago, when she had finally succumbed to the disease that was riddling her flesh, consuming her from the inside out. It was her brother's grief, yawning and unfillable, that she remembered, inconsolable next to her father's stoic wooden mask and her own utter exhaustion. Then and now, it had felt like a dream. Her every nerve-ending hypersensitive to each look of pity shunted her way, to the light and the air itself, which had felt too heavy on her skin and in her lungs. Kate had willed herself to sit at the pew and not run away. She had barely taken in the service that she'd spent days organising. Her brother and father, both devastated in different ways, had not been equal to the task, so she had stepped in, handling the funeral arrangements, glad for the admin of death to occupy her mind. It was only weeks and months later that the true weight of the day had hit her.

She pulled her mind back to the service, which was ending; the celebrant making her final remarks and inviting mourners to join the family at the Royal Hotel for refreshments. A simple ceremony brought to a close without fuss. Kate rose with the crowd. She had taken the afternoon off from work and there were no calls on her time. She spotted her brother in between the bobbing heads of the throng, and made for his disappearing back.

3

'Luke.' She rose on tiptoes to hug her brother, tightly. 'You all right?'

He grimaced. 'Not sure I've taken it in properly, to be honest. Ant is the last person I would have expected to do that. But then, what would I know. It's been so long since I've seen him.' He took a deep pull of his beer.

Kate didn't reply. Luke was right, you couldn't presume to know a person whom you'd hardly seen since high school. It was impossible to discern the vagaries of a human soul and the demons people carried.

'Have you spoken to Frank? The poor bloke. What a head-fuck.'

'Not yet,' Kate replied. 'I wanted to give him some space. He looks completely overwhelmed.'

They both gazed across to the far side of the room, where Frank Reed sat at a table, his mobility aid tucked nearby, a cup of tea and an untouched plate of sandwiches in front of him. He was being pressed upon by people from all sides, who had arrived straight from the chapel to the function room designated by the Royal for the wake. Mourners eager to do their duty by the family, before turning with relief to attend to their parched throats and growling stomachs.

'We'll see him at the end. Let him have a couple of drinks first.'

'Do you think he'll stay on in town?'

Kate sighed. 'No idea.'

Frank's wife had passed away when Ant was only a toddler, and it had always been Frank and Ant against the world. Now, for all intents and purposes, he was alone.

'One of his sisters will probably take him in,' she said. 'But who knows. He's stubborn. He won't want to move away from Esserton.'

Kate glanced at her brother. 'What about you? Are you heading back tonight, or staying on for a bit?' She had rung Luke earlier in the week to tell him about Ant's funeral, but he'd never returned her call. While it was a relief to have him here, she still had no idea of his plans.

'Yeah, I might hang around for a week or so maybe.'

'Oh, that's great. It's good your work is being so flexible.'

He didn't reply, burying himself in his schooner.

'So, I'll go ahead and organise a lunch for Saturday?'

'Yeah, why not. I guess I'll have to meet the happy couple sooner or later.'

'You'll like him. Caleb is honestly the best thing that's happened to Dad in years.'

Luke made a noncommittal reply, once more concentrating on his drink.

'Where are you staying, by the way? You're more than welcome at ours. You can have Archie's room, or Geoff can set up the sofa bed in the lounge room—'

'It's all good, I've booked into the Arms. Thought it would be easier all round.'

Kate nodded. The River Arms Hotel was a renovated heritage pub on the banks of the Tweed. Of course, her brother would prefer his privacy and the chance to stay out till all hours. He had chosen the right accommodation for that.

'Luke! Luke Grayling. I thought it was you. What's it been like, six, seven years? Fuck, look at you, bro. You haven't changed a bit. Still a fucking scruff nut, eh?'

A wide-set bear of a man barrelled into Luke, gripping him in an embrace. He had the look of a once-handsome man gone to seed. Marcus Rowntree, the son of Eric Harrington, an actor of some renown who hadn't quite reached the heights of Hollywood but had still made the rounds of Australian TV. Kate saw traces of his father's famous good looks in Marcus's tired eyes and rough, bearded face. He wore a thinner version of the famous smile that had made Eric Harrington a household name. He was like a blurred imprint of his father; a smudged facsimile of the real thing.

Back in high school, Kate recalled, Marcus had held ambitions in that direction, too, but they had never amounted to anything. There had been an uncredited walk-on role in an episode of *Neighbours* (man number two in bar), a couple of bit parts in a commercial for a soft drink, and a few lines in a young adult show, but his acting career, such as it was, had fizzled out before it had begun, never in the same league as his celebrity father, whose genes he shared but not his surname.

'I think the last time I saw you was at your mum's funeral, wasn't it? Fuck, man, how have you been?'

Kate met Luke's eyes over Marcus's shoulder. He had never been one for tact.

'Hey, Marcus, I'm good, man. How are Fi and the kids?'

'Ah, me and Fi, that didn't work out. You know how it is. She and the kids are down Uki way now.'

'Shit, mate. I'm sorry. I didn't know.'

'How would ya, mate? You never visit us anymore. Big-city boy now, eh? Too good for us.' He ruffled Luke's hair, only half joking, an undercurrent snapping behind his humour.

Luke laughed, trying to move the conversation on. 'So, how old are the kids now?'

'Teddy's eight and Jasper's six, would you believe it? I see them every other weekend, but the rest of the time it's all for me, brother.' He grinned, making a hang-loose sign with his hand. 'And how have you been, Kate?' he asked, his dark ringlets swinging as he turned to her. 'Big police chick, now, eh? I keep seeing you on TV... On all those press conferences and shit.

Better watch my p's and q's in front of you, eh?' He cackled at his own joke.

'It's good to see you, Marcus. I'll let you two catch up,' Kate said with a smile. Even as kids, Marcus had been the least likeable of the trio. Always trying just a tad too hard.

Kate moved away. She had clocked one of her own friends standing in line at the bar. Sarah Osmond was another graduate of Esserton High who seemed to have inherited a life of hard graft and heartbreak. While Kate in her early twenties had been pursuing a police career down south, Sarah had remained in Esserton saddled with caring for her sick, single mother, and getting her younger sister through her final years of high school and on to university in Brisbane. Their mother had passed away when Nadine, the younger Osmond sister, had been a year into her marketing degree. And then there had been the body-blow of Nadine herself.

'Sarah, I wasn't sure you'd be here.'

'Kate.' Sarah's smile was sad. 'I had to. Ant was like family.'

Ant's connection to the Osbornes went deeper than blood. Sarah and Ant had together survived Nadine. There were fathoms of water under that bridge. Kate took in the dark circles around Sarah's eyes and the tired lines etched deep into her face that her foundation couldn't quite conceal. Sarah's normally pale complexion, framed by ash-blonde hair that fell in straight sheets to her shoulders, looked almost sickly today, like she was minutes away from collapsing.

Kate took her arm. 'Sarah, you look like hell. Why don't you sit down for a minute and let me get you a drink?' She led her to a chair and returned with two lemonades.

'Drink that, you need the sugar.'

Kate watched her friend as she sipped her drink, relieved to see a blush of colour returning. They had been close in the early years of high school but had drifted apart in the last years before graduation, gravitating into different social cliques. Since Kate's return to Esserton almost four years ago, they had reconnected in fits and grabs. A dinner and movie here, a girls' night out there. The fact that they'd both experienced the loss of a mother to cancer had forged a bond of sorts. Kate had found Sarah easy to talk to about that particular hole in her heart. But she had barely been there for her friend over the last few months. Sarah had been dealing with the fallout of what had happened to her sister, and Kate... she had been navigating her own challenges. The birth of her second child, returning to work and being thrust into one of the biggest cases of her career. She had been entirely preoccupied, with no emotional energy to spare for her friend.

The guilt washed over her now. She should have done more. While Kate had her family, Sarah had hardly anyone to turn to. Her friend had remained determinedly single all these years, and the twin absences of her mother and sister seemed to dominate her life. If not for her work as an aged-care nurse, which required her to visit various elderly clients and retirement homes in the area, Kate doubted whether Sarah would leave her house at all – the same aging, fibro-clad homestead she had once shared with her mother and sister.

'Had you spoken to Ant, recently?'

Sarah wiped her palms on her pants. 'Even after everything with Nadine, he never stopped calling. Every week without fail. We'd spoken only a few days before. And a couple of weeks before that, he dropped in for a meal when he was in town visiting his dad.'

Kate felt her stomach dip. It was Nadine's sister's ex, Ant, who had made a point of checking in with Sarah, rather than Kate herself.

'It turns out, he's the one who needed to be supported,' Sarah continued. 'And no, before you ask me, I had no idea he was thinking of doing that. He sounded the same when he called. A bit sad and trying to be cheerful. But I thought that was because of Nadine. It never occurred to me... I never thought he might be thinking of that. God!' Sarah squeezed her eyes shut and Kate reached for her friend's hand.

'He was such a sweet boy. It's such a waste.'

Kate didn't respond. Who knew what had driven a seemingly healthy and well-adjusted man to take his own life? Ant had died two and a half weeks ago, and Kate had heard the basic details of how it had occurred through her police contacts in Queensland. He had chosen to secure a bag over his head to induce unconsciousness followed by hypoxia, helped along by a healthy dose of sleeping tablets and alcohol to ease his final moments. Clean, painless and relatively quick.

'Mr Reed—' Sarah had sprung to her feet to greet Ant's father, who was shuffling over to them, supporting himself on his mobility walker. Kate caught the whiff of alcohol and the staleness of age. Frank had been in his forties when he had become a father to Ant. Thirty-five years on, he had shrunk into an old man.

'Thanks for coming, my girl.' Frank took Sarah's hand and she hugged him firmly, her height towering over him. The absent ghost of Nadine seemed to hover between them. The girl who should have been here.

'Now, remember what I told you. I've got all Ant's stuff from his apartment just sitting in boxes at the house. I want you to come over and pick something that you'd like to keep as a memento. He would have liked that.'

'I will, Frank, I promise. How about I come around in the morning? I'm not working tomorrow.'

'That's the girl. That would be lovely.'

Frank's rheumy eyes turned to Kate and a claw-like hand reached for her wrist. 'You're Grayling's daughter, aren't you? You're in the police.'

Kate nodded kindly. 'I am.' She offered Frank her condolences and asked if she could pull up a seat for him to sit down.

He waved away her offer. 'I don't need a chair. But I need to speak with you.' A slightly feverish look had come over his face. 'About Ant. This whole thing. Everyone's saying it's suicide, but I know it wasn't.'

Sarah caught Kate's gaze, giving her a rueful look as if to say, *good luck*.

Before Kate could respond, a fresh-faced young woman in a well-cut jumpsuit, obviously a niece or relative of some kind, had reached his side. 'C'mon, Uncle Frank. Don't work yourself up. Mum's looking for you.' She smiled at Kate, whispering, 'Sorry' over his head.

Frank ignored his niece, his eyes trained on Kate. 'Don't you believe a word of it. My son didn't kill himself. He would never do that. You need to make them look at it again. That's not what happened.'

'Mr Reed, the coroner has already come to a decision. Ant died in Brisbane and it's a matter for the Queensland Police. There's nothing I can do.' Kate's tone was gentle, trying to lessen the sting of her words. The man was at his most vulnerable. Logic and reason were less than useless.

'I don't care what they said, you hear me? My Ant wouldn't do that. I know my son. They got it wrong. I'm telling you. They have it all wrong—'

'Sorry, mate, on your left.' One of the waitstaff had bustled past, balancing a tray of sandwiches, heading for the food table. Another couple of staff followed behind with a tray of mini-quiches, party pies and bottles of juice.

The niece used the distraction to press a hand on her uncle's shoulder. 'C'mon, Uncle Frank. Let's go back now. Your tea will be getting cold.'

She nodded to Kate and Sarah and manoeuvred around her uncle, hooking her arm firmly around his.

Kate saw Frank Reed's shoulders sag with resignation. His eyes slid from her face and he allowed himself to be led away, looking small and fragile, like a lost child.

4

Friday

'He's here.'

Kate looked up from her desk and rose to her feet with her colleagues. Like her team, she too was curious about their new station head. A southerner, of course. The Northern Region Command had been at pains to bring in an outsider with no obvious links to the district.

Acting station head, she reminded herself. Esserton had yet to secure a permanent replacement for their departing chief inspector, Andrew Skinner, who had stepped down under a corruption cloud with internal investigations still ongoing. They had been *ongoing* for the past three months, and Kate wouldn't be surprised if they remained that way, spinning their wheels for many more. She had heard through the police grapevine that Skinner had been offered a plum management position with a private security firm in Victoria somewhere. So much for probity.

Leo Esposito. Memories flooded her, both butter-warm and crushed glass.

The door opened to reveal a middle-aged man, easily topping six feet, with the slight stoop of a person used to bending down to accommodate people lower in height. She had forgotten how he did that. He wasn't starting work today, a Friday. This was just a meet and greet, she gathered, so he could get straight to work on Monday. What a trooper.

'Chief Inspector.' Kate held out her hand and found it clasped in a firm, dry handshake. 'Detective Sergeant Kate Miles.'

'Sergeant. It's good to meet you.' Sharp, intelligent eyes appraised her for a couple of seconds before moving on. The look had been so quick, she'd barely had time to register the soft hazel of one and the faded grey of the other. His two-toned eyes. There was a time when those disparate colours had held her in their thrall, laughing, cajoling, pleading. No more. There was no acknowledgement. And she was glad.

Kate watched as he moved on to the next officer in line, Constable Greg Darnley, an Esserton Station stalwart, dependable, loyal and discreet, his sun-worn face and neck covered in freckles, his uniform pressed to angled perfection. The mess with Skinner had rocked Darnley. It had affected them all, but Greg was old school. He still believed in the police as an institution. Of the principles they were all meant to stand for. Service to the public, upholding the law without causing undue harm. Skinner's blatant corruption, essentially in plain sight, had been a hard pill to swallow. The entire station was tainted by association and it didn't sit well with Darnley. She nodded briefly as he caught her eye.

Her gaze swung back to Esposito as he moved down the line, exchanging brief remarks with each officer. The years had marked him. A scattering of salt had joined the rich pepper of his hair, and deep, tired lines seemed etched into his face like fissures in stone. She wondered what changes he had registered on her. Had he known she was stationed here when he accepted the position? Had it made a difference?

He still gave the impression of an overworked accountant, slightly dishevelled and easy to underestimate, though Kate knew he was anything but. Over the years, she had kept tabs on him. Not obsessively, but a check every now and then on the police intranet. He had never been a slouch. Moving up the ranks from a detective sergeant at the Kings Cross Police Area

Command to a chief inspector at Surry Hills PAC, alongside stints at the State Crime Command, Organised Crime Group, and continuing his role as a regular guest instructor at the Police Academy in Goulburn. Those were the highlights. But Kate knew there had also been some close shaves.

There was the shit fight that had gone down in Nowra six years ago. An operation that had been the brainchild of Esposito's team at Organised Crime. The fallout from that particular mess was still playing out in the courts in the form of a compensation claim against the New South Wales Police. Esposito's team, she'd heard, had been put through the wringer during the critical-incident investigation that had followed. And yet here he was, out the other side seemingly unscathed, his career and reputation intact. Without a doubt, he had seen plenty and navigated much more to get to where he was. Kate had the impression of a keen political mind at work behind his unassuming manner.

Kate also noted that he had remained single after his divorce. She would have to begin again with this man. Establish a holding pattern for however long he intended on sticking it out here; until the permanent position was filled.

'Good to meet you all. I realise that the nature of events over the last few months hasn't been easy for this station or for all the staff here. There's been a lot of upheaval and uncertainty, and I know you've been placed under considerable pressure and public scrutiny.' His eyes brushed across the assembled faces. He had a politician's voice. Confident, reasonable and assured; calibrated to persuade, reassure and engender trust.

'My job is not to put any more strain on you by micromanaging or telling you how to suck eggs. You obviously know how to do your jobs, since the station has been running perfectly well without a commander for some months. My job here is to keep the boat afloat until the position of chief inspector is advertised and filled in the new year, and to provide a smooth transition to whoever takes over the role. I'm also happy to lend my knowledge to the team where it can be of use. Please think of me as a resource that you can utilise while I'm here. Although I may be an ignorant outsider, I'll do my level best not to exhibit it too much.'

This earned a murmur of chuckles around the room.

'Let's try to make this as painless as possible for everyone involved.' With a nod, he dismissed them and retired to Skinner's old office. The temporary admin assistant, loaned from the district head office for a few weeks to help sort through Skinner's files and get the office space prepared, trooped in after him.

Kate returned to her cubicle. The desk opposite, which her ex-partner, Josh Ellis, had occupied so recently, sat idle. Kate was still getting used to his absence around the office. It had been a few weeks since his departure, and yet, a part of her expected to see his perfectly groomed features and well-cut suit sauntering along the corridors, like he had just stepped out of a spa session, refreshed and rested. Even now, during case briefings, she half looked for his mocking glance among the assembled faces and anticipated his acerbic asides designed to needle. She was glad he was gone, but a strange muscle memory of their time together remained, as though it was stuck-on mould that she couldn't quite scrub out. He was her worst critic and it was his voice she heard when she second-guessed herself. He had pushed her on every case they had worked on together, daring her at every turn to prove him wrong and making her fight for each victory. She had become a sharper detective in the process, and at times she found herself missing his naked ambition breathing down her neck, willing her to work harder.

Josh had put in for a transfer within weeks of Skinner leaving. It hadn't surprised Kate. Esserton had lost its appeal. Since arriving at the station earlier in the year, Josh had spent months ingratiating himself with Skinner and getting into his good books, seemingly finally working him out. Skinner's sudden fall from grace had left Josh reeling; months of internal manoeuvring with nothing to show for it. He had preferred to move rather than play the game again.

A second empty desk sat a few feet away from Josh's. That of Constable Roby, a young officer she had taken under her wing in the last few months, who was spending some much-deserved leave with his family in South Australia.

'What do you reckon, Sarge?' Constable Vickie Harris had propped herself, uninvited, on the side of her desk. Kate took in the young constable's bob, coloured a deep burgundy, just on the right side of the force's strict dress codes. She noticed that since Josh had left, Vickie had been sidling up to her more often, trying to make conversation. They had never been particularly close. Vickie had been Josh's favourite both at work and at play. But now, Vickie too was having to adjust and rebuild loyalties.

'He seems all right.' Kate kept her response short. She was hardly about to engage in speculation about Esposito with a junior officer.

'You believe what he said about letting us do our own thing. He'd be the first boss in history if that was the case.' As she spoke, Vickie's eyes grazed across the neighbouring desk, empty of Josh's effects but already starting to fill up with old paperwork – an ad-hoc dumping ground for files.

Kate wondered if Josh had remained in touch. Probably not.

'He has to say something, I suppose,' she answered.

'Yeah, I suppose.' Vickie stood up to leave just as abruptly as she had appeared.

Kate's phone beeped with a message.

> David O'Connell. He's a constable at Boondall.
> You can trust him. Also, you owe me a drink.
> Several, in fact.

She smiled. The message was from an old colleague. They had attended the academy together, but Celia had ended up moving to Queensland and now worked in the Domestic and Family Violence Command in Brisbane.

Kate glanced at the mobile number that Celia had forwarded. She was still uncertain whether she would even make use of it. Frank Reed's distress yesterday had been palpable, but it didn't mean she wanted to start messing around with an interstate case outside of her jurisdiction.

Her phone buzzed again.

I trust you're not poking your nose into something you shouldn't be.

She smiled at that. Sometimes her police friends knew her too well.

5

Kate parked the car and sat in silence, not quite ready to leave the comforting cocoon of the family sedan, with its familiar smells of old Happy Meals, spilled juice and biscuit crumbs. The engine ticked over as she took in the building across the road. The River Arms was ablaze with light, red-and-silver tinsel adorning its doorways and balustrading in festive cheer, music and laughter spilling out into the night. It was Friday night at the height of the pre-Christmas, office-party season, and the pub was pumping.

The Arms had always attracted the crowds, with its prime position along the river and extended trading hours; away from the heart of town and the scourge of noise complaints. The imposing building was over seventy years old, and had survived more than its share of floods before the construction of an earth-and-rock levee embankment had finally secured its foundations and beer cellar. The grand old dame had been restored to its former glory, complete with a revamped wrought-iron balcony with sweeping views of the river.

The door to the sports bar opened and a couple of young guns lurched out, the shorter of the two barely making it to the pavement before heaving the night's damage onto the bitumen. His friend's raucous cackle filled the night. 'Fucking piss-weak, bro.'

Resentment swilled in her belly like a bucking wave. It was her night off and her brother had been back home less than two days. And yet, here she was: called in to mop up the aftermath of too much alcohol and testosterone.

She sighed, exiting the car and jogging across the road. Avoiding the sour pool of vomit, she headed inside just as the last strains of a rock anthem abated, switching to something moody and melodic. Young people hung around in loose groups, smelling of beer and sweat and spent excitement, not quite ready to let go of the night.

She spotted the messy mop of Rick Garret, the popular barman and owner of the Arms, well into his fifties, but able to pass for someone decades younger in the right light. He caught her eye and pointed to the doors that led to the back terrace. 'Mitch and Dom are with him.'

She raised a hand in thanks.

At least Rick had had the sense to call her directly rather than ring the station. She knew there would be a favour in it for him at some point. But then, wasn't there always.

She took in the sloping grounds dotted with outdoor tables and chairs, the trees swathed in twinkling fairy lights and spotlighting, creating soft shadows and hidden alcoves. At one of the far tables, she spotted three huddled figures. As she approached, the largest of the trio unwound himself from his seat. Dom, the River Arms' bouncer and head of security, was, as the saying went, built like a brick shithouse, with designer stubble, dreadlocked hair and dark-tanned skin. He could be morose and dour or the life of the party, depending on the time of day you caught him. Kate had come face to face with Dom's temper on more than one occasion over the years, when the police had been called to attend disturbances at the pub. His face cracked into a smile when he saw her, and she breathed a sigh. Dom was in a forgiving mood.

'Your little brother isn't as much of a hotshot as he thinks he is.'

'What happened?' She glanced at the two men who remained seated and recognised Mitch, the bistro chef, still in his work clothes but finished for the night. He nodded briefly in her direction before returning to his cigarette. Next to Mitch sat Luke with his head thrown back, holding what looked like a frozen bag of vegetables to his left eye. A bloody nose was visible underneath the bag of home-brand peas, corn and carrot.

'Bit of a bust-up with one of the lads from the Sub. Big unit with a punch on him. Reckon he would have kept going if I hadn't turned up, heh?' He ruffled Luke's hair and laughed as Luke swatted his hand away.

Kate got the impression that the encounter had been a fairly one-way affair. The Submariner was the local backpackers' place, chock-full in the summer with interstate and overseas tourists. She wondered what beef her brother could have got into with a backpacker. Or was it the usual: too much to drink, a look or word taken the wrong way, sparking into senseless violence? The tedious bread-and-butter of police work on any given weekend.

'Any injuries to the other bloke?'

'Nah, I don't reckon. Just some lads letting off steam, you know. Nothing serious.' Dom winked at Kate. 'I'll leave you to it, then.'

Kate turned to her brother. 'Ready?'

Luke grimaced and stood up, holding out the packet of veg, now semi-defrosted and soggy, to Mitch. Kate could see swelling around his cheek and temple. By tomorrow morning, it would be a perfect black eye.

'Nah, mate, it's all yours. On the house,' Mitch said.

Luke followed Kate without a word.

-

'So, are you going to tell me what happened?' They were in her car, gliding past silent, sleeping houses.

He'd agreed to stay the night at hers rather than back at his accommodation, mainly to get her off his back, she suspected. He would have to be there in the morning for their family get-together, anyhow. And this way, she could keep tabs on him and make sure he turned up for lunch.

He now lay sprawled in the passenger seat, his body angled away from her, facing the window and the night beyond. One hand lay over his face like a shield, the limp packet of vegies on the console between them. She could smell the musk of him, a jolt that took her right back to their childhood and his teenage years.

She glanced at his hunched body and felt a stab of sympathy. In the half-light of the car, he looked even more like the skinny teenager she remembered, lounging next to her on the couch, sharing bags of Doritos and watching rented movies.

She saw him reach for his swollen cheek, gingerly touching the puffed skin with his fingers.

'How's your face? Do you want me to take you to the hospital?'

His hand fell. 'Fuck, Kate. Just drop it, would you. You're not fucking Mum, all right.'

A wrench in her stomach. Harsh but fair. Her mother, she certainly was not.

THEN

He was hot from the dance floor. Pushing his way through the heaving crowd, he stumbled out into the first-floor verandah to catch his breath. The outdoor area had been set up as a chill-out space, all lounge chairs and artificial turf, beneath endless inky skies. Globe lights were strung across pale timber pergolas and sheer gauzy curtains hung down from their frames.

The music from inside sounded softer out here; the muted bass reverberating deep inside his bones. A pleasant buzz hummed through him – the shots of tequila and the pills he had downed earlier doing their work.

He hadn't gone too hard. He knew how to pace himself, how to hit that sweet spot. Just enough of a chemical high to dull the edges of reality and cushion the world. He felt carefree and untethered. A little bit horny and with enough confidence fizzing in his blood to do something about it; to take a risk.

He breathed in the balmy evening, moving to the balcony to look down at the famous Surfers boulevard. Families and tourists were moving along the Esplanade, some turning curious faces up towards the packed venue and pumping music. This end of town was known to host parties for various celebs and football stars. He half smiled at a couple of backpackers in light summer shifts over bikini tops, who craned their necks as they walked past for a stickybeak. *You wish, honey.*

He could hear the crash of waves and shouts of laughter coming from the beach beyond. Maybe he too would end up there at the end of the night. He turned his back to the ocean and leaned against the balcony wall, chugging on a Heineken and watching her.

She was standing at the centre of the space with a group of friends, seemingly in conversation but actually checking out the field. He had caught her glancing his way, her eyes roving over his sweat-soaked T-shirt, the corner of her mouth hitching into a secret smile. She was standing just below a string of lights, appearing to glow in their soft amber warmth.

He had noticed her almost as soon as she'd arrived. It was hard not to. With a shimmering handkerchief top, secured across her bare back with little more than thin strappy ties, over a black denim mini, every red-blooded male at the party had noticed her entrance, as she'd intended. She smirked in his direction and flicked her hair, her eyes lingering on his for a beat too long for him to misinterpret.

He smiled and stepped in the direction of the group.

6

Saturday

'Are you going to finish that?'

Caleb rolled his eyes as Kate's father removed the remaining cutlet from Caleb's plate onto his own. Gray smiled and gently nudged his boyfriend's shoulder as he popped the food into his mouth.

Kate blinked away a memory of her father doing exactly that when her mother was alive. Stealing the last cutlet from her plate, a habit she had pretended to despise but actually had loved, flattered by her husband's attention for her cooking. She caught Luke's expression. The barest hint of a raised eyebrow above a swollen and red-raw eye. It was still jarring. These small flickers from their past being re-enacted in the present day with a new actor in the role.

'Why is it called a *cutlet*, by the way?' Caleb asked, looking around the table.

'No idea,' Kate replied. 'That sounds like a question for Siri.'

'Can I ask, Mummy? Can I?' Archie, her five-year-old, had leaped to her side. Too late, Kate realised that she had let slip the dreaded word.

She surrendered her mobile, letting her son loose on the phone-assistant app. Within seconds, the query had changed from *cutlet* to *buttlet* and Archie was in hysterics, rolling on the floor laughing. Amy, her almost eight-month-old, who was parked on the floor surrounded by toys, commando-crawled towards her brother and tried to grab the phone with a delighted cry. Archie held it out of her reach but relented at a look from Kate, letting his sister have a turn. Amy promptly put the phone in her mouth just as Siri said, *I'm not sure I understand*, making Archie laugh even more.

Sri Lankan *cutlets* were not a cut of meat, but crumbed fish croquettes made with tuna or mackerel with potato and spices. Fiddly and time-consuming, her mother had only gone to the trouble on special occasions. They were Gray's favourite and Kate was glad she'd made the effort, though it had taken her all morning, following her mother's go-to bible for Sri Lankan cooking passed down from her own mother: the *Ceylon Daily News Cookery Book*, dog-eared and displaying its vintage. She had gone all out, preparing a full array of rice and curries, re-creating the greatest hits from her mother's repertoire.

'Good job, Kit,' Gray said, mopping up the last of his food. 'Just a bit more chilli next time.' He winked. The running joke in the family. Kate, who had taken after her Sri Lankan mother in appearance with her brown skin and dark hair, had an aversion to chilli, the dreaded spice making her sweat and her sinuses weep. Meanwhile, Gray and Luke, the fair-skinned contingent of the family, breezed through without a care, crunching down raw chillies like they were nothing at all.

She poked out her tongue at her father as Geoff entered the room holding up a bottle of Adelaide Hills shiraz.

'Anyone for a top-up?' her husband asked.

Kate declined. She was on call this weekend. Gray, the designated driver, also shook his head, while Caleb and Luke held up their wineglasses.

Kate took in her brother's hangdog appearance, still suffering from his excesses at the pub. Luke had remained in his clothes from the night before, reeking of old beer and cigarettes. She didn't think he needed any more alcohol, but she held her tongue. Kate had yet to get the whole story of what had happened last night. He'd dodged all her attempts at conversation in that direction. He hadn't slept much, having been woken up in the early hours by Archie, who'd made a beeline for the TV to watch his weekend cartoons while scooping Coco Pops from a bowl. Archie had been unruffled to find his uncle snoring on the couch, merely moving his breakfast to the floor and settling in for the morning.

When Kate had found them later, Archie had been snug against his uncle on the lounge, seemingly unaffected by Luke's unwashed and bruised appearance. They were both engrossed in an episode of *Bluey*, Archie occasionally explaining various details. Luke had managed to avoid all opportunities to chat by determinedly hanging out with the kids all morning. Not that Kate minded. It had allowed her and Geoff to concentrate on the food, and the kids to roll all over their uncle with impunity. She had to admit that he was actually great with the kids.

Kate's eyes shifted from her father to her brother, hoping they would manage to get through the afternoon without incident. It wasn't like Luke was home very often. His past trips had been brief in the extreme, mere stopovers to meet obligation, more often than not bypassing Gray altogether. It would be nice to have one positive family interaction to save into the memory banks.

So far, Gray had managed to stop himself from commenting on Luke's appearance. The family, it seemed, had collectively agreed to not notice the golf-ball-sized lump on Luke's inflamed face. Kate had hoped that Caleb's cheerful presence would help to rub the spiky edges off their family grievances, allowing Gray and Luke to navigate each other without tripping over old wounds. But she could see her father's expression slowly darkening, his belligerence growing. Gray had expected Luke to make an effort with Caleb, and his disappointment was clear, slowly curdling into anger.

Luke was currently at his aggravating best, spending his time at the table wordlessly stuffing his face and checking his phone. Her brother was in a mood and was deliberately baiting Gray. And he was succeeding.

'How's work going, Luke?' Kate tried her best to pull him into conversation. She had never really understood her brother's profession as a financial services consultant. She knew he worked in the heart of Sydney's CBD, in one of those shiny, ultra-modern, steel-and-glass towers. Hull-Hayward Financial, the firm he worked for, regularly featured in the Fortune 500 company list. But what he did on a day-to-day basis remained a mystery. Something to do with markets and investment strategies, he'd once tried to explain, though her understanding remained opaque on what it actually entailed. All she knew was that the job seemed to reward him with money to burn.

'Fine. The same.' He barely looked up from his screen.

'Did you meet with Marcus after the funeral?' Kate persisted. Her brother grunted.

'How's TwitFace going, mate? Must be interesting since that's all you've done all afternoon.' Gray had had enough.

Kate exchanged glances with her husband, a plea to intervene. He took the hint.

'Right, everyone ready for dessert?'

Luke hadn't responded to his father's jibe. Not a muscle had changed in his demeanour, his fingers not missing a beat in their relentless scrolling.

'Mate, why even bother coming home if all you're going to do is sulk in a corner. Your sister went to a lot of trouble today. The least you can do is get your head out of that bloody phone.'

'Naughty word! Daddy, Grandpa said a naughty word.'

'Father, dearest. Two words. Fuck. Off.'

'Luke—'

'Uncle Luke said a naughty word!'

Kate's phone trilled loudly in Amy's lap, as Gray half rose from his seat, shrugging off Caleb's warning hand. His chair scraped loudly on the timber floors.

'If you've got something to say, just say it, why don't you?' Gray's voice was dangerously tight.

Amy whimpered, sensing the sudden charged atmosphere of the room. Kate scooped her up and grabbed the ringing mobile, wiping the drool on her T-shirt.

'That's just the problem, isn't it? You still need other people to explain it all to you.' Luke stretched his legs, pointedly relaxed, and faced his father from across the table.

'What? You've got an issue with Caleb, is that it?'

'I've never had a problem with Caleb. Only with his dickhead of a boyfriend.'

Kate fumbled over her mobile. 'Hello,' she answered, trying to tune out her family.

'Okay, that's enough,' Geoff cut in. 'Luke, mate, you need to pull your head in, all right. There are kids here. Just settle down or you're going to have to leave. Your choice.'

'Fine by me, Geoffrey, my man.' He rose from the table, tucking his chair neatly back into place. 'This party was getting stale, anyway.'

'Detective, sorry to bother you over the weekend.' Kate heard the clipped voice of Constable Vickie Harris on the line, not sounding the least bit sorry. 'Just got a report of a—'

'Sorry, could you hang on a sec, Vickie.' Kate lowered her mobile to call out to her brother, 'Luke, just wait a minute, would you?'

'Thanks for the meal, sis. For the record, I thought the chilli level was just right.' He waved to her and exited the house through the back screen door, sliding it gently closed behind him.

Fuck.

'Detective?' Vickie sounded impatient.

'Sorry, Constable, can you repeat what you just said?'

'We've had a report of a body being discovered at a property out Byangum way. Porter Drive. Lot eighty-two... Sarge, you there?'

'Yep, I'm here. Can you repeat that address?'

Vickie obliged. 'The ambos and forensics are on their way now.'

'And the deceased. Have we got an ID?'

'We do, Sarge.'

Watching her brother's retreating figure, Kate felt her world tilt as Vickie's words came down the line.

7

Kate pulled up along the gravel driveway and sat for a moment, listening to the engine tick. She needed to gather her thoughts before facing whatever shitstorm was waiting. Ahead, an ambulance, a couple of patrol cars and a forensics vehicle created the usual line of first responders, tracking the direction of tragedy.

She glanced at her phone, checking for nonexistent messages, her mind drawn back to the capital-D drama that was her family. To the lunch that had imploded. Luke storming out. Her father shutting down and contracting into himself in silent fury. Geoff and Caleb trying to plaster over the wreckage with berry pavlova.

She exited the car, swapping the remains of the air conditioning into the heat haze outside, where the Northern Rivers weather was doing its best to air-fry its inhabitants, the mercury stuck determinedly in the mid-thirties. The air felt scorched, the dryas-dust bushland just waiting for an excuse, like some idiot's stray cigarette, to crackle into flame. The fire danger rating signs were permanently dialled to screaming red, and the local Rural Fire Services up and down the state were on high alert.

'Sarge, you're here. I can show you the way, if you like.'

Constable Harris, looking decidedly worse for wear in the heat, met Kate as she walked up the dirt driveway. Harris's face was slick with sweat, ruby-coloured strands of hair sticking to her skin, and damp patches marking her uniform. The constable swatted away a couple of droning flies.

Kate nodded towards the brick-veneer homestead, its front door ajar. 'Anyone inside?'

'No one. The patrols checked when they first got here. Found the front door wide open, like that. Nobody else has been into the house. It hasn't been cleared by the crime-scene officers yet.'

Kate took in the blue esky and empty longnecks that littered the verandah. A straggly row of Christmas lights had been hung across the front deck; tinsel wound clumsily along the timber railing. She felt something tighten in her belly.

'He looks like he had company,' Harris said, motioning to the beer bottles.

'That, or it was a standard night in,' Kate remarked, scanning the grounds. 'Where's Fiona?'

'She took the kids to the property next door. She didn't want the boys to see. Darnley is with them,' Harris added.

Kate nodded. Darnley was experienced, empathetic and calm in an emergency. She was glad the family was being seen to by him.

'They're in the back paddock,' Harris said, pointing over her shoulder.

Kate followed Constable Harris as she led the way along the side of the house. Unkept gardens housing an empty clothes line fed into a couple of desultory rolling paddocks, clear of stock, their once-verdant pasture dulled into olive-grey and brown by the heat. Bushland fringed the paddocks in a dense semicircle, the velvet-green flanks of Mount Nullum rising in the distance.

Ahead, she took in a ute parked haphazardly in the middle of the paddock closest to the house, its driver's door flung open. Three mountain bikes – one adult and two kids' – were attached to the back tray of the ute with a metal grip. A temporary forensic canopy had been set up alongside the stock fence that separated the pasture from the paddock beyond. A blue-plastic-garbed CSO moved into view and crouched beside a motion-less figure by the fence post, photographing the scene. Kate looked away.

'The boss is here, too,' Harris noted. 'I phoned him after I called you, and he insisted on coming down.'

Kate nodded. She wasn't surprised that Esposito was making an appearance. He was taking his posting seriously, and a suspicious death on the very first weekend of his new job warranted an in-person look-see. It would be an early test of his professed intentions to abstain from micromanaging. Kate didn't think it likely. If there was credit to be had, she had no doubt that he would be claiming his share and stamping his name on this new jurisdiction.

She spotted him, donned in forensic gear and standing slightly to the edge of the crime-scene activity, speaking on his phone. Esposito noticed Kate, greeting her with a nod and ending the call. He waited while she pulled on booties, coveralls and gloves, and signed into the forensic log, before gesturing for her to lead the way.

As they passed the stationary ute being photographed by the forensic officers, she noticed that the keys were still in the ignition. An open beer can was stuck to the drinks holder of the centre console, and what appeared to be a garment, possibly a top of some kind, was scrunched up on the front seat. A mounted spotlight was attached via a bracket onto the upper frame of the driver-side window.

Kate approached the body, forcing herself to take in the sight. A male in his mid-thirties, his cheeks and chin covered over by a rough beard. He was shirtless, dressed only in a faded pair of knee-length gym shorts and thongs, which had slipped partially from his feet. She wondered in passing if the man had been wearing the clothing balled up inside the ute. A T-shirt he'd discarded at some point during the night because of the heat, maybe? The man's body was flung back on the ground, a fist-sized wound blooming across his chest. One of his legs was bent, resting awkwardly against the metal wire of the fence line. Flies buzzed around in a frenzy, the grass and earth beneath his body stained a dark, oily crimson. A .22 rifle lay by his side, apparently where it had fallen. Kate noticed the spent cartridge expelled by the rifle, at the base of the fence post. An unopened beer can, the same brand as the one inside the ute, was balanced carefully on the post.

'Do you recognise him?' Esposito's glance was sharp, searching.

Kate recalled the bear-like man chugging on a long neck, and enveloping his friend, her brother, in an embrace.

'It's Marcus Rowntree. He's a local.'

'Do we know anything about him?'

'He's a chippie. Does odd jobs around the place. Fencing, a bit of labouring sometimes.' Kate sidestepped the question. She knew what he was asking, but she couldn't answer him properly yet. Her brain was still catching up to what she was seeing.

Just two days ago, she had commiserated with Marcus and her brother at the wake of their school friend's funeral. And now, Marcus too was dead. Luke, it seemed, had lost both of his childhood friends in a matter of weeks.

'Anything else I should know about his identity?' Esposito's voice was more insistent now.

He already knows. No doubt Harris had fed him the information when she called Esposito, unable to resist handing out that morsel in her efforts to get on his good side. Wasn't that why he was here? So he could be on the front foot on a case that had all the ingredients of a story that could explode onto the front pages.

Kate met Esposito's glance. 'Marcus is Eric Harrington's son. The actor.'

Esposito nodded, unsurprised. Kate could see him assessing the implications and potential ramifications for the case.

Eric 'The Prince' Harrington. Two-time Logie winner and a stalwart of soaps and teledramas over the past three decades. Anyone with a passing interest in Australian TV would recognise the name. A connection to Eric Harrington meant the press would flock to the story, pouncing on it like seagulls over dropped chips on the beach. Weeks out from Christmas, with little to occupy the press, this was going to hit the headlines.

'Is there a reason he didn't go by *Harrington*?' Esposito asked.

'Rowntree is his mother's name. I understand that the relationship between father and son was complicated,' Kate said carefully. She wasn't sure why, but she didn't feel ready yet to reveal what she knew of her brother's friend. It felt like a betrayal, somehow, of her teenage memories of Luke, Marcus and Ant. For as long as Kate could remember, Marcus had worn his insecurities about his father like a scratchy second skin. With Marcus gone, it was his mother's story to tell. She would leave it to Celeste Rowntree.

Esposito marked her with a look, but moved on. 'What about suicide? Is it a possibility?'

Kate recalled what Marcus had let slip at the wake about his breakup with his wife. Was he depressed enough to go down that route?

'Maybe,' she replied. 'Suicides tend to aim for the head rather than the torso, but it does happen. This seems more like an accident to me, the way he's fallen with his leg caught on the fence like that.' She nodded to the spotlight mounted to the driver-side door of the ute. 'It looks like he was out shooting last night, most likely rabbits,' she said. 'And he'd been drinking. The gun could have gone off accidentally, maybe while he was trying to climb the fence. Stuff like that is more common than you'd think.'

Esposito grunted and turned to speak to the CSO.

Kate faced the opposite direction, away from the body to the empty paddock beyond fringed by thick-knitted vegetation. She exhaled slowly, unsure why Marcus Rowntree's body laid down on the ground had rattled her so badly. She had seen her share of dead bodies, and this was not even close to being in a state that would normally cause her concern. And yet, taking in the bloody bullet wound, the blowflies defiling his eyes and mouth, all Kate could think of was the young boy who had played with her brother and had once screwed up his courage to ask her to his Year Ten formal.

8

Kate surveyed the home that Marcus had occupied with his family for years before Fi had up and left with the kids. The two-bedroom, one-bath, single-storey red-brick cottage slumped in the heat. Inside, the scuffed floors and furniture with ancient food stains told the story of a dwelling well used to young kids.

An undecorated plastic Christmas tree took up one corner of the lounge room, looking strangely forlorn in its naked state. A cardboard box of decorations sat at its base. Had Marcus been waiting for his boys to arrive to decorate the tree? She glanced inside the box without disturbing its contents, taking in the paper-chain decorations, angels and stars made with paddle-pop sticks sitting among store-bought tinsel and baubles. Multiple years' worth of Christmas craft from the boys' preschool and primary years. It seemed that some of the boys' memorabilia had remained in their father's possession.

A couple of forensic officers were meticulously combing the house, searching for signs of a suicide note, bagging any spare ammunition rounds for comparison purposes and collecting any electronic devices that might have recorded the final thoughts of its owner. Each room was being photographed, and suitable surfaces such as the empty beer bottles on the front deck were being processed for prints to help determine if Marcus had entertained any visitors the night before. If Marcus hadn't been drinking alone, it was possible that there had been a witness to the accident or its direct aftermath. She wouldn't be surprised if someone had taken off in shock after seeing something like that. Very few people reacted in the way they expected to in moments of crisis.

At the primary scene, two additional CSOs were busy cataloguing firearms evidence around the body and processing Marcus's vehicle. It had been found to be drained of battery from the door being left open and possibly the spotlight being on all night. So far, three bullet rounds had been discovered in the far paddock, between approximately twenty to twenty-five metres from the fence line where Marcus's body lay slumped, presumably shots he had fired at stray rabbits and missed. A total of five spent cartridges had been recovered, three near the driver-side door of the ute and two near the fence post beside the body. The firearm had been taken into evidence after being rendered safe and the live ammunition rounds removed. The rifle, spent cartridges and recovered bullets would be subject to ballistic testing to confirm a match against the weapon.

Kate took in a height chart pencilled onto the kitchen door frame, marking the growth of the two boys. The names *Teddy* and *Jasper* carefully scribbled in lead tracking up the architrave in increments. Her eyes trailed the kitchen counters, not dirty, exactly, but not rigidly clean, either, like the rest of the house. Passable on the surface, as long as you didn't look too closely. A few unwashed plates and a handful of cutlery lay in the sink. In the corner, a full bin sat waiting to be emptied, patrolled by a pair of flies zigzagging the room. A used saucepan sat on the electric stove, marked by congealed bacon fat, a faint hint of fried bacon still permeating the air. Had Marcus cooked for anyone last night? Kate swatted at a stray fly and addressed one of the passing blue-clad forensic officers. She could feel the heat emanating from the woman inside the airless room.

'Anything?' she asked.

The CSO shook her head. 'Nothing so far. No obvious notes or messages. We've collected his laptop and phone for anything digital.'

'Are the bedrooms okay to look around?'

42

'Yeah, you're right to go through. They've been photographed and searched.'

Kate nodded and followed the corridor to the back of the house. She entered the master bedroom first, a musty, unwashed smell reaching her nose. The sheets and doona on the bed were rumpled and Marcus's work clothes lay in a pile on the floor, where he had discarded them the previous day. Scanning the room, she took in a narrow, mirrored wardrobe, and a chest of drawers with a flat-screen TV propped on top. The bedside table on Marcus's side held a TV remote and a glass of water, its surface skimmed with dust motes.

Next to the family bathroom stood Ted and Jasper's room, which was set up with bunk beds that were clad in matching Spider-Man bedspreads, twin dressers and three stacked plastic storage boxes filled with books and playthings. An entire box was dedicated to Lego. *Star Wars* movie posters and various kids' artworks competed for space on the walls. This was by far the cleanest room of the house and looked like it hadn't been occupied in a while, going by the film of dust that coated the windowsill and the storage-box covers. She wondered at Marcus and Fiona's co-parenting arrangements. Maybe the boys didn't do sleepovers.

And yet, she noted that the bedspread on the bottom bunk appeared rumpled, the pillows not quite aligned, as if the bed had been made haphazardly. Pulling the blanket off the bottom bunk, she found creased sheets below, and a tiny rust-coloured mark on the pillow case, like a small bleed from a graze or shaving cut. A faint smell clung to the bed clothes, a mixture of sweat and citrus spice interlaced with sandalwood. A man's cologne, maybe? She wondered suddenly if Marcus spent time in the boys' bedroom. Maybe occasionally falling asleep in their beds, to feel close to his sons.

In the aging bathroom, which could do with a good scrub, she opened the medicine cabinet, observing the expected Lynx, shaving cream, hair gel and other sundry items. She brought each one up to her nose, picking out a trace of sandalwood in a half-empty bottle of aftershave, though not quite the scent she had noticed in the boys' bedroom. She placed it carefully back on the shelf.

—

Kate waited patiently for Louise Askall, Marcus Rowntree's nearest neighbour, to finish setting down a jug of iced tea and a plate of biscuits – baked that morning, they had been informed. She watched as Ms Askall poured glasses of cold tea for those gathered: Kate, Constable Darnley and Fiona Rowntree. She was a statuesque, middle-aged woman with glossy waves of auburn hair tied into a messy bun. Her movements were stiff, made awkward by shock. She offered the plate of shortbread around, everyone declining.

They were gathered in Ms Askall's living room, a homely space filled with lived-in furniture and books overflowing from shelves into piles on the floor. A wide bay window provided views of an immaculate front garden, planted entirely with Australian natives and drought-tolerant succulents, evergreen despite the heat. Two young boys squealed and giggled as two large chocolate labradors bounced around them. Inside the house, Kate and Darnley faced Mrs Rowntree across the coffee table on opposing floral couches.

'Thanks, Louise,' Kate said, as the woman went to sit down. 'We can take it from here.'

'Yes, of course,' Ms Askall murmured, taking the hint and picking up the plate of untouched biscuits. 'I'll just take these to the boys. See if they're hungry.'

Fiona Rowntree smiled at her friend as she turned to leave the room. Ms Askall squeezed her shoulder in a gesture of solidarity and Fiona clasped her hand in return.

Louise Askall had given the police a statement, essentially confirming that she had no useful information to provide about the tragedy next door. A semi-retired university lecturer, she lived alone, her property separated from Marcus's by a thick corridor of bushland. She had no direct views of his house or the dirt track that provided entry to his land. She had gone to bed early just before 9 pm, had apparently fallen asleep almost immediately, and had not heard the sounds of any gunshots. She clarified that she used audio aids to fall asleep and that it was possible the recording she'd played last night could have muffled any sounds from outside. She had also confirmed that rifle shots from her neighbour's land were not uncommon, with Marcus often taking pot shots at feral animals around his paddocks. The police were still canvassing other properties around the area to narrow down the timeframe for when the shooting had occurred.

'Thank God for Louise.' Fiona Rowntree's voice was small. She was curled into the couch, her body coiled around a cushion, as if trying to shrink into herself. A smaller target for the pain. She had hardly moved from the spot since Kate had arrived, her head turned towards the window, her eyes hyper-vigilant of her sons. Her hair was tied into a ponytail, grey roots starting to peep through from beneath her DIY colour job.

'I don't know what I would have done without her. She's been keeping the boys occupied with the dogs. They're meant to be spending the day with him. I haven't told them yet... They didn't see...'

Kate nodded, relieved to hear that the boys, at least, had been spared the sight of their father. 'Mrs Rowntree, I'm so sorry you had to witness that. We can provide you with the details of some counsellors. It would be a good idea to speak to someone about this. It's not something you want to process by yourself.'

'Fiona... You can call me Fiona. I know who you are. You knew Marcus. You should call me by my name.'

'Fiona, I understand you and Marcus separated a few months ago. Can you tell me how he's been in that time?'

'So, you *do* think he did this to himself? You do, don't you? Is that what you're thinking?' She searched Kate's face for answers.

'At this stage, it does look like an accident, but we do have to look into all scenarios, if only to rule them out. A self-inflicted injury is one possibility we have to consider.' *You saw the body. You know why.* Kate didn't need to say the words. She could see it in Fiona's eyes. The thought had crossed her mind, too.

'Fuck, I can't believe this. I was meant to be getting a wax today. That's where I'm meant to be right now.' A hysterical giggle escaped her and she gulped it back.

'Tell me about how things have been between you and Marcus, Fiona.' Kate repeated her original question.

'Good. Fine. I mean, not brilliant, obviously. He was really upset at first, but I thought things were getting better. He seemed to have accepted it, that this was how it was going to be. He was getting used to having the boys over every other weekend. And, I don't know. Things just seemed… calmer.'

'So, he didn't agree to the separation at first? Was he ever violent or aggressive towards you and the boys? Maybe threatening self-harm to convince you to come back?' Kate was thinking of Ms Askall's preliminary statement to Darnley, which the constable had apprised her of before she had sat down with Fiona. Ms Askall had confirmed that she had known the family when Fiona and the boys lived with Marcus. Apparently, Marcus had changed over the last few months, growing testier with Louise as she had remained friends with Fiona through the couple's separation. Ms Askall believed that Marcus was nursing a grievance against his ex-wife, but he hadn't struck her as suicidal. *But then who did?*

Fiona shook her head, stalling for time. 'I know what you're going to say. How it's going to sound. But it wasn't like that. He never once hit me or the kids. He had a short fuse, is all. But it was all bluster. He would drink and rage for a bit, but he would come around in a few hours. It was just his way of coping. It doesn't mean he was violent or *coercive* or whatever it's called.'

When Kate didn't reply, she ploughed on, determined to prove her point.

46

'That's not why I left, just so you know. We'd just run our course. We were kids when we got together. It was a lifetime ago. There was nothing there anymore. He and I both knew it, but yeah, of course it felt like a failure. Plus, he didn't want to lose the kids.'

'So, Marcus was helping you out with the boys? Did they sleep over at the house?'

'We didn't have a formal arrangement.' She bit her lip. 'Marcus would sometimes take the boys to the footy or the park when he had time on the weekends. But they didn't do sleepovers. The boys have issues with sleep. Teddy especially gets really bad night terrors and Marcus wasn't the best at dealing with it. The kids haven't slept in the house since we left.'

'And Marcus was happy with that? With his level of access to the boys and how everything was going between you two?'

Fiona flicked her head, an almost imperceptible movement. 'When he got drunk, he would leave messages on my phone. Nothing aggressive, just sad, you know? He wasn't a good sleeper, just like the kids, and he'd end up in the back paddocks shooting at the rabbits. Or just sit in the ute and call me.'

'Did he ever threaten to hurt himself? Mention suicide?'

'Yes, but I never took him seriously. That was just what he did when he had too much to drink and had worked himself into a mood. He could be a sad drunk. It was more than just me and the kids. There was all this stuff he kept bottled up about his father and the acting stuff, and God knows what else. That was another reason why I couldn't stay with him. He never dealt with that stuff. It was eating him up inside.'

'Are those messages still on your phone, Fiona? Can we listen to them?'

Fiona nodded, her expression fixed. 'I've deleted some, but there are a few there.'

'Did he happen to call you last night?'

'No.' Her answer was swift and definite. 'The boys and I were home all night watching movies. I would have noticed if

47

Marcus had called.' She rummaged around in her bag and placed her mobile on the coffee table between them. 'Here, you can check if you want. No texts or calls or anything.'

'Thank you. We'll need to look through your call records and we appreciate you being so helpful.'

'Have you... Did you find a note?' Her dark-brown eyes drilled into Kate's. Frightened of the response but needing to know.

'Nothing yet. But sometimes people leave messages on their laptops or their phones. His devices are password protected. Do you happen to know what he may have used as his passwords?'

'The kids' birthdays,' she replied without hesitation. 'That's what he used when we were together and I doubt he's changed them.' She recited the dates so Darnley could write them down. 'It'll be the years they were born or a combination. That's his go-to.'

'Thanks, Fiona. We'll try those. You said Marcus didn't call you. But what about social media? Did he happen to message you or maybe post something?'

'What? You mean like, leave a goodbye post online?' Her eyes widened in shock. 'It'll be a Facebook post. That's all he's on.' She reached for the phone on the table and began tapping furiously. 'Hang on, he did post something last night, at 8.46 pm.' She screwed up her face, a small, sad smile playing on her lips. 'It's nothing. Just selfies of him drinking on the deck. There's no text description. Here, take a look.'

Kate accepted the proffered mobile and scrolled through the five photos that Marcus had posted. All drunken selfies. In each, he was holding aloft a beer bottle and smiling or making a face at the camera. His last communication with the world. Seemingly happy and without a care. The post had garnered six likes.

Her fingers froze on the final photo. It appeared to have captured the half-blurred image of someone else in the background. The person's face was out of shot, but they were bending down to pull a can of something from an esky on the floor. Marcus had not been alone last night.

Her skin prickled as she zoomed in on the man's maroon-print T-shirt. She had stared at that exact shirt, smelling of smoke and sweat all morning. The person Marcus had spent his last hours on earth with was her brother. Luke.

9

'*Police were today called to a property on the outskirts of Esserton, south of Murwillumbah in the Northern Rivers, New South Wales to attend the scene of a man found deceased as a result of firearm injuries. The man in his thirties was found alone in a paddock that backs onto his property, and investigations are underway to determine whether the death was the result of misadventure or suicide. Police have yet to release the identity of the body, noting that they are still in the process of notifying family.*

'*In other news, bushfires are continuing to burn uncontrolled in the state's north-west. Emergency evacuation orders have been issued for—*'

Kate listened, taking in the location of the fires and silently calculating their distance from Esserton. In her memory, bushfires of the scale and ferocity that seemed to occur in the south had never been a feature of this region. Until now. All the old certainties were coming to an end. The planet was finally calling their pestilent species to account.

On screen, the newsreader had moved on to a story about a compensation case against the NSW Police. Years'-old mugshots and the forever-young photograph of a fourteen-year-old boy, his hair brushed back and his uniform immaculate for his high school photo, smiled from the TV. She realised with a start that this was the Nowra case, one of the ghosts from Esposito's past. According to the newsreader, the court was due to deliver its findings before Christmas, possibly as soon as this week. Despite herself, her thoughts flickered to her boss. How would he be feeling? Was he okay?

It was no longer her business, she reminded herself. It hadn't been for a long time. She reached for the TV remote and deliberately switched channels, cutting the newsreader off mid-sentence.

'Do you mind?' she asked her husband, settling on a Christmas cooking show. Geoff shrugged, unbothered, only half an eye on the TV.

The kids were finally in bed and they were crashed in the lounge room, Geoff on the couch and Kate on the floor, surrounded by the remnants of wrapping paper and partially wrapped Christmas presents. It was a task that fell to her, Geoff being a truly terrible gift-wrapper, specialising in scrunching and tearing rather than neatly folding. Reaching for a new roll of reindeer-print paper, she sipped on her glass of white wine embellished with a couple of ice cubes against the heat, for the umpteenth time wishing their house had air conditioning. Even with the ceiling fans on and the French doors thrown open to capture as much breeze as possible through the insect screens, the heat trapped in their eighties' brick bungalow remained oppressive. Maybe they would need to bite the bullet on that particular expense.

Her eyes turned to her husband, whose attention was, as usual, on his mobile, his headphones on, scrolling endlessly and occasionally laughing out loud at whatever he was watching. In the months since Kate had returned to work, and Geoff had shrugged back on the mantle of full-time, stay-at-home care duties of the kids, she had noticed her husband becoming increasingly dependent on his phone in his downtime, addicted to the various posts, memes and videos offered up by the apps' algorithms. Her husband could easily give Luke a run for his money when it came to screen time.

She understood that it was an escape. A respite from the real world, and the career stalemate he found himself stranded in. Geoff was still sending out applications to architectural firms to regain a spot on the ladder, but the nibbles had become few and far between. His sudden job loss some six months back – a decision by management to reassess all contract positions – had accelerated her own return to work. The adjustment this time around had felt more fraught and fragile, compared to that first with Archie. Alongside mutual affection and comfort, their marriage was coloured by compromise and resentment, threads of bitterness over choices made, and their effect on his career opportunities compared to hers.

With Amy getting old enough for day care and Archie starting school next year, she had hoped that he would be able to re-enter the workforce and find some professional fulfilment. But it was taking longer than they both had imagined. He was competing against applicants with full résumés, not chequered histories of extended care leave and part-time, contract work. The online world provided an outlet from all of that.

Gazing at her husband lying relaxed against the cushions, a small smile playing at his lips, Kate decided to leave it. She turned her attention instead to the presenter on TV, currently rolling a cream-filled chocolate sponge into a roulade in order to create a Yule log. She found the complicated steps strangely comforting, even though she could never hope to re-create the recipe. It was the simple satisfaction of watching someone skilled at their job completing a task well.

It was a relief to focus on something other than the news, though she'd felt compelled to watch the 6 pm broadcast to make sure that Marcus's identity had not been revealed. The entire team was under a strict embargo to prevent the connection with Eric Harrington getting out to the media before the families on both sides had been informed. Kate didn't blame Esposito for being nervous. Esserton was still a small town with connections running deep, and it was easy for such things to spread. Nevertheless, she had felt annoyed on behalf of the team. It was a matter of professional pride that the detail was not leaked by anyone from Esserton Station.

Thankfully, they had managed to get in contact with both families. Kate had visited with Marcus's mother, Celeste

Rowntree, to break the news, while Esposito had liaised with the South West Metropolitan Region Command in Sydney to organise for officers from Ashfield Station to inform Eric Harrington. A press conference would be convened late tomorrow so that Marcus's identity could be released with both family members in attendance. Eric Harrington had agreed to fly over. It would be a chance to see how Celeste and Eric interacted in each other's company. From speaking with Celeste that afternoon, Kate got the strong impression that the relationship between the two remained unresolved, despite thirty-five years of water under the bridge.

Kate had taken a uniformed constable along with her to meet Celeste at her tiny fibro cottage in Uki, which also served as her place of work as a massage therapist. Kate had been expecting windchimes and crystals, but she had pulled up to a neatly swept front path and a discreet sign ('Massage by Celeste') that was concise and to the point.

The woman who had met them at the door was lean and fit in the way of yoga instructors, all long-limbed, sinewy muscle, a striking upright posture and relaxed strength. She was dressed in a cotton T-shirt over loose-fitting harem pants, with a plain silver chain sporting a third-eye pendant clasped around her neck. Her short, dark hair was interspersed with blonde streaks, and her face was devoid of make-up. Although weatherworn and lined, her face was attractive, with intelligent grey eyes and the kind of wide, sensual lips that could transform a face when swept into a smile.

'Ms Celeste Rowntree?' Kate asked, holding up her ID.

The eyes that met hers were watchful, like this wasn't the first time she had had to deal with unpleasant news.

'Is this about Marcus?' Her voice held no surprise, and for a second, Kate was sure that she had already found out somehow. But if so, she was handling the news remarkably well.

'Can we speak inside, Ms Rowntree?'

Celeste made a movement of impatience and stepped aside, allowing Kate and the constable to enter what was the waiting

53

area of her business. A two-seater couch took up one wall, and a round glass table was stacked with magazines and a tray holding a clay water urn and tumblers. Posters of human anatomy identifying acupuncture and chakra points, as well as various prints featuring bamboo and stacked stones, lined the walls, while soft music played in the background. The air held the smell of incense and massage oils.

'Well, what's he done now? Don't tell me it's another incident at the pub. Or has Fi finally bitten the bullet and called you lot in. I mean, I assume that's why you're here?'

So, there was clearly more to the story of Marcus and his marriage than Fiona had led on. 'Ms Rowntree, I am here about Marcus, but it's not to do with anything he's done—'

'The kids are fine? And Fi?' she interrupted.

'Yes, Fiona and the boys are all fine…'

Celeste exhaled as if she had been holding her breath since finding the police at her doorstep.

'Celeste, I'm sorry, but Marcus was found dead at his property this afternoon. It appears he died from a gunshot wound. It was Fiona who found the body.'

She took it better than Kate had expected, going pale and very still but not losing control. Kate led her to the couch while the uniformed officer got Celeste a cup of water from the clay urn. She accepted it without protest, holding the cup with both hands though not making any move to drink from it.

'Did he… did he kill himself?' she whispered.

'It's something we're looking into. But based on how the body was found, we believe it's more likely an accident, though we'll be examining all possibilities. A report will be prepared for the coroner.' Kate caught a flicker of emotion in Celeste's eyes. 'You don't believe it could have been an accident?' she asked.

Celeste turned her head. 'No, no, it's not that. It's just… I had the thought, what if he'd been with the kids? He bought that stupid .22 to teach the boys to shoot rabbits. It was one of the things I was most terrified of. The kids in the house with the gun. He could be such a child, overconfident, blasé, just irresponsible, you know? You can do that when you're single, but not when you have kids.' She shook her head as if to flick away an old memory, then looked down at her untouched cup and placed it back on the glass table. 'Anyway, whatever happened, I'm glad it's over. It's all for the best this way.'

The atmosphere shifted as Kate watched the woman. 'Why do you say that?'

Celeste snorted. 'Isn't it obvious? Why do you think Fi left him? Don't think because I'm his mother that I couldn't see him for what he was. I'm a realist, Detective. I did my best with him. And God knows, maybe I didn't do a good enough job. No doubt Marcus thought so. But it's not an excuse, is it? To terrify your wife. To take out your insecurities on another human being?'

'He was violent towards Fiona?'

'He never actually hit them, as far as I know, but there's more than one way of being violent, isn't there? He could be frightening when he wanted to be. There was plenty of broken crockery and smashed furniture. But that's how he justified himself when he blubbered and begged for Fi's forgiveness afterwards, that whatever he did, he would never strike them. And she accepted his excuses.'

She caught Kate's eyes. 'I've been so afraid something like this would happen, but I never expected it to be him. God, I've been so scared for those kids and Fi. Despite everything, she loved him and refused to see what was right in front of her. But I could see it. I saw all of him. He's got his father's genes. Weak and entitled. Thinks the world should fall at his feet, just because he wants something.'

Eric Harrington, the rich, good-looking 21-year-old from Sydney's Northern Beaches who had got a local girl pregnant while on holiday with his family in Murwillumbah. Kate had gleaned the details over the years through snippets heard at barbeques; gossip exchanged among the adults over warm white wine and honey-soy skewers. Eric had returned to Sydney to finish his acting degree at NIDA, the prestigious National Institute of Dramatic Art. Celeste at nineteen had opted to keep the baby, bringing up Marcus with the help of her family. Eric's parents had softened the blow with the regular inflow of money, though not with their presence. Or so the story went.

Celeste obviously still nursed a grudge against her ex-partner. No doubt it also helped to deflect her own guilt. It was much easier to blame her son's deficiencies on his absent father, rather than taking stock of her own hand in his upbringing.

Celeste marked her with a look. 'Don't think I don't remember you. I know who you are. You're that Luke Grayling's sister. You think you know Marcus from the teenager he was at school. But Marcus grew up. And you wouldn't like what he turned into as an adult.'

As she folded wrapping paper around a Lego set, Kate mulled over Celeste's remarks, thinking over Marcus's trajectory and the resentments he must have accumulated along the way.

Marcus had been sixteen when Eric Harrington had begun a slow but sustained better-late-than-never campaign to reinsert himself into his son's life by throwing money at the problem. There had been trips to Sydney, father-and-son interviews in women's magazines, and behind-the-scenes invites onto sets. Rumours had been rife that Harrington would help pave a career for his son, nudging him towards the right producers and onscreen projects.

Even though by then Kate had been absorbed in her new life as a young probationary copper in Grafton, she had been kept up to date on the local gossip by her mother. Their weekly phone chats had been peppered with insider details that her mum had needled out of Luke. *Marcus thinks he might get an audition with* Home & Away! *Eric is taking Marcus with him to the Logies. He's going to be on the red carpet!* Her mother, like everyone else in town, had been low-key obsessed with all things Harrington.

But as quickly as it had begun, it had all fizzled out. Out of the blue it seemed, Harrington had made the decision to try his luck in America. He had broken the news of his move to Marcus at his eighteenth birthday; an extravagant and raucous affair that Harrington had paid for. A whole beachfront restaurant rented out for the night at Surfers on the Esplanade with a flash DJ and a bottomless tab to soften the blow. Luke had only shared select details of the party with her afterwards, but it had been enough.

Eric had left the country two weeks later, stepping out of his son's life as rapidly as he had decided to re-enter it, exiting stage left when a better offer had presented itself. Marcus had discarded his thespian aspirations soon afterwards, switching to an apprenticeship in carpentry, as far away from his father's world as he could get. The life he thought he had been promised, gone in an instant. Kate wondered just how deep his feelings of ill-treatment ran, and exactly how he had vented those feelings while he had been alive.

Her attention returned to the TV chef, who had moved on to a recipe for easy, three-ingredient chocolate truffles. It looked simple enough. Maybe she would give it a go this Christmas – get Archie involved. The rolling of the chocolate balls in cocoa looked right up his alley.

'Oh, shit. Have a look at this.' Geoff's words knocked Kate out of her reverie. 'Did you tell Luke about Marcus?'

'Yeah, why? Marcus was one of his best friends. He deserved to know before it all got splashed in the news.'

'Yeah, but did you tell him to keep quiet about it?' He held out his phone to her.

Kate grabbed the mobile, her stomach plummeting. On screen was her husband's Twitter feed. Geoff and Luke, it seemed, followed each other on the app, and there was a tweet posted by her brother less than an hour ago.

@LukeThoughtThat When you lose both your best friends from childhood in the space of two

weeks. FU Universe. #ValeAnthonyReed #Vale-
MarcusRowntree

The picture attached showed a high school photo of Luke
with Ant and Marcus. The three teens wore identical grins as
they posed for the camera, their arms slung across each other's
shoulders. So far, the tweet had gained a couple of hundred
likes and dozens of comments.

The story had leaked. And it was because of her. *Fuck*.

10

'Holy shit. I cannot believe your dad got us this.'

Luke tumbled in through the doorway after Ant and Marcus, his eyes taking in the salmon-coloured walls of the two-bedroom apartment that Eric Harrington had booked for the three boys so they would have a place to crash after the party tonight.

'I call shotgun!' Marcus ran directly into the larger of the two bedrooms and leaped straight onto the double bed, causing an avalanche of piled-up cushions to tumble to the floor. Luke laughed. He didn't care where he slept. The smaller of the two bedrooms with its two single beds suited him fine. Standing at the window, he thought he could just make out a sliver of the Pacific Ocean in the distance. And beyond the hotel walls, the Gold Coast lay waiting.

'Marcus, have I told you how much I love your dad?'

'Fuck yeah, he's a bloody legend,' hollered Ant.

Marcus came into the room, holding a bottle of Bundy in one hand and a two-litre bottle of Coke in the other. 'Boys, we are getting wasted tonight.'

–

Luke stood in the shower, the hot water raining over him. The harder he tried to avoid them, the more his memories seemed to be pressing to the fore. As if some sort of dam had been breached. He stepped out of the shower and sniffed, automatically recoiling at the smell of day-old sweat, booze and smokes. He had scrubbed hard, emptying the complimentary shampoo bottles onto his head and body, but the discarded pile of clothes in the bathroom corner remained. Notes of his own feral stench were still finding their way to his nostrils.

Back in the room, he stripped his bed entirely, finding a couple of spare blankets in the closet and replacing his pillows with cushions from the sofa. Now that he was showered, he found the smell that still clung to the sheets intolerable. Balling them up into a pile on the carpet, he sat down on the side of the bed, still undressed apart from a towel around his waist, suddenly drained. The burst of activity had sapped him of his energy.

Marcus is gone, Luke.

Bitterness clung to his throat. He rose, heading without thought to the minibar, his fingers closing on the cold comfort of a beer. He swallowed too quickly, coughing as the liquid burned. Rummaging in his toiletries bag, he found a strip of paracetamol and popped a couple of pills, chasing them down with the beer. His shiner still throbbed like a bastard.

A couple of hours ago, his sister had pulled him out of bed, banging incessantly at his door at the Arms. He'd been asleep, having crashed almost the minute he'd arrived back at his accommodation after the train wreck of a lunch. At first, he had assumed that Kate wanted to berate his behaviour from that afternoon. But she had said nothing on that score, instead following him inside his room and breaking the news about Marcus, simply and without fuss. He guessed she'd had plenty of practice.

He's dead, Luke. We found his body in the back paddock. It looks like a firearms accident.

Luke had been sluggish and disoriented from sleep, and it had taken several more turns of Kate's patient explaining before the words had broken through. And even then, the information had just sat there on the surface of his brain like dog shit on a carpet, something odious that didn't belong.

He had felt Kate's eyes on him, assessing and observing. 'You were with him last night.' It wasn't a question.

'Yeah, he texted me after the funeral. Invited me over for a couple of beers after he finished work on Friday.'

'Were you with him for long?'

'A few hours, maybe. I went around about six, or a bit after. Not that late, but he was well tanked by the time I got in. He said I should have got there earlier.'

'Yeah, well knock-off time for Marcus is probably more like three-thirty, four. He had a few hours' head start.'

Luke had smiled at that.

'Can you remember when you left?' Kate asked.

'Nine-thirty, I think, or maybe just before. Something like that.'

'So, you didn't stay on and have a meal with him or anything? Did he show you around the house?'

'What? No. I mean, I used the toilet, and yeah, Marcus knocked up some bacon rolls in the kitchen, but we mostly hung out on the front deck.' Her questions had felt casual, but he knew his sister. He had felt her light probing touch even under the cloak of sisterly concern.

'How was he? Did he seem all right to you?'

Even then, he had understood what Kate was asking him. She had given the impression that Marcus's death was likely due to misadventure. That sounded about right. Marcus had always been a fucking idiot. Never one to care too much about safety or instructions of any kind. Yet the police were evidently looking into all possibilities. Like the way Ant had chosen to go.

'Honestly, Kit. I have no idea,' he had said finally. 'I haven't seen or spoken to him in so long, I don't know what he's like anymore. As far as I could tell, he was normal. I mean, a bit antsy and hyper, but you know that's how he was, even at school.'

Luke thought back to how it had been with Marcus; the sense of danger and volatility his friend had carried tucked just below the surface. Wasn't that why all the girls had loved him?

61

'He didn't seem upset to you? About Ant or anything else?' His sister had been gentle but persistent. Her modus operandi.

'We didn't speak about Ant, actually. He mainly wanted to reminisce about his acting days. Typical Marcus, still not over it.' They had spoken about other things, too, but that didn't matter now.

'What about Fi? Did she come up in the conversation at all?'

Luke had spent the evening sitting out on Marcus's deck as the light had faded and the chorus of insects had begun, feeling like an ice lolly slowly melting in the humidity. Sucking on beers and slapping away mosquitoes, listening to Marcus droning on. The complaints, the grievances. Everything was someone else's fault. He could have been somebody, if only the world had not stood in his way. No one understood. No one cared.

Marcus, it was clear, hadn't changed one bit, he had just got older and flabbier and more embittered. At eighteen, his complaints had felt justified. There had been real fire behind his anger. Now he just sounded sad. Within half an hour of arriving, Luke had cottoned onto why Marcus had asked him over. He was a new audience for Marcus's rants. Everyone else had no doubt heard it all before and was no longer willing to oblige him.

'Yeah, he seemed pissed off about Fi, though he didn't say much about her. Just an impression I got when he spoke about the kids.' Luke recalled the resentment he had seen flashing in Marcus's eyes, becoming more evident with every beer he had knocked back. 'I didn't ask him for any details, to be honest. I didn't want it to become a whole thing.'

'How did he sound when he spoke to you about the kids?'

'I don't know, Kate. Fuck! What is this? It feels like I'm in a bloody police interview.' He had flared up at her then, deflecting his rising anxiety with anger.

'I know, Luke, and I'm sorry. But you were the last person to see him before he died. We'll need a statement from you for the coroner's report.'

She had departed soon afterwards, leaving behind the weight of her words like an unwanted guest.

He would be questioned and dragged into a police investigation. He had no choice, but he could feel the resistance growing, the need to escape gnawing inside him. This shouldn't be his problem. He had left these people behind. Those phone calls from Ant that he'd never bothered to return. The messages he'd listened to and deleted. Years on and it was as if nothing had changed. They seemed to still live in each other's pockets. Claustrophobic and intertwined.

Except, he reminded himself, they didn't anymore. Both of his childhood friends were gone. Dead before their time.

His room lay in semi-darkness; night slowly edging out the long hours that had been stretched and extended by daylight savings. Laughter and voices reached him through the open balcony. A warm breeze drifted in from the river, bringing with it the scent of the bistro: burgers and chicken parmigiana. His mobile vibrated on the desk. He thought it had rung earlier as well, when he had been in the bathroom, but he made no move to get up.

'Going to take the kids mountain bike riding tomorrow.'

He remembered Marcus's petulant face breaking into a smile as he'd motioned to the bikes rigged up to the back of his ute.

'Jasper's been bugging me for weeks. They're going to love it.'

11

Sunday – two weeks to Christmas

'The tweet's been deleted. It should never have happened. I apologise.'

Kate sat stiffly at the table, watching as her new boss ground liberal portions of cracked pepper onto his eggs benny. This was new. They had never done this when they were together. Theirs had been stolen moments and hurried conversations, slick skin and crumpled sheets.

It wasn't what she had expected, being called to task over breakfast at a café, but Esposito had his own way of doing things. It was all very civilised. He had insisted on shouting her coffee and had remembered her old order, a skinny cap. It had felt like a punch to the guts. Tasting the sweet, grainy chocolate dusting felt like visiting a younger version of herself. A sweeter, more naïve version. After that first sip, she had let it sit untouched in front of her. He wasn't to know that she had moved on from cappuccinos. Although he would have, if he had bothered to ask.

Esposito had made small talk until his meal had arrived, enquiring about everything from her kids to her early career in Grafton. It was a ploy to make her uncomfortable, dragging out the suspense under a veneer of polite chitchat, and it had worked. She had broken first, blurting out her apology about Luke's tweet.

He had not answered, concentrating on popping his poached eggs, the yolk running lemon-bright across his toasted sour-dough, and taking an unhurried mouthful, slowly masticating and swallowing. After sipping his coffee and wiping his mouth on a paper serviette, he had settled back into his chair. Only then did he assess her with a look. She had to admit he was good.

'No point apologising to me. It's Eric Harrington you'll have to contend with. Hopefully, he won't feel the need to get his people involved.' His tone was conversational rather than accusatory. She had no idea what he meant by Harrington's *people*. Lawyers, presumably, or the PR brigade.

Luke's tweet had made the news. Although she had made him delete it last night, when he had finally picked up his phone, it had been too late. The photo Luke had posted of Marcus had been recognised by too many.

This morning, she had woken up to an online news report that featured a screenshot of Luke's deleted tweet and photo, front and centre. The news story also made use of an old *Woman's Day* profile piece of Eric Harrington dug up from the late nineties, which pictured Eric posing with Marcus alongside a quote about how much he regretted not spending enough time with his son while he was growing up with his mother in the Northern Rivers. With both images published side by side, it was clear that the Marcus from Luke's tweet was the same teenager who was smiling beside Eric Harrington in the old article. While the news site had been at pains to state that the identity of the deceased man had yet to be formally released by the police, it had done a good job of connecting the dots. Much had also been made of Luke having deleted his original tweet, with speculation around whether it had been at the behest of the Harrington family or the NSW Police. The article was being picked up by multiple news sites and social media was alight with the news.

'It's not the tweet I'm worried about,' Esposito went on, his tone even more measured and thoughtful. Kate would have infinitely preferred a shouting match to this excruciatingly civil tiptoeing.

'I'm more concerned about why a senior detective would consider it appropriate to share details of an active investigation with a person directly connected to the case. Going off Marcus's Facebook post, which you detailed in your report, Luke Grayling was the last person to see him alive, was he not? You're his sister and you deliberately visited a key witness alone, unaccompanied by another officer. I see conflict-of-interest red flags everywhere.'

Kate bit her lip, the worry she had been clamping down on flaring white-hot in her belly. She had wanted to be the one to inform her brother, rather than have him find out through the papers with everyone else. She had known without a doubt that he would take that as a betrayal. It just never occurred to her that Luke would feel the need to tweet the information out to the world, the self-absorbed twat.

Internally cursing, Kate rose to defend her brother.

'Sir, that's unfair. There's nothing so far to suggest that Marcus's death was anything but accidental or possibly self-inflicted. There was no sign of a struggle or defence injuries that would indicate someone else was involved, least of all my brother. I accept that visiting Luke alone was less than ideal. I see how that could be construed. But I was acting as a sister, not as a police officer.'

'Interesting. And here I was thinking we haven't ruled anything in or out as yet. As I understand it, none of the forensics are in and the autopsy is yet to be completed. I'd say there are still a few t's that need crossing before the death is written off as accidental.'

The look that Esposito gave her made her flush. 'I'm not writing anything off, sir. I understand that the investigation has only just started.' Annoyance was starting to build inside her rib cage, bricks of indignation cemented in by defensiveness. The criticism, she felt, was disproportionate to the offence. Was this a byproduct of Esposito's experience at the hands of the Critical Incident Investigation team? Was he now so tied to the book that there was no room for compassion or leeway?

She took a deep breath. 'Luke had two best friends at school. The three of them were inseparable. My brother had just attended the funeral of one of them – Anthony Reed – only a couple of days ago. When I found out about Marcus, I knew I had to let Luke know. It was the least I could do, to break it to him in person. To be clear, I didn't share any details of the investigation and I only saw him after we'd made contact with Marcus's family on both sides.' She added the final detail, though it sounded less remarkable out loud.

Esposito grunted and reached for his coffee, raising an eyebrow as he lifted the cup to his lips, those mismatched eyes boring into hers. 'And?'

'Sorry?'

'And, did your brother give you anything useful on Marcus?' he asked, impatience threading his words. He wanted a heads-up on Luke before he came in to provide a formal statement later today.

'Not really,' Kate replied, detailing what Luke had told her. 'They haven't seen each other in years, so Luke wouldn't really be able to judge Marcus's moods. But for what it's worth, Luke didn't get the impression that Marcus was suicidal.'

'And would you say your brother is confident using a firearm?'

Kate sucked in a breath before answering. 'Yes. We were taught to shoot as teenagers. Our granddad had a property and he used to take us rabbit shooting.'

A memory slid into place. Nights hunting with their grand-father. Luke hating every minute of it, from the cold steel thrust into his hands to their pop's sneering laugh when he inevitably missed. Kate made the shot every time, but that never made any difference. Their pop's objective had been to hound Luke into submission. To make a *man* out of his grandson. He would force Luke to carry the dead rabbits, foisting their soft weight on him, blood oozing down still-warm fur. The kill sometimes so fresh the rabbit's body would jerk involuntarily, one last synapse still firing, making her brother flinch, and earning him a shout of derision. Luke was a good shot, but he would aim slightly off in defiance. He wouldn't kill for his grandfather, no matter how much he was bullied.

Shaking off the image, Kate waited for more questions, but her boss merely sat there. Silently chewing and sipping his way through his breakfast, allowing her to stew in the awkwardness of the situation, exactly as he intended.

–

Kate was at her desk when Luke arrived at the station, accompanied by Constable Darnley, who had picked him up from the Arms. The interview was to be conducted by Esposito with Darnley as his second. Esposito, it seemed, had become part of the furniture. She, of course, was not invited to attend. She would read the transcript later.

Kate hovered in the corridor while Luke was being questioned, waiting until he was finally allowed to leave after reading over and signing his statement. She caught Esposito's eye, taking his small nod as permission to leave with her brother. Not that she needed his authority, but it was nice to see that he had a heart.

'Let me buy you a coffee.'

Luke didn't reply, stuffing his hands in his pockets and striding ahead without a word. She knew that he was pissed off at her. Like a confused toddler, he blamed her for the situation he found himself in, caught up, however tangentially, in a police investigation. It wasn't easy fronting up to a police interview, even if it was in the capacity of a witness. This was her world, not his. He was scared and grieving, and he was taking it out on her.

They ended up at the strip of cafés and restaurants that hugged the esplanade with views of the Tweed River. She steered them to a tiny coffee shop, ordering iced coffees for them both. They sat outside under the awning, trying to find cool relief in the hint of breeze that skimmed the surface of the river.

'How did it go?' she asked, her eyes trained on the water, allowing him space.

'Fine.' He shrugged. 'Just the same as what you asked me, but in more detail, I guess. I didn't tell them anything I hadn't told you.'

'I'm sorry I couldn't be in there with you. It's just protocol...' She trailed off, feeling a pinprick of guilt. Esposito was right. In talking to Luke ahead of time, she had given him a heads-up of the type of questions he should expect, time to prepare. She dismissed the thought. This was her brother, not an actual person of interest. Taking in his bruised left eye, the skin underneath now a deep charcoal, she wondered if Esposito had questioned him about his injury and how Luke had answered. She was still in the dark about it. She scanned his luggage-crumpled clothes and hunched shoulders. Her brother looked exhausted.

'I had to hand over my clothes from Friday night,' he blurted out. 'They won't find anything. Marcus's blood or whatever the fuck they're looking for. When I left there, he was fine. Just sitting on the deck on his tenth beer for the night.'

His hands were jittery on the table. Kate covered them with hers to still their movement. 'It's just procedure, Luke. For elimination purposes. I believe you. I know they're not going to find anything. That's the point. The tests will prove you correct.'

He looked down at her fingers trapping his own. She released them as he went to speak. 'What happens now? When's the funeral?'

'The body won't be released until the autopsy is complete. So, it'll be about a week, I'd say. Maybe longer. Will you fly back for it?' she asked softly. She was almost sure he would refuse. He had a 4 pm flight to Sydney this afternoon, and no doubt he couldn't wait to leave Esserton. The last few days had taken their toll. She was certain he would use his job as an excuse to not return for Marcus's wake.

'I was thinking of changing the flight, actually,' he said, his hands now fiddling with the paper straw of his iced coffee. 'I thought I might stay on for a bit, at least until the funeral.' He must have seen the obvious surprise on her face, because he bristled immediately. 'What? I've got heaps of leave owing.'

'Nothing. No, I think it's fantastic,' she said, trying not to sound too enthusiastic. 'It'd be great to have more time with you.'

'Yeah, well, I feel like a redo of the family lunch may be in order.'

They stared at each other and simultaneously burst into laughter.

'Oh, man, I thought Dad would combust right there at the table.' She chuckled. 'You've really got it down to an artform, winding him up.'

'He makes it too easy.' He smirked.

'You know, he'd love you to visit his new place in town. It's pretty cool, just a small townhouse. Caleb's helped him decorate.'

'He seems all right, Caleb, I mean.'

'He's more than all right. He's been brilliant for Dad.'

Luke grunted in reply, the memory of their mother flitting between them.

'I know the last few years haven't been easy, Luke. You could talk to someone, you know?'

'Stop, Kate. Fuck, you're like a reformed smoker, the way you evangelise. Just because you've found the church of fucking therapy, it doesn't mean we all need to, all right?'

Kate tamped down her fury at Luke's sudden outburst and rose to her feet, gathering her things. 'Well, I'm sure you're fine to get back to the Arms. So, I guess I'll call you.'

12

'Mr Reed, what are you doing here?'

Frank Reed was sitting in the reception area of Esserton Station. Kate had been summoned by the duty officer, having been informed that she had a visitor waiting. It wasn't a good time. Eric Harrington, who had flown in from Sydney, along with Celeste Rowntree were assembled in Esposito's office. Both had lately returned from Tweed Heads, where they had viewed Marcus's body at the Northern District Base Hospital morgue accompanied by officers from Esserton. A press conference on Marcus's death was scheduled to commence in less than half an hour.

'Have you spoken to the Queensland Police? Are they going to reopen the case?'

Kate hesitated, half irritated, half torn. He seemed to have spruced himself up for the occasion so he would be taken seriously. A clean, collared shirt was paired with a mostly clean pair of pants. His hair was wet and combed back, and he had attempted to shave, badly. Clumps of stubble that his trembling hands had missed stuck out along his jawline. And Kate could smell the undercurrent of stale alcohol that seemed to seep from his pores, the result of years of pickling that couldn't be brushed away with a single morning of mouthwash and soap.

'You said you were going to look into it for me.'

She had promised no such thing. Kate wiped the sweat from her brow and discreetly looked around. The last thing she needed was Mr Reed to be bailed up by a journalist. For his pain to find vent in the papers. The story would run and the journalist would vanish, and then what? Frank Reed would still be left as he was, without relief, the news cycle having moved on.

'Mr Reed, it's good to see you. I didn't realise you were coming in today.'

'If I had told you, would you have seen me? I know you think I'm being too emotional. But he was my son, Detective. I know my Ant, and he wouldn't do this.'

She relented. An overemotional parent. Kate had been accused of that and much worse as a new mother juggling work and home life. Derided for inserting sentiment into decision-making. As if the very act of being a parent made her less rational, less objective. She had sympathy for Mr Reed. His instincts about his son were based on accumulated knowledge absorbed over a lifetime.

And yet. Kate did not want to feed him false hope.

'Mr Reed, you have to understand that my hands are tied. You know I can't get involved in a police investigation in another state.' But what about the Queensland Police contact Celia had passed on? Kate had sent an initial text but hadn't bothered to follow it up. There had been so many more pressing matters to deal with.

'Why are you lying to me? I know you helped that other family. The inquest has been reopened for that young man who died in the floods because of your investigation. What's so different about this? Why won't you do this for Ant?'

'Mr Reed—' she began, trying to find the words to explain. The case he was referring to had happened in their own police district. Yes, it too had been in response to a request by the family, but Kate had been asked by one of the police hierarchy to review that case. Here, she would be on her own.

He raised a hand to stop her from going on. 'You've said your piece. You're not going to help me. I get it.' His eyes held disappointment before they clouded over, retreating inwards, like he was closing up shop. He rose to his feet, refusing any help, and shuffled painfully towards the door.

72

'Mr Reed, will you be right to get home? I can get someone to drive you—'

'Kate, here you are. I was looking for you.' Esposito had appeared from the doors leading to the back offices. His voice was polite, but there was a bite of impatience held in check.

'You know...' Frank Reed had turned around. 'Ant always thought you were stuck-up at school, thinking you were too good for us. Too high and mighty for Esserton. I see nothing's changed.' The automatic doors slid open and swallowed Mr Reed into the searing heat outside.

'Everything all right?' Esposito glanced from Kate to the departing figure, his annoyance sharpening into interest.

'Everything is fine, sir.'

'Good to hear. We're on in ten.'

As she made to leave, she realised that Mr Reed had left something behind under his seat. A plastic shopping bag.

She addressed the duty officer. 'Constable, can you try to catch him and return this, please.'

—

The minute she stepped into the room, set up with mics with a dozen or so mingling reporters, Kate felt a visceral heat travel through her body. Media conferences had never been her favourite pastime, but she had become increasingly averse to the task since her own personal life, and that of her father, had been dragged into the broadsheets during a high-profile case earlier in the year. The private grief of families she could handle. It was the unpredictability of journalists that made her want to run for the hills.

A light hand on her forearm made her start. She found herself facing the wide shoulders and tanned face of Richard Markham from the *North Coast Leader*, the local rag. He loomed above her, Kate's face reaching somewhere mid-torso. They had helped each other out in the past year. Kate had pointed Markham to the source who had broken the story on the

Esserton Police corruption scandal. It had been picked up by all the national dailies, making Markham hot property for months on end. She recognised the expression on his face: apologetic but determined.

'Can we talk?'

'The briefing's about to start.'

'This won't take long. Trust me, you'll want to know.'

She led him back out through the same door and walked him to an empty stairwell.

He didn't wait for her to speak. 'Listen, we know it was your brother behind the tweet and we're running a piece tomorrow.'

'Right,' she said, her voice tight. Markham was a local, not born and bred but close enough. Of course, he would have figured it out first. Not that it would have been hard. Luke's Twitter handle didn't identify him, but the photo he had posted would have done the trick. She assumed Markham had dug up an old Esserton High School yearbook, which would have named her brother alongside his two best friends.

'I argued against it. I personally don't think it's worth wrecking our relationship with the station.' He paused. 'But one of our photographers snapped Luke going into the station this morning and you walking out with him. John was hanging around trying to get a lead on the first pictures of Harrington.'

Panic roared in her ears. *Fuck! It was happening all over again.*

'I don't think anyone else has cottoned on yet, but fair warning, I'll be asking you about him in there. If your brother is a person of interest on this, that's a story. I'm sorry, Kate, but there's obviously a conflict of interest here if you're the lead detective on the case. The story practically writes itself. Luke knowing Marcus's identity before anyone else did and tweeting about it, well, that's a clear link to you. How else could he have got the information?'

'Sarge, they're waiting for you.' Constable Darnley came into view, looking between Markham and her with curiosity.

'As I said, fair warning,' Markham repeated, then strode back to the briefing room.

13

Kate looked down at the ancient cattle dog that lay splayed by her feet on the worn timber deck. She leaned over to rub the dog's belly, and her fur, coarse like brush matting, came away in clumps in her hands.

'How are you, Boof? How come you're not chasing me today?'

The dog's collar declared her to be *Billie*, but she had been called Boof for so long that it was the only name she answered to. Boof's tail thumped once, twice and lay still, exhausted by the effort. Kate felt the shallow rise and fall of Boof's chest. Her breath sounded laboured, and her once-sturdy body was bulging with cancerous growths. Just a few months ago, Boof would have been racing beside her police-issue Nissan Patrol, barking her head off and doing her level best to get run over. Kate felt a pang for the freewheeling mutt that was not long for the world.

The screen door flung open and Sarah Osmond emerged, carrying a couple of Coronas with lime wedges sticking out of their necks. Handing one to Kate, who was sitting cross-legged beside the dog, Sarah flung herself onto a frayed cane chair. The homestead was devoid of decorations. Sarah's mother had passed away a week shy of Christmas and celebrating the season had never been a priority for her friend.

'Cheers, big ears.'

Same goes, fuck nose. Their old high school bottoms-up.

Kate smiled and clinked her bottle against Sarah's. Pushing the lime into the amber liquid, she took a deep swig. It was ice-cold and went down exactly right. She leaned back against the weatherboard cladding, feeling its warmth seeping into her skin. Although the sun had dipped behind the roofline, the heat clung to the air, fetid and heavy. In the distance, framed by the verandah posts, her eyes took in the familiar view of Mount Nullum, its verdant slopes rising to the south.

She took another long draught of her beer. She'd definitely earned it. It had been a bastard of a day. Markham had been true to his word, relentless in his questions about Luke's connection to the case and the detective in charge. Esposito had taken the lead, confirming that Luke had indeed been helping the police to establish a timeline around Marcus's last hours, and thanking the families for their understanding over the untimely release of Marcus's identity into the public domain. To his credit, Esposito had tried his best to move on and deflect attention from Kate as far as possible. But the damage was done. In the end, it had been Eric Harrington, the veteran actor, expert at reading an audience, who had turned the course of the press briefing and redirected the attention of the journalists. His tearful statement recounting Marcus's life had silenced the reporters, reminding them of the grief crowding the room, beyond the particulars of a tweet. The concluding questions had been directed to the family, mostly to Eric, once it had become clear that Celeste Rowntree, sitting statue still, would provide only single-word answers.

When it was over and Ms Rowntree and Eric Harrington had departed – Celeste back to Uki and Harrington to his accommodation in Murwillumbah – Kate had waited for Esposito in his office. Scanning the room, not yet embellished with personal touches since its last occupant had departed, she had thought of all the previous times she'd been called in there to defend her position and fight to maintain a seat at the table. She had steadied herself for the battle to come, but Esposito had surprised her.

'You're not off the case, if that's what you're thinking. I can't afford a detective of your experience to be sidelined just because your brother happens to be a friend of the deceased.' This had been the reverse of the bruising, abrasive encounter she'd had with Esposito that morning when he had dressed her down in between mouthfuls of eggs and coffee.

He had given her a short smile, his face for a moment settling into the younger version she remembered. 'Go home, Kate. Let's see what this Markham bloke publishes tomorrow and we can take it from there.'

Esposito's tired face had stayed with her, his tie loosened at the collar and a five o'clock shadow bruising his jawline. It had been a hell of a way to begin a new placement, she reflected. And yet he was still there at the station, even though technically he wasn't even meant to start until Monday.

A strange feeling had risen within her as she had left the station. Esposito's apparent support was not unwelcome, but she could feel the strings attached, winding languidly around her and tugging firm, threatening to strangle. She had to remind herself that she didn't know him anymore. Had she ever known him? To trust him once again would mean walking unseeing into an abyss, without a clue of how deep and how far she could fall.

'God, I just can't believe it.' Sarah's voice cut through her reverie. 'First Ant and now Marcus. What the fuck is happening?'

Kate didn't reply. The mention of Ant made her think of the plastic bag Mr Reed had left behind at the station, containing a thick sheaf of papers held together with a bulldog clip. When the duty officer had tried to return the bag, Mr Reed had told the constable to *keep it and give it to the detective*, saying he had printed it out for Kate. It was a copy of the Queensland Coroners Court report into Ant's death. Kate had thrown the bag into the car with the rest of her stuff without a second glance. Ant would have to wait his turn, until she had a better handle on his friend's death.

Her gaze moved to Sarah, watching her friend tap a nervous beat on her bottle with the thin gold band of her mother's onyx ring. Her nails were cut so short they looked red-raw. Calling in at Sarah's on the way home had been a spur-of-the-moment decision, but she was glad she had come. This was a drink with a mate who was hurting just as much as Luke.

'How… how are the kids going?' Sarah's face was set. It was the right thing to ask. The polite and caring thing, but Kate could tell she didn't want to know the answer. It was too hard to hear.

Kate shrugged. 'As you'd expect. They don't really under-stand what's happened, yet. It's going to take years of therapy to set right.'

'Sometimes even years of therapy isn't enough.'

Kate could hear the sadness behind that statement. She knew that Sarah was thinking of Nadine, and all the years that Ant had tried.

She had a sudden memory of Sarah chiding her younger sister at Mrs Osborne's funeral, urging a bottle of water on the inebriated twenty-year-old who was barely holding it together. Almost all her life, Sarah had acted as both a parent and sister to Nadine. Even though she didn't have kids of her own, Sarah understood the heartbreak of being a parent.

'At least the kids will know it was an accident. Nothing to do with them. Who knows, maybe this was the better solution. For the kids and Fi.'

Kate glanced sharply at her friend.

'What? Anyone who was paying attention could tell where that was heading.'

'I didn't know you kept such close tabs on Marcus and Fi.'

Sarah sighed. 'You don't remember, do you? I've known Fi for years. She used to babysit Nadine, back in the day. I've known for a while that Fi and Marcus weren't working. And Fi won't admit it, but I have no doubt there were other women in the background. And they were probably there for a while.'

'I heard he had a temper on him.'

'He could be aggressive, yeah,' she sighed. 'When Fi still lived there, his skill set very much leaned towards destroying their furniture and punching holes in the plaster board. I ended up donating a few things from here: the bunk beds that Nadine and I used to sleep in and Mum's old desk, and a few odds and ends the boys could play with. He never hurt the kids, as far as I could tell. But he was vindictive, and he wasn't above using the boys to get back at Fi when he could.' She hesitated for a second before continuing. 'There were occasions when Louise Askall or I would take it in turns to visit when Marcus had the kids and he would make a point of not returning Fi's calls.'

'Did you do that often? Check up on the kids like that?'

'Probably Louise more than me. She mostly worked from home, so Fi would often ask her to.'

Kate reflected on her conversation the previous day with Fiona. Marcus's wife had been at pains to play down her relationship woes with her husband, but Sarah's take seemed to mirror Céleste Rowntree's observations about her son's family. It seemed Fiona had been warier of her husband than she let on, especially around the kids. Louise Askall also appeared to have held back from revealing all she knew, presumably out of a sense of loyalty to Fiona. She made a mental note to check in with the neighbour again.

'What's Louise Askall's story? Do you know much about her?'

Sarah shrugged. 'Not really. Fi introduced us a couple of years ago when she moved to the area. I think she's originally from around Toowoomba way. Fi loves her. She's been great with the kids.'

'But you're not keen?' Kate asked, picking up on a slight reserve in her friend's voice.

'No, I didn't say that. She seems perfectly nice.'

'Wow, that's a ringing endorsement.'

'Oh, shut up.' Sarah laughed. 'She's fine. She's been a great support for Fiona living so close.'

'But...'

'Oh God, it's nothing,' Sarah said, now with a trace of embarrassment. 'It's like she tries too hard or something. Wants to be good at everything. Like she'll put out biscuits and pretend they're homemade when they're obviously store-bought. I mean, why lie about something like that? It's so unnecessary.'

Kate smiled. People lied about so many things. Big, small and every size in between. That was how society rubbed along, to get ahead, to not hurt someone's feelings, to get through an awkward conversation, to make small talk, to protect your loved ones, and to hide your mistakes and misdeeds.

'How'd you know the biscuits weren't homemade?' she asked.

'Oh, I know.'

Kate laughed but didn't contradict her friend, who had been a baker all her life, right from a toddler, keeping her mother company in the kitchen.

'Okay, apart from her biscuit deficiencies, is there anything else I should know?'

Sarah rolled her eyes. 'Well, she's renting the place. You know that's the Massedons' old place, right? It exchanged hands a few times after they sold it, but it's owned by a couple in Noosa now, and their daughter stays over sometimes. It's apparently part of the deal for the house. The daughter's studying at Southern Cross in Lismore, and if she needs a place to stay during the uni holidays or whenever, she gets to use the studio flat above the garage. Louise reckons it's how the owners keep an eye on the place.'

'And do you think there was anything going on with Marcus and this girl?' Kate asked, cottoning on.

'I couldn't say,' Sarah replied. 'I only met her the one time a few months back, and she seemed nice enough. I think her name was Kerrie or Kirsty or something. To be honest, I don't know if she visited often enough for Marcus to have tried anything. But I do know he preferred them young. That's where his eyes would go when he surveyed the room at the pub or RSL. You could pretty much bet on it.'

'Lovely,' Kate remarked. 'Listen, Sarah, it would be great if you could come into the station and put this all in a statement, about Marcus and Fi's relationship.'

'What, why? We're just talking, aren't we?'

'We are, but you obviously knew the family well, and it would be helpful for us to have all this on file. It gives us background on Marcus's state of mind and will assist us with the coroner's report.'

Sarah grunted. 'God, you really sound like a copper some-times, you know that?'

Kate laughed. 'It's because I am one.'

'Yeah, but it's like you've inhaled a cop show or something, the things you say.'

Kate snorted, a dribble of beer escaping her lips. 'What can I say? I aced the police course on speaking like a fuckwit.'

'It shows.' Sarah grinned. 'Do you think you'll ever do anything else?' she added.

'What? Something other than a copper?' Kate was silent for a beat. 'I honestly don't know. It's not something I think about, not really.'

'Geoff would probably prefer it. He'd sleep easier.'

'He would. But then we wouldn't have any money, so there's that.'

She was being flippant. But it was easier than delving into that particular iceberg, which continuously lurked just below the still waters of her marriage. She knew that Geoff would love her to give up the police force for a profession that posed less strain on their family life and removed his constant worries about her welfare and safety. But that would mean throwing away all the years of slog, the slow and patient climbing, dealing with all the bullshit and dick swinging and bureaucracy to prove her worth. It felt like so much of her life and identity were tied up with proving herself against those jeering voices that told her it was her skin colour, her gender and her father's influence and not her ability that had got her there. To give it all up now felt nigh-on impossible.

Kate took in the bags under Sarah's eyes and the tired slump of her shoulders. Did her sudden interest in Kate's job reflect her friend's own dissatisfaction with the direction her life had taken her? Seemingly wedded to her job as a geriatric-care nurse, in the town of her birth and living in the same house that she had grown up in. There didn't seem to be any men friends, or for that matter any women friends, on hand. And all Kate's past attempts at inquiry had been met with polite but determined deflection.

'How are you getting on at work?' she asked, putting the onus back on her friend.

Sarah screwed up her face. 'Oh, so we've come around to me, have we? Got to that part of the visit.'

'What do you mean?'

'Your checklist to make sure your sad and lonely friend is okay.'

'So, you admit that you're sad and lonely.'

'Piss off.'

'Yeah, but seriously, Sarah. It would help to see someone. To talk about things.'

'Let's not, all right?' Sarah's response was an echo of her brother's.

Kate swallowed the last of her beer. Sarah was coping the best she could. Just as they all were.

She rose, surrendering her empty bottle and pulling her friend into a tight hug. Breathing in her scent, she realised with a pang that Sarah had gone back to wearing Chanel. The perfume Sarah's mother had gifted both sisters on their respective sixteenth birthdays. Sarah had stopped wearing the perfume when her mother had passed. Maybe this was a good sign.

'Make sure you call me, if you need anything.'

THEN

'Mate, you need to slow down.'

'Fuck off, Grayling. It's my fucking party, isn't it? I'm the goddamn birthday boy. It's all for me, brother.' Marcus cheered loudly, swaying on his feet. He threw his head back and chugged on a bottle of Grey Goose, sucking on the vodka like it was water.

He stumbled on his feet and Luke caught his friend before he fell. He pressed Marcus down, forcing him to take a seat at one of the corner tables. Luke sat down beside him and motioned for the vodka.

'Atta boy.' Marcus grinned and passed him the bottle, laughing as Luke took a generous gulp of the crisp, smooth spirit.

'Good, innit? It's the top-shelf stuff. Nothing but the best for his fucking loser son.' He turned and screamed the last bit at the packed dance floor, his words drowned out by the music and noise of the hundred-plus revellers.

'C'mon, mate. There'll be other auditions. It happens to everyone. You can't get every job.'

Marcus laughed, a bitter, angry sound. 'Fuck the audition, man. You think any of that shit matters? Do you know what he told me? He's off to LA. Doesn't know for how long. A few years at least, he thinks. He's fucking leaving me. Again. So long, dickhead. It's been fun, but I got offered fuck-loads of money, so off I go. You'll be right, won't you? Going back to your tiny, useless life.'

'Marcus, I'm sure it's not like that—'

'Of course it's fucking like that, Grayling. Don't tell me what it's like and not like. You wouldn't have a clue with your perfect bloody nuclear family. This party. All these people – who I don't even know, by the way. All his friends, not mine. This is all for him. So he's surrounded and there's less chance of a scene. Forever a buffer between him and his needy fucking son.' He pointed towards a packed table littered with drinks at the other end of the room, where Eric Harrington was holding court surrounded by friends, admirers and hangers-on.

Luke froze, uncertain how to respond. Marcus didn't share. He didn't get into his feelings. Marcus was confidence personified. He attacked life like it was a banquet laid out entirely for his gratification. He was all about parties and tequila shots and pulling chicks. Luke didn't know how to deal with this version of his friend. Drunk and hurting, his soft underbelly exposed for all to see.

Marcus was muttering something under his breath, the words whispered so softly that Luke wasn't even certain he had heard them properly.

'… did it for him. All for him… make him proud.'

And suddenly Marcus was crying, soundless, apart from deep, hacking breaths, his torso shaking and his face contorted, his hands clamped to his forehead.

'Marcus, mate.' Luke pressed a hand to his shoulder.

Marcus flinched as if he'd been burned. He swatted Luke away and rose unsteadily to his feet, pushing through the crowd towards the entrance.

Luke let him go, knowing instinctively that Marcus wouldn't want to be followed. He'd be back once he'd had a chance to pull himself together. Whatever else Marcus was, he wasn't stupid. He was skint and Luke was certain that his friend would never ditch his own bash for another, when this one offered free everything.

He lifted the bottle of Grey Goose to his lips. Eric Harrington was a shitty parent, but he knew how to throw a party. It felt like everyone from town had travelled up to Surfers for the night. All their mates from Year Twelve, like a second schoolies for the newly minted eighteen-year-olds, a last hurrah before settling down to uni courses, apprenticeships and real life. Even a scattering of kids from Years Ten and Eleven seemed to have snuck in. All the Esserton townsfolk were trying not to gawk at the various almost-celebrities and soapie stars Eric had lured over from Sydney. His eyes roamed the packed space and smiled as he caught sight of Ant Reed with a girl on his lap, seemingly superglued to her face.

There was a burst of laughter and his eyes found the source: soft hair on tanned skin and that damned sparkly top, which moved with her body. He would be happy to look at her all night. Her eyes appeared to trace across him before she excused herself from the group and moved to the outside terrace to light up. Luke smiled, his stomach doing a little back flip and all thoughts of Marcus falling away. Reaching into his pocket for his own pack of smokes, he stood up, steadying himself against a sudden light-headedness, and followed her out.

14

Monday

From her back deck, Kate took in the early-morning sky, bright azure and blinding. The air was utterly still and breathless. It was not even seven o'clock and yet exhaustion was stealing through the trees, their crowns bowing in surrender. Even the morning birdsong seemed listless and subdued. The day bracing itself for another scorcher.

She sucked on her coffee and leaned against the railing. Beside her, the deflated form of a blow-up Santa, Geoff's big Christmas decoration purchase for the year, lay flat and motionless, biding its time until the evening when the automatic timer and air compressor would bring it to life. Usually, she enjoyed this time by herself. Breathing in the day before the world had really woken up. Focusing on the tasks that were ahead of her: dropping Archie at preschool and then driving to Tweed Heads for Marcus's autopsy. But today, it was her phone, and more specifically the online news, that was taking up her attention.

She turned back to the article displaying Markham's by-line. The facts presented were all technically true. At no point did the article accuse her or the Esserton Police of outright negligence or bias. It was the way each piece of information was arranged, lined up one after the other just so, which made it impossible for readers to be left with any other impression.

Fact one: Detective Sergeant Kate Miles and Luke Grayling were siblings. Fact two: Luke Grayling had been privy to the death of his childhood friend, Marcus Rowntree, well before the information was released to the public, as evidenced by his (now deleted) tweet. Fact three: Kate Miles was the detective in charge of investigating the circumstances of Marcus Rowntree's death. Fact four: Esserton Station had confirmed that Luke Grayling was one of the people assisting the police with their investigations. Fact five: Following his police interview, Luke was spotted at an outdoor café in Esserton, enjoying a relaxed iced coffee with his sister. Fact six: Esserton Station had recently been embroiled in a corruption scandal involving its previous station head, Chief Inspector Andrew Skinner. All the dots leading to one conclusion.

The images that accompanied the article did the real damage. Luke heading out of the station with his head down, his hands thrust deep into his pockets, the dark bruising around his eye still visible despite the angle of his face. And a second photo of Luke and Kate seated at an outdoor café table, laughing. No doubt plenty of other photos had been taken, when they had been facing each other silent and sullen. But the newspaper unsurprisingly had chosen to go with the photo that had captured their one moment of levity, a joke at their father's expense, which had broken the tension. The photo that would create the worst impression, making them look insensitive and uncaring in the face of a friend's death. A second article followed, detailing the known facts of the case, accompanied by copious quotes from Eric Harrington's tearful press conference, as well as an old image of Harrington with a teenage Marcus posing on the red carpet.

If she was being honest, it wasn't as bad as she had expected. Maybe Markham had pulled back due to their history. She had read much worse, although no doubt her brother wouldn't see it that way. She had called him last night to give him a heads-up, and to prepare him as much as she could. He wasn't picking up this morning, though she had tried multiple times. He shouldn't be dealing with this alone, but instinctively, she knew that she shouldn't be the one making the trip to the Arms. Now was not the time for another photo of Kate and her brother to end up in the papers. She texted her father, instead, and Caleb a minute later as a precaution. She knew she could rely on Caleb even if her father proved bull-headed.

–

'The cause of death is a single gunshot wound to the chest by a .22 long rifle rimfire round, which entered the chest cavity, perforating the heart's right ventricle, and penetrated into the left, where the projectile was retrieved. The cause of death is intrathoracic haemorrhage resulting from a rupture of the heart tissue. A Ruger 77/22 bolt-action rifle was recovered at the scene and is assumed to be the weapon fired, subject to ballistic confirmation.'

Graham Barlow, the senior forensic pathologist at the Northern District Base Hospital, cleared his throat, a long-drawn-out sound that seemed to go on forever, as he concentrated on his computer screen. After spending the majority of the morning in the mortuary suite, observing Marcus's body being catalogued in every way possible, Kate had joined Barlow in his office to extract the edited highlights of his findings. Sometimes he was happy to oblige, but often he would insist she await his formal report, mostly, she thought, just to piss her off.

Today it seemed he was in a benevolent mood, and despite the growl in her stomach that informed her it was well past lunchtime, she made herself focus.

Her mind flicked back to the remnant of the bullet found in Marcus's body. A couple of hours ago, she had watched Barlow retrieve it using plastic forceps to prevent scratch marks on its metal surface. The .22 unjacketed lead projectile was so deformed and fragmented that ballistics would have a job matching it to the weapon, but she reminded herself, that they also had the spent cartridges found on site for comparison.

'Rigour is fully established and signs of lividity with blanching is present along the deceased's back, buttocks and underside of his thighs and legs,' Barlow continued. 'The body also exhibits the presence of blowfly eggs in multiple cavities, as yet unhatched. Based on these factors, I would place the postmortem interval at between twelve and twenty-four hours from when the body was discovered on Saturday afternoon. Later than that and I would expect to see hatched maggot larvae and signs of rigour dissipating.'

'The body was called in at 2 pm on Saturday, so we're talking anytime from approximately 2 pm on Friday to around 2 am on Saturday morning?' Kate asked.

'As I said.'

'We have a witness who says the victim was still alive at 9.30 pm,' she said, thinking of Luke's statement. Actually, Kate mentally corrected herself, Marcus's Facebook post at 8.46 pm provided the most accurate evidence of when he was alive. While she had no reason to doubt Luke's version, her detective instincts reminded her that his statement was uncorroborated.

'That is your domain, Detective. I think you'll find that 9 pm on Friday remains within my estimate.' Barlow's eyes narrowed at her over his computer screen. His fingers drummed on a packet of cigarettes, a none-too-subtle reminder that she was keeping him from the real love of his life, and that his patience was running thin. She took in the stark, emaciated image on the packet, health warnings of the risks of smoking, which seemed to have no effect on Barlow, though he could easily pose for one of the shots with his gaunt figure and death pallor.

She shook away his words. He wouldn't be Barlow if he wasn't trying to antagonise her or show her up.

'What about the manner of death? On site, it looked like the gun may have gone off accidentally when he was trying to get across the fence. He was drinking pretty heavily, and apparently he wasn't the most responsible or safety conscious of blokes.'

'We'll have to wait on blood screens and toxicology, of course, but yes, based on the empty beer bottles documented in the scene photos, I think we can safely assume that alcohol was a factor in affecting his motor coordination and reaction time.'

She noticed that he hadn't answered her question. 'Are you thinking suicide?'

'Marcus Rowntree is six foot two and has an arm length of ninety-three-point-five centimetres, so he would certainly have been capable of reaching the trigger and shooting himself with this rifle model, which has a barrel length of fifty-point-eight centimetres. However, in suicides, I would expect a contact or close-range bullet injury because they're usually holding the muzzle close up to the skin. With no intervening clothing, for a contact injury, that would mean evidence of muzzle imprint, searing and skin tearing. For a close-range injury, there should be signs of gunpowder carbonation – or soot – marking the skin around the bullet entry site, hair singeing, and even unburned grains of powder injected directly into the wound. In this case, there is no soot and the skin around the entry site shows more of a *tattooing* pattern. Small puncture abrasions from unburned gunpowder grains marking epithelial tissue in a radial pattern,' he explained. 'Tattooing without carbonation is more characteristic of a gunshot from further away. I would estimate up to a hundred centimetres away, again subject to confirmation by ballistics.'

He caught her eyes again, waiting for her mind to catch up.

'You're saying the gun was fired from about a metre away? That means he couldn't have held the gun himself, either deliberately or by accident.' The knowledge settled in her chest like a dead weight.

'That would be my professional opinion. The entry wound is backed by fingerprint evidence recovered from the weapon. It's been wiped clean with only a single set of partial prints that match Marcus Rowntree's right index finger and thumb close to the stock near the safety. As I understand it, Marcus used this weapon fairly regularly, in which case I would expect many more prints. If I had to guess, I would say his fingers were pressed to the gun after the fact.'

Kate nodded, trying to sort through the emotions crawling inside her. Her brother was the last person they knew to have seen Marcus alive. After visiting with Marcus, Luke had travelled back to the River Arms. There would be security footage from the pub confirming when her brother had got back to his accommodation. She had been called to the Arms around 11 pm that night when he had got into an altercation with a random backpacker, after which, at her insistence, he had stayed at her place. That still left at least an hour or so unaccounted for between the Facebook post and when Luke had arrived back at the pub.

Barlow had not finished. His words droned on over her scurrying thoughts. 'The body also exhibits what look like postmortem injuries along the right lateral side near the hip and buttock. A group of five to six contusions, yellowish-brown and bloodless in appearance. Given their positioning and pattern, I would say the injuries were sustained while the body was in a supine position. Possibly from being kicked—'

'Marcus was kicked while he was on the ground?'

Barlow gave a her a look, his annoyance clear. 'If you would let me finish… The pattern of injuries is contained to a defined area, indicating that the body didn't move or react on contact. Normally, you would expect a victim to curl up or move in response to repeated blows. This positioning and injury pattern suggest the blows were incurred postmortem when the victim was on his back and incapacitated.' He eyed her again, but Kate stayed silent this time, waiting for him to finish. 'So, it appears that your offender not only shot Marcus but kicked him after he died for good measure.'

Unbidden, Kate's thoughts flew to the dark volleys her brother had been sporting on Friday night. If Marcus had been kicked after being shot in the chest, it was very likely that traces of blood would have made their way onto the offender's shoes.

'There was some clothing and shoes submitted yesterday. From a witness who was last seen with the deceased. Has the testing on that commenced yet? Have they found any traces of Marcus's blood or anything else?'

Barlow looked at her like she was a child. 'Not my department, Detective. You need to check directly with forensics – although if they were only submitted yesterday, I think you may need to lower your expectations a tad and wait your turn.'

Kate bit back a retort, but she knew he was only speaking the truth. Even as she had asked the question, she knew what the answer was going to be. And yet, the panic had reared and it had tumbled out.

Only one thought kept pounding through her brain. Based on the autopsy results, Luke was currently their prime suspect in the homicide of Marcus Rowntree.

15

Kate's mobile blared as she reached the car, her father's words audible even before the phone touched her ear.

'Have you seen the news?'

'Do you mean about Luke? Yeah, of course, I sent you the link this morning,' she said.

'Not that one, the article that's just gone online. They've interviewed the bloody backpacker that Luke got into fisticuffs with on Friday night.'

Another pebble of anxiety dropped into Kate's stomach. 'Is it bad?'

'Well, they've made him sound like a violent git who decked a bloke unprovoked, so yeah, I think it's quite bad.'

'Fuck.'

'Did you ever find out what exactly happened that night?'

Kate sighed as she fell into her seat and fiddled with her seatbelt. 'Not a word. You know how he was on Saturday. Well, he was worse on Friday night when I picked him up.'

There was a beat of silence before her father replied. 'Yeah, and that's the other thing. The article has got onto the fact that it was you who turned up at the pub to deal with Luke.'

'Right.' She could see what the paper was doing. It was doubling down on the impression it had created with the first article: that Luke was unreliable and that Kate, his big sister in the police force, was in the habit of cleaning up after his mistakes and smoothing out his path with the law. She wondered idly who at the pub had given out the information. Had it been Dom, the bouncer, or Rick Garret, the owner? Her bet was on Rick. It had the feel of a quid-pro-quo arrangement that Garret would be in on, his eyes perpetually on the next mutually beneficial opportunity. It wouldn't surprise her in the least to see a write-up of the Arms' revamped bistro menu in an upcoming addition of the *Leader*.

'Have you spoken to Luke? What's he saying about it?'

'I haven't seen him—'

'What? What do you mean? I asked you this morning—'

'Kate,' Gray cut in, his voice taking on that particular edge, which said, *I am the parent, not you*. 'He's not answering his phone and when I turned up at the Arms, he'd already checked out. Maybe he decided to go back to Sydney, after all.'

Shit! It wouldn't surprise her if her brother had decided to cut and run. When they had spoken yesterday, he had seemed sincere about wanting to hang around for Marcus's funeral, but that was before he'd woken up to his face in the news.

'Okay. Well, if you get on to him let me know, will you?' She rang off before her father had a chance to reply and punched in Luke's number. But just like this morning, it went to voicemail. Kate hung up without leaving a message. She should really speak to Esposito before she had any further communication with Luke.

Once the news went public that Marcus's case had turned into a murder investigation, the coverage on Luke would turn even further. She realised that Markham's articles had set Luke up perfectly for the carnage to come. If her father and Luke believed the current news coverage was bad, they had no idea of what was in store.

—

Kate probably could have sent a uniform for the security tapes, but something in her just needed to see exactly what her brother had been up to on Friday night. She told herself it was only so she would have a concrete timeline to take to Esposito. It was definitely *not* because she was trying to discover all she could before she was most likely booted off the case. She could hardly argue no conflict of interest, the way matters stood.

The dark, wood-panelled interior of the Arms' sports bar was cool and deserted when she made her way inside. It seemed it was too early even for the regulars. Rounding the corner to where the chimes of the pokies chirped and squabbled, she spotted the true locals, a couple of hunched silhouettes moulded to their stools, beers warming by their side, their eyes glued to the false promise of the bright lights. She headed for the bistro, empty apart from an elderly couple tucking into the daily lunch special.

Pausing outside the door to the kitchen marked *employees only*, she pushed it open, walking in on a couple locked in an embrace.

'Ah. Sorry, guys.'

'Fuck, you've got the worst timing, Sergeant.' Dominic Tohu, the Arms' head of security, groaned and reluctantly pulled away from his boyfriend. They were braced against the stainless steel of the kitchen counter; the bistro chef, Mitch Cosgrove, tucked snugly between Dom's legs. Mitch gently untangled himself when he noticed Kate.

She raised a hand in apology. 'Sorry, I did call.'

'It's all right. I should get back to work, anyway.' Mitch smiled.

'Yeah, you don't want to keep the hordes waiting.' Dom rolled his eyes and turned to Kate. 'The security footage?'

Blowing Mitch a kiss, he motioned for her to follow him into the corridor. 'You couldn't have waited ten minutes?' He adjusted his crotch as they walked.

Kate supressed a laugh. 'Dom, I truly am sorry. But you told me to get here by two.' She strode after him and into a back office.

Inside, Dom made his way to a desktop setup, his fingers moving across the keyboard. The screen came to life, a chequer-board of live security feeds from about a dozen or so separate cameras. She recognised the view from the side entrance leading to the carpark where she had stowed her vehicle, as well as several angles showing the floor area of the sports bar, the pokies, the bistro, the landing leading up to the Arms' accommodation and the beer garden out the back.

Dom handed her a USB. 'It's all on there. The footage from Friday night. I've got you all the cameras from 9.30 pm till closing. There's footage of Luke from the camera in the parking lot, the bar floor and the beer garden from about 9.50 pm onwards, and of you as well when you got in around eleven.'

She accepted the thumb drive, placing it into an evidence bag and labelling it.

'Rick's aware that you've asked for the footage,' he added.

A warning of sorts, she guessed. His way of telling her that it was the pub owner who had blabbed to the newspapers. But then, she had surmised that already. 'Do you know what happened with the backpacker?'

He sighed, shaking his head. 'By the time I got to them it was all over and Luke was down. I got the impression that he may have been trying to intervene in an argument between the bloke and his girlfriend. She was pretty insistent that they get out of there.'

'Is it captured by the footage?'

'Nah. They were out the very back of the beer garden. The camera doesn't reach that far. But there'll be other footage of them from that night. I can have a look, if you like.'

'Thanks, Dom. Could you also print me some stills of their faces, if you find anything good.'

'Not a problem.' He brought up the footage and silently scrolled for a few minutes. 'Will these do?' He pointed to the screen. When Kate nodded he sent the capture to the printer.

'Have they been back to the Arms since?' she asked.

'If they have, I haven't seen them. You could check at the Sub, they might still be there.' He hesitated. 'Listen, Sarge, I'm sorry about the papers and everything. Luke's a decent bloke. It's too bad he's got caught up in all of this.'

'I understand he checked out this morning. Did he happen to mention where he was going?' She forced herself to say the words. To admit out loud that their family had no idea where Luke was.

'I don't think anyone saw him leave. His room was empty and his swipe card was in the key box.' He paused again, seemingly wanting to say more, but the moment passed.

'Was he alone, do you know? Can you check this morning's footage?'

Dom complied, turning back to the computer and rewinding through this morning's video. He paused at the recording from the first-floor landing, which showed Luke carrying a holdall and walking towards the stairs at 9.42 am. One of the bar-area cameras had caught a glimpse of him, just a slice of his right forearm and holdall as he had passed through at 9.43 am. The last footage was of Luke exiting the pub soon after via the carpark entrance. The camera was angled to cover the venue door rather than the carpark in general, so there was no footage of Luke driving away in his hire car. If Luke continued to avoid her calls, it would be easy enough to check on the car-hire returns at the airport and flights back to Sydney.

'I can make a copy of this footage as well, if you like?'

'Thanks, Dom. That would be great.'

They walked back out together, Dom insisting on accompanying her. As they approached the bar, she caught sight of a tall figure dressed in jeans and a long-sleeved work shirt, leaning against the counter and ordering a drink. *Richard Markham*, doing his best grizzled farmer impression. *Fuck no.*

Dom paused, using his bulk to create a barrier so Markham wouldn't see her if he turned around.

'Actually, why don't I show you out through the back way?'

16

The Submariner Youth Hostel was difficult to miss. Its entire external wall was covered in a mural depicting a giant orange submarine swimming in an ocean of psychedelic coral. Various iconic Australian animals – a kangaroo, koala, emu, wombat, and crocodile – grinned maniacally from the submarine's portholes. Kate assumed the garish tangerine colour had been chosen by the owner to avoid any comparison to another quite famous submarine, though she imagined the reference would be lost on the venue's largely gen Z clientele.

Kate ventured inside, taking in the internal setup. Cheap and cheerful, a tad run-down and a bit loud in its colour scheme, with a reception plastered with tourist brochures and maps. The twenty-something man at reception sported a red Santa hat and a short-sleeved print shirt, several buttons undone. Kate held out her police ID, taking note of the name tag clipped to the front of his shirt.

'Zach, I'm trying to find a couple of guests who I understand are staying at the hostel.' She held up the security footage still that she had obtained from Dom. It showed the couple Luke apparently had argued with on Friday night, waiting to order drinks at the bar. The young woman was about five foot two, with wavy brown hair, and wearing a strappy summer dress. Her boyfriend towered over her in the image. Kate figured he must be well over six feet, sporting a buzz cut and muscle shirt with a full sleeve of tattoos on his right arm. Seeing the photo, it made even less sense to her why Luke had thought he could take this unit on.

Zach made a show of looking at the printout. 'Ah, look, we don't want any trouble.'

'No trouble, I just need to speak to them. Can you confirm if they're currently guests at the hostel?'

'Ah, yeah, that looks like Sam Delaney and Ben Keeling. They checked in on Friday and are booked in till Wednesday, actually.'

'They around at the moment?'

'Yeah, I think so. Maybe check around the kitchen or the common area?' He waved his hand vaguely.

'And their room number?'

'Thirty-two. It's a four-share, but only Ben and Sam are occupying it at the moment. It's just down the corridor to your right.'

'Thank you, Zach.' She handed him her card. 'If you do see them around, can you let them know I'd like to speak to them.'

'Um, yeah. All right.' He accepted the proffered card like it could bite him and placed it by the phone.

Kate made her way down the corridor.

At number thirty-two, she raised a hand to knock, but the door swung open before her knuckles had the chance to connect. A young woman started in surprise. Brown hair framing large, expressive eyes and a pale face dusted with freckles. A wide empire dress swamped her curvaceous body, the hem stretching below her knees and sleeves down to her wrists, despite the heat. She held herself unnaturally still. Her posture reminded Kate of her father, when he had broken his collarbone earlier in the year. He had held himself with just such rigidity, every unnecessary movement causing a spasm of distress to flicker across his face.

'Oh, sorry. Were you coming in? Are you staying here, too? Only they said we could have the room to ourselves, at least until tomorrow.' Her expression immediately took on a more worried countenance.

'No, I'm not staying here. I'm Detective Kate Miles with the Esserton Police.' She held up her ID, watching as the young woman's expression changed rapidly from relief to startled panic. It was obvious her name rang warning bells. Very likely Richard Markham had cautioned Sam and her boyfriend of this very possibility.

'You're Sam Delaney, right?' she persisted. 'I wondered if you had a few moments to speak? I was actually hoping to catch both you and your partner, Ben Keeling. Is he around?'

'Ben's not here. And we don't want to speak to you.' She went to close the door, but Kate was quick to wedge her body into the opening. The movement had cost Sam. Kate didn't miss her sharp intake of breath and the flinch of discomfort that crossed her face. Was Sam Delaney hiding injuries beneath that voluminous dress?

'Are you okay? You seem to be in a bit of pain. Do you need to see someone?'

'What? No, I'm fine.' The look of alarm was back on her face.

'Okay, well, Sam, I wanted to speak to you both about what happened on Friday night at the River Arms. I understand Ben got into an altercation with another patron, is that correct?'

She opened the door wider at that, a look of determination swamping her earlier anxiety, in defence of her boyfriend.

'That's not what happened. Don't make it out like it was Ben's fault. It was the other guy, poking his nose into our business, when it had nothing to do with him. He shouldn't have got involved. You can't blame Ben for getting upset.'

'I'm not taking anyone's side. I'm just trying to understand what happened—'

'Don't do that. Don't pretend as if you don't know exactly who he is. We know it was your brother. Richard warned us that you might come here. You only care about what happened because it made it into the news. This is about protecting your brother's name.'

Kate hesitated; the girl wasn't far wrong. Still, she ploughed on.

'It's in the news because that's what you chose. And you're absolutely right. It was my brother that night who somehow found himself at the other end of your boyfriend's fist. But none of you chose to make a complaint to the police. Not you or Ben or my brother or, in fact, the venue. So yes, I'm playing catch-up. And yes, I have a vested interest. But that doesn't mean I'm not open to hearing what actually happened.'

The woman glared at her. 'That was a lovely story, Detective, but I'm not stupid. Ben and I have nothing to say to you. Now please go, before I do decide to make a complaint. About police harassment.'

She waited pointedly until Kate had moved back from the door and slammed it in her face.

Fuck! She had ballsed that up completely.

17

'Do you believe your brother capable of this?'

Kate looked at her boss for a long time before answering. She had walked into Esposito's office the minute she had got back to the station and laid it all out, not omitting a single detail, from Barlow's autopsy opinion, to her brother's Friday-night special at the Arms, and the fact that she currently had no idea where her brother was holed up.

'If you're asking me if my brother's capable of killing someone, then of course my answer is yes.' She met Esposito's unwavering gaze.

She knew the effect of her words, the implications of her candour. If he was ever called to give evidence, Esposito could be compelled to repeat her words on record, possibly in a court of law, where this version could be manipulated and manhandled by a lawyer. And yet here she was, deciding to go all in. To lean on their history and put her faith in this man. She was letting him know that she was trusting him with her career and her family. *God, she hoped she was right.*

'But then, I believe everyone is capable of killing someone,' she continued grimly. 'Given the right circumstances, of course. Yes, Luke could have done this in the spur of the moment, in anger or accidentally, but he wouldn't have been able to hold it together for days on end. Not after killing a lifelong friend. I know they haven't been close in the last few years, but still. Going back to his accommodation, getting into a random fight with someone at the pub, coming home with me and then sitting through lunch with the whole family. There is no way he wouldn't have broken down.'

'So, you're saying nothing in your brother's behaviour in the past few days feels off or emotionally amiss.' Esposito kept his tone even. He wasn't trying to call her out or trip her up. He just needed to know.

A sudden irrational urge to laugh overcame her and she clamped it down.

'Kate?'

'Sorry, sir. I was just thinking that everything about my brother's emotional wellbeing has been slightly off the last couple of days. He was coming to terms with the loss of one of his oldest high school friends. Plus, he had to deal with us.' Kate pointed to herself. 'Our family has a history, to say the least. Luke's constantly on edge when he has to deal with us. But that's actually my point. He wears all his emotions on the outside. His grief, his frustrations, his anger. If this was him, he would have been an emotional wreck. He would have confessed straightaway. You've met him and interviewed him. You would have got a feel for him. You know what I'm saying is true.'

'In Luke's statement, he says he saw a vehicle turning into Marcus's property as he was driving back into town. He says he saw it in his rear-view mirror. A dark-coloured sedan turning left into the driveway, which he had pulled out of only moments earlier. Couldn't give us any more details than that. It's convenient don't you think, given the circumstances he now finds himself in.'

Her stomach swooped, something unpleasant squirming and snapping. Luke hadn't mentioned anything about seeing another car when they had spoken.

'I don't know anything about that. This is the first time I'm hearing about a car.'

Esposito watched her closely. 'He said he only remembered after he'd spoken with you at the Arms on Saturday evening.'

'Well, he was asleep when I got there, so I'm not surprised he forgot that detail.'

She held his gaze and the seconds ticked.

'Okay,' he said.

'Okay?'

'Okay, meaning I'll go with your instincts. For now,' he said with emphasis.

Kate exhaled, relief tripping through her veins. Close enough.

'However, it's not going to be sufficient for the AC,' he said, referring to the assistant commissioner of the Northern Region Command.

She nodded, knowing what was coming. She had been prepared for this. Of course, until her brother had been found and cleared of the investigation, she could not be involved. The chain of command would have been clear with Esposito on this point. Already, her presence had muddied the water and the media was watching. She needed to get out of the way, so that the team could build a clean case with admissible evidence.

'Sir, I have some leave owing. I think it would be easiest if I step back for a bit. For a week, maybe two. Give the team some breathing space.'

Esposito nodded. She was both frustrated and relieved that he didn't argue. It was pointless, anyway. They both knew that they would find themselves at this same juncture, eventually. Might as well rip off the Band-Aid now.

'It's not just you stepping back, Kate. The AC's office would like a new detective to take charge of the case. They've put forward a name, in fact. Josh Ellis from Byron Bay. I understand that he worked at Esserton for some months until his recent transfer. They thought he would be best placed to take over the case, given his familiarity with the area and the team. State Crime Command detectives are also available to assist as necessary through Tweed Heads.'

'Okay. Yeah, that makes sense.' Kate swallowed. She saw how Ellis would seem like the perfect choice. He was a political player and would keep the higher-ups fully briefed. Esposito, it seemed, had been busy over the weekend ensuring everyone was in the loop. They hadn't come up with this contingency on a whim. She wondered if this plan had been in train even when she was invited to breakfast yesterday. It was the Eric Harrington effect. The case was high profile and getting attention. The powers that be wanted to stave off any fuck-ups.

'Has Detective Ellis agreed to the proposal?'

'I understand that someone from the AC's office has broached the subject with him. That's how I got given his name. I'll need to call him to confirm the arrangements.'

She nodded. It seemed that Ellis would remain her own personal millstone, the one person she couldn't quite shake off. Kate had been in this position before, finding herself edged out of a case she was leading. But at least this time it would be on her own terms. She wondered idly when Josh would arrive back in town.

'You'll be kept informed of the case, Kate. Especially as it relates to Luke. I'll make sure of that.'

Kate knew this was a platitude. From now on, only those aspects of the investigation that were cleared for release would be revealed to her. Her last task as the case lead had been to assign Constable Greg Darnley, discreet and loyal to a tee, with the job of following up on Luke's hire car and checking on departing flights to Sydney from nearby airports. So far, there was no indication that Luke had left the area. If he had done a runner, it had not been by plane. If necessary, the next steps would be a call-out on his licence and registration, and a location trace on his mobile phone. Josh no doubt would take care of it.

'We'll need to search your property and your father's. Just routine. I'll have a couple of uniforms go home with you.' Esposito's words sounded oddly formal.

Kate nodded. Of course, they needed to confirm that Luke wasn't hiding away at either her or her father's residence. The most detailed search, she knew, would be saved for her father's rural property, currently unoccupied and sitting on the market awaiting a buyer. For a person who was familiar with the bush, there were plenty of places to camp out for a while. She didn't think that was her brother. For her money, he had hunkered down at a friend's or at an Airbnb somewhere. Booked online, a place that didn't ask too many questions.

'Can I explain to the team before I go?'

'I think it's only fair that you do.'

'Also, Sam Delaney. The backpacker whose boyfriend Luke got into an altercation with on Friday night. It's worth doing a welfare check. I think her boyfriend may have done a number on her.'

18

'You sure about this? Last chance to change your mind.'

'You want to back out?'

'Bro, I already told you. It's no skin off my nose. Nothing linking me to this prick. You're the only one it could affect.'

Luke stayed silent. From the window of the Subaru Forester, he watched a man leave a noodle house on the opposite side of the road and make his way down the street holding a carrier bag with a couple of takeaway containers. He wore a faded surf shirt, cargo shorts that hung off his flat-as-a-tack bum, and rubber thongs on his feet. His pale face and thick flaxen hair were obscured by a peak cap, pulled down. He walked while scrolling on his phone with his free hand. Luke knew that at the end of the block the man would turn right, cross through a small bush reserve and then turn left into a quiet residential street, where he would head for a modest, double-fronted brick house four dwellings down. The message that Luke had received from a friend almost a week ago now had proved correct. The man had indeed gone to ground.

'You sure it's the guy?' Dom Tohu asked him, mistaking his silence for hesitation.

For a brief second, her face came back to him. Stripped raw by hurt-fuelled rage. 'Yep, it's definitely him.'

'Right, then. Head up to the carpark by the beach. The one we passed on the way. There're no cameras there. I shouldn't be more than fifteen minutes.'

19

Tuesday

'Still not answering?'

Kate shook her head, trying but failing not to let her panic show. 'I think it's switched off. It's been almost twenty-four hours since he left the Arms. Why can't he just call and let us know he's okay?'

'It's not something he's used to, Kate. His name getting splashed in the papers. He just needs some time to process it all.' Geoff squeezed her arm. 'He'll get in touch when he's ready. It's going to be fine.'

Kate hummed, not answering. She knew Geoff meant well, but he didn't get it. The longer Luke stayed away, the worse it would look. She knew from experience that you needed to get on top of this stuff early. Nip it in the bud with your truth before the silence festered with other people's thoughts and speculations. When you left a vacuum, it got filled with shit. And it was much harder to reverse the public's mistrust and bad impression, once created. Luke burying his head in the sand and disappearing would just make the police and the media assume he had something to hide. Especially once Josh Ellis was back on the team. He would be unrelenting in his pursuit of the obvious solution, and Luke would be right in his crosshairs.

Kate didn't want to think of the alternative possibility. She knew it was playing on her father's mind, too, though neither wished to acknowledge it. She didn't really believe the prolonged absence meant Luke had done anything stupid, but still, she just wished he would call and put their minds at ease.

Geoff nudged her untouched plate of toast. 'So, this period of leave. Are you planning on doing anything in particular, or will you just be moping around the house pissed off at Luke?'

Kate smiled. 'Probably the latter.'

'Good to know. I'm glad you're not planning on wasting time, at least.'

Kate laughed, biting into her cooling toast. 'Don't worry, I can organise the kids if there's something you need to do. I am at your service,' she said through a mouthful of peanut butter on rye.

'Well, as it happens… I actually do have something on this week.' A smile played on his lips, his expression almost shy. 'I've got a job interview this Thursday, via teleconference,' he clarified. 'A senior architect position with Carter Group.'

Her eyes widened. Even she had heard of that name. Carter Group was a large architectural consultancy firm with headquarters in Melbourne and regional offices across the eastern seaboard. Geoff had mentioned the firm numerous times over his career, usually in frustration when they had outbid him on a project tender. She could tell that he wanted this, although he was trying to keep his emotions in check. After such a long spell of unemployment, he was doing his best to not get his hopes up, or to jinx anything.

She scooted around the breakfast counter to pull him into a hug. 'Geoff, this is brilliant. When did this happen?'

'I got the call yesterday. I meant to tell you last night, but you know with everything going on…' his voice trailed off.

Of course. Last night, her professional and personal problems had taken precedence, per usual, forcing Geoff to swallow his own news.

'What's happening? What's happening?'

Archie had appeared in the kitchen, carrying his empty cereal bowl from the lounge room, where he'd been eating his breakfast while watching cartoons, his morning routine. He looked between his parents, an expectant smile on his face, wanting to be brought in on the news.

'Daddy's got a job interview, mate. How exciting is that?'

'Oh.' Archie frowned. 'Will you be coming to Little Kickers today?' he asked, referring to his weekly indoor soccer lessons at the local community centre.

Geoff laughed. 'Of course, matey. Wouldn't miss your class for the world.'

Satisfied with his father's response, he patted Geoff on the arm. 'Well done, Daddy,' he said, before running back out to catch *PJ Masks*.

'Yeah, well done.' Kate planted a soft kiss on Geoff's forehead. 'I'm sure you'll crush it.'

—

'We got a couple of officers from Cronulla to check on his address. There's no one home. The occupants of the units on either side don't believe that anyone's been around for days. If Luke's back in Sydney, he hasn't been to his apartment. Is there anyone else you can think of that we should check with?'

Kate chugged on her takeaway coffee cup and shrugged. Her brother's personal life was something she had zero details on, apart from knowing he had one. An active one, at that. Luke had never had a problem pulling a date. He could be effortlessly charming when he wanted, and he had one of those faces and easygoing personalities that people were constantly making room for and giving second chances to. For years he had sailed through life, seemingly skimming the surface without raising expectations, and never being called to account. There had been a revolving door of partners over the years, and Kate had no idea if Luke was currently in a relationship.

'I wish I knew, Greg. He doesn't really share much about that part of his life.' He didn't share much about his life at all, if she was honest.

Constable Darnley sipped from his reusable cup without saying anything.

She had 'bumped into' him at Shot Shop, a newly opened café within walking distance of the station that guaranteed a decent brew. She knew she had a good chance of finding Greg here. After his daughters had surprised him with an espresso machine for his birthday a few months ago, Darnley had, almost overnight, swapped his instant Blend 43 for coffee snobbery. Now he was a regular at the café, with its sustainable, ethically sourced blends and the team of baristas who knew him by name. Plus, it was an excuse to join his wife, Vanessa, who managed the clothing retailer next door, for a quick break.

Kate had made a beeline to the café after dropping Archie at preschool. Darnley had spotted her immediately, displaying no surprise to see Kate perched at one of the corner tables, nursing a latte with Amy tucked into a child seat. Vanessa, long-limbed and at least an inch taller than her husband had smiled broadly on noticing the pair, coming over immediately to start cooing over Amy, who was happy to oblige with a smile that showcased two newly erupted bottom teeth.

'Oh my God, she is such a little cutey,' Vanessa gushed. 'Is that a tooth I see, Missy?'

Kate smiled. Vanessa and Darnley's two daughters were well and truly grown up and both studying at university. The parents were empty nesters and Vanessa predictably missed the baby stage, now that it was all nostalgia and none of the reality. The coffees were called at the counter and Vanessa looked disappointed.

'Oh, I've got to get back. But, Kate, you should come over for a meal sometime with the family. We'd love to have you.' With a quick peck of her husband's cheek, she left, collecting her macchiato on the way.

Darnley had moved to sit at Kate's table, smiling at Amy and gently tickling her cheek as she gurgled at him. He'd guessed Kate's game before she had uttered a single syllable, his expression kind and without judgement as he waited. Wasn't that why she had sought him out? Because he was considerate enough to not dismiss her outright but smart enough not to reveal anything that would compromise the investigation.

The words – *Is there anything new?* – had spilled out of her mouth. It had only been a few hours since she had been cut off from the investigation and yet she was desperate for news. Not only was her brother not answering his phone, but he seemed to have also dropped out of his social media accounts. According to Geoff, Luke had not reappeared on his socials since his infamous tweet on Saturday night. Not having access to the police network to locate her brother was doing her head in.

'It looks like he's turned off his mobile, so no luck with the mobile tracking,' Darnley offered. 'And nothing on his vehicle, yet. According to the hire firm, Luke called on Sunday and extended his rental for an extra week, so we assume he's still driving the same car, but he seems to be keeping off the main roads and highway.'

Kate concentrated on wiping food off Amy's hands and face. She had packed a fruit snack for her daughter and Amy had managed to mash the soft banana between her fingers and smear it all across the surfaces of the high-chair. As she cleaned up bits of fruit from Amy's hair, her mind picked over what Darnley had said.

The car-hire extension made sense. Luke had told her on Sunday that he'd made the decision to stay on for Marcus's funeral. She also understood why he would want to disappear for a while, stay off his phone and socials. Fall off the grid for a few days until the dust from the press fallout settled. She just didn't understand how he'd managed to slip through the cracks quite so successfully. Luke had once been a local, but Kate had thought that her brother had cut those ties, fairly ruthlessly. Apart from Marcus and Ant, had her brother retained any old friendships that he could now call on?

Darnley watched her deal with the mess Amy had made. 'Sergeant Ellis will be in the office by tomorrow morning, at the latest. Esposito received confirmation.'

Kate nodded. She would give him a call once he arrived. Get the conversation over with, to let him know that she was available to answer any questions or provide whatever support she could.

'When are the families being told?' The case was now being investigated as an unexplained death and the families needed to be informed.

'Esposito is meeting with Fiona and Celeste Rowntree this afternoon and afterwards with Eric Harrington. Barlow's preliminary report came through overnight,' he added.

'And the media?'

'There'll be a press conference later today.'

'Did you get a chance to speak with Louise Askall again?' She knew she was pushing her luck, peppering him with questions like this, as if she had a right to the answers. But he seemed happy enough to oblige, for the moment at least.

'Harris followed up with her on the rental situation,' Darnley replied. 'She confirms that the room over the garage is sometimes used by the daughter of the family who owns the property. But she says the girl hasn't used it in months, and as far as Louise knows the girl never met Marcus. Anyway, we're checking with her, directly. She lives on campus at Lismore. It's on the list.'

Kate nodded, avoiding Darnley's eyes. She walked her fingers along Amy's forearm, making a game of it, as the conversation stalled. She was grateful to the constable for speaking with her and sharing what crumbs he could. For giving her the time of day, even though he didn't have to. It might well be the last time she was able to meet with one of the team so openly.

By the end of the day, the news would be out. That a new detective had been brought on board, to curb any further allegations of conflict of interest. Because her brother had been identified as a person of interest. The reality of it struck her anew. The media was going to have a field day. Not only would her brother's life be picked apart but so would Kate's and her family's. It would be just another excuse to bring up the recent corruption saga, and all of her father's history when he was the station head at Esserton.

'There's something else, Sarge.' Darnley interrupted her thought spiral. He hesitated, catching himself, but deciding to continue.

'I got on to Luke's work yesterday afternoon.' He watched her carefully. 'It turns out he was let go from his firm a week ago. Last Tuesday.'

Darnley's words pinged around in her brain without any place to go. Her brother had been fired, and he had kept it from her, from all of them. In fact, he had lied to her deliberately, speaking of accrued leave rather than admitting the truth.

What was he ashamed of? The mere fact of losing a job or something worse? Darnley obviously knew. Sufficient details of Luke's termination must have been provided by the company. However, it was information that he wouldn't be sharing with Kate. Even as she knew this to be the case, she felt a beat of resentment towards the constable for holding out on her.

'Is Esposito planning on releasing that detail at the media conference?'

'I honestly don't know, Sarge. But I doubt it. It's not relevant.'

The look he gave her held pity and she tamped down a sudden urge to scream.

20

Kate scrutinised the contents of her father's fridge, picking out a Corona. One of the side benefits of her dad going out with Caleb was that the fridge was stocked with proper beer, not just her father's standards.

'Want one?'

'Nah, I'm still going.' Gray pointed to his stubbie of Carlton Draught.

Kate nodded, busying herself with slicing off a wedge of lemon for her beer. Bunty, her father's supremely pampered tabby, watched her from his nest of cushions on the couch. 'Sorry, mate,' she said. 'No food tonight.' The cat flicked his tail in disgust. He was still grumpy and unsettled by the recent move and had refused to be patted when she had arrived.

She had driven over to her dad's after helping Geoff with the kids' evening routine. Like Bunty, she was still getting used to his rented townhouse in Esserton, which was modern and compact and a far cry from the country cottage vibes of his previous property. The place still had an unfinished feel with many of Gray's belongings yet to be fully unpacked.

Taking a grateful swig of her beer, Kate joined her father on his balcony, where twilight was rapidly waning into night.

'Before I forget, a message from Archie: it's his preschool Christmas concert next week. It's on all week to allow as many parents and family to attend. So whatever day works for you is fine. Two o'clock,' she reminded him. 'He's been practising *Aussie Jingle Bells* for weeks.'

Gray laughed. 'Yep. Don't worry. Got that in the diary. Caleb's coming too.'

'Perfect. He'll love having you both there.' She took a sip of her beer before adding, 'He expects Luke to attend too. Apparently, Archie invited him when he was over on Saturday, and Luke said yes.'

Their eyes met, but neither spoke, the silence between them straining with unsaid things.

'Did you watch the news?' her father finally asked, deciding to take the plunge.

'I saw it.'

'I thought the new bloke handled himself well.'

Kate agreed. Esposito had conducted the press briefing with minimal fuss, outlining the current investigation status and that Kate had stepped back from the case. Luke had been identified as a person of interest, and members of the public with information on his whereabouts were being asked to contact the police. There had been no mention of Luke's employment woes. The tide of questions afterwards had been fierce and unrelenting, but Esposito had navigated each without being rattled. Not once had he thrown Kate under the bus, or implied that Luke was anything more than someone they wished to speak to once more.

'The newspapers tomorrow should be interesting,' Gray remarked.

'We know what's coming. We just need to ride it out,' she said, feeling less confident than she sounded.

'I take it you haven't heard anything from Luke?'

'Not a peep.' She took another long swig of her beer. 'You heard what Esposito said. The last sighting is the security footage of him leaving the Arms on Monday morning. I spoke to Darnley today.' She relayed all the constable had told her. 'Everything points to him still being in the area. But he must be getting help. He can't have disappeared this neatly without assistance.'

She could feel the worry she had been holding onto all day unfurling as she spoke. She was with her father and finally she could share the full extent of her fears with someone who felt the same way and wouldn't minimise or downplay them.

'I hear they're bringing Josh Ellis back to run the case.'

'How'd you know that?' Kate frowned. Esposito hadn't named Ellis in his briefing.

'I still have friends in the force who tell me things, on occasion.'

'Did your *friends* give you a heads-up about Luke's work?'

'What about it?'

'Apparently, he was fired from Hull-Hayward last week. I have a feeling Darnley has more details, but they're not saying, so whatever it is, it's not good.'

'What? But he never said.'

'Well, it's not like you two are the best at talking when you're together.' The words shot out before she could bite them back. 'Sorry, Dad. I shouldn't have said that—'

'It's okay. And you're right, I've never tried very hard to push past his defences. He knows which of my buttons to press and I let him. It's easier to be angry, I guess, rather than doing the hard work of trying to resolve the mess.'

Kate sat in silence, a bit stunned at her father's level of self-awareness.

'What? You think you're the only one with experience in psychoanalysis?' He gave her a small smile. 'Actually, Caleb might have helped me a bit, to work all that out.' He studied her carefully. 'The real question is, what are we going to do about it?'

'What do you mean?'

'C'mon, Kate. You're not telling me you're actually entertaining the possibility that Luke may be involved in any of this? You know your brother. He can be a dickhead, but there's no way he's killed someone. So I'm asking you again, what are you going to do to help him?'

'Of course, I don't believe Luke killed Marcus. But I can't do anything about it. I'm no longer involved in the case.'

'Kate.'

'Don't Kate me, Dad. You know why I can't. It's a straight conflict, that's exactly why I stepped back from the investigation. If my meddling results in the case not being able to be prosecuted, that's my career down the tube. This isn't some piddly case that no one's going to notice. This is Eric Harrington's son.'

'Kate, it's family. We have to do something.'

'What? What exactly do we do? What are you even asking me?' She stood and strode back inside in frustration, her father following close behind. Disrupted by their sudden reappearance, Bunty dropped lightly to his feet and loped out of the room.

'We could work out who did this to Marcus. Talk to his family and Eric. Or at least try to find where Luke's hiding out. There are people I can reach out to in the force. We can't just sit around, Kit.'

'Do you even hear yourself?' She rounded on him. 'What? We go all private eye and solve the case behind the team's back? It's not the bloody movies, Dad. This is real life and it's my job on the line. I can't run some kind of half-arsed parallel investigation. The minute I go anywhere near people involved with the case, I'll be in breach. You know that.'

Her father huffed and looked away.

'You know what would actually help? Not some amateur PI shit, but getting Luke a lawyer. Because, trust me, he's going to need one when they finally find him. Why don't you use your contacts to organise that?'

'Fine. All right. Forget I asked.'

She heard the disappointment in his voice. 'Would you have done this?' She glared at him. 'Risked your career and everything you'd worked for?'

He sighed, all the fight suddenly draining from his face.

'That's all I ever did, Kate.'

21

She ended up at the Royal Hotel, fuming and not yet ready to go home, taking her frustrations out on the pool table. She could rely on the Royal being relatively sedate on a Tuesday.

She ordered a drink and retired to an empty pool table at the back, breaking the rack and watching the balls scatter across the surface, none of them sinking. The conversation with her father had left a tangle of emotions: anger at him for expecting the impossible of her, guilt that she wasn't doing enough to help her brother, and unease that Gray would go off and do something stupid that would make everything worse. For the first time in what felt like forever, she had a boss who appeared to be on her side. She had given him her word and she needed to give the team space to do its job.

She knew it all stemmed from Gray's pathological need to feel useful, to be the one to fix things. But his so-called contacts weren't going to be of any use in this case. Luke was a person of interest in a murder investigation involving the son of a celebrity. The die was not cast in their favour. The police command was going out of its way to ensure the case was watertight, without any hint of internal interference. There was no special consideration coming their way. Her father should know this. It was his desperation speaking.

It was an unfair expectation to place on her. It shouldn't be all on her, anyway. What about Luke? Where the fuck was her brother? Why was he absent from his own life? Even Luke, with his utter self-absorption, had to realise this disappearing act wasn't helping his case.

Her phone buzzed and she glanced at it automatically. A text from an unknown number.

> Detective, I hope you don't mind me contacting you in this way. Your number was forwarded to me by Frank Reed, Anthony's father. Mr Reed mentioned that you were looking into the circumstances surrounding Ant's suicide and I wanted to reach out so you had my contact details. I was a friend of Ant's and a fellow welfare worker. If you have any questions, I would be happy to speak with you. Cheers, Jacob

She remembered that name. A sweaty red face came back to her, distressed and nervous, shuffling his notes at the lectern. Wasn't that the person who spoke at Ant's funeral? Kate stared down at the message, irritation battling against obligation. Maybe she could make the time to call him back this week.

She put her phone away and lined up her cue stick, swearing as the green ball she was trying to sink bumped off the pocket and spun sideways.

'Not having any luck, Miles. I remember you being a better player.'

She looked up to find a man in jeans and a light-blue linen shirt, looking like he had stepped out of a menswear catalogue, his stubble perfectly groomed and his hair mussed just right. He sucked on a bottle of pale ale and smirked at her over his drink. Detective Sergeant Josh Ellis looked exactly as she remembered, freshly put together and dripping in self-confidence. Some things never changed.

'Josh, I heard you were getting in tomorrow.'

'Finished up work this arvo and I thought, why wait? It's an easy drive up.'

'Couldn't stay away, huh?' she joked half-heartedly.

'It seems that way.'

'How are you enjoying Byron?'

'It has its perks,' he replied, taking a sip of his beer, his eyes not leaving her face.

She knew he had transferred to an equivalent position to hers in Byron. One of the reasons he had left. So he could finally take up a role he felt was deserving of his skills, rather than playing second fiddle to her in Esserton, and of course, he had managed to bag a plum location in the process. The look he gave her said it all. She sighed. Less than a minute and their interactions had already assumed a spiky edge.

'I'm glad it's working out for you.' She motioned to the pool table. 'Care to join me?' It was silly, she knew, to pander to his competitive side. But then bullshit one-upmanship had been a feature of their relationship from the start. It almost felt like coming home.

He grinned, setting down his beer. 'Always.'

She let him rack the balls, setting up a new game, waving her hand to indicate he could break first. He broke the rack and sank three balls in a row before it was her turn. She aimed, feeling her body tense and focus on the task at hand. She called and sank two before the game switched back to Josh. They sparred back and forth, a silent battle of wills. Neither willing to give an inch. Each concentrating harder because they were battling the other. It was both annoying and predictable that she played better under his scrutiny. When he won by two points, she decided to call it. There was no need to prolong this pissing contest.

He offered to buy her another round and she accepted. A soft drink only, knowing she would be driving home. They settled at a table, Josh's win having put him in a good mood, a glass of wine replacing his beer.

'So, this new boss... Leonardo Esposito.' He rolled the name, threading it with a hint of derision. 'What do you make of him?'

'He seems all right, so far.' Kate's reply was noncommittal. She sensed that this was about their previous boss, Skinner, whom Josh had come to admire before his fall from grace. She didn't want to get into a comparison between Esposito and their old boss. Her own preference was clear.

'I looked him up, you know, before accepting this... role.' He had glanced at her prior to settling on the word. 'Did you know he was involved in the Nowra thing?' Josh wasn't ready to let go of the topic of Esposito.

'He wasn't part of the team on the ground.' Her tone was sharper than she had intended. Why did she feel the need to defend Esposito?

Josh quirked an eyebrow at her, a hint of amusement on his face. 'The coroner didn't differentiate, did she? She was just as scathing of Organised Crime Command for the planning of the op as the team that stormed the property. Some would say more so.'

Kate sipped her drink and winced, the too-sweet lemonade not even close to what she needed to get through this conversation. Somehow, even in this discussion of an old police incident that had nothing whatsoever to do with them, she found herself on the opposite side to Josh. Forever sparring for the sake of it.

Kate knew the case he was talking about. She would have known about it even without Esposito's involvement. It was familiar to every NSW Police officer. The incident had become legendary for all the wrong reasons; inserted into their training and refresher manuals on the many ways in which an op could turn sideways on the day. Lessons learned based on the critical-incident investigation and coronial findings that had followed.

The name of the two brothers came back to her. Alexis and Leon Fincher – career criminals both with priors for assault and various drug charges. The twins had been the object of a strike-force operation six years ago targeting their property in Nowra. It had gone wrong in the worst possible way, resulting in lethal force being used against Alexis and his teenage son, Raff, who had been fourteen at the time. The teen had been shot in the chest while attempting to defend his father by aiming a handgun at officers. Except, as the critical-incident investigation had later uncovered, the pistol had been a replica and empty of bullets. Alexis had been pronounced dead at the scene, while the boy had been flown to Randwick Children's Hospital to undergo emergency surgery, which he had never recovered from. Eight days later his mother had made the difficult choice to turn off her son's life support.

Following the inquest, in which the coroner had had a number of choice words to say about the actions of the police, the Fincher family had launched a compensation case against the NSW Police in relation to the death of Raff. Kate recalled the news report she had seen only a few days ago that a verdict on the case was imminent.

'You know, I heard Fincher's no longer in Sydney. Apparently, he's been on the losing end of a turf war with a rival drug gang for the last couple of years and he's been lying low. There's even a whisper that he may have headed north, possibly even up our way.'

Kate didn't answer, refusing to engage. She knew that Josh had little interest in Leon Fincher's whereabouts. He just wanted Kate to ask him how he had come by the information so he could casually mention his Sydney contacts. Rumours and titbits gleaned via one of his three older brothers, all police officers in Sydney. Well, she didn't give a shit.

'Might mention it to the boss when I see him. See what he says,' Josh persisted.

'You haven't met him yet?'

'Nah, only spoken over the phone. He sounded like an accountant. Very… precise.'

Kate chose to ignore this. 'Have you spoken to the team?' she asked, careful not to sound too eager.

He took a sip from his glass of red wine before answering. Studying her. 'Yeah, I met up with Darnley just before and he ran me through the basics. I have a briefing with Esposito in the morning.'

She nodded, forcing herself to stay silent, to leave the questions to him.

'Do you know where your brother is?'

Kate knew it was coming and still she flinched. 'I don't.'

'What about your father's property? Plenty of places to hide out there. And his two – what do you call it – Airbnb cabins?'

'They've been searched. What do you think? That was the first place the team looked after we realised he'd gone AWOL. Plus, Dad's new place in Esserton and my house, of course.'

He took a long drink, almost draining his glass. 'It's nothing personal, Kate. I had to ask. I'm not here to judge either way. I'm just here to follow where the evidence leads.'

'I know that,' she gritted out. God, he could be such a pompous arse. 'And I'm not asking for any special consideration. I want this sorted as quickly as you do.'

'Fair enough. Okay, well if it's not Luke, who are your picks?'

'Seriously? We're doing this here?'

'Yeah, why not? I know it's hard to believe, but I respect your opinion. Don't always agree with it, but that's a different matter.' He grinned.

She stopped herself from rolling her eyes. 'Marcus's wife, Fiona Rowntree, had the most motive. He was violent towards her, which is why she left him, though she denies that's the reason. There's plenty of corroboration that he was an abusive partner from Marcus's own mother, Celeste Rowntree and two family friends, Louise Askall and Sarah Osmond. I think Fiona was certainly capable of shooting her husband in self-defence. She says she was alone at home with the boys. But it's possible that she drove over to her husband's late that night while the kids were asleep. Maybe they got into an argument. I don't know. My gut feeling is that it wasn't premeditated. She's genuinely devastated for her two boys, that they've lost their father. I don't think she would have planned that.'

'Anyone else?'

'Celeste Rowntree.'

He raised his eyebrows. 'Marcus's mother?'

'Yeah, I think she's a possibility. She knew what was going on between Marcus and Fiona and she didn't have the best opinion of her son. I think if she felt that Marcus was a threat to her grandchildren, she may have taken that course of action. But then again, she was pretty composed when I spoke to her, so we'd be talking stone-cold nerves. But I think it's possible.'

'That it?'

'There are his friends and workmates, of course. I didn't get a chance to follow up his contacts to check on any existing issues or animosities, but the team might have since. In theory, anyone could have visited him that night and got into an argument. Luke says he saw a car turning into Marcus's property that night. A dark-coloured sedan. The vehicles of Marcus's contacts will need to be cross-checked.'

'Ah yes, the unknown stranger theory, who conveniently arrived on scene after your brother left it. A call-out for that car has been on the news hasn't it, without any hits. Funny, that.'

She didn't bother to reply.

'In your statement, you mention that Luke slept on your couch that night, after you picked him up from the River Arms around 11 pm?'

'Yeah, that's right.'

'Can anyone verify that he remained asleep on the couch all night? Did you or anyone else sleep in the same room with him?'

'I… He was alone in the lounge room. So no, I can't say definitively that he stayed put all night, though that's what I believe. I would have heard something if he'd gone out again that night.'

Josh stared at her, his expression unreadable. Was he getting a kick out of this? To finally have her in his power and interrogate her like a petty criminal. To find the cracks in everything she said in good faith.

'Luke seems to have been having a tough time, recently. What with losing a close high school friend to suicide and getting fired from his job. He'd been there what, five, six years? From what I understand, he was making good money. On the promotion track and then suddenly bam. Goodbye, dream job. It's understandable that he was in a volatile place emotionally that night. That fight he got into at the Arms. Does that seem in character to you?'

Kate glared at him. 'What's your point, Josh? Plenty of people lose their jobs and get into pub fights. These things don't make you a murderer.'

'I'm merely pointing out to you, Kate, that your brother's emotional state was probably a bit off that night. Just the kind of state that's likely conducive to arguments and lashing out.'

Kate ground her teeth but remained silent. This was Josh's technique, she reminded herself. This was what he did. How he got results. Of course, he needed to test the evidence and try to find the holes in it. He was just doing his job. Luke was innocent. She had to hold onto that belief.

'Do you know why he got dismissed from Hull-Hayward?'

She felt the hard thump of her heart but forced herself not to react.

'Apparently, your brother recorded an intimate video with one of his colleagues. It was consensual, but it seems to have gone south fairly quickly. She's accusing him of using the images against her.'

Kate stared at him, utterly floored. Ice pooling inside her belly.

'The colleague went straight to HR and it's been referred on to the police. Sydney City PAC are handling it. Luke was let go, subject to a non-disclosure agreement.'

She still gaped at him, her mind scrambling to process the information.

'So you see, Kate. I think your brother was actually under immense pressure. Probably at breaking point when he happened to visit an old school friend for a drink.'

22

Wednesday

Person of Interest Named in Rowntree Death

From illicit love affairs to corruption scandals, ex-Chief Inspector Arthur Grayling and his daughter, Detective Sergeant Kate Miles, two generations of the Esserton Police Station, are no strangers to controversy. It appears that a third member of the Grayling brood, Luke, son of the former and younger brother of the latter, has now stepped into the spotlight. Luke Grayling was yesterday named by Esserton Police as a person of interest in the ongoing investigation into the death of local resident Marcus Rowntree, son of renowned actor Eric Harrington.

The body of Marcus Rowntree, thirty-five, was discovered at his property in Byangum on Saturday with a gunshot wound to his chest. Though initially thought to be self-inflicted, detectives yesterday confirmed that enquiries were being expanded. Police now believe that Marcus was killed by a person or persons unknown sometime between approximately 8.30 pm on Friday night and the early hours of Saturday morning. It is understood that Luke Grayling, a high school friend of Marcus Rowntree, visited Marcus on Friday night for drinks and is the last known person to have seen Mr Rowntree alive. The *Leader* can confirm that since his initial questioning by police on Sunday morning, Luke Grayling has gone to ground, with his current whereabouts unknown to police. Luke Grayling is wanted for questioning and police are asking anyone with information to contact Esserton Station or to ring Crime Stoppers.

Meanwhile, Sergeant Kate Miles has been removed as the lead detective, with Sergeant Josh Ellis from Byron Bay Station being brought in to run the case. Before his recent move south, Detective Ellis worked out of Esserton and played an instrumental role in the investigation surrounding the death of local infant, Sienna Ricci, earlier in the year. His familiarity with the area and the team is expected to allow for a smooth transition of the inquiry.

This publication previously raised concerns regarding the obvious conflict of interest arising from Sergeant Miles remaining on the task force given her brother's direct connection to the deceased. It appears that these probity issues are finally being taken into account in the handling of the case going forward. Whether these measures are too little too late to ensure the case is untainted for prosecution remains to be seen.

Marcus Rowntree's death follows the passing by suicide of his high school friend, Anthony Reed, whose funeral was held in Esserton less than a week ago. Police have called the circumstances of both men's deaths tragic, especially so close to Christmas.

Keep reading for our exclusive profile on *Luke Grayling: What We Know So Far.* Follow the links below for a recap of the peppered history of the Grayling-Miles family.

Kate couldn't help herself. She clicked on the next article, the 'exclusive profile' on her brother, without pause. Under a photo of Luke, which appeared to have been nicked from his LinkedIn profile, the piece laid out various statistics about her brother: his age (thirty-five), schooling (Esserton High), degree (Bachelor of Business and Enterprise at Southern Cross University), and current place of residence (Cronulla, Sydney). Her heart dropped when she got to the 'employment' section, her eyes flying across the damning words.

> The *Leader* understands that Luke Grayling, until a week ago, was employed by Hull-Hayward Financial, a leading financial services firm with head offices in Castlereagh Street, Sydney. The firm remains listed as Luke Grayling's current employer on his LinkedIn profile. In response to questions put forward by the *Leader*, representatives from Hull-Hayward have confirmed that Mr Grayling's employment contract was terminated last week for reasons that remain undisclosed. However, the *Leader* can exclusively reveal that the circumstances surrounding Luke Grayling's termination have been referred to the Sydney City Police Area Command for investigation.

A final section ominously titled 'social life' appeared to catalogue Luke's various dating exploits over the years, probably based on interviews with the most juvenile of his male friends so that the resultant quotes were as moronic as the article had intended, painting a picture of a fuckboy, eternally playing the field and looking for his next pull. She had no idea how many additional quotes or friends had not made it into the article, but what had been carefully curated and presented had succeeded in continuing the hatchet job that the paper had begun two days ago, dismantling Luke's reputation one sentence at a time.

Selected images from Luke's private Instagram account had been included for effect, evidently shared by the same so-called friends, showing him partying and posing with various women, never the same ones twice. She glanced through the stream of comments below. An argument was brewing already between those denouncing his behaviour outright, and various 'boys will be boys' type comments, all of it sickening for different reasons. She clicked out of the browser. No doubt social media would be alight with far worse.

She stared at her blank computer screen without moving. *Markham*. His name created a sour taste in her mouth. To think that only a few months ago she had thought them on the same side. Somehow, he had got on to the story about Luke's employment. But how? Had someone from Esserton Station tipped him off? Could it have been Darnley or Esposito? She didn't believe so. Her thoughts slipped back to her conversation with Josh. His obvious antagonism. She wouldn't put this past him, but then he'd only just arrived in town. Richard Markham would have needed time to put this article together. She thought about the Sydney City PAC. Markham had worked for one of the national dailies in Sydney before his move to Esserton. No doubt he still had police contacts at the central Sydney station. Was that where the leak had originated from? Kate felt instinctively that Markham had learned far more about Luke's termination than had been revealed in the article. That explained the paper's decision to portray Luke as a sexist playboy, so when reports of the video came out, they had laid the groundwork on his character.

Not that Kate was blind to the finer points of her brother's personality. But she had sufficient experience of the media, being on either side of a story at various points of her career, to recognise a take-down when she saw one. She debated whether to call Gray, but decided against it. She wasn't ready for round two of that particular conversation.

Her mobile buzzed as if she had manifested it. Two texts. One from Vanessa Darnley sending a couple of dates of when they would be free for a barbeque catch-up before Christmas, and a second from an unknown number. She read the latter text, digesting the message. It was an invitation to talk. *Why not? She had nothing else to do.*

She was on the phone drafting a reply when she heard the sounds of Geoff navigating Amy's stroller at the front door, having returned from dropping off Archie at preschool. Kate rose from her seat at the kitchen counter to greet them.

'Hey, how'd he go?' she asked, making for Amy, who was bouncing up and down in her stroller. She snuggled her daughter, blowing raspberries into her neck as Amy shrieked and giggled.

'It was a good day.' Geoff smiled.

'Oh, excellent,' she said, relieved, making faces at Amy. She unclipped her daughter and placed her on the floor by her playpen so she could crawl around.

Archie's drop-offs had become hit and miss lately. Some days he was happy to attend, while on others it would take quite a bit of reassurance, cuddles and wiping of tears before Geoff and Kate could pry his little fingers off their clothes and safely leave him.

Archie's behaviour had become noticeably unsettled both at home and at day care in the preceding months. Kate knew it was a stress response to the multiple upheavals the family had experienced that year: Amy's birth, Geoff losing his job, Gray having a car accident, and Kate surviving a firearms injury, as well as her ongoing workload, which meant she was regularly missing-in-action at home. It was his way of reacting to the unrelenting worry and uncertainty he had felt swirling around him within their household. Archie had become less comfortable with change and more rigid with his routine.

She worried constantly about how he would cope with the transition to school in only a few short months. *Where had that time gone?* She and Geoff had visited the local primary school last month, attending the kindy orientation with Archie, his nervous hand firmly grasped in Kate's. He had been fitted for his new uniform. The yellow shirt and grey shorts had ballooned over her son's slight frame, even the smallest size extending well below his knees. Another *first* that had felt so far in the future and was now careening towards them.

Geoff's words brought her back to the present. 'How's the stuff on Luke?' he asked, nodding towards the open laptop on the counter.

'Same shit, different day,' she said her thoughts still on Archie.

She and Geoff had become so conscious about not discussing potentially triggering subjects around their son. Distressing world events or family problems. And now here was news of his uncle being plastered all over the papers. A familiar guilt coiled her insides; the weight of unintended consequences on her family.

She had no idea where her brother was, and short of searching Esserton house to house, she didn't know how to improve the situation. She could think of no better excuse to run away from her problems.

'So, I was thinking,' she said. 'I actually have to see someone in Brisbane today. It won't take more than half an hour max. Why don't we all go and make a day of it? We can take a picnic and hang out at South Bank. Maybe get the final bit of Christmas shopping sorted.'

Geoff glanced at her, a smile tracking across his lips. 'Sounds good to me.'

23

It was so very easy to drift off. Luke lay splayed in bed in nothing but his jocks, the overhead fan turning lazy circles above him, a curl of smoke rising from the spliff between his fingers. His new accommodation was old school and his host wasn't much of a talker, but then all Luke wanted from the world right now was for it to stay the fuck away from him, so that suited him fine.

Most importantly, living here meant access to some truly excellent weed. A flash new indica blend from the hinterland that leached the anxiety from his body, leaving him boneless and relaxed in a way he hadn't felt in years. He knew for a fact that he was being overcharged. There was a mercenary edge to his host's hospitality, getting his money's worth from the city slicker. But Luke didn't care. He would happily pay double for the privilege, if it meant he could escape the heavy-metal thrashing inside his brain for a few blessed hours. This batch was doing wonderful things to him, cushioning and cocooning his mind from the outside world. Every time he felt his thoughts starting to spiral, the spark of anxiety flaring in his bowels, he would reach for another joint. It was as good a way as any to spend his money.

Luke brought the spliff up to his lips, inhaling deeply and holding the smoke in his lungs, allowing it to do its work. He exhaled. In his drug-sated state, he found he could probe the scar tissue of his life without too much blowback. Ant and Marcus. And especially... Payton Cavanaugh.

It wouldn't be quite so bad, if he could just stop thinking about her. If she would just take his calls. So he could explain and apologise. But she had blocked his number weeks ago. In a funny way, the searing pain of losing her had almost protected him from all the rest of the shit, keeping the enormity of everything else at bay, because his brain and body were still too busy processing the crater-sized void that Payton Cavanaugh had left within him.

Payton with her pencil skirts that rose up her thighs, an extra button undone on her blouse when she called him into her office to run through the monthly reports. Those legs that never quit and those eyes that looked straight through him, daring him to make a move. She'd known exactly what she was doing. It was a game. And he'd been happy to play along. God, had he been happy to play along.

It had never got in the way of their professional relationship. She knew exactly where she was headed. She was on track to make section director in a couple of years, followed by a posting to the Asia-Pacific office in Singapore, her end game. He was a little fun she was having along the way. Luke had no illusions about where he stood in the grand scheme of Payton's life. He wasn't special, or even the only plaything she retained for her entertainment. If his feelings took a battering now and then, it was all grist to the mill. He didn't care, as long as he got to spend time with her. He knew the rules and played by them.

Until the conference in Byron. And fucking Tristan Gill.

Now, looking back, they probably hadn't been as discreet as they'd assumed. The plentiful cocktails hadn't helped. The team had congregated to socialise and decompress after a day of heavy-going seminars and presentations, and it was likely clear to anyone with eyes that there was something going on between them. If not the giggling and the none-too-subtle brushes against each other at the bar, the eye-fucking across the room surely would have done it. She had worn a sheer asymmetrical number that had simultaneously covered everything and yet left little to the imagination, and it had the effect on him that she'd intended. While the rest of the party had headed out to dinner, they had returned to her hotel room to camp out for the night.

And it had been glorious. She had been glorious.

He thought they'd got away with it, too. Until Tristan Gill had mooched into Luke's room in the morning with that shit-eating grin on his face, trying to get Luke to spill the beans on exactly how he'd spent his down time with their finance manager. Luke had resisted, pretending to check for messages on his phone, parrying each of Tristan's jabs and dirty jokes, and finally physically escaping to the en suite. By the time he had hopped out of the shower, Tristan was gone.

Two weeks later, Luke had been called into an emergency meeting at Hull-Hayward with the firm's head of HR.

THEN

'Wakey, wakey, hands off snakey.'

Luke opened his eyes a crack and swatted Ant's hand away as his friend tried to ruffle his hair.

'Piss off,' he attempted, but it sounded more like 'Pish oghf.' His mouth felt dry and furry, like he'd swallowed a wad of cotton wool, and tasted like he imagined bin juice would if it had been left out to marinate in beer and vodka. He squinted against the bright sunshine pouring from the apartment windows, raising his head and immediately groaning as the movement elicited a dull pain deep inside his skull. Fuck, he felt like an entire fleet of trucks had driven over him.

'What's the time?' he croaked, slowly rising into a sitting position on the couch he'd fallen asleep on.

'Almost eleven. So, you should definitely be up. And don't worry, I've done a Maccas run,' Ant said cheerfully.

His upbeat Mary Poppins act was doing Luke's head in.

'What's going on?' A sleepy voice sounded as the rumpled form of Marcus emerged from the master bedroom.

'Ah, the main man is awake, too. Morning. Breakfast is served.' Ant gestured with a flourish at the various paper bags and styrofoam packaging lined up on the dining table. 'We have hotcakes and coffee and all variety of McMuffins.'

'What are you so happy about?' Luke grunted, lifting himself off the sofa and heading for the food. He unwrapped and took a huge bite out of a sausage McMuffin.

'Gentlemen, you are looking at a freshly laid lad.' Ant made an exaggerated bow and grinned at his two friends. 'Yours truly spent the night at Ally's at her lovely share house in Parkwood. She just drove me back here, and we swung past the drive-through. You're welcome.'

'Fucking well done, Antsy.'

Marcus high-fived his friend as Luke asked, 'Who's Ally?'

'The girl I hooked up with last night. Where've you been, bro?' Ant smiled broadly at his friends.

Luke nodded, suddenly recalling the pretty, copper-haired girl he had seen Ant locked in embrace with at the party.

'Don't worry about our Lukey,' Marcus answered. 'His evening plans didn't quite pan out, did they? What went wrong, Lukey? Did she get cold feet after she figured out what you had to offer?' He fisted his groin for effect.

'Fuck off,' Luke growled as both Marcus and Ant roared with laughter.

'Ahh, don't be like that, Lukey. Better luck next time.' Marcus teased, his voice loud and grating.

Luke said nothing as hazy images from the previous night sparked in his mind. He'd done all right. Marcus, as usual, had no fucking idea. He took another savage bite out of his breakfast muffin.

The old Marcus was back, he noted. There was no hint of the teary, angry young man who'd confessed his deep hurt about his father the previous night. He wondered if Marcus would even remember or want to acknowledge their conversation. Not that Luke was stupid enough to bring it up with him. Especially when Marcus was like this. All bravado and sneer, overcompensating for whatever it was that he couldn't face and was running away from. It was moments like this when he wondered what it was that actually bonded him to his friend, and whether he, in fact, needed Marcus in his life.

'But forget about Luke. Two out of three scores ain't bad, heh?'

'What, you hooked up as well?' Luke asked, his attention diverted back to Marcus in an instant. 'When?'

Marcus winked at him with a wolfish grin. He grabbed one of the takeaway coffee cups and raised it in a toast. 'All in all, a fucking excellent eighteenth party, eh, boys?'

Ant followed suit immediately. Luke was the last to raise his cup. A slow, reluctant salute to his two best friends.

24

'Constable O'Connell?'

A trim, middle-aged man looked up from his perusal of the menu. A full head of hair brushed back with just a hint of grey spotting his temples, wearing chinos and a dark polo. Even off duty, he looked every inch a police officer, sitting upright and tall on his seat. Clear blue eyes marked her through frameless spectacles.

'Detective Miles, good to finally meet you. You can call me David.'

He half rose and they shook hands.

'David, I wasn't sure you'd agree to this,' Kate said, moving to sit opposite him in the corner booth he'd secured.

'Well, to be honest, I wasn't going to. But Celia can be persuasive as hell and I couldn't really turn down a celebrity now, could I? I don't know many people who make the front-page news.' His face crinkled into a grin to undercut the offence of his words.

'Didn't realise I was making the Queensland news, too?'

'Ah, well, true bullshit gets plastered everywhere.'

She laughed. It was a small nod of solidarity, but she'd take it.

'Would you like something to drink? I'm getting an iced coffee. They brew it proper here.'

'Oh, great. Make that two,' she said.

He moved to the counter to order, waving away her offer to pay. She leaned back against her seat, breathing in the sugar-laden warmth of the hole-in-the-wall Fortitude Valley café.

She had been surprised when David O'Connell had texted that morning. She had messaged him days ago, though it felt like much longer, before all the saga with Marcus Rowntree. She had received his details from Celia, her contact within the Queensland Police. Kate had never received a reply and with everything that had happened since, she hadn't thought to pursue it. It was a fool's errand, anyway. As a kindness to Frank Reed, she had reached out to the officer who had dealt with the aftermath of Ant's suicide.

David slipped back into the seat opposite her, setting two tall glasses on the table: strong, filtered coffee mixed with sweet condensed milk, topped with ice. One sip and she was in heaven.

'Bloody hell.'

'Right?'

'Not sure I'll be able to go back to normal coffee after this.'

'Told you it was good.' He slurped from his own glass before facing her. 'Okay so, Anthony Reed. What's your interest?'

'Nothing beyond keeping a promise to his dad. His father is adamant that Ant would not have killed himself. I'm a family friend and Frank's convinced that because I'm a detective, I can get the case looked at again.' She caught the expression on his face. 'Trust me, I've tried to explain to him that I have no jurisdiction, and even then that there's a process to follow. But, well…' She threw her hands in the air. 'He won't listen. So, this is my compromise. I was hoping that if I tell him I'd spoken with you, that may be enough for him. I appreciate you being here and giving me your time.' Kate met his gaze, trying to impress on him that she wasn't here to show him up or try to poke holes in his case. She was in his territory and reliant on his good will.

David sighed. 'Mr Reed seems like a good man. How exactly do you know him?'

'Actually, Ant went to school with my brother and with Marcus Rowntree.' She saw David's eyes widen as he made the connections. 'All through high school, it was the three of them: Luke, Ant and Marcus. It's hard to say no to his dad when you've known him practically all your life.'

'Have you seen the coroner's report? The findings were made available to Mr Reed.'

Kate nodded. Before leaving the house, she had skimmed through the pages that Frank Reed had printed out for her. 'Mr Reed shared a copy of the report with me.'

'So, you know what it says.'

'I read the findings, but I'd be grateful if you could take me through the details.'

He sighed again, making sure she knew this was a waste of time. 'Anthony Reed was found in his residence, an apartment dwelling in Chermside,' O'Connell began. 'Police were called in when he didn't turn up to work on Monday and he wasn't answering his phone or email. We were able to gain entry to his unit with the assistance of a neighbour who had a spare key. Mr Reed was found sitting on the couch in his lounge room with a plastic oven bag – like the type used for roasting a turkey – covering his face, secured to his neck with a rubber band to create an air seal. A glass of whisky was on the side table next to him, along with a half-empty blister pack of sleeping tablets. The alcohol was later identified as a Lark Distillery, Tasmanian single malt. The man had good taste.' He gave a small smile.

'There was no note,' O'Connell continued, 'but his browser history showed access to various suicide-related websites in the months prior. The autopsy confirmed the cause of death to be hypoxia resulting from carbon dioxide inhalation from the lack of fresh oxygen supply. Toxicology matched the active compound in his blood stream to the pills found on scene. Fingerprints found on the plastic bag, blister pack and whisky glass also matched those of the deceased. The overwhelming evidence pointed to suicide with no significant contraindications, and the case was classified as such.'

'That seems pretty conclusive,' she said, mentally ticking off the details she had read in the report. 'Thank you for taking me through it.'

He nodded, draining his coffee and burping quietly.

'I understand you were the attending officer? That mustn't have been easy.'

He shrugged.

'Well, anyway, I appreciate you going through it again for me today. As you say, it seems pretty cut and dry.'

He cleared his throat. 'Listen… er… I'd be happy to speak to Mr Reed myself. The detectives dealt with the family. I didn't realise that Mr Reed was having such a hard time accepting his son's death. It might help to speak to someone who was there… You know, someone who actually saw his son and can answer any specific questions.'

Kate studied him. 'That's really kind of you. I think that might actually help. I can ask him.'

'I understand what he's feeling, you know. My brother… well, he went the same way when he was a teenager. Not the pills and the plastic bag part. He used a rope to hang himself.' His eyes slid away from Kate. 'For ages, I didn't believe it. Not my brother, you know? Not Pat. I was so angry at my parents for accepting it. For not demanding that the police do more. To find out what actually happened, who really did that to him. I was convinced. Absolutely certain. But eventually, I had to face the truth. Just like everyone else had. That it had been Pat's decision. It was almost harder, you know? To finally let go of my version and accept reality.'

His words sat in the stillness between them. Beyond their booth, the café bustled, customers streaming in and out and staff calling out orders. He met Kate's eyes with a look of sadness.

'I get it. I was Frank Reed, fifteen years ago.'

25

Carrying Amy on her shoulder, Kate walked with Geoff back to their car. The heat of the day had left her with a slight headache, but she didn't care. It had been a good day. Geoff bumped her shoulder softly as they walked together, the impromptu outing having loosened something between them. For a few hours of sand, water and ice-cream on the bank of the Brisbane River, they had given each other permission to not think of anything beyond the present. She smiled at him over Amy's slumped head. The plan was to head home, pick up Archie from day care and have an easy night in, maybe even order takeout for dinner.

Nearing Archie's preschool, Kate remembered that her phone was still switched off from earlier. She had turned it off after rejoining Geoff and Amy following her chat with David O'Connell, a deliberate line in the sand for a few hours. Several notifications went off in quick succession and she registered four missed calls from an unknown number, all clustered just after midday, over two hours ago.

She dialled the number for her voicemail, raising the mobile to her ear.

Her brain screeched to a halt as she recognised the flustered and panicked voice of her brother.

'*Kate, it's me… Can you call me back, please? On this number.*'

'*Kate, Fuck! Why aren't you answering your phone? Just please, call me, will you? I can explain.*'

'*Kate… please. I don't know what to do.*'

The final recording was just several seconds of silence before cutting out.

—

As she pulled into the driveway, Kate caught a glimpse of Dominic Tohu's muscled frame, opening the screen door wide and hurrying down the porch steps to meet her. The single-storey orange brick bungalow at the south end of town looked nondescript and ordinary. A standard family home with a double lock-up garage and a basketball hoop attached to the side. Kate had got the address out of her brother when she had called him back.

Her initial relief at finding out Luke was safe had morphed into anger. She could feel the heat of her emotions bubbling under her skin. Luke had been here all this time. Just a few blocks away from her own house, where she had been worried sick, climbing the walls and unable to sleep, worrying over her brother's whereabouts. She had driven over in her own car, after Geoff had dropped her home.

'Where is he?'

'Sarge, can we have a word before you go in?' Dom looked agitated and stressed. Perhaps for the first time, unsure of himself.

'Save it, Dom. I've called it in. Detective Ellis is on his way.'

'You're going to turn him in? That's why we called you, so he could speak to you and explain.'

'The time for explanations was about three days ago.' She rounded on him as she walked up the driveway. 'What the fuck was Mitch thinking, hiding him away? You know he could be charged with hindering an investigation.'

'It wasn't like that, Sarge. I'm telling you.' Dom rushed ahead of her, blocking her path and forcing her to stop. 'Luke just needed a place to crash and Mitch offered him a room because his folks are away for a few weeks and there's plenty of space to spare. I swear, we thought the police had already spoken to

Luke and he just needed a place to lie low until all this media stuff blew over.'

'It was on the news yesterday evening. You can't pretend you didn't know.'

'Mitch and I were both at work, a full twelve-hour shift. He only saw the news this morning when he woke up late. And he called me straightaway. We didn't know what to do. You were the only person Luke wanted to call.'

Yep, she was first on his list when he wanted something. No thought to the numerous missed calls she and her father had left on his phone since Monday morning. Her eyes took in the front façade of the house. The curtains firmly drawn across each of the windows. Where even was her brother now? Why was he letting Dom Tohu do all the talking for him?

'Well, I'm flattered. Meanwhile, all I've done is try to contact him. Three days of dead air and suddenly I'm his favourite person.'

'Sarge, he forgot his phone charger when he flew up from Sydney. He borrowed one from a staff member a couple of times when he was staying at the Arms. The battery finally carked it when he got here, and he didn't do anything about it.'

'Bloody hell, of all the excuses. He couldn't borrow one of your phones to make a call?'

As she moved to step around him, she heard the sound of vehicles pulling up at the front of the property.

Dom flushed but still held his ground, his voice becoming an urgent whisper. 'Sarge, he's been out of it all this time, all right? Mitch was just trying to help him.'

Kate met his gaze. She understood now. For the last few days, Luke had been escaping the world with the help of chemicals, most likely pills and cannabis supplied by Mitch Cosgrove. Dom was trying to look out for his boyfriend. She assumed that they had spent the morning getting rid of the evidence, but he was also looking for assurance from her should Luke give Mitch away.

'Kate, you're here.' She heard Josh's voice behind her and she turned to face him. 'I wasn't sure if you would be.'

Kate nodded. 'I was just about to head in.'

'Best that you don't.' Josh's eyes roved between Dom and Kate. 'I take it Luke's in there?'

'Yeah,' Dom confirmed, stepping aside to let Josh through.

'Have you spoken to him?' His question was directed at Kate.

'Only on the phone.'

'All right, well it would help if you stay out here.' He pointed a finger at Dom. 'I'd like you to come with me, Mr Tohu.'

'Can I speak with him?' Kate asked, hating that it sounded like she was begging.

'Later, maybe.' Josh didn't look at her.

He strode forward with Constables Harris and Darnley in his wake. Darnley nodded towards her, but Harris kept her eyes trained to the ground. Kate moved to the corner of the garden, pulling out her phone and seeing a text from her father. She had called Gray straight after listening to Luke's voicemail. Gray, it seemed, had heeded her advice and organised a lawyer. The text said he was heading to the station now. So, Luke would be supported. That at least was a relief.

She heard the screech of a car turning too quickly into the street. Her heart sank as she saw Richard Markham scrambling out. There was no place to hide even if she wanted to; the front yard of Mitch's parents' house was an ode to buffalo grass without a tree or shrub in sight. He caught sight of Kate straightaway, acknowledging her with a brief salute that she didn't return. If Markham was here, other journalists wouldn't be far behind. She glanced around. The presence of the police cars had woken up the neighbourhood. Heads were peeping out of front doors and residents were starting to gather in small groups.

There was a scuffle at the front door and Kate turned to see her brother being led out by Constable Darnley. Something flipped in her stomach. He was wearing boardshorts, a white T-shirt and a pair of scuffed trainers, the years stripped away. He looked like the teenager she remembered from seventeen years ago. Darnley led him to the waiting paddy wagon, helping him into the back seat as Markham snapped the exclusive photos, which would no doubt turn up in tomorrow's news; print and online. At least he wasn't handcuffed. It wasn't much, but it would mean something when the photos got splashed across the papers.

Kate tried to catch Luke's eye, but he kept his head down. He must have seen her, though he made no move to acknowledge her. She could only watch as a uniformed officer joined Darnley in the front of the vehicle and it drove off with her brother bundled inside.

26

God, his head was woolly. That last toke while waiting for Kate to turn up had been a mistake.

Not that she had helped anyway. She hadn't even bothered to walk inside the house. Couldn't bear to be in his presence. The job came first. Her reputation. How it would affect her. Just like she had been with that bloody tweet. She'd called in her cronies and then stood by watching from the sidelines as they had led him out. God forbid she got her face in the paper again in the same frame as her loser brother. She'd learned that lesson.

He knew the officer had said something or asked something, but he couldn't remember what. Something about his hire car being impounded for forensic testing. Fuck knows what the excess was going to be on that one. He rubbed his bloodshot eyes. The station interview room was hot and stuffy, and his brain felt like it was slowly curdling and grinding to a crawl.

The officer was speaking again. He heard the mention of Marcus Rowntree.

Marcus. Marcus. Marcus.

God, he'd had enough of that name. He wished for the thousandth time that he'd never bloody agreed to drinks with him that Friday. He'd only gone because he'd felt sorry for the idiot. Still stuck in fucking Esserton, and blaming the whole world for how his life had turned out – everyone but the sack of shit that he saw in the mirror each day. All Luke had done that evening was sit in a chair and drown his stomach full of Carlton Draught to try, as he'd been doing for weeks, to remove the image of Payton Cavanaugh from his mind. He'd barely listened to Marcus's ramblings. Bullshit that he was still hung up on from his high school days. At one point, he'd started reminiscing about his eighteenth birthday and Luke had switched off entirely. And now he was stuck here, trying to answer questions about that night to these police officers.

I don't remember because I didn't care enough to listen. Until a few days ago, Marcus Rowntree had been a miniscule footnote in the story of his life.

At least he could defer most of the questions to his purse-lipped lawyer, who Luke could tell was none too pleased at the state of his client. Elliot Ramsay, the apparent hotshot lawyer his father had organised, who had driven all the way down from the Gold Coast. The frown line on his forehead deepened and little huffs of impatience would escape his lips every time Luke's attention drifted. Like right now.

'Luke, mate...'

It was the constable, Greg someone, who had driven him to the station. Luke turned at the sound of his voice, focusing on his slow drawl and kind eyes. He seemed like a nice bloke, this officer. He'd be the kind of person you'd want to have a beer with after work. Luke could imagine him being a good dad, someone who'd play down on the floor with his kids and load the dishwasher without being asked.

'Luke, we were asking you about when you got back to the River Arms on Friday night. We understand you had a bit of an argument with one of the other patrons.'

'What? Oh, yeah. He was being a dick to his girlfriend.'

The backpacker's face suddenly came back to him, furious and overcome like a rutting bull, just before he'd decked Luke square in the face. He had fallen, dragging a schooner of beer with him, soaking himself and splashing the said girlfriend. He remembered lying on the grass and laughing uncontrollably, which had pissed off bull-boy even more. Luke had run the risk of being seriously hurt if Dom had not seen it all and calmed the situation with his bigger bulk and height, re-establishing the pecking order. Luke had escaped with a bloody nose and a black eye.

'How was he being a dick?' It was the other officer this time. The smartly dressed detective. He sounded keyed up and annoyed. The same suppressed irritation of his lawyer. They looked a bit alike, too, now that he thought about it. Like maybe one was just an older version of the other, with their matching fitted suits, expensive-smelling cologne and designer haircuts. Maybe they were friends outside of work.

'How was he being a dick, Luke?'

The detective sounded pissed off now, and Luke made an effort to focus on his words.

'He was on his girlfriend's case. Putting her down for what she was wearing. And she looked nice, man. Just had on a normal dress. But he was at her. That she was showing too much skin and needed to go on a diet so he wouldn't be embarrassed to be seen with her. Shit like that. The guy was being a tool.'

'So, you were defending the lady's honour?' There was a thread of steel to his voice.

'Yeah, man. He deserved it.'

'And you had no problem getting into a fight, did you? Is that how it went with Marcus, too? Did your drinks with him also end in a physical altercation?'

'I've already told you. I never touched Marcus. I left him the same way I found him, drinking and sweating on his front deck—'

Elliot Ramsay caught Luke's eye and signalled for him to be quiet. 'Detective, it appears we're going around in circles. Are we here to answer questions about Mr Keeling, or are we back to the Marcus Rowntree matter? May I remind you that it was Mr Keeling who assaulted my client during that incident? I fail to see how this relates to the investigation on Marcus Rowntree.'

'It does relate to the matter at hand,' the detective snapped. He opened his file and retrieved some papers, which he slid across the table to Ramsay.

'Both Mr Keeling and Ms Delaney came into the station this morning to make voluntary statements, copies of which are before you. They both assert that Mr Grayling was behaving erratically and was in a highly emotionally charged condition when he deliberately provoked Mr Keeling into an altercation on Friday night.'

'What the fuck? I wasn't behaving erratically—' Luke interrupted before a look from Ramsay shut him down again.

The detective resumed as if he hadn't spoken. 'Mr Grayling has stated that he travelled directly to the Arms after visiting Mr Rowntree on Friday night. It begs the question, doesn't it? What happened at Marcus Rowntree's property to result in your client being in such an agitated state upon his return?'

Ramsay did not say a word, merely took his time carefully reading each statement. 'Detective, while I admire your initiative, we both know these statements don't change the fact that you are yet to present a single piece of physical evidence linking my client to Mr Rowntree's death.'

Ramsay stared the detective down.

'To reiterate our position, my client has already made a complete and voluntary statement about his movements and whereabouts on Friday night, and unless you have any specific or new information linking Luke to Marcus's death or are proposing to lay charges, we have nothing further to add.'

From that point on, Luke had replied with 'no comment' to each of the questions put to him by the two police officers, until the interview had been suspended.

–

From across the glass sliding doors that separated Caleb's kitchen from the back patio, Luke watched his sister and father engage in a furious whispered conversation. He couldn't hear what they were saying, but he could guess. He blew out a spiral of smoke, wishing it was a spliff – a Mitch Cosgrove special. Leaning his head back on the swing seat, he closed his eyes, feeling weightless and utterly drained. A headache reached from deep inside to pound at his temples.

If it wasn't for the anxiety cramping his insides, it would almost be peaceful. Above him, countless stars were scattered like rice grains across an indigo canvas. Every time he visited home, he marvelled at the vastness of the skies visible from this part of the world, unaffected by light pollution compared to the suburbs of Sydney. He felt cocooned within Caleb's lush, tropical garden sprouting like a jungle around him; palms and crotons fighting for space among heliconias and cordylines, the night chorus of insects in full swing.

Luke had been deposited at Caleb's front door almost an hour ago, having been driven straight there by Elliot Ramsay, after they had slipped out of Esserton Station via its rear entrance to avoid the gathered media. The family had made the executive decision that there was less chance of Luke being discovered by the press at Caleb's place in Terranora rather than at either of their houses.

He hoped Caleb wouldn't come to regret his offer to share his home. His father's boyfriend had been nothing but gracious since Luke's appearance, despite everything that had gone down only a few short days ago at his sister's. He was out right now picking up takeaway for them all, getting out of their way so they could talk in peace. But being stuck in the kitchen alone with his dad and sister was the very last place Luke wanted to be.

The sliding door opened and he glanced up. *Fuck. They couldn't even give him ten minutes.* Kate walked towards him with a couple of beers in hand, her signature peace offering.

'Thought you could do with some alcohol in your system.' She gave him a half-smile and motioned for him to shove over so she could sit beside him. 'Weed, smokes and beer. Three for three.'

'You forgot the painkillers.'

'No drug in the world can stop you from being painful, brother. You're immune to all medical science.'

Luke rolled his eyes and accepted the beer, taking a sip. 'Fuck, what's this shit?'

'Low-carb beer. They're Dad's. I think he's on a diet for Caleb.'

Their eyes met and they both dissolved into laughter. Cackling like teenagers more than the joke deserved, the tension from the last few days dissipating into the balmy night.

'Don't tell him I told you. But I think he's joined a gym, too. In Murwillumbah. I saw the membership card in his wallet.'

Luke snorted into his beer. 'God help us.'

'Yeah, but look who he's got to keep up with. Caleb's got some serious RDJ vibes going, don't you reckon? Hot in that kinda scruffy way?'

Luke laughed. Now that Kate mentioned it, in the right light, Caleb could sort of pass for a longer-haired, stockier version of the famous American actor, Robert Downey Jr, star of the *Iron Man* movie franchise.

'So, this is where you're hiding.' The man himself appeared suddenly and Luke almost choked on his beer.

'Food's up if you're hungry. I didn't know what you'd like, so I got a bit of everything.' He handed a bowl each to Kate and Luke, filled to the brim with rice and Thai curries, with cutlery sticking out of the top.

'This is perfect. Thanks, Caleb.'

'What can I say. Getting takeaway food is the least of my skills as Iron Man.' He winked and headed back inside, smiling serenely.

'Shit, I'm never going to live that one down, am I?' Kate grimaced.

'Never, ever.' Luke grinned and tucked into his green curry, feeling instantly better as the food hit his system.

'So, how was Ramsay today? He seems like a bit of a dick.'

Luke had known it was coming. He'd been waiting for his sister to turn the conversation.

'He is a bit,' he replied. 'Didn't say much on the drive here. Had no idea where he was taking me. He spent most of the trip on speakerphone telling off a builder about renovation delays at his house.'

When they'd arrived at Caleb's, Ramsay had cornered Gray in a hushed conversation for a few minutes, before leaving straight afterwards, gliding away in his gunmetal-grey Lexus NX with a promise to call if there were any developments.

'But was he all right at the station? Dad said he comes from a policing family, so he's got an insider's track into the system. He's moved to the Gold Coast, but apparently most of his cases are still south of the border.'

Of course, Gray had scoured his network and called in a favour. But for once, Luke was glad. He had to admit that Gray had come through with the goods in finding Ramsay. Luke had been in no shape this afternoon to take on the likes of that detective. And Ramsay had shielded him, making quick work of the police officers. And then he'd rounded on Luke in the car, furiously and at length, for attending a police interview in his condition, for not taking his situation seriously enough. That's the bit Luke had left out when he'd recounted his time with Ramsay to Kate.

'Yeah, he was a gun in the interview room. Ran rings around the detective. Josh someone. He said he knew you, actually,' he added. 'The detective, I mean.'

Luke's mind drifted from the quiet stillness of Caleb's garden back to his last conversation with the detective, after his formal interview had concluded.

Luke had been waiting in the corridor in sight of a uniformed officer as Ramsay had used the room to make a couple of phone calls. The high from the weed was starting to wear off and he could feel the heaviness in his limbs, his eyes fluttering shut even as he stood leaning against the white-washed wall. He'd jumped when the detective had slid into place beside him, seemingly out of nowhere.

'Still here, mate?'

'Yeah, just waiting for Elliot. He's on the phone in there.'

Josh studied him, as if trying to make up his mind about something. 'You know, your sister and I used to be partners. I don't know if she ever told you. You should ask her about Sam Delaney.'

'What do you mean? Why would I do that?'

The detective marked him with a hard look. 'Out of interest, Luke, when you decided to insert yourself into Sam Delaney's life on Friday night, did you consider what she might have wanted? Did you stop to think whether your blundering might have made things worse for her behind closed doors? Having to deal with her boyfriend's bruised ego? All you did was push her straight into the path of his anger. So thanks for that, mate. You're a bloody hero, you are.'

A loud smacking sound of a palm making contact with skin jerked him back to the present.

'Yeah, I know Josh Ellis,' Kate said, flicking the dead mosquito off her.

'Yeah, well, he said I should ask you about Sam Delaney. He reckons me getting into that fight with her boyfriend made things worse for her. Is he right? Did Ben Keeling hit her?' Luke hardly dared to look at his sister. There seemed to be no end to the girls that he somehow hurt with his decision-making, good, bad or otherwise.

'Luke.' Kate's words were careful. 'You're not responsible for Ben Keeling's actions. Your heart was in the right place, trying to defend her. It was just one of those situations that you could walk away from.' She shrugged.

'But she couldn't.' He finished her sentence for her, suddenly feeling sick. Placing his bowl on the ground, he took a deep draught of his beer.

'Luke, there are many things we need to discuss. Things that you need to properly worry about. But Sam Delaney isn't one of them. That situation is outside of your control. Right now, we need to talk about Marcus and whatever's happened at your work.'

THEN

I know he's started to guess. I can tell by the way he yields control when we're intimate. How he makes no comment when I turn on a night light when we go to bed. Complete darkness is not an option. He hasn't suggested we visit home in over a month now. I thought I had managed to cover up my little panic attack at the pub that last weekend, stumbling outside in a cold sweat on the pretence of needing a smoke, but apparently not.

Plus, I know he's been on the phone to her, getting advice, planning and devising. I can guess their subject. Yet another round of counsellors, clinics and rehab programs. Good luck finding one that we can afford. The Medicare cow has been squeezed so dry, its teats are chapped and sore. And yet here I am, still trying to convince myself that this toke, this pill, this glass will definitely be my last. Definitely.

He wants an explanation. They both do. Something neat and tidy that they can fix. *Why are you like this? What has made you this way? Why won't you let us help you? Just talk to us.*

Platitudes and wishful thinking. The truth does not set you free. It just creates more complications. They think they want to know because they believe my problems will not affect them. That my Pandora's box will have no bearing on their lives, or friends or memories. It'll just help cure me, with no collateral damage. But that's bullshit. Because of course it'll capsize the comfortable stasis of their lives. My problems will suddenly become theirs. Tainting their recollections and forcing them to question, to choose and sever. It's easier this way.

And what makes them think I want to talk about any of it? If half a dozen counsellors have failed, why do they think I'd want to vomit up that ugliness onto them? I can barely face it myself, and never sober. I have spent a lifetime running away. Only succumbing, when a random trigger takes my body hostage, stripping away the years in a millisecond. All it takes is a smell, or a look, or an unexpected touch. Like the other day at Coles, when a man stepped a beat too close, reaching for a packet of Twisties in the chip aisle. His proximity, bulk and body odour working to instantly upend my world. My brain cramping and my flesh seizing up like cement. My world narrowing to a suffocating square meter of space inside a supermarket. Reduced to shallow panic-breathing until control resurfaced. Some old biddy having to ask me to move because I was blocking the aisle.

Only in moments of deep relaxation can I go back there. Under the trance of a needle, when the chemical high both breaks down my barriers and cocoons me from the pain.

Once upon a time, I hooked up with a guy at a party. My friends wanted to move on to a different venue, but I was having fun and decided to stay. He was cocky and brash but it was working for him, or at least I thought so at the time. His confidence was a turn-on. It felt good to have his eyes trained on me. I recognised him, of course, but I don't think he made the connection, or not for a while, at least. I guess, a year away from home, a hair straightener, dye job, and new clothes will do that. I was strutting out the brand new me, and I liked that he couldn't stop looking.

He offered me a place to crash for the night and I said yes.

We were pissed when we got back to his unit. He lit a spliff and we smoked it on his bed, talking shit. All surface stuff, nothing too deep, which was fine by me. I think we both drifted off. I sort of woke up a bit later and thought he had left the room. It sounded like there were voices coming from the sitting room, at least I think that's what I heard. I was still pretty out of it.

It was later in the night that I felt him kissing me. The room was pitch black. I responded at first, but something felt wrong. He was going too fast. His hands were pushing up my skirt and pulling at my undies. I didn't want that and I tried telling him, but he ignored me. He just kept shushing me and calling me *babe*, his voice rough and insistent, telling me how good I looked and how he'd wanted me all night. He pinned me down. Didn't care that I was crying or that he was hurting me. He had his palm over my mouth, ready to press down, if my cries became too loud.

Afterwards, he planted a hard, sloppy kiss on my lips and rolled off me. I remained there, crumpled and motionless, exactly where he had left me. As small as I could make myself. There, but not there; the shadow of him still imprinted on my flesh even though his weight had lifted. There in the saliva cooling on the parts of my skin where his tongue had probed, in the folds of my mini bunched uncomfortably under the small of my back, and the slick of liquid leaking from between my legs. I heard him getting up. The sound of the bedroom door swinging open and closing.

I took my chance, grabbing my things, grasping around on the carpet for my discarded shoes, and feeling my way out of the dark room into the living area. I heard a toilet flushing somewhere to the rear and didn't wait for him to reappear. I ran for the door, past the small dining table scattered with empty spirit bottles obviously stripped from the mini-bar and the common area with its L-shaped sofa and flat-screen TV. A street away from the apartment block, I managed to hail a taxi that didn't mind the fare up to Brisbane, back to campus. It cost a bomb, but at that point it didn't matter.

It was only months afterwards that it occurred to me to wonder about the figure I had seen crashed on the couch when I had fled the unit.

27

Thursday

A loud squawk jolted him awake. It was followed by another, and another. A chorus of crowing, one on top of the other, each full-throttled caw apparently trying to outdo the one before.

Luke reached blearily for his mobile: 5.11 am. *Brilliant.* The room was still dark, hovering between shadow and the first veins of peach-pink dawn. He swore, burying his head under a pillow, and yet the insistent bird chatter made it through. It was the sound of his father's chickens. Caleb had offered to rehouse the chooks when Gray had relocated into town from his rural property. The coop seemed to be positioned right underneath Luke's window. *Fuck this shit.*

He grabbed his pillows and stalked out, intending to get some shut eye on Caleb's oversized modular sofa. He paused at the entry to the lounge room, which gave way to a generous open-plan kitchen, spotting two figures already by the counter. His father and Caleb.

Gray was folded into his boyfriend's chest, Caleb running soothing circles along his back. Their hushed voices drifted towards him.

'He'll come around. He just needs a bit of time.'

'How much time? How long do I have to pay penance for?'

'You're his dad. It's forever, of course. That's the cost of parenting.'

His father grunted.

'It's his loss, you know,' Caleb said, tilting his father's head up so their eyes met. He bit Gray's lip lightly, the touch deepening into a slow kiss.

Something rose in Luke's chest and he turned abruptly away. A soup of emotions he wasn't sure he was ready to tackle head-on. Had he ever seen his parents being intimate in that way? All those times he had walked in on their quiet moments. Sharing a blanket while watching late-night TV on the couch, his mother rising at the crack of dawn to get Gray breakfast before he headed out on shift, his father placing a cup of tea beside her and kissing her forehead as she sat reading in her favourite armchair. At their best, his parents had enjoyed the comfortable intimacy of friends, and at their worst, they'd been two strangers forced to share the same living space. Even as the impulse to bat for his mother stirred within him like a well-worn note, Luke recognised that his heart wasn't in it. He'd seen the way Caleb looked at his father and registered his own reaction to it. Something uncomfortably close to jealousy at what his father shared with his boyfriend. Something he had so recently found and let slip through his fingers.

When he started awake a couple of hours later, the sun was streaming through the blinds and he could smell coffee in the air. In the kitchen, he found Caleb alone in his work clothes: a green polo bearing the logo of his landscaping company, cargo pants and boots. He pointed to a carafe of freshly brewed coffee, motioning for Luke to help himself.

'Hope the chickens didn't wake you? The ladies can be a noisy bunch at the crack of dawn.' He grinned as Luke sank onto one of the stools at the island bench.

'They were all right,' Luke mumbled.

'I think it's the dog next door.'

'Sorry?' Luke asked, pouring himself a mug of coffee.

'The neighbour's lab. When he goes out to relieve himself in the morning, the chooks arc up and start a racket to warn each other the dog's about. I think I'll have to move the coop away from the fence line.'

'Yeah, that makes sense.' He looked around. 'Ah… is my dad awake?'

'He got up early and decided to head home to get a few things done. He'll be back later.'

'Okay,' Luke said, feeling unreasonably relieved that he wouldn't have to deal with his father first thing. Clearly, he wasn't the only one good at avoiding difficult conversations.

Caleb studied him. 'You got anything on today?'

'Not really. Hide from the national press. Stay away from social media. Try not to shoot any friends. You know, same old.'

'Maybe you can add having a wee chat with your dad to that list.'

'What, to the things I'm *not* planning on doing?'

'Luke, I don't pretend to know what's gone on between you and your father. Given what a stubborn bastard he is, I assume a lot… But he's trying, all right. Just give him a chance.'

Luke nodded, his face tight, the conversation he'd overheard that morning still fresh. He sipped his coffee, focusing on the burn of the hot liquid at the back of his throat.

'All right, I'll be out all day. There's food and beer in the fridge and I've written out the Wi-Fi password for you.' Caleb collected his keys and took his used coffee cup to the sink.

Luke had to grimace at that. It was like being a teenager again. Being told the house rules. He forced himself to speak. 'Listen, Caleb. I meant to say last night. I really do appreciate this. Letting me stay here and everything. Also, I wanted to say sorry about the other day at Kate's…'

Caleb waved him off. 'Water under the bridge.'

'Yeah, well, I just wanted you to know that day wasn't about you. It's just me and Dad. We haven't quite mastered the art of being in the same room.'

'Yeah, I noticed.' He came up beside Luke, went to place a hand on his shoulder and seemed to think better of it. 'For the record, Luke, you're not the only one with a complicated family. If you're trying to win that award, trust me, you're not even in the running. Your family may not be perfect, but they're doing their best to help, which isn't a luxury that everyone has.'

'And what if they can't help me?' Caleb was almost out of the kitchen when Luke spoke, his voice small and ragged. 'What if I can't really undo what I've done?'

'Well, I'd say your dad is a good person to speak to about how that feels. He's been trying to make up for the mistakes he made with you and Kate for the better part of his adult life.'

Luke rolled his eyes, more out of habit than anything. Caleb shrugged and left him to it.

The front door closed behind Caleb and Luke felt the weight of the day sink in. He guessed he had a couple of hours max to himself before Kate got here. He knew his sister and she had a deep-seated inability to leave anything the fuck alone. Plus, he had an interview with the City of Sydney Police the following day via video link, because the Esserton cops didn't want him leaving the area for now. So, Ramsay would be around later this evening, no doubt with his father in tow, to discuss strategy.

In a way, it would be a relief to talk about what happened to people with no vested interest. Maybe they might even believe him. Not that it would make the slightest bit of difference to the person at the centre. The life he had blown up and had no chance of repairing.

He reached for his new phone. The Esserton Police had his actual mobile, apparently checking his call history and location data against the account he'd given for Friday night. If he had, in fact, stayed all night at Kate's, collapsed on her couch nursing his black eye. Good luck to them finding anything that would disprove his statement. Last night on their drive over from the station, Ramsay had agreed to stop at a grocery store so Luke could purchase a cheap Nokia to tide him over.

Despite his vow not to get on social media, he logged on immediately. Not using his own profile, of course, but his dummy Instagram account, the one on which he only posted arty food shots, with no reference to his real life. He had followed Payton using the dummy account almost a year ago now, months before they'd begun their thing, and she had followed back. It hadn't been to stalk her, exactly. It was just because he'd already been half in love with her by then and was still no closer to having a real conversation with her. The dummy account and follow-back had been his 'in' to discovering something about her life. So the next time they met, he would have something to say that might actually interest her, rather than being struck senseless the minute she entered a room and her perfume drifted his way.

And it had worked too. It turned out she was an indoor-boulder enthusiast, and that she had a penchant for northern Italian cooking. They were things he'd been able to research, going so far as to join a local climbing gym to get familiar with the basics so he could speak about boulder problems with some level of confidence the next time she was within his orbit. She had seen through him, of course. He'd exhausted his knowledge in less than five minutes, but it had been enough to make her smile and pique her interest. The next time, he'd blurted his love for Ossobuco alla Milanese and she'd laughed, a full-bellied, throaty sound, and whispered in his ear that she might just cook it for him one day, if he was lucky.

And so it had begun. Luke scrambling to keep up with her. Doing his best to be good enough. Marvelling at his luck and trying hard not to fuck things up. Though he had anyway. In the worst possible way. He had hurt her. Even when he had been so sure that it was he who would be destroyed by her.

He looked up her Instagram feed now. No new posts or stories. She had fallen off social media, just like he had. He scrolled through her old photos, his eyes feasting on her smile, the tiny scraps of exposed skin, as she posed with friends and family, made funny faces and giggled at the camera. The only parts of her face and body that remained accessible to him.

He logged off Instagram and into his dummy account on Twitter, his breath catching as he read the first tweet that came up on his feed.

> @Stella!!LivesHere 1/ So fucking sick of this shit. My BF was at the top of the world & now she can barely function. Intimate vid shared w/out consent by her a88hole boyfriend from work with their co-workers.

> @Stella!!LivesHere 2/ Her confidence & mental health are destroyed. No idea how many work-mates have seen the images. She used to live for her job, and now she's a fucking shell of the smart, confident woman I used to know.

> @Stella!!LivesHere 3/ This is what men do. They take what is given to them in trust and use it to destroy you. If you think things have changed since #metoo think again. #itsstillhappening #teachy-oursons #Ibelieveher

> 523 replies 620 retweets 1.6k likes

Payton's best friend, Stella Oeste. Savage, uncompromising and with a mind like a blade that could eat you up and spit you out in seconds. She had scared the shit out of him the only time they'd met, when he'd accompanied Payton to an art gallery opening. He'd felt her eyes lancing him, cataloguing every nervous smile and attempt at conversation. Stella had, of course, already unfollowed and blocked him on Twitter, but he could still access her public feed from his separate account.

And this tweet was doing numbers – not celebrity numbers, but it was getting there. Messages of support and solidarity. Other women sharing their own stories of breaches of confidence from the sick fucks in their lives. There were a few *shouldn't she have expected this* type comments, questioning why the woman had allowed herself to be recorded in the first place, which were quickly shouted down by replies pointing to victim blaming and the double standards that existed around women enjoying sex. He could feel the frustration and rage sparking off the women's words.

His fingers scrolled down the feed, dismay and despair vibrating through his body with every damning word. It was finally sinking in. People who knew Stella would be able to work it out. He couldn't hide out for much longer. No job, no friend, no acquaintance would want anything to do with him. His life was about to implode.

28

'What time are they calling you?'

Geoff eyed the wall clock. 'Ten-thirty,' he confirmed, a small, nervous smile playing on his lips.

'You're going to be great. You know that, right?'

The footage of Luke Grayling – *the younger sibling of a senior officer at Esserton Police Station* – being led into the back of a paddy wagon had made the news. Not only had Markham taken photos, but he'd also managed to record the moment of Luke being bundled into the police vehicle on his phone, footage that was now doing the rounds online and on TV.

Kate smiled brightly at her husband, willing him to redis-cover the enthusiasm and confidence he had held for this job opportunity only a few nights ago. Before her family had once again made front-page news. She knew that Geoff was worried the publicity would affect his job prospects. Big firms were averse to negative press coverage of any kind. The fact that the whole mess had nothing to do with Geoff or his abilities as an architect was beside the point. It was just another way she seemed to be unwittingly obstructing his career. Jesus, this job. With every passing day, it seemed to take more from her family. Momentarily, her conversation with Sarah about whether she would ever consider another profession flashed through her mind like a mirage, before she packed it firmly away.

She reached out and squeezed his hand. 'Please, don't worry about Luke or anything else. Just focus on the interview.'

He nodded, rewarding her with a smile that looked pained.

Kate drained her mug of coffee. 'Okay, I'll organise the kids and we'll get out of your hair so you can concentrate. Good luck. You'll be brilliant, I know it.' She kissed him and left the kitchen to round up Archie for preschool.

—

'Stop fussing. It's only ice-cream.' The words were slurred.

Kate felt her hand being pushed away as she tried to dab the spilt blob of strawberry ice from Aunty Iris's blouse.

'Sorry, Aunty.' She raised another spoonful, but Iris shook her head, indicating she was done.

'It hurts everywhere. I want my pain medication. Where are my pills?'

'The nurse said you already had your pills for today, Aunty. They'll start working soon.'

'I want Sarah. She knows what I need. Where's Sarah?'

'She's not working today, Aunty. She might be on tomorrow. I can check for you.'

'No, she was here before, tidying up in the bathroom.'

'The orderlies do that, Aunty. Sarah is a nurse. She only deals with the patients,' Kate said, trying to explain.

Iris made a dismissive sound. 'I want Sarah,' she repeated mulishly.

'I'll check with the staff,' Kate said to placate her, shrugging away the momentary hurt. Not quite jealousy, but something close. She knew that Sarah was popular with the residents. Kate didn't mind that Iris enjoyed Sarah's company. She only wished she could comfort Iris with her own presence. She resented Sarah's easy ability to raise a reluctant smile from Iris when she had been trying in vain for weeks.

Kate quickly wiped a line of creamy liquid from Iris's chin before she could object and tucked the knitted quilt higher up her body. Iris gave her an irritated wave, motioning towards the TV. Kate pointed the remote and turned up the volume. She understood that this was Iris's way of saying she'd had enough for a while.

'Just going to get a bite to eat for lunch, Aunty. We'll be back soon.'

Kate caught Luke's eye and signalled for him to follow her out.

'That's it?'

'For now. She needs a break. We can go back in a tick.'

She pushed Amy's pram to the nearby courtyard, making for the shade of a large London plane tree. Removing Amy from the confines of the pram and setting up a picnic blanket, she sat down with Amy, pulling out her favourite toy: a sensory book on farmyard animals, full of bright, noisy pages to poke and prod at. Luke joined them, smiling as Amy squealed with delight when he pressed the rubber snout of the pig on one of the pages, making it oink.

'I thought you said she was better.'

'She is. That's her better. A couple of months ago, she could barely speak.'

Aunty Iris, not a relative by blood, but family in every way that mattered. A friend of their mother and an adopted grand-mother to Kate and Luke, Iris had been a permanent fixture in their lives growing up. Now in her early nineties, she had been a sprightly, engaged and fiercely independent resident of the Scottsdale House retirement village. Usually found reading on the side terrace, whatever the weather, or enjoying the centre's activities, yoga, choir and chess club. Or getting one of her visitors, usually Geoff, to sneak in some McDonald's. That was until a stroke had struck her down eight weeks ago, affecting movement and speech and confining her to the high-care nursing wing of the facility.

Iris hated being bed-bound, and having to rely on others for her basic needs. It grated on her pride, and made her increasingly fractious when interacting with friends and family. Kate had worked out that Iris did better in short spells, so she rationed out her visits in ten-minute stints, to give Iris space and avoid tiring her.

'Don't ever get old,' she'd whispered in Kate's ear as she had bent down to hug Iris during her last visit. There was nothing she could say to that. Bodies broke down and illness struck when you least expected it. It would come for them all, eventually.

'It's strange seeing her like that.'

Strange was not quite the word she would use. Awful. Heart-breaking. Distressing. There were a hundred other words that came to mind.

'She looks really... fragile.'

'Yeah,' she replied shortly.

'What did the doctor say?'

'That she's as well as can be expected and at her age she's unlikely to recover from another one.'

'Right.'

They lapsed into silence, each caught up in their own memories of the past, when Iris had been a force of nature, descending on their house on those days when their mum had been unable to move, when the door to her bedroom had remained closed for days on end, and their dad would sleep in the lounge room and eventually give Iris a call. She would bustle in, whipping the house into shape, prepping meals that could be frozen for the week, organising the shopping and laundry, and somehow coaxing their mother back into the world. Iris had been more present than their paternal grandparents, whom Gray would never call upon for help on any of their mum's 'rest days' out of loyalty to her. It was Iris who had witnessed the inner workings of their family, providing support without judgement.

Regardless of the circumstances that had brought Luke home, Kate was glad that he was here. She watched him turn the pages for Amy and make funny animal noises for her. Kate didn't want to ruin the moment, but he would need to talk to her at some point. She hadn't pushed him last night, but enough was enough.

'So, are we going to talk about what happened at Hull-Hayward?'

'Kate, don't start, all right. I thought we were just here to see Iris.'

'Luke, c'mon. You need to spit it out. Is it true you shared some sort of video?'

'What?' His head snapped as if she'd punched him.

Kate's expression softened. The look her brother had given her was hollow, almost desperate. She couldn't remember ever seeing him like that. What the fuck had he got himself into?

'Luke,' she tried again, 'whatever this is, however bad it is, we want to help. We're not trying to interfere, just trying to understand.'

'Kate, this isn't one of your cases, all right. I don't need to tell you anything. It's my private business. Ramsay has the details. He's dealing with it.' His voice sounded defeated.

'Luke, you can't just refuse to talk about it or pretend it's not happening.' Kate could feel her patience snapping, the frustration from the last few days boiling over. 'We're your family. We have a right to know. You're not the only one this affects.'

'And there it is. I was waiting for it.' He pushed himself up, his sudden movement knocking over Amy's sippy cup. She gave a surprised squawk and he planted a quick peck on her forehead as an apology, then turned towards Kate. 'That's really the only thing that matters, isn't it? You and your squeaky-clean police career.'

'Oh, come off it. You cannot be this naïve. Of course, all of this impacts our family. And it's not just me. Geoff has a job interview today. The first one he's had in months, and he's petrified that all this media attention is going to impact his chances.'

'Oh, so now Geoff being unemployed is also my fault,' he hissed.

'Luke, wake up, would you? If you don't clear your name, this stuff is going to hang around all of us like a bad smell.'

'God, who needs enemies when you've got family like this. As per usual, Kate, I thank you for your fucking belief in me.' He rose to his feet. 'I'm going to wait in the car.'

29

'Mum, look. Boof's licking Amy. Muuum, look. Look at Boof.'

Kate turned to see Sarah's dog lick the square of watermelon that Amy had been eating. Amy and Archie were set up on the timber floor of Sarah's kitchen, a plate of cut fruit between them. Kate had laid out a towel for them to sit on to catch the mess. Her daughter giggled as Boof wolfed down the sweet fruit, licking the juice running down Amy's arm.

The dog now tried her luck with Archie, but Archie swung his bowl away, laughing. 'No, Boof, it's not for you.'

Sarah gently manoeuvred the dog outside as Kate washed Amy's hands and got the kids resettled with a new plate of fruit. At Archie's insistence, she moved the kids next to the door so they could still see and speak to Boof through the insect screen.

After dropping her brother back at Caleb's house, Kate had driven around to Sarah's with the kids, collecting Archie from preschool on the way. Luke had not spoken a word during their return trip to Terranora, inserting his earbuds to discourage any attempt at conversation. It had been a relief to see the back of him.

The oven dinged and Sarah pulled out a perfectly baked tray of sugar cookies, which she moved to a cooling rack. The room seemed to swell with heat, the warmth of the oven increasing the already sweltering temperature, and Sarah's newly redis-covered perfume adding a sickly scent on top. It didn't seem like a day for baking, but then Kate never questioned Sarah's small rituals, which were always strictly observed. Especially today.

'You okay?'

Sarah smiled, concentrating on setting up her mixer and the ingredients that went into the frosting. Icing sugar, butter, vanilla and lemon juice. Just like Sarah's mother would have made it.

The entire kitchen and the house itself remained almost identical to when Mrs Osborne had been alive, as if Sarah couldn't bear to change anything without her mother's permission. The original three-piece lounge suite sat where her mother had arranged it all those years back, and the side tables still displayed Mrs Osmond's old books. On the walls hung a selection of photos, younger versions of the sisters frozen in time. Sarah dressed for her Year Twelve formal, her pale hair in an elegant top knot, with Nadine grinning by her side, her face framed by a halo of tight blonde curls. Their mother had favoured informal shots over posed photos. Kate had forgotten how alike the sisters had looked, especially as teens. The same hazel eyes, thin lips and aquiline noses peered out of the images; Nadine's with the addition of a small bump on the bridge of her nose, the result of a childhood dirt-biking accident.

Kate watched as Sarah checked her mother's recipe book, though she was sure Sarah knew the quantities off by heart.

Even when the cancer had been at its worst, Mrs Osborne would find solace in baking. Although by the end, she had no appetite for what she had cooked, and Sarah had to perform most of the steps with her mother looking on, the mere act of being in the kitchen had brought comfort. And Sarah had carried on the tradition, re-creating her mother's favourites. Especially, the sugar cookie recipe, a treat for Nadine, reflecting the last time her mother had felt well enough to bake. Five days later, exactly a week off Christmas, she had succumbed to her illness.

Sarah had got into the habit of baking the cookies for Nadine each year as a means of remembering their mother and ignoring the Christmas season. Kate regarded her friend; pity laced with impatience. Even this year, when there would be no sister to enjoy the fruits of her labour, Sarah had still persisted with the cookies. Sarah finished with the electric mixer and held out the metal beaters.

'Okay for the kids to have a lick?'

'Yeah, go on.'

Sarah passed the beaters on to Archie and Amy, who accepted them with enthusiasm.

'It's nice that you're still doing this,' Kate said, careful to keep her voice neutral. She began to gather the various mixing bowls and used utensils as Sarah filled up the sink with hot water.

'Rocky road in November and sugar cookies in December.'

'You still made the rocky road?' Kate asked, both surprised and saddened.

'Just a small tray for her birthday.' Sarah smiled briefly.

Kate returned to the dishes. Homemade rocky road: Nadine's favourite. Of course, it shouldn't surprise her.

Nadine. The sister who had never got over her mother's death. Who had bombed out of university and lurched from one party drug to another to salve the pain, until addiction itself had become the knot she couldn't escape. Sarah's gesture, this whole baking routine, seemed so utterly pointless and self-punishing.

It suddenly struck Kate how many life-changing tragedies her friend had endured. The two women in her family, Ant and now Marcus. Her eyes moved to Boof, breathing heavily outside. Another loss that wasn't far off.

'How's Frank doing?' Sarah's voice cut through her thoughts. 'He keeps calling me, you know. Asking me to convince you to relook at Ant's case.'

'Oh, shit, sorry. I didn't realise he was hassling you, as well.'

'He's no trouble. He's just lonely, that's all.' She cleared her voice. 'So, are you going to look into Ant's death?'

Kate made a face. 'Not really. I mean, I followed up with a contact in Queensland and she put me on to the attending officer who found Ant that day.'

Sarah's hand slipped and one of the dishes fell back into the sink, splashing her. 'Shit, sorry. Wasn't concentrating. What were you saying?'

'The officer who discovered Ant,' Kate repeated. 'I just met up with him the other day and he took me through what they found. And there's nothing out of the ordinary there. It's suicide. Just like the coroner's report stated. I just haven't had a chance to meet with Frank yet, with everything that's been going on. I'll make sure to visit him this week.'

Sarah nodded. 'And Marcus? Any news there?'

Kate shook her head. 'I'm staying out of it. I have to with Luke...' She waved her hand, not wanting to complete the thought.

'But they don't really think it's him, do they?'

Kate shrugged. 'I'm no longer in the loop, Sarah. I only get told what they're happy to release to the public.'

'How is he, really?' Sarah asked. 'I saw in the paper about him losing his job?' She lowered her voice with a quick glance towards Archie.

'Oh, God. Let's not talk about it. The least said about that mess, the better.'

'So, all that stuff about him and the girls he's dated, and about the Sydney Police looking into it? It sounds pretty serious.'

'Yeah, well fooling around with a sex video is pretty serious.' It flew out before she could stop herself. 'Shit, forget I said that. I really shouldn't have said anything.'

'A sex video? Fuck.'

'The worst part is, I'm not even really that surprised. Luke's never had trouble getting girls, you know? And he's always been kind of careless with their emotions. I honestly don't know how bad it is. But it's definitely not good.'

'That's... a lot.'

'Yep. And I'm trying to keep an open mind. I don't actually know his side of the story because he refuses to talk to me. It's all with the lawyer.'

'He called me today,' Sarah said.

'Luke did?'

'Yeah, about an hour before you arrived. He wanted to chat about Iris. He told me about your visit this morning.'

'It's the first time Luke has seen her since the stroke. It was a shock to the system.'

Sarah nodded. Kate didn't need to explain any of this to her. Sarah had spent a lifetime helping families cope with the physical and mental changes wrought on their loved ones by age. Iris's challenges weren't new or any worse than what she had managed for countless other people.

'Did he say anything else?'

'Not really.' She hesitated. 'He sounded a bit out of it, to be honest.'

Kate stiffened. So, Luke obviously still had access to his contacts.

'Actually, I said he could come over for dinner on the weekend. I hope you don't mind. He sounded kind of sad on the phone—'

'Here you go, Sarah,' Archie interrupted them. He returned the beaters, which had been licked clean.

'Thanks, mate, you've both done an excellent job. Even better than Boof would have done.'

Kate's phone pinged with a text message from Geoff. 'We'll have to get going soon, bud. Can you also collect the fruit bowls, please, mate, and bring them up to the sink?'

As Archie ran off, Kate turned to Sarah. 'You know you're welcome at ours for Christmas, right? Why don't you bring Boof along and stay over.' It was a standing offer, one her friend had refused steadfastly each year.

Sarah bumped her softly. 'Thanks, Kate, but we'll be fine. Boof and I, we like our own company. We'll find something to do.'

30

Kate ordered a Great Northern and took the beer to a quiet table at the Crest Bar inside the Esserton RSL. She wasn't perfectly convinced that she should be here. In meeting with Eric Harrington, she would be going against her agreement with Esposito of not meddling with the investigation or speaking to witnesses. But it was difficult to refuse a celebrity and his voicemail message had piqued her curiosity. Geoff's urging had done the rest.

'Go, the kids will be fine. Just make sure to get a selfie with him.' He had winked.

Geoff's interview had gone well, and nothing could dampen his mood. He wouldn't find out the results for a couple of weeks, but he was quietly optimistic. She hoped this meeting with Harrington wouldn't take too long so she could return home and celebrate her husband's win.

Sitting at her corner table, its surface slightly tacky from a quick not-quite-wipe by a staff member, she watched as Harrington worked the room. A handshake and a clap on the shoulder, shared reminiscing about Harrington's most famous role, a long-running series about a down-and-out football coach, devilishly handsome and forever unlucky in love, which was still doing the rounds on streaming services. A schooner pressed into his palm, a quiet word of sympathy, if they remembered. These were his people. Where his glory days were still remembered. Not a has-been who couldn't get a call back from producers. There was a reason he had chosen this venue.

He had to be in his late fifties now, she guessed. His compact physique kept mostly in check by regular visits to the gym, the once abundant hair receding at the top and sides, and the familiar square jawline loosening into the beginnings of a chook neck. As he smiled and exchanged a few words with a couple of women who seemed to melt under his gaze, Kate thought she could see snatches of the old heartthrob visible in this thicker and older version.

'Detective Miles.' Eric Harrington had made it to her table and pulled up a chair.

'Mr Harrington.'

For a man who had only recently lost his son, he looked composed and well rested. But maybe it was a mask he put on for the crowd. As he sat down opposite her, she could see the heaviness around his face, the automatic smile that didn't quite reach his eyes.

'How's your holiday?'

'I wouldn't exactly call it that.'

'Listen, I don't believe for a minute that Luke had anything to do with Marcus's death. I'm sorry your family's been dragged into all of this.'

Kate regarded him. When it came down to it, Eric Harrington didn't know her family from a bar of soap. How could he be so sure that her brother had nothing to do with his son's death? Was he just naïve, or was this his standard mode of operation? Buttering her up to get what he wanted. Whatever that was.

He seemed to intuit something in her expression because he half smiled, a sad little grimace. 'I don't remember many of Marcus's friends, but I remember your brother and the other boy... Ant, was it? I heard he's passed on, too.' He paused, reaching for his drink. He drank deeply, half emptying the glass before resuming. 'I remember them from Marcus's eighteenth. Thick as thieves, they were. I liked what Luke tweeted about Marcus, you know, before he took it down. And that photo he posted of the three of them together.'

Had that been a subtle nudge? Eric Harrington had been good about the whole tweet debacle. He hadn't created a fuss or made an issue of Luke's ill-timed release of Marcus's identity to the public. Was this a gentle reminder that Kate owed him?

'I thought we weren't here to speak about the case,' she said with a smile, in an effort to keep the conversation light.

'You're right. You're right. Not another word.' He mimed zipping his lips shut.

There was a silence as they both concentrated on making a dint on their lagers.

'So, what can I do for you, Mr Harrington?'

'Straight to business, ha-ha. I like that.'

She waited. For all his assumed jocularity, he was ill at ease.

Again, he made for his beer before speaking. 'Marcus's kids, Ted and Jasper, I'd like to meet them.'

Kate stared at him. Her confusion must have been obvious, because he hurried to fill the silence.

'I've never actually spoken to Fiona, Marcus's wife. Marcus made sure to keep his family separate from me. Even now, dealing with the police and everything, our paths haven't crossed. It's just been Celeste, and she'll barely look at me, let alone take my calls. I'd like to see Fiona and the boys. You know, meet them properly.'

'You didn't keep in touch with Marcus after he got married?' Kate asked, surprised.

'I should have made more of an effort,' Harrington replied. 'I did try. But Marcus was so angry when I left for the US. He seemed to think I should have taken him with me to LA.' He shook his head in disbelief. 'Marcus had no clue. I was travelling all the time, auditioning for every project I could, trying to get a break. He thought my life was one party after another. But it wasn't like that. Nobody knew me in America. I was starting from zero, trying to get my face in front of producers. I was pushing forty and competing with every fresh-faced wannabe actor going round. Do you know how hard it is to make it in Hollywood?'

Kate didn't answer and Harrington went on, too invested to stop.

'I tried for six years and barely got enough parts to make my rent. In the end, I just had to call it quits and come back home. Meanwhile, Marcus just wanted me to throw jobs his way, to talk to people I knew and get him parts. It doesn't work like that. Well, it does sometimes, but you have to put in the hard yards, too. And you have to have some talent—'

He bit his lip, realising too late that his last words sounded like a petty insult hurled at his dead son.

'Anyway.' He swallowed. 'After he found Fiona, he seemed happy. Settled, even. I thought he was okay.'

'How long has it been since you last spoke with Marcus?'

'It's been years. I tried visiting him a few times when I was up this way for auditions and projects, but he would have none of it. I even tried connecting with him on Facebook. But he wouldn't accept my bloody friend request. Ha. You know, he never even invited me to his wedding? Or informed me when his boys were born? I only found out later through a friend. Not Celeste. She won't say boo to me if she can avoid it.'

Silence fell as Harrington seemed to battle something within himself.

'Marcus cut me off. Not that I didn't deserve it... But he made it clear that he didn't want me near his family or his sons.' His voice wavered. 'I thought we'd have more time to fix things... After he became a father, I thought he'd come around, you know? Realise how hard it is to live up to your children's expectations.'

Eric Harrington skolled the remainder of his drink, then coughed and cleared his throat, suddenly conscious that he'd revealed too much.

'Mr Harrington, you can just ask the detective in charge, Josh Ellis, or Chief Inspector Esposito. They'll be able to pass on your details to Fiona.'

'Yes, I know. I've already asked Detective Ellis, and he said he's spoken to Fiona but nothing's come of it. You're a local and you know the family. I just thought if you could speak to Fiona or Celeste…' He ran a hand across his face, a gesture of helplessness.

'I know what you're asking, but you have to understand, even though Luke and Marcus were friends at school, I don't know Fiona or Celeste particularly well. Me speaking to them isn't likely to have any more impact than Detective Ellis. And Fiona probably just needs a bit of time to get her head around everything. It doesn't mean she's not going to get back to you.'

'I know. I know. That's why I haven't pushed. She's grieving and trying to look after the boys. But… if you could just touch base with her. Ask her if it's okay to visit them. I won't take much of their time. Half an hour, ten minutes, even. I'd just really like the chance to get to know my grandkids.' His voice broke at the last words.

Her resolve faltered. This man, who not a minute ago had stalked the room like a big cat, suddenly looked so small begging her for a favour. And there was no reason why she couldn't help him. Or at least try.

'I'll speak to her,' she said.

'Thank you.' He seemed to sag with relief.

'Can I get you another?' he asked, motioning to her drink.

'No, I'm still going. I need to head soon, anyway. I'll let you know how I go,' she said.

He nodded, taking the hint and moving away.

Kate chewed over Harrington's request as she finished the last of her beer, realising she would need to check in with the station before she did anything. Sighing, she rose and made for the exit.

In the sports bar, she manoeuvred past a group of men shouting at their football team on the wall-mounted TV and fell in behind a tall woman with closely cropped blonde hair, millimetres off being fully shaved, who was walking briskly towards the sign pointing to the ladies. A faint scent of bruised flowers and bergamot trailed in her wake. When the woman turned and disappeared behind a corridor, Kate spotted someone else come into view.

Esposito. In jeans and a cotton shirt with his top buttons undone and the sleeves rolled up, probably having just finished a bistro meal, the tiniest smudge of gravy still visible on his chin. In an instant, she was transported to the cafeteria at Goulburn, sneaking looks at Esposito sitting at the instructors' table with the other training personnel, laughing between bites of schnitzel.

She made to leave, but he'd already seen her.

'Kate.'

'Sir. I was just leaving.' She was suddenly painfully aware of the clothes she was wearing. The soft cami and denim skirt that didn't quite reach her knees. Without the armour of her work suit, she felt exposed.

'Are you alone? I mean, is your family with you?'

'No, they're at home. I had an appointment with someone.' She didn't explain. Didn't want to get into a whole thing about Eric Harrington right now.

'Well, I was about to grab a drink for the road. Do you want to join me?'

This wasn't a good idea.

'Sure. Why not.'

He gave a soft grin, as though he hadn't expected her to agree.

'Corona with lime?' Again with remembering her old favourites. Except this drink preference had lingered.

'Actually, I'm driving. Just a lemon, lime and bitters would be great, thanks.'

There, she had established a boundary. She needed all her faculties to deal with Esposito.

He ordered their drinks and ushered her to a table outside in the beer garden, away from prying eyes, she noticed. *No. He was her boss, for Chrissake. She was almost twenty years older and hopefully at least that many years wiser. This wasn't happening again.*

He swallowed a glug of red wine, his eyes sliding off her. Was he nervous, too?

'How's Ellis going with the case? Any updates you're allowed to share with me?'

'Straight to work, I see.'

'Is there anything else we need to discuss?'

He sighed. 'I was hoping we could chat about other things, yeah.'

She stilled, then sipped from her glass, the bubbles rising and tickling her nose.

'I've thought about you, you know.'

'Leo. Let's not do this.' *Leo.* How quickly she had reverted to his given name. The name that for years had tasted like dust on her lips. A pebble of hurt that had rolled around in her chest whenever she'd heard that name mentioned. It had taken her years to still that pebble and forgive herself for being young and inexperienced, and for jumping heart-first. To come to terms with the fact that he had been married. That he'd kept the truth from her for months. Never outright lying – he'd held on to that distinction. Just never telling her the whole truth. So that, in the end, he'd broken two hearts for the price of one.

'I heard about your accident. I wanted to call you…' His eyes grazed over her left shoulder, where the slight puckering of skin indicated the place where a bullet had sliced through her flesh some months back.

'I'm glad you didn't. I had a lot going on at the time. I didn't need any more complications.'

'So, you still think of me as a complication.' He smiled, the cheeky grin of old that used to make her stomach catch. She regarded him now over her drink. The smile had lost its shine. It was sadder and more calculated. And it had lost its power over her.

'I think of you as my boss, nothing more—'

'Kelly's left me. Over three years ago now,' he blurted. It was clumsy, but it was also an overture. An offer of sorts, if she chose to go there.

She finished her drink, sucking on a piece of ice and crushing it between her teeth.

'I'm glad we had this chat, if only to clear the air. The thing we had, it's in the past. It's not something that can be re-created.'

Adrenaline coursed through her and she felt lightheaded, finally getting to speak the words she had thought about and rehearsed in various forms over the years. 'I don't know what's going on with you. Maybe you're still hurting after Kelly. Maybe you're just lonely. But you can't use me to fix that. I'm married and I have a family.'

She met his eyes so there would be no doubt. 'It's over, sir. It's been over for years.'

THEN

Ant felt the buzz of his phone in his pocket but ignored it. It would be just another message from Jacob asking where he was.

> you coming tonight or what

> wtf bro

> you're being a dick you know that right

> what are we meant to tell her

He was being rude. He knew that, but he didn't care. He was meant to be in Fortitude Valley right now, meeting up with Jacob and Rita, his girlfriend, along with her workmate, Chrissie. One of those excruciating blind dates that his loved-up couple friends insisted on foisting on him. Jacob had been showing him photos of Chrissie all week, scrolling endlessly through her Instagram feed to point out yet another image of her on the beach, on a bushwalk, baking sourdough. She seemed nice enough, wild ringlet hair and kind eyes, with one of those light-up-your-whole-face smiles. He had been looking forward to meeting her. Maybe he would still be able to make it up to her, assuming he could ever convince Rita to pass on her number, after tonight. But he couldn't think about that right now.

Nadine. That was what mattered tonight. He needed to find her.

> I'm sorry. I can't anymore. I just can't.

He'd almost resisted when he'd seen her text. He'd almost convinced himself that he could get in his car and drive to the pub where his friends were waiting, and spend the night conversing with a girl he didn't know, trying to feign interest in the minutiae of her life, remembering to laugh at her jokes, when in reality his attention would be anywhere but there.

Nadine. Nadine. Nadine. The pounding in his brain and the pool of acid in his stomach would not abate until he knew she was safe. It was always this way and always would be. Until the day when one or the other of them actually went through with what they threatened. For Anthony to finally absolve himself of responsibility for her. And for Nadine to take her own life.

Not that she would ever do it; he was convinced of that. This was the way she called him back to her. The knotted thread that bound them together, never quite snapping, regardless of how frayed the edges had become. The lightest tug and he found himself strung to attention. She was like the long tail of a bout of flu that he couldn't quite shake off. A tail that had lasted something like seventeen years.

The suburban streets were dark now, as the final brushstrokes of the setting sun drained from the sky. He'd been driving around for two hours, checking on her usual haunts but coming up empty. The share house had been a non-starter. They hadn't seen her in over a week. A week. Had he really not checked on her for that long? A worm of fear dug inside him, and he could feel sweat curdling in his armpits.

There was too much history between Nadine and him. That was the problem. He had allowed himself to get too close, convinced himself that he could help her. He had talked with her, nursed her, yelled at her and pleaded with her. He had washed the vomit from her make-up-grazed face, forced air into her grey, unresponsive body and rushed her to emergency. He had laughed with her, drunk with her and danced with her. He had loved her. Before her first relapse and then her second and her third, he had convinced himself that she would be all right. That together they would be able to work through her demons.

In his darkest moments, he wondered if their strange entangled relationship, this dependence on each other, was what was keeping her from truly getting better. Whatever she attempted, whichever murky depths she descended to, he was there to pick up the pieces. Each time was a test. To see if he would come and prove her wrong.

… I am worthless I am scum I am nothing I haven't done a thing right my entire life I just take up space and it hurts to breathe and it hurts to exist and it hurts to talk I am so sick of myself I am sick of hearing myself whine whine whine why can't I get on with it and move on like every other person I just want it to stop I just need silence just blessed blessed silence…

All the endless hours of counselling. The scratchy, hate-filled pages of self-loathing in her journal. The cuts sliced over and over into soft flesh in places only he could see. If he abandoned her, it would be the confirmation she needed to make the final leap. *I told you so.*

Maybe she never would. But he'd never had the courage to call her out. To challenge her bluff. She had become his conscience. While Nadine was alive, Anthony could believe that he was a good man.

Ahead, against the sulphur glow of a street lamp, playing fields loomed. Netball courts and soccer fields backing onto a patch of bushland that was the pride of the local Landcare group. He remembered this place. An old drainage ditch had run the boundary of the bush block. When he'd last visited over six years ago, Nadine had been in a good place, and they'd come together, combining their efforts to look for an acquaintance.

And now here he was, retracing old memories. He parked the car and jogged towards the oval, the winter air sharp on his skin. In the distance, a game of netball was ending, the teams shaking hands and hugging it out. He made for the bushland edging the aging playing fields, green couch grass marked with expanding patches of brown.

Holding his phone torch aloft, he peered into the scrub, trying to make out movement. The last time he was here, the place had been covered in accumulated rubbish, plastic bags, fast food containers, condoms and used needles. But it had obviously experienced a facelift.

'Fuck, Nadine.' He stabbed her number as he followed an informal track that seemed to push its way into the bush.

From somewhere ahead, he heard the squeaky strains of REM's 'Shiny Happy People' and he felt his stomach drop. Nadine's ringtone. He broke into a run, stumbling over the uneven ground, frantically following the direction of the sound. Abruptly, the song cut out, the call having gone to voicemail. He swore and rang her number again, waiting for the tune to restart.

He found her curled under the base of a tree, in an oversized jumper and leggings, her knees tucked to her chest like a baby, one of her sleeves rolled up and the arm outstretched. Fear jolted his chest. She was motionless, not reacting to his touch or voice and he knew, without needing to see it, that there would be a needle nearby.

31

Friday

Kate crunched on an icy pole, feeling the lemony ice melt on her tongue and numb her teeth. Beside her, Archie bit into his chocolate Cornetto, going straight for the tip of the cone – in her opinion, foolhardy and overconfident. She watched, fascinated and bemused, as he managed to coordinate the demolition of his ice-cream from both ends without a major mishap.

'Wow! That was impressive, bud. Good job.'

Archie grinned and high-fived her.

Gray, who was tackling his own Cornetto, laughed. 'Maybe I should try it that way, too.'

'You've got to be fast, Grandpa.'

'I can see that.'

They were sprawled on the grass under the shade of a large Moreton Bay fig, overlooking the still expanse of the Tweed River. Kate had left Geoff on Amy duty so she could have some one-onone time with Archie at the park, which was a rare treat these days. She had invited Gray to join them so Archie could hang out with Grandpa without competing for attention with the baby. It would allow Archie some breathing space and get Gray out of the house, and away from stewing over Luke's police interview with Sydney via video link.

It was a scorcher of a day. Getting on to midday and the sun's glare seemed to sting her eyes despite her sunglasses. Even the wind blowing across the water was hot and airless. Archie had done well with the play equipment, but his endless energy had started to flag. He lay in a floppy heap on her lap, damp with sweat.

'Drink some water, bub.' She pressed Archie's bottle into his hands.

'Did you know anything about this woman at Hull-Hayward? Ramsay won't tell me anything.'

Gray's mind was never far away from Luke. Both Kate and her father had offered to accompany him to the station, but Luke had refused. He only wanted his lawyer.

'No idea. I take it Luke's not speaking to you, either.'

'I'd have more chance getting something out of a corpse.'

'What's a corpse, Grandpa?'

'Nothing, mate. Grandpa's being silly.'

'Is Uncle Luke in trouble?'

Gray met Kate's eyes over Archie's head. He opened his mouth to reply, but Kate got there before him.

'He is, mate. But we're trying to help him through it.' This thing with Luke was going to be with them for a while. There was no point in trying to avoid it. Archie was going to hear about it at some point, and she had to address it head on, so it didn't add to the weight of his fears.

'Did he do something bad?'

'We're not sure of all the details, mate. But we think Uncle Luke made some mistakes. Everyone's allowed to make mistakes, you know that, right? But you need to take responsibility. That means admit when you've done something silly and to say sorry to the people you've hurt. That's the only way you can learn from your mistakes and try to make things better.'

Archie was solemn as he listened to her. The explanation was probably a bit beyond his age, but she wanted Archie to know that she was taking his question seriously, not trying to fob him off.

'Okay, but do we still love him?' His little face was tense, wanting to know where his uncle stood within the family. Archie had been there when Luke had walked out of their lunch. He'd seen the anger and distress in the adults' faces, the tension and resentment pinging off them. The answer to this question meant the world to him.

'We do, mate.' It was Gray who answered, his voice quiet. 'Very much.'

The crunch of gravel under wheels made Kate turn, and she watched as a police-issue Commodore slotted into place beside her sedan in the small, unsealed parking lot attached to the playground. Josh Ellis unfolded from the car, elegant in a mauve checked shirt rolled at the elbows, his suit jacket discarded – a concession to the heat.

'Detective Ellis. Long time no see.'

'Chief Inspector.' Ellis nodded a greeting at Gray.

'Dad, can you—' Kate motioned to Archie.

'Go. Go.' Gray waved her off. 'C'mon, mate.' He held out his hand to Archie. 'I can push you on the swings.'

Kate joined Ellis and they walked a few metres, seeking shade underneath one of the foreshore gums.

'I got your message,' he said.

'You didn't need to meet me in person. You could have just called me back.'

'I felt like getting out of the office.' He shrugged. 'So, you said you met up with Harrington?'

His tone was even, but she felt his reproach. She had reached out to Josh because Esposito wasn't an option, especially not now with the way things stood between them. She understood why Josh had come to see her. So he could berate her in person, if necessary.

'It was nothing to do with the case,' she clarified. 'Harrington wanted to talk to me about his grandkids. He'd like to meet them.'

'Yeah, he's already said and I've mentioned it to both Fiona and Celeste. I don't think it's their priority at the moment.'

'He's asked if I could have another go and speak with Fiona.'

Josh frowned. 'A woman's touch and all that shit. God forbid a mere man could handle such a request with sensitivity.'

191

'Josh, don't get up me. I'm telling you what he asked.'

He sighed. 'You can try if you want. Just keep it contained. Nothing about the case.'

She nodded. They both knew that keeping Harrington on side and not telling tales to the higher-ups, or worse, the media, was part of the job. She debated whether she should ask after Luke. Josh had to know whether or not Luke was still sequestered at the station, stuck in an interview room. She hesitated but decided against it.

Josh's mobile chimed loudly and he answered the call. A brisk back and forth followed, and a minute later he rang off.

'That was your mate, Darnley,' he said.

Kate didn't take the bait, waiting him out.

'He's been trying to track down Luke's mysterious, dark-coloured sedan. The one he says he saw turning into Marcus's property that Friday night. Seems Darnley's got himself a lead. Apparently, one of the apprentices at the building site where Marcus was working prior to his death owns a metallic-grey Nissan. He's going to check it out later.'

Kate nodded, appreciating that he was keeping her in the loop. 'Out of interest, how is the case going? I know you can't say too much.'

'Chasing up a few things,' he conceded. 'It seems Marcus was a bit of a player. Those blokes from the Arms, Dom and Mitch, were very helpful in volunteering a whole bunch of information about Marcus. Anything they could do, to avoid a charge of drug possession and supply.'

'Oh yeah?' she said, her interest roused.

'Yeah. Apparently, he wasn't the best around women. Could get quite handsy and a tad aggressive when drunk, especially when they didn't reciprocate. According to Dom, there have been a few incidents over the years with him crowding women in the corridor near the women's toilets to cop a feel or force a kiss. He's mainly hit on young backpackers and tourists, very rarely any locals, but who knows? He may have pissed off one too many women or their boyfriends.'

Kate thought back to when she had first visited Celeste to inform her about Marcus's death. She had made a retort about her son getting into altercations at the pub. So, this was what she had meant: fisticuffs with disgruntled men defending their partners. She was definitely a mother with no illusions about her son. Kate marvelled at how none of the incidents with the women themselves had reached the police over the years. A combination of a pub owner who was charming as hell, and no doubt generous with the free booze, and a transient tourist population that didn't want the hassle of getting involved with the police while on holiday. Marcus had evidently known whom to prey on.

'Sounds promising,' she said.

'Also, that Louise Askall woman is squirrelly as hell.' Now that he had started blowing off steam to Kate, Josh couldn't seem to stop. *Just like the old days*, she thought.

'How do you mean?'

'Giggly. Over the top.' He shrugged, as if it was self-explanatory. 'I reckon she had a crush on the bloke. On Marcus, I mean. That's why she made such an effort with the kids and Fiona, to have a ready excuse to drop in on him with his wife's blessing.'

Kate stood silent. Sarah too had been lukewarm about Marcus's neighbour. Josh's instincts could be right on the money about this one.

'She doesn't have an alibi for that night. We only have her word that she was asleep,' she said slowly. 'An affair turned sour, you think?'

'Could be,' Josh said. 'She was definitely alone at her place. We checked with the daughter of the property owners, a Kirsty Lee. She confirms Askall's story that she hasn't stayed at the house in a couple of months at least.' He paused for a second, gathering his thoughts. 'I got the impression Askall's not particularly enthusiastic about the girl. Harris looked her up on social media. She's definitely a looker. And young.'

'Right in Marcus's sweet spot,' Kate finished the thought for him, thinking back to the suspicions that Sarah had hinted at, though not articulated in so many words. 'Are you thinking Marcus tried it on with Kirsty while she was staying at Louise Askall's? And what? Louise was jealous?'

'Maybe. It's a possibility. Askall's version is that Marcus had never met the girl but I'm not so sure. I've got Harris heading down to Lismore tomorrow to check-in with Kirsty. To get her take on Marcus, and if she thinks there was anything going on between him and his neighbour – mutual or one-sided. Let's see if another chat is needed with Louise after that.'

Kate nodded. For all the niggles between them, she had never doubted that Josh was a competent police officer. He knew how to cross all the t's.

Josh met her eyes and seemed to recollect himself. Apparently realising that he had spent more time with Kate than he'd intended. 'Let me know how you go with Fiona,' he said, rather tersely, and she watched him leave in a spray of gravel.

32

Luke waited as the detectives sitting at the conference table in Sydney some 800 kilometres away went through the preliminaries via video link. He watched as they organised themselves, deliberately taking their time. His chest felt tight and he resisted the urge to loosen the top button of his shirt. On Ramsay's advice, Luke had chosen to wear his work uniform to the interview: slacks and a long-sleeved business shirt rolled up at the sleeves.

He focused on the older woman detective on screen in her well-fitting jacket with bangs and deep-aubergine highlights through her shoulder-length hair. He thought the hair was a recent style choice. Luke could see her catching herself on the laptop, and he could tell she wasn't quite used to this version of herself. Had she tried a new look for someone she loved? Perhaps for someone who had stopped noticing her. Or maybe it had been for a special occasion. An anniversary, or more likely a wedding, which allowed her to mentally justify the expense of a 250-dollar haircut. Luke wanted to reassure her that she looked good. *Give yourself leave to enjoy this*, he wanted to say.

The male detective sitting next to her was younger, obviously junior, taking his cues from her. Respectful, like he had nothing to prove and was happy to learn. Had Luke looked like that when he had sat next to Payton? Just happy to be there. There was never any doubt who was top dog if Payton was in the room.

'Mr Grayling—' The male cop was speaking. 'As mentioned, we are investigating an allegation made against you relating to image-based abuse. We have a statement from a Ms Payton Cavanaugh, finance manager at Hull-Hayward, which relates to an intimate video that was recorded of her while you and Ms Cavanaugh were in a sexual relationship.'

He felt his stomach drop. So, it was true. Payton had made a statement to the police. That meant he really had lost her. That despite his multiple texts and voicemail messages, she had chosen to believe the worst of him. A part of him understood. She needed to blame someone. Payton had lost so much, while he had escaped reasonably unscathed, so far at least. But then again, she *knew* him. She had to know that he would never do that. To anyone, but especially not to her. Never to her. And yet, here they were.

'To start from the beginning, Mr Grayling, did you record an intimate video of Ms Cavanaugh during the course of your relationship with her?' the detective asked.

Luke exhaled. 'I did. And it was consensual,' he added.

'And this was recorded on the night of the eighth of November at a work retreat in Byron Bay. Is that correct?' the detective continued.

'That's correct,' Luke said, without looking up.

God, that night. In the hotel room after the conference. He couldn't believe it then. He still couldn't, in fact. That she had allowed him to watch and then to film her as she had explored her own body, his name falling from her lips. God, it had been the horniest thing he had ever witnessed, bar none. But he had also known what it meant. How vulnerable she was making herself. How much trust she was placing in him. She had given herself freely and he had destroyed her.

'To be clear, Detectives, my client denies ever sharing the video with any external parties.' It was Ramsay jumping in.

The detective ignored his interjection, pretending to check something in his notes. The female detective looked up. Erin someone – why was it that he could never hold people's names in his head? Luke thought she already looked tired of the interview.

196

'We're going to get to that, Mr Ramsay,' she said shortly. 'For now, can you explain to us, Mr Grayling, how your relationship with Ms Cavanaugh began? She was more senior to you in the firm, is that right?'

'Yes, but we got to know each other through various work functions. We hit it off and started going out about three months ago.'

'And would you say you were happy in the relationship? Did your work dynamic change as a result of you becoming a couple? She's a manager, isn't she?'

'Yes, but of a different section. I didn't report directly to Payton. It didn't make any difference to the way each of us performed our roles. She was higher up than me in the firm, but so what?'

'You tell us, Mr Grayling.' She eyed him calmly. 'An intimate video like that. It's leverage, isn't it? With that on your phone, you could pretty much ask for whatever you wanted. Help with a promotion. Financial assistance. Maybe even slow down her progress up the ladder if she was getting a bit too uppity.'

'What? I would never do that. I cared about her. I would never use it to tear her down.'

'And yet, a few days after you recorded that video, Ms Cavanaugh states that she began receiving abusive and obscene WhatsApp messages on her phone from an unknown number. She was going to delete the texts and block the number, except they kept referring to a video of her. To details that only a person who had viewed the video would be privy to. Or the person who had recorded it.'

'No. That wasn't me. That's all Tristan. That fucking prick. It's all him. I never sent Payton any abusive messages. You can check my phone. I handed it to the Esserton Police. You'll see that I never sent anything like that.'

'We'll be accessing your mobile and laptop, Mr Grayling. A warrant for your personal devices was provided to Mr Ramsay yesterday. And as your phone was surrendered to Esserton

Police, our colleagues have shared the call history and message transcripts obtained from your mobile—'

'And you didn't find anything, did you?' he interrupted. 'I told you, I didn't message that stuff.'

'The messages were sent from an unknown number,' the detective reminded him. 'People use spare phones all the time. For activities they'd rather keep separate from their personal phones. As it happens, there was no record of the messages on Mr Gill's mobile, either.'

'He's the one using a burner phone, not me. Fuck, don't you get it? I had the real thing. Payton was my girlfriend. Why would I want to wreck that? She was the best thing going in my life. This... all of this, is Tristan.'

The detective observed him for a moment, her expression impassive. No doubt she thought he was a deadshit, but she had years of practice keeping her emotions in check and not allowing her true feelings to show.

'Mr Gill maintains that you willingly shared the video of Ms Cavanaugh with him and collaborated in setting up the link to allow third parties to view the recording. He asserts the two of you came up with the idea together.'

'No. That's a lie. He's a fucking liar. I never did any of that. I had no idea he had that link going.'

Fucking prick. Tristan had been sharing the video as a password-protected link to be viewed by various co-workers he thought would appreciate the show. Luke hadn't really noticed what was happening at first, but within a couple of weeks of the Byron conference, the winks, wolf whistles and random claps on his back in the men's toilets had become too frequent to ignore. It had come to a head at Friday-night drinks, when he'd been subjected to some particularly pointed comments, the lewdness increasing as the alcohol had flowed. *Jesus, Lukey, can you convince my girlfriend to do that, too. Mad props to you, bro. You're my fucking hero. When's the next video, player?*

Seeing Tristan smirking in a corner, trying to keep a straight face, it had suddenly hit him. *No. No. No. Oh fuck, fuck, fuck.*

But it was too late by then. All at once, it had made sense. Why Payton was not answering his calls or texts. Why she seemed to have dropped him like a piece of garbage, without explanation and without notice. Of course, she had found out. Something like that would scorch through the office like a wildfire. It had reached Payton's PA via one of the many co-workers Tristan had tried to show the link to, assuming that all men would be titillated and laugh rather than be appalled by the footage. Tristan had been stood down within days, and Luke shown the door soon after. Payton had left the firm on extended leave.

'Listen,' Luke said. 'You can look at all my devices. All my internet history. You'll see I had nothing to do with setting up that link. I wouldn't even know where to start. Tristan's the tech head. He's on his bloody computer all the time. This stuff, it's all him.'

'Okay, leaving the link for a minute, how do you explain the video coming into Mr Gill's possession, if you were the only one to have a copy?' The male detective had taken over again.

'He did it himself.'

'Excuse me?'

'Tristan was at the Byron conference. He knew I'd hooked up with Payton. He came into my hotel room the next morning, hassling me for details. He wouldn't leave even when I kept refusing to tell him anything. I ended up escaping into the bathroom for a shower just to get away from him. I think that's when he went through my phone—'

'Your phone's not password protected?'

'It is, but it's a swipe code. Tristan was a mate. He'd seen me using it hundreds of times. It was an inverted Z. I've changed it since, but at the time it was simple. He probably could have guessed it just by the finger marks on the lock screen.'

He sighed, looking away from the detectives. 'I think he sent the video to himself on WhatsApp. Once he'd downloaded the file onto his phone, he deleted the message from our chat. There's a "this message was deleted" notification on my WhatsApp from that date. I only saw it weeks later. I don't use that app very often. So he knew it's not something I'd notice. I know I can't prove it, but that's what happened.'

The detective held his gaze for a long time. 'Thank you for letting us know. We'll make sure to look into it.'

Luke nodded but held no hope. He and Ramsay had already gone back and forth on this issue. The messages on WhatsApp were end-to-end encrypted, not stored on servers, and only visible to the sender and receiver on their devices. Once deleted, they were unlikely to be recoverable, especially if they had also been deleted from the device's backup storage, which he had no doubt Tristan would have taken the precaution of doing. Unless police digital forensics were able to connect Tristan to that bloody online link, it was just Luke's word against Tristan's.

Would his co-workers come to his defence, he wondered, to testify that it had been Tristan and not Luke who had been spruiking the online link? That he hadn't cottoned on to what was happening even as the bawdy locker-room teasing had become coarser and harder to ignore? Would they remember that Luke had tried to maul Tristan that Friday night when the penny had finally dropped, and it had taken three of his work-mates to hold him back as Tristan had laughed and laughed? Or would they all fade into the background, not wanting to get involved?

Luke tuned out as Ramsay began to question the officers on the likely charges that would be laid, pushing and arguing the details. His thoughts started towards Payton and instead of executing an immediate mental U-turn, his usual strategy to spare himself the heartache, he made himself grit it out, letting the white-hot pain wash over him. However bad this was for him, he knew it was immeasurably worse for Payton. Yes, his career would take a hit but, ultimately, he would survive this. Even gain a level of notoriety in certain quarters, distasteful as that was to contemplate. But this was going to follow Payton around. No doubt the video had already made its way to external porn sites. She would never be able to escape its sting, and he would always be the man who put her in this situation through his carelessness. Why the fuck hadn't he stored the video in a password-protected folder, the minute he'd left her room?

I'm sorry, Payton. I'm so fucking sorry. The useless words that would thrum inside his head forever.

'Speaking of Mr Gill...' The male detective's voice rose, cutting across something Ramsay was saying. 'We had an online interview with him two days ago. He's staying in Lake Cathie for a few days. Both of you seem to have headed north, for some reason.'

Luke's attention snapped back to the present. He thought of the WhatsApp message he had received from a friend over a week ago, informing him of Tristan's whereabouts. It was an innocuous message along the lines of *the bastard has fucked off north somewhere near Port Macquarie*. It was a small gesture of solidarity that had arrived on his phone on the evening that Luke had been terminated from Hull-Hayward. A tiny sign that someone else believed him over Tristan. That message had been enough for him to work out where Tristan was hiding; from the bits and pieces Tristan had mentioned over the years about his aunt's old holiday house at Lake Cathie, twenty minutes south of Port Macquarie and four-and-a-half hours' drive south of Esserton. That message had been deleted too, and he hoped would be unavailable to the police when they scoured through his phone. It certainly hadn't existed long enough on his phone to be captured by his device's 24-hour backup frequency.

He remained silent now, waiting for the question.

'Mr Gill appeared to be suffering significant facial injuries when we spoke to him. He looked like he'd been in a fight. Or more like he'd been bashed. He insists that he sustained the injuries himself, by falling down the back steps of his accommodation at Lake Cathie. Do you happen to know anything about this?'

Luke could feel Ramsay stiffen beside him. This was definitely new information to the lawyer. He thought about Stella's tweet, in which she had detailed what Payton was going through. The fun-loving, confident, ambitious woman who had been stripped of everything. And then he thought about the blow-by-blow account that Dom had given him of his encounter with Tristan Gill in the dark bushland reserve near his place. How Tristan had whimpered and begged for him to stop.

Luke had no regrets.

'I haven't seen or spoken to Tristan since he left Hull-Hayward. I have no idea where he's been staying… Lake Cathie, did you say? Never heard of the place.'

33

Kate made her way to the small green space that made up the village centre of Uki, a picturesque artsy settlement on Kyogle Road in the foothills of Wollumbin. Over the phone, Fiona had agreed to give Kate ten minutes of her time when she collected her boys from their local primary school at Uki, and Kate had accepted. Dropping Archie back at home, she had made her way to Uki in time for school pick-up at 2.50 pm.

On the opposite side of the road, groups of parents were gathering near the school entrance, awaiting the afternoon bell. Kate had been surprised to hear that Ted and Jasper had gone back to school so quickly, but apparently, Celeste had been firm that the boys' usual routine be maintained as much as possible.

She spotted Fiona Rowntree emerging from the general store with a cloth bag of shopping and walked over to her. In the handful of days that Kate had last seen her, Fiona seemed to have become thinner. Her skin appeared shrink-wrapped tight around her bones and her white cotton dress was hanging off her frame. She hid herself behind large sunglasses, shoulders hunched, closing herself off from any passing glances.

'Detective, I don't have much time. The boys will be out soon.' She nodded towards the school.

'Fiona, thanks again for seeing me. How have you been? How are the boys?'

She flinched at the mention of her sons. 'Teddy's not eating. I can just about get him to drink some milk, but that's it.' She gestured to her grocery bag, opening it so Kate could see inside.

It held a tub of ice-cream, several bars of chocolate and a packet of biscuits. 'I'm willing to try anything, at this point.'

Kate took in her pinched face. She guessed that Ted wasn't the only one not eating.

'I'm sorry to hear that, Fiona. There are counselling services you can access for the boys. You should have been provided with a list of practitioners.'

Fiona waved away her words. 'We got the details,' she said. 'The other detective made sure we received it all. In between questions about my movements on Friday night. Is that what you all really think?' she hissed. 'That I would leave my kids alone at night to drive to their father's house and shoot him in cold blood. And what? Just drive home again, and make them pancakes the next day like nothing was wrong. I mean, what kind of monster do you think I am that I would do that to my kids? My own boys… Jesus!'

You'd be surprised. What she actually said out loud was, 'I'm sorry about the line of questioning, but it's routine. We need to speak to everyone who was close to Marcus—'

'We're grieving.' Fiona stepped closer, crowding her space. 'Both me and Celeste. And you treat us like we're the suspects. As if Celeste would have done anything to hurt her son.' Her voice trembled before she regained control. 'She's his mother, for fuck's sake. You know, you can be disappointed in your loved ones. You can even not like them very much. But that's very different to being capable of shooting them down.'

Kate stood her ground. It was clear that Josh had pushed both women hard while questioning them. That didn't mean he was wrong. She had done her share of putting family members and persons of interest under pressure during cases. It was often, though not always, the way to get a result, and it was Josh's go-to strategy. Only time would tell if he was right.

'Fiona, I understand what you're saying and I don't disagree with you. But I'm not here to speak to you about the case. Not directly, anyway.'

'What? What do you mean?' She stepped back from Kate, wariness replacing her earlier anger, her body tensing for the new blow.

'Did Detective Ellis tell you that Marcus's father, Eric Harrington, has been asking after the boys?'

Fiona screwed up her face. 'He did mention that, yeah.'

'Eric has asked if he could meet with you and the boys, to establish a relationship with his son's family.'

'What, he wasn't able to fly up all these years and make an effort to see us? To meet his grandkids and talk to his son? Suddenly, now that Marcus is dead and the media is here, he's all concerned about being a grandfather?'

'He says he did try to visit a few times but that Marcus cut him off. Made it clear that he didn't want Eric in his life, which is why he kept his distance.'

'You're his errand girl now, are you?'

'Fiona, I'm not making any claims for Eric. I'm just here to pass on a message because he has no other way of reaching out to you and Celeste. I don't pretend to understand the intricacies of his relationship with Marcus, but Eric is mourning too, in his own way.'

She watched the woman before her, as she tried to keep it all together. Fiona was a heaving mass of emotions. Grief at having to support her sons through the death of their father, alongside spiky anger about what he had put her through while he was alive. Relief that there would be no more second-guessing, navigating, placating, de-escalating and putting up with her husband's behaviour, interspersed with shards of real sadness over the death of her partner, or at least the version she had fallen in love with. Grief was confusing and contradictory, an everchanging chimera that glowed a different colour of emotion every time it was held up to the light. Kate was loath to add to this woman's load, but she needed her to remember that others were grieving too.

'Please, just think about it, all right? He is the boys' grand-father, after all.'

Fiona nodded, a tight little movement of her head. That was the best she was going to get right now, Kate surmised. The school bell rang on cue and Fiona hurried across the road to meet her boys at the school gates.

Kate watched as groups of blue-uniform-clad students streamed out of the school, chattering and laughing in groups. She saw Fiona waving at two boys, tall and sturdy with ringlet hair, taking after their father. She hugged them tightly and they walked together towards her car parked on a side street, Fiona holding out the grocery bag for her boys to see. Kate noticed that she barely spoke to other parents, choosing to keep her gaze trained on her children so as to avoid eye contact.

'It's so awful, isn't it?'

'Pardon?'

'What's happened to that family. You were just speaking to Fiona, weren't you? The poor thing. She looks so devastated.'

A woman in colourful, flowing garments, wearing numerous clinking jewellery, bangles, necklaces and a nose ring, had moved to stand beside Kate. Her hair was arranged in long beaded dreadlocks and her skin was deeply sun-worn.

'I'm Essie, by the way. My son Nix is in the same year as her eldest, Teddy.' She motioned to a boy with long dark hair talking animatedly with a friend at the school gates. 'Actually, sorry, that's Taj, my younger one.' She looked around and pointed to another boy with his hair in a ponytail, who had just reached the gate. 'That's Nix. Now that they're both growing their hair, it's so hard to tell them apart.' She tittered and then quickly added, 'You're a police officer, aren't you?'

'I am. Sergeant Kate Miles. It's nice to meet you.'

'You too.' The woman half smiled. 'I've got a brother-in-law who's a copper in Queensland. I can tell.'

Kate waited. The woman obviously had something to say, since she had gone to the trouble of starting a conversation.

'So,' she began, visibly gathering up her nerve. 'This is probably speaking out of turn, because I know Fi would never admit to it in a million years. The things she avoided seeing when it came to Marcus could fill a small continent. But you should know that he was a player. Constantly trying to pick up if he could, behind Fi's back.'

'Fiona wasn't aware of her husband's behaviour?'

'Oh, I'm sure she was, but she just never wanted to know.' She glanced quickly at Kate. 'Look, I understand this may not be relevant to how he died, but you never know, do you?'

Kate nodded.

'On the day he died, that lunchtime, he was trying to sweet-talk some woman at the Cresty, even though he was telling Fi he wanted to get back together with her. My brother was there having a counter lunch and saw him. Just shameless.'

As the woman spoke, Kate felt her mobile vibrate. She glanced at the screen, frowning slightly as she saw her father's name. She let it go to voicemail, but a text popped up almost immediately: *CALL ME* in all caps. Kate had been with her father only an hour or so ago. Why the urgent need to speak with her? Had something gone wrong with Luke's interview?

'I'm sorry, I have to get this.' She said, moving away and dialling her father's number.

'Kate,' Gray's voice had an edge to it. An unfamiliar hesitancy. 'Have you seen the news?'

'No, why? Is it to do with Luke, again?'

'It's nothing to do with Luke.'

34

Ahead of Kate, a bus lurched to a halt, making a last-minute decision to pull up for a young passenger who had been running and waving frantically. Kate braked hard, swearing and swinging her car around the jutting back of the bus. With a clear path ahead of her, she pressed her foot down.

The news footage, which she had viewed on her phone only a few minutes ago, swam to the surface of her mind. A young reporter standing outside a residential street, her face shiny from the brittle heat. '*A call to emergency services shortly after 2 pm... Unconfirmed reports of an officer down... Police and emergency personnel have descended on a house in east Esserton... Reports of shots being fired...*'

An officer down. A thousand bull ants swarmed under her skin. She glanced at her silent mobile. Her calls to Josh and Esposito were going unanswered. *An officer down.*

Aging, timber-slatted houses came into view, marking the outskirts of Esserton. She turned east, speeding through the quiet residential streets, rendered almost empty by the relentless heat. '*Police have established a cordon, blocking access to Bell Mont Lane, both from Eltham Road to the north and from Haines Street to the south.*' The reporter had gestured behind her as she had spoken the words, though the street in question was not visible in the footage. Kate guessed she was camped several streets away, kept well back from an active and unfolding incident by police.

She knew Bell Mont Lane. It was a tiny byway providing rear vehicle access to the garages and carports of the long residential blocks that backed onto the lane, and whose houses fronted the streets parallel – much in the way of more expensive real estate in the trendy inner-city suburbs of Sydney. She recollected the skinny alleyway fringed by rear and side fences, overhanging greenery and a few front driveways of properties that had been subdivided into dual occupancies. At the beginning of the year, when the weather conditions had been very different and it had been all hands on deck, she had assisted in a flood-rescue operation at that very location, the street then resembling a canal-scape of swirling muddy brown. She had been over five months pregnant at the time as she had helped residents ferry pets and belongings across the metre-high water.

She blinked and the view outside her vehicle reformed into the sun-baked streets of Esserton. She had to be getting close as there were signs of people gathering, moving as if with one mind to the source of the commotion, attracted like flies to a dung pile. Concern and curiosity mixed with a frisson of something else, the thrill of unexpectedly finding themselves in the middle of a drama. The inevitable iPhone warriors, collecting content for their feeds.

Her phone buzzed and she checked it automatically, expecting to see Ellis or Esposito on the caller ID. Instead, it was a text.

> Detective, I'm sorry to keep bothering you. I hope this will give you a reason to speak to me.

She didn't process the words immediately and then she realised. It was Jacob, Ant's friend, whom she still hadn't made time to call back. A link to what looked like a Google drive document was attached to the text. *For fuck's sake.* She swiped the message away.

Parking as close as she could manage, Kate approached the outer cordon, which was marked by two patrol vehicles that blocked the road, keeping onlookers and the media at bay. Holding up her ID to an officer she didn't recognise, she gained entry and made her way along the intervening streets, past tense-looking police and waiting ambulance personnel towards the inner cordon that she knew would be set up at the mouth of Bell Mont Lane.

'Kate, what are you doing here?'

Josh was striding towards her, irritation marking the sharp lines of his face.

She ignored his annoyance. He was safe. Her eyes swung past him, catching the unmistakable figure of Esposito huddled in conversation with an officer who was strapping on a bullet-proof vest over his plainclothes. Relief flared once more. She had known all along it couldn't have been him. And yet, the irrational part of her mind had feared the worst. That version of herself from all those years ago, which she kept small and tucked away, had reared despite everything, a tiny protesting hand against the thought of Esposito being hurt. But it was fine. Her boss was right there in front of her, whole and intact.

'Kate,' Josh addressed her again, snapping her attention back to him.

'I saw it on the news. I wanted to be here. Don't make me leave.'

The *please* hung in the air between them.

His lips curled in distaste. 'Not up to me, is it?'

Kate followed Josh's gaze to the grizzled and balding man speaking to Esposito. She recognised the sturdy bulk of Nick Demetriou, a negotiator who worked out of Tweed Heads – the district head office. She knew him by sight, but she'd never had an occasion to work with him. Now looking prop-erly, she noticed several officers in dark fatigues who appeared to be setting up a forward command post with comms and laptops. TORS, or Tactical Operations Regional Support – local officers with part-time training in tactical ops – who had accompanied the negotiator from Tweed Heads.

'It's a hostage situation?' she asked, even though the answer was clear.

'Yeah. Esposito is forward commander and TOU have been called in. They are en route. Should be here before six.'

Kate glanced automatically at her watch. Just on 3.15 pm. The hard pebble in her stomach felt heavier. Things had to be serious if Tactical Operations Unit officers were being flown in via PolAir from Sydney.

'They think it's Fincher.'

'What?' She stared at Josh, incredulous. 'The drug dealer?'

He nodded, his hostility forgotten for the moment. 'Didn't I tell you there was a rumour he'd taken off up north? Turns out, I was on the money.' Josh nodded over towards Esposito. 'Leo was on the blower to the commissioner's office straight-away. The lessons of the past and all that. TOU were deployed immediately. We do nothing apart from securing the scene until they arrive with their snipers and everything else.'

She shook away her irritation at Josh referring to Esposito by his first name. 'But how are you sure it's him?'

He hesitated, then said, 'We've got footage. One of the neighbours managed to get a recording on his phone.'

She asked the question, fear scrabbling at her throat as she said the words. 'Who's the officer? Who got hurt?'

He was silent for a beat before answering. 'We think it's Darnley.'

Her mind went blank. 'And…?'

Josh shook his head.

She listened as if from a great distance as he recounted the details. A roar of sound was building inside her ears. Every word that Ellis spoke was like salt on exposed flesh. *He's dead. He's dead. He's dead.*

'Sergeant Ellis?'

Kate looked up at the interruption, taking in a uniformed officer accompanying a middle-aged woman who looked fearful and out of place. Kate saw a version of herself from a few minutes ago, trying hard to keep the panic at bay by the sheer force of will and telling herself that everything would be all right. The woman was neat and compact, with short hair, and wearing a pharmacist's smock over navy slacks. Kate thought she recognised the logo from a chemist in town weaved into her top. On any other day, she would be the brisk, cheerful pharmacist assisting you with your prescriptions and advising on cold-andflu meds.

'I have Mrs Casey from number fourteen,' the officer said.

Josh seemed to have been waiting for the woman. 'Mrs Casey, right this way.' He ushered her towards Esposito and Demetriou, and Kate followed without being asked.

'I only got your message a few minutes ago.' The woman seemed anxious to explain herself as she kept pace with Josh. 'I was out Tyalgum way on a pharmacy run, delivering prescriptions. To some of our older customers, you know, who find it difficult to drive in. I wasn't checking my phone.'

'It's all right, Mrs Casey. You're here now.'

'Where are my boys? Have you got them? Are they safe?'

Josh introduced Demetriou and Esposito to Mrs Casey without answering her questions. Demetriou greeted her gently, while Esposito took in Kate's presence without a word.

'You're Mrs Vivian Casey of fourteen Bell Mont Lane?' Nick Demetriou asked.

'Yes, yes. That's right. What about my boys, Tom and Logan? I can't get a hold of Tommy. It just keeps going to voicemail. Logan's not at school today. He's at home with a sore throat and Tommy is meant to be watching him while I was at work.' She was babbling; explanations and justifications tripping over each other. 'Today is Tommy's TAFE day. He does it online and he's supposed to be home, all day.'

Demetriou didn't reply. Instead, he held out a police tablet open to an image of Leon Fincher, a surveillance photo taken some years ago, which showed Fincher sitting at a café wearing sunglasses and speaking into his mobile. 'Mrs Casey, do you know this man? Is he a resident of your house?'

'What? Yes. Yeah. That looks like Gareth. I mean, he looks older now than in this photo. He has a goatee and longer hair.

But that looks like him. Why? What's happened? What's he done?'

Demetriou swiped through to another photo. A much grainier image, zoomed in and cropped to only show a face in profile. The man in the photo had rough facial hair lining his upper lip and chin, his long hair tied in a ponytail. His face was twisted in an angry snarl.

'Is that the same man, Mrs Casey? The man you know as Gareth?'

'Yes. I think so. That's definitely him. That's Gareth Cooper.'

'How did you come to know him, Mrs Casey?'

'Who, Gareth? He rents the granny flat at the back of our place. He moved in about two months ago.' Her tone was impatient. 'Listen, I'm not going to say another word until you tell me what's going on. Has Gareth done something to my boys? Please, just tell me.'

Nick Demetriou observed her and glanced at Esposito. They appeared to come to an unspoken decision, and Demetriou spoke.

'Mrs Casey, the man you know as Gareth Cooper is known to police by the name of Leon Fincher. He's a criminal with links to organised crime and drug syndicates. At approximately 2 pm this afternoon, we believe that Mr Fincher got into an altercation with a police officer, who was at this location carrying out routine enquiries. The altercation resulted in the police officer being shot. It seems your younger son, Logan, was with Mr Fincher at the time. Right now, we believe that Mr Fincher has barricaded himself and your son in the building at the back of your property.'

'No. No. No.' The words came out in a disbelieving whimper. Mrs Casey's hand covered her mouth and her eyes tripped between Esposito and Demetriou, as if trying to detect the lie. 'We don't know if your elder son, Tommy, is in the house. Our calls have been going to voicemail. Is there any possibility he could be at a different location? There's a grey-black Nissan Pulsar parked in your driveway. Is that your son's vehicle?'

'That was my husband's old car. Tommy drives it now.' Mrs Casey's voice was a whisper. 'If the car's there and he's not at home, it means he's out with Ruby. His new girlfriend from Burleigh Heads. Her father gave her a brand-new Mazda6 for her birthday. Can you believe it?' Derision momentarily replaced her worry. 'If you ask me, Tom is more in love with that Mazda than with its owner.'

For a second, Kate lost track of the conversation. The *grey-black Nissan Pulsar*. Her eyes automatically sought Josh's face, but he wouldn't look at her. It didn't matter. Their conversation from a few minutes ago had brought her up to speed.

The vehicle was the tip that Constable Darnley had been following up on. A small detail that had shaken loose during the course of his routine enquiries into Marcus's work life and colleagues. During a conversation with Marcus's building contractor boss, Darnley had learned that Tommy Casey, an apprentice on Marcus's crew, drove a dark-coloured Nissan Pulsar. It wasn't much, but it was the first hint of a connection between one of Marcus's associates and a *dark-coloured sedan*. And Darnley had not hesitated. With the apprentice not answering his mobile, Darnley had decided to drive out to Tommy Casey's address himself, to see if he could find the young man to have a chat. And that's when all hell had broken loose.

Kate bit her lip, tasting the tang of blood. Darnley had been here because of Luke. If Tommy Casey turned out to be the person Luke had seen, it could help prove her brother's story that Marcus was still alive when Luke had left him that evening. Darnley had pursued the lead because he was a meticulous and diligent officer, yes, but also because of his loyalty to Kate. And now because of Kate and her family, Darnley was dead. A career police officer. One of the most trusted and experienced members of the team. A husband and father of two. Her friend.

She thought of the unanswered text that still sat on her phone from Darnley's wife, about a catch-up before Christmas. *Jesus Christ. How the hell were they going to break the news to Vanessa?*

She heard Demetriou speak again and she forced herself to concentrate.

'Have you got a number for Ruby?'

'No, but I know her Instagram account.' Mrs Casey pulled out her phone and tapped on the screen before holding it for Demetriou to see.

'Okay, that's good. I'll need you to message her. Tell her that if Tommy is with her, he needs to get in contact, immediately.'

Mrs Casey typed quickly, showing the final message to Demetriou before hitting send. They waited but the message remained unread. 'It says she's not online at the moment.'

Demetriou nodded. 'Mrs Casey, let's get back to Fincher. How did you come to rent your property to this man? Was it through a real estate agent?'

'What? No. It was nothing like that.' Her eyes flicked between the gathered faces, suddenly a shade nervous. 'The place isn't really a granny flat, to be honest, even though I call it that. It's just our back shed. Simon, that's my husband, was renovating it. He was hoping for an Airbnb-type setup, you know. It was his project before... before he passed away.'

Vivian blinked and took a deep breath before continuing. 'Since Simon died eight months ago, it's been tough, financially. There were a lot of medical bills and... other things. I just needed the cash, so I listed it on Gumtree. It's a cash rental. The building hasn't got council approval or anything, so I couldn't put it through a real estate agent. But Tommy started his apprenticeship and he did his best to fix up what his dad hadn't finished.' She looked at Demetriou. 'Gareth... I mean, this Fincher person, he was the first to reply to the ad.'

'Do you have a contact number for him?' Demetriou asked quickly. 'Is the back shed connected to a landline?'

'The shed doesn't have a phone. But I have the mobile number he gave me.' She recited it out.

Demetriou dialled the number, his phone on speaker. It went straight to an automated voicemail. Either the line was busy or Fincher had switched off his mobile. He swore under his breath and turned back to Mrs Casey.

'What's he like as a tenant? Did he get on with your children?'

'He kept to himself. I barely spoke to him. Only a few words in passing when he came into the house to hand in his rent. Same with Tommy. Of the three of us, Logan probably got on with him best.'

A fluttering of unease flared within Kate at Mrs Casey's words.

'… He was always running around the back to help Gareth or Fincher or whoever he was—' She shook her head, impatiently. 'His car is some kind of classic Holden or something, which he's forever tinkering away with. I don't think they spoke much. Logan mainly watched while Ga— while *he* worked on that car. Maybe handed him a tool now and then. It was harmless, honestly.' Her gaze stumbled across each of the police officers, pleading her case.

'It's because he misses his dad. That's the kind of thing he used to do with Simon, messing about with the car and in the garden. Logan just turned thirteen. I didn't have the heart to stop him. I did speak to *Fincher* about it, but he said he didn't mind. That Logan was easy and reminded him of his nephew.'

The flutter in Kate's belly reared again. She could see that Mrs Casey's words had also made their mark on Esposito. Demetriou's expression was grim.

'Mrs Casey, have you been inside the granny flat since Fincher began living there? Could he have been keeping any weapons or firearms in there, for example?'

'What? No. I never saw anything like that. There's no way I would let anyone like that near my sons. Are you saying this man has a gun and now he's got my Logan?' Her face crumpled. 'Oh, God, you have to do something. You have to get him out.'

'That's the plan, Mrs Casey. That's what we're trying to do.'

Mrs Casey jumped as the mobile still in her hand vibrated. 'That must be Tom.' She answered it, not bothering to glance at the screen. 'Hello… Tom—' Her eyes widened and she gave a kind of muffled scream. 'It's him,' she whispered. 'It's Gareth.'

35

'Put it on speakerphone,' Demetriou commanded, his voice suddenly utterly calm.

Mrs Casey did as she was asked. A voice, more high-pitched than Kate had expected came through the mobile. 'You there, Vivian? I said, I'm sorry you've been dragged into this.'

Demetriou motioned for her to answer, while mouthing to the technical officers to record the audio.

Mrs Casey once again complied, her voice sounding both tremulous and determined. 'Have you got my Logan?'

'I do and he's fine.'

Mrs Casey gave a little moan. 'But why? Why do you have Logan? He's done nothing. Please, just let him go—'

'Are you with the police?' he cut her off. 'I need to speak to the person in charge.'

'No... wait. What about Tommy? Have you got him, too?'

'Tom's not here, Vivian. Logan's been alone in the house for hours. Now, hand the phone over, or I'll be hanging up.'

'Please... wait. Can I speak with him?' Mrs Casey had turned away from Demetriou, who was gesturing sharply for her to pass over the phone. She shook her head, her whole body hunched over the mobile. 'Please, Gareth. Only for a bit. I just want to hear his voice.'

'Fuck, woman. It's not that complicated. You do what I ask or I hang up.' The line cut off and he was gone.

'Shit. I'm sorry. I'm sorry.' Mrs Casey burst into sobs, her body shaking with a mixture of adrenaline and fear.

Kate moved to place an arm around Mrs Casey's shoulders and she slumped into her. Demetriou reached for the phone and redialled the number. Unsurprisingly, it went straight to voicemail – the automated message they had previously heard. Kate helped Mrs Casey to walk across to one of the ambulances where a paramedic assisted Mrs Casey to a seat and found her a bottle of water.

'Just rest here and have a drink.' Kate motioned gently to the water by her side and waited until Mrs Casey had taken a few slow sips.

'You did great. Better than great. Fincher will call again. Trust me. The fact that he wants to talk is a good sign. And Inspector Demetriou is a great negotiator. He'll be doing everything he can to bring your son home safe.'

Mrs Casey nodded through her tears and reached for a tissue in her bag to blow her nose. Kate directed a nearby female constable to sit with Mrs Casey and returned to the group.

She found Demetriou and Esposito in mid-argument.

'—and you didn't think that was important enough inform-ation to share?' Demetriou sounded pissed off. 'Sir,' he added as an afterthought.

'I'm telling you now. The commissioner knows and has briefed TOU command,' Esposito replied.

'Of course.' Demetriou muttered something under his breath and stalked away to speak to one of the TORS officers.

Kate caught Josh's eyes with a questioning look, but he didn't react.

'Did Fincher call back?' she asked.

Esposito turned to her. 'Aren't you meant to be on leave, Sergeant?' The heat in his voice made her flinch.

'Sir, Darnley is part of the team. I don't want to be watching this on the news.'

He stared at her for a long second, before finally speaking. 'The houses within the perimeter are being evacuated. You can assist with that.' He moved away from them, walking in the opposite direction to Demetriou.

'What was that all about?' she asked Josh in a low voice.

'It turns out that the judgement on the Finchers' compensation claim came out this morning at 11 am,' Josh explained.
'The judge came down on our side, said there was insufficient
evidence to prove negligence on the side of the TOU operatives
in relation to the death of Fincher's nephew. They reacted
per their training against what they perceived to be a real and
eminent threat to life.'

'Right,' Kate said, comprehension dawning. 'And Fincher
knows this?'

'He must have got the news from the lawyers or through his
family. The police media unit has put out a press release and it's
made it onto a few of the online news sites.'

And once the press realised who was behind today's siege, it
was going to be front-page news, Kate thought. Her mind flew
to Darnley, with a twist in her guts. Of all the days to go up
against Fincher. He had been primed and itching for a fight.
Darnley the individual had not mattered. Only the uniform
he'd been wearing.

Again, her mind flew over what Josh had recounted prior
to Mrs Casey's arrival: what the neighbour who had rung triple
zero had witnessed from his upstairs balcony when he'd stepped
outside for a smoke. The patrol car he'd seen pulling into the
driveway opposite, and the officer who had stepped out to
examine the dark-coloured sedan parked on the lawn. The
officer had begun a conversation with a young boy who had
been in the front yard at the time, pointing towards the vehicle.
They had been interrupted by Fincher, who had emerged from
the side of the house, where he had been working on his
car, exhibiting a rage entirely out of proportion to what was
happening. He had screamed at the officer to stop speaking to
the boy and to get off the property, a sawn-off shotgun clearly
visible by his side. Darnley had reached for his own Glock, but
it had been too late. Fincher had fired without hesitation at
point-blank range.

A 25-year career ended in a matter of moments. Darnley had not stood a chance. Kate closed her eyes, breathing in deeply. 'Does Demetriou think Fincher will try to use the boy as leverage?'

'Well, Fincher didn't run when he had the chance, did he? Instead, he grabbed the boy and stayed put, waiting for the cavalry. He must have a reason.'

'Maybe it's a good thing Vivian got a chance to speak to him. Maybe she'll make him remember what it feels like to lose a child.'

Josh grunted and didn't reply.

—

An airless heat pressed onto the assembled group, afternoon dipping into evening without relief. Kate scanned the officers who stood sweating in full tactical gear, Kevlar vests and helmets, conferring with Esposito and Demetriou. The addition of TOU officers from Sydney, flown to the Murwillumbah airfield and driven straight to scene, had swelled their numbers. It was 6.16 pm: four hours and counting.

Kate picked out Josh Ellis standing slightly outside the main circle with Constable Vickie Harris by his side, their sleeves almost touching. At any other time, she would have stopped to wonder if they were back together, with their on-again off-again relationship being as regular as the shifting tides and the subject of endless office speculation. So much so that Constable Grant, at one time, had set up an unofficial betting tab on it, until Harris had found out. Today, the scrap of would-be gossip fell away to dust. None of that would ever be important again. How could they possibly go back to the easy office banter that had existed at the station, after this?

Demetriou cleared his throat to get their attention.

'Okay, the situation in short is this. We have an officer deceased, and a single shooter who's been positively identified as Leon Fincher. For the past eight weeks, Fincher has been renting out the dwelling at the rear of number fourteen going by the name of Gareth Cooper. He's currently holed up there with a young hostage, a thirteen-year-old male – Logan Casey – the younger son of the property owner, Mrs Vivian Casey.'

The negotiator's voice was clipped and tight as he tracked each of the assembled faces in turn. Red skin bulged above his collar and sweat patches marked a line of heat beneath his armpits. A wall of grim, stoic faces stared back at him.

'The altercation between Fincher and Constable Darnley was witnessed by a neighbour who was smoking on his upstairs balcony at the time and had a full view of the street, including number fourteen opposite. He rang triple zero and also had the presence of mind to record the incident. He only managed to film the tail end, but it was enough to get a positive ID of Fincher.'

His gaze swept across to where Kate stood with the rest of the officers from Esserton, acknowledging their loss, before turning to a waiting laptop and clicking 'play'. The shaky smart phone video began, zoomed in to its maximum capacity. The footage appeared to show the partial view of a shipping container backing onto the rear fence of number fourteen at the end of a narrow gravel driveway. It looked to have been converted into a habitable shed of sorts with the addition of a sliding glass door that opened onto a small timber landing. A man in jeans and a black T-shirt could be seen pushing a young boy inside through the sliding door, following him in. The door was slid shut and a curtain pulled across to hide the occupants from view.

The footage was less than six seconds in length, but it had been sufficient to capture the profile view of Fincher, his face contorted with rage, which Demetriou had shown Mrs Casey earlier. The version shown to Mrs Casey had been cropped to hide the view of her son and the shotgun held by Fincher to his torso. The neighbour had been too far away to capture any sound. The only audio they could hear was the recorder's own shocked reaction. *Fuck. He's got the kid. Fuck.*

Right before the video ended, the footage zoomed out again, for a brief second taking in the front view of the entire property. As Demetriou pressed 'pause', the image froze on the small weatherboard house set forward on a grass block, a grey-black sedan parked on its front lawn. A sagging, knee-high timber fence delineated its front boundary, while Colorbond metal sheets rose on either side, separating the land from its neighbours. A driveway travelled the length of the fence line on the right-hand side of the house, providing access to the shipping container at the back. Kate could see a sky-metal-blue Holden Torana sitting up on jacks: the vehicle Fincher had been working on when Darnley had pulled in. His police patrol sat neatly parked on the driveway, blocking the exit. The only indication of its owner was a hint of black on the ground peeking out from behind the front wheel of Casey's Nissan Pulsar. Possibly the polished tip of his black leather boot or just a shadow. Kate blinked. If you stared hard enough at the spot, you could convince yourself of anything.

'Fincher has only made contact twice so far. Both times ringing Vivian Casey's mobile. He won't answer our attempts to contact him. And we've been trying for the past three hours. It's all on his terms. This is the recording of his last phone call, made fifty minutes ago.' Demetriou clicked out of the video and pulled up an audio file in its stead. He hit 'play'.

'Demetriou.'

'Hello... You the police?'

'This is Inspector Demetriou. Am I speaking with Leon Fincher?'

'...Are you... you the person in charge?'

'I'm the negotiator on site, yes. Can you tell me if Logan is safe? We'd like to know if anyone is hurt?'

'The boy's fine... all right? He's fine... He doesn't need anything.'

'Okay, that's good to hear. What about you—'

'Fuck, mate, just listen, all right... Just listen... Cut the fucking negotiator crap for a second.'

There was a pause and scuffling sound as Fincher seemed to move away from the phone. A couple of beats later, he was back on.

'I've got something to say. So just listen.' This time he seemed to be reading off a script. 'Six years ago, your friends cost me two lives. My brother and his son. I've redressed one of those debts today, but there's one still owing. Our family deserves compensation and a public apology. Right from the top. The commissioner needs to take responsibility for what you all did. Five hundred thousand. The original compensation sum. Or I'll be forced to call in that final debt. The same way you took away my brother's child.'

The phone rang off and the silence that followed felt as loud as if someone had been screaming.

'So, he sounds delightful.' The remark had issued from the TOU commander at the front, a confident GI-Joe type standing square and tall, at home in his bulky kit. Kate had caught his name earlier, Inspector Adam Locke, an action-hero name to suit his persona. The attempt at gallows humour fell flat.

As TOU lead, Locke had assumed the role of Tactical Commander, taking over the coordination of the police response within the inner perimeter. Upon arrival, Locke had moved straight into a briefing with Esposito, Demetriou and select TORS personnel, along with senior police command patched in by teleconference. This meeting was to lay out the course of action, vetted and authorised by the chain of command.

Esposito now moved to speak. 'We believe Fincher to be in a highly volatile state and unravelling,' he said, his voice deadly serious. 'We could wait him out, see if he'll call back, and try to negotiate – he hasn't, after all, provided a deadline. But we believe realistically, the chances of bringing him around voluntarily are low. We have the usual options of turning up the pressure by switching off the utilities. But again, given his state of mind, I think it would only place Logan in more danger.'

Kate tamped down a bubble of unease that seemed to erupt in her rib cage as she watched Esposito speak. His manner was calm and measured, though she could hear the thread of steel that marked each word. She knew why the powers that be had appointed him forward commander for the operation. It was his patch and he was of senior rank; an experienced and capable officer. And yet, there was Esposito's history with Fincher. Could her boss be entirely objective when it came to him? Could any one of them, when it came to it? Even Kate could feel the heady pull of rage, the need for vengeance so palpably close to the surface. It would be so easy to give in. She wondered idly how many of the current TOU personnel had been part of that original operation in Nowra. If they gave any thought to how their actions and the fates of six years ago had led them here.

Kate shook herself as she heard a question raised by a female TOU officer.

'Are we thinking of using family, sir? Is he likely to speak to anyone?'

'Fincher's only remaining relatives are his sister-in-law and mother,' Esposito answered. 'The former now resides in the States. She left the country a year after her son's death, leaving the compensation suit in the hands of her lawyers. Fincher's mother is ancient. She lives in a nursing home somewhere in Bankstown in Western Sydney. Regardless, Fincher isn't going to be swayed by his family – particularly, I'm sorry to say, any female relatives. Trust me. He doesn't work that way.'

Esposito paused momentarily to collect his thoughts. 'Fincher's demands are pie in the sky. He's not an idiot. He must know that no one's going to agree to his terms. This feels like a last hurrah, which is what worries me. If Fincher's not expecting to come out alive, then he's got nothing to lose. This whole thing has been irrational and reckless from the start, fuelled by emotion, not any plan. The longer it drags on, the more likely Fincher's going to do something stupid. You've heard the tapes,' he added. 'He's getting worse. He sounded far more agitated the second time he called.'

'He'll have taken something,' Demetriou commented. 'He's bound to have some drugs in that shed. If he's trying to psych himself up, he'll be reaching for whatever chemical assistance he can find. He's strung out and paranoid, and it'll only keep going downhill.'

'Thoughts, Inspector?' Esposito turned to Locke.

'I agree with your team's assessment,' Locke said. 'Based on what we know of Fincher and his actions to date, he presents a real and escalating risk to the hostage. We need to go in sooner rather than later. Our primary concern is the kid's welfare.' He turned to Demetriou. 'Let's run through the site options.'

Demetriou turned once more to the laptop, bringing up a satellite view of the street and the house. 'The dwellings to the rear and either side have been evacuated, and there are officers stationed at the properties where safe cover is available.'

As Demetriou pointed to the houses, Kate thought about the bewildered residents she had helped evacuate from the properties surrounding number fourteen. An elderly man in his eighties, who had been dozing in his living room, his hearing aids turned down low. The man had been frightened and confused at finding police officers at his front door, not understanding what was happening, and fretting over a pet cat that they'd been unable to find. Next door she had disturbed a young mother who had just settled her twin toddlers in front of a Disney movie. Her initial curtness had turned quickly to clumsy panic when she had realised the seriousness of the situation, hustling her two girls out in record time.

'Apart from the dwelling directly opposite where the neighbour took the recording, the only other two-storey house in the vicinity is number eighteen.'

On screen, Demetriou pointed to a boxy, double-storey brick dwelling that was separated from number fourteen to its left by an intervening bungalow and tall hedging along the side boundary.

'Two of the upstairs bedroom windows of number eighteen face the Caseys' property. There's a small bathroom window cut into the top right-hand wall of the shipping container. We have spotters at number eighteen at the moment and they can see the window. That's your best option for getting eyes inside.'

Kate stared at the properties on the laptop screen. The thirty-metre distance between the dwellings, and the thin, single-pane glass fronting the shipping container window, she knew, would not be a problem for the TOU team's high-powered, scoped rifles. She listened in silence as Locke asked a few more questions working out with Esposito and Demetriou the best options for ground access when the time came.

Four TOU operatives peeled away to number eighteen to take up their positions. The remaining officers, the ground team, spoke together in undertones, checking their weapons, testing comms and adjusting their equipment. Two German shepherds from the local dog squad sat panting by their handlers. Kate knew that they would be deployed to bring Fincher down at close range, if it came to that.

Within minutes, the radio crackled, confirming that the TOU operatives were in place. 'We have clear eyes from two locations. No one is visible at present. The bathroom appears to be empty.'

'Copy that,' Esposito replied.

It was now a waiting game, ticking down the minutes until Fincher ventured into the loo. Kate could feel the sweat pooling underneath her blouse. Her phone vibrated, but she didn't bother to check it. Later. Everything else could wait. A lone kite soared in the darkening skies, the heat of the day still lingering and shimmering in the air.

Ten minutes past. Twenty. Thirty. Forty-five.

The radio burst into life, making Kate jump.

'There's movement. The door has opened and Fincher has come in with the boy—'

'Have you got a clear shot?' Esposito's voice was tight.

'Negative. The boy is in the way.'

'How does he look?' Esposito asked.

'A bit roughed up. It looks like he's been crying. Fincher just shouted something at him and slammed the door.'

Kate felt her stomach drop, glad that Mrs Casey wasn't around to hear this. She had been persuaded to await any news at a friend's house close by. She would be near enough to be back on scene straightaway if anything changed.

Next to Demetriou, Vivian Casey's mobile trilled loudly and they all stared at it for a moment, motionless.

At a look from Esposito, Demetriou answered the call, placing the receiver on speaker.

'Wos happening? Have you got any news? When's the money going to go through?' Fincher's words sounded slurred.

'Leon, what you're asking for, it's not a simple matter. These things take time. These kinds of requests need to go up the line. It needs approval from a lot of people.'

'Fucking bullshit… You think the police minister or the fucking premier can't get this done with a click of their fingers… Five hundred thousand is nothing. Bloody play money.' Here his words became muffled. And they heard him shout away from the phone receiver, 'Oi, you finished? Hurry up in there.'

'Is that Logan? Is he all right?'

'The kid's fine. Stop worrying about him. And start worrying about my cash.'

Demetriou seemed to make a decision to switch tack. 'Leon, I have to be honest. What you're asking for is unreasonable. You must know that…'

On the radio, the TOU operative's voice came back on line. 'Fincher has reopened the door. He's coming back inside…'

'… The minister isn't going to grant you that kind of request. But if you give yourself up now, and give up the kid, that will work in your favour. You've killed a cop, Leon. There's only one way this can go. It's all a numbers game now. How many years you can shave off by showing compassion for the kid—'

'I have a clear shot. Authority to proceed.'

228

'Who fucking showed compassion for my family?' Fincher screamed down the phone.

'Clear to proceed. Take the shot,' Esposito gave the order.

'… What about my brother and my nephew? Who gives a shit about the—'

There was a sound like a whip cracking followed by a dull whump and a muffled whimper of surprise.

'Target is down. Confirming target is down.'

On Locke's directive, the waiting ground team surged forward to storm the dwelling.

From somewhere a high-pitched scream rose, sounding tiny, like it was coming from far away. It took a few moments for Kate to realise that it was Logan, his panicked cries issuing from the phone.

36

From the small timber landing of the converted shipping container, Kate watched as an ambulance pulled up along the front of number fourteen, sedate and unhurried. There was no rush. Once the crime-scene officers were done inside, Fincher's body would be transported to the morgue in Tweed Heads. The portable outdoor lighting set up by the CSOs illuminated the first responders that had taken over the property. Evening had fallen abruptly, like a swift change of scenery on stage. The scene was now set to *dealing with the aftermath*. The machinery of death set in motion.

Seeing Fincher in person, diminished and pathetic, sprawled where he had been shot, half inside the bathroom and half outside on the cheap timber laminate floor, death having bled his face of menace and bravado; it was all something of an anticlimax. Kate had wanted someone more commanding, evil incarnate, to hang her pain on, and to warrant the enormous law-enforcement effort that had descended onto the street. Instead, he was just another man, entirely unremarkable, broken by bullet wounds and leaking fluid into the grout lines between porcelain tiles. A bit shorter and flabbier than he had seemed in the video footage, with the beginnings of a receding hairline. A quick search of the small flat so far had uncovered a couple of unregistered handguns and several baggies of methamphetamine pills.

Kate forced herself to walk back down the driveway to the front lawn, where a second set of CSOs were gathered. When first entering the property, she had moved deliberately past this location, keeping her face averted from Tommy Casey's Pulsar. But she couldn't avoid it forever. Enclosed in forensic overalls, she rounded the vehicle to take in her fallen colleague, his essence long gone to wherever these things disappeared to. The empty shell left behind was blood-encrusted and motionless. A mannequin staged to look like her old friend, wearing his clothes and his five o'clock shadow, but holding nothing of his warmth or laughter or grace. Just a cooling lump of bone and tissue, liquefying from the inside, the inexorable work of his body's microbes well underway; blowflies doing their bit from the outside, violating, probing and feasting.

Her stomach rolled, white heat travelling up her throat, the hastily swallowed sandwich from hours ago threatening to reappear. She turned away, leaving the body to others, tearing off her plastic coverall and retreating around the corner to a neighbouring fence line, where she rested her clammy forehead and waited for the nausea to pass.

She heard more sounds of retching and turned to find Constable Harris emerging from behind a stand of trees further down the street. At the rate they were going, the neighbourhood was going to be plastered with the heartsick offerings of their team. She silently held out a packet of tissues to Harris, taking in her blotchy face and red-rimmed eyes. Harris accepted with a grateful nod, wiping her mouth and blowing her nose.

'You all right?'

'I think so, Sarge. It was just seeing him like that. I just...' Her voice trailed off.

'I know. I feel the same.'

Grief had started to enter her body, replacing the adrenaline that had previously held sway. It was starting to sink in, thick and tar-like, squeezing her chest and making every breath an effort. It was mixed with something else. A feeling of dread that was coiling through her body, strangling each organ along its path.

Harris was saying something, holding out the near-empty packet of tissues.

'Keep it,' Kate said, not really listening. Her eyes were on a small commotion at the end of Bell Mont Lane, where uniformed officers appeared to be trying to hold back a young man from accessing the street. *Tommy Casey.*

An ambulance carrying Logan and his mother had already left for Esserton Central Hospital, accompanied by Josh. Logan would not be questioned tonight. That would happen in the upcoming days, once he'd been examined and cleared by medical staff. Did Tommy not know where his mother and brother were? She realised that Vivian Casey's mobile was still in police custody. Had Tommy been able to get in touch with his mother?

She made her way towards the uniformed officer, who was leading a protesting Tommy back towards the outer cordon through which he seemed to have slipped. She could understand why the officers were inclined to deny him entry. A powerful funk of dope and alcohol clung to his skin, and he was jittery and on edge.

'You're Tommy Casey, right?' Kate asked.

His head snapped towards Kate. 'Where's my mum? Do you know where she is? I got all these messages from her, but she's not answering my calls. What's happened? No one's telling me anything.'

Kate nodded towards the officers. 'It's okay,' she said. 'He's fine, I can speak with him.' At the far end of Bell Mont Lane, she led him towards a neighbouring property, its boundary demarcated by a squat retaining wall. Tommy's gaze roved to where the police activity was concentrated on his own front yard.

'We need to talk, Tommy. Take a seat if you want.' She pointed towards the low wall ledge.

He chose to stand, reaching into his pocket and pulling out a packet of smokes. Lighting a cigarette with fumbling fingers, he took a deep drag, trying to hide his frayed nerves behind a cloud of smoke. His eyes skittered back to the house, seemingly unable to look away. 'Is Logan all right? I heard people talking. That Gareth held him hostage. Is that right? Did that happen?'

Kate nodded and Tommy blanched.

'Where were you today, Tommy? Your mother says you were meant to be home looking after Logan.'

'My girlfriend, Ruby, came over and we went for a drive. We weren't going to stay out for long. But we ended up at Casuarina Beach. I forgot to charge my phone, and Rubes had left hers in the car. We lost track of time and we had no idea what was going on.'

Kate thought she had a pretty good idea of how Tommy and his girlfriend had passed their time. All the while, his kid brother had been in fear for his life in the company of a man who had run out of options.

Almost as if he had guessed what Kate was thinking, Tommy blurted out, 'Logan's old enough to take care of himself. He hates me hanging around, anyway. He likes being by himself, especially since Dad—' He stopped abruptly and took another deep drag.

Kate made no reply. Tommy's actions had been irresponsible, but no worse than any other teenager who had sought the pull of a girlfriend and the escape of drugs and alcohol to get through a tough patch in their life. No one could have foreseen Fincher's actions.

'Where is he now?' Tommy asked.

'Your brother's been taken to Esserton Hospital and your mum's with him. He's not hurt,' she added. *Not physically, anyway.* God knew how long it would take Logan to heal from the psychological scars he had earned from witnessing two men being shot down in front of him.

'I should go, then. Get to the hospital.' He looked around, seemingly at a loss.

'Have you got a ride?'

'Ah no. Ruby dropped me off a couple of streets away. She didn't want to come in with me...' he trailed off.

'It's okay. I can organise an officer to drive you. But before you go, Tommy, I need to ask you a couple of questions to clarify some things.'

She knew this could wait. Josh would no doubt interview Tommy at some point, but there was no guarantee that she would be invited to sit in on that. The dread in her chest was rising again, drumming a beat all of its own against her rib cage. She needed to know now. And only Tommy Casey could give her the answer.

He looked at her, more curious than concerned.

'Do you know why the police officer from Esserton Station... Constable Greg Darnley...' she forced herself to say his name, 'drove around to your house this afternoon?'

'No idea. Wasn't it something to do with Gareth? When we were driving back here, the news on the radio said that he's actually some ex-con or something. That Gareth isn't even his real name.'

'Actually, Tommy, Constable Darnley drove out here today to see you.'

'Me. What? Why?' That had got his attention. He stilled, the cigarette suspended halfway from reaching his lips.

'He'd tried calling you today, but you weren't answering your phone. That's why he drove out here. He rang your boss at the building site and got your address.'

'Yeah, I told you. My phone died when I was out with Ruby. And I had it on silent before that because I was online for TAFE. I think there was a couple of missed calls when I checked, but I never call back unknown numbers. It's just scammers.'

Except today it hadn't been. Had Darnley left a voice-mail? Would it have made a difference to Tommy? He was from a generation who used texts and DMs; who were suspicious of phone calls and flinched away from the obligation to make conversation. Another bit of bad luck that had directed Darnley's decision to drive out here.

'So, what did he want? Why did he want to speak with me?' Tommy asked.

'He was actually trying to work out your movements for last Friday night. From about 8 pm onwards.'

'Last Friday. That's easy. I drove up to the Goldie, straight after work. My best mate's birthday. I stayed over at his all weekend in Main Beach. Drove home late on Sunday arvo. You can ask him. I got to his place around four-thirty, quarter to.'

He must have seen something flicker in her expression because he pushed on. 'I'm telling you, there were plenty of people in the flat when I got there. You can check with them. We spent the night at every pub and club that would have us.'

'Did you happen to drive anywhere near Byangum that night?'

'What? Why would I do that?'

'A vehicle that looked like yours was seen turning into a property off Porter Drive in Byangum around 9.30 pm on Friday night and we're interested in speaking to that person on an unrelated matter.'

'Someone saw my car? That's not possible. I told you. I was up in the Gold Coast that night.' He was getting agitated now.

'Not your car. A dark-coloured sedan. Constable Darnley was following up on various leads, and you were one of them.'

'But a dark-coloured sedan could be anyone. Why was he after me?'

'We thought you may have known the victim. He worked at the same job site as you, as a chippie. Marcus Rowntree.'

'Hang on, you're trying to connect me to Rowntree's death? Jesus Christ, that's a reach. As if I would go anywhere near him. He was a complete dick.'

'You weren't friends, then?'

'He was a wanker, man. Had tickets on himself and thought he was all that. I wouldn't hang out at his place if you paid me.'

She thanked Tommy and accompanied him back to the cordon, directing an officer to drive him to the hospital to his family. She then texted Josh to let him know that Tommy was on his way.

The pressure in her chest thrummed harder. So, the Tommy Casey lead had turned out to be nothing, after all. They were still no closer to finding out who had driven into Marcus's property that night after Luke had left. It was fine. Leads fizzled out all the time. They were back to square one.

Except, they had lost a man finding out.

–

Kate pressed her finger to the doorbell and held it there. She could hear it pealing through the darkened house, followed by voices and footsteps. A corridor light was switched on.

The front door swung open and she gazed at Caleb, bare-chested in boxers and her father similarly dressed but with the addition of an old dishevelled T-shirt. She had got them up from bed. It was past ten o'clock, after all. That was well past midnight in these parts.

'Kit. What are you doing here? Geoff said you were on your way home.'

She had multiple missed calls from her family on her phone, from Luke, from her father, from Geoff. But she had returned only one of them, to Geoff. Of course, he had kept her father appraised of what was going on.

'Where is he? Is he awake?' She pushed past her father and Caleb into the hallway.

'Who are you after?' A hint of annoyance threaded Caleb's voice.

'Luke,' she answered, her impatience growing, past caring that once again Caleb was being thrust into a drama not of his making. *This is it. This is the family you've joined. One fuck-up after another.* 'Is he in the guest room?'

'Kit, we don't need to do this now. His case can wait till tomorrow. After you've had a chance to rest. It's been a big day for you.'

A big day? Really? Placating her like she was in kindergarten. Kate turned away, stalking down the hall towards the bedrooms, not trusting herself to speak. *Christ*. Did her father really think she was here to unpack her brother's interview?

'Is he here?' She thrust open a door, flinching as it crashed loudly into the wall, no doubt leaving a mark. The room was empty, set up as a small home study with a table, office chair and bookcase.

'What's going on? What's happened?'

The next door up had opened, and Luke stumbled out in gym shorts and a tank top. He caught sight of her and squinted. 'Kate?'

She advanced towards him, anger making her movements fast and fluid. Her hands were on his chest, shoving him hard against the doorframe.

'Did you really see a dark-coloured car?'

'Kate, what the fuck?'

'Hey—' Her dad's voice.

'Did you see the car?' she said, her voice dangerously low and enunciating every word. 'Or was it just something you made up?' She leaned in close, right up in his face.

'What are you talking about? Get the fuck away from me.' He swatted at her and she could smell the unmistakable earthy odour of weed on his breath.

'The dark-coloured sedan you saw in your rear-view mirror when you left Marcus's place. Did you really see it?' she repeated.

'What? Yeah. I saw it. I saw a car.'

'You definitely saw it turning into Marcus's driveway? It wasn't to another property? It wasn't up the road a bit? Or on a different road altogether?'

'What? No. I mean, yeah. I... You're confusing me. I thought I saw a car when I was driving back from Marcus's place. I already told your boss.'

'I know what you said.'

'Kate, what's wrong? What's going on?'

'Did you kill him?'

'What?' Her brother looked like he'd been slapped.

'Kate. That's enough.' Her father's voice was loud and strident. His *dad* voice that he used to shut down an argument. But she wasn't a mouthy teenager living at home anymore.

'Did you kill Marcus?' she repeated, speaking over her father.

'Of course not. How could you even think that?' Luke was staring at her like he was seeing her properly for the first time.

'I don't believe you.' Her voice was like a knife slicing between them, severing something.

'Kate—'

'My friend is dead,' a scream that sucked the air from the room, 'because of you. He was chasing your fucking phantom car.'

She rounded on him again and he backed away, stumbling through the doorway into his room.

'There's no fucking car, is there? You just made it up so we'd look elsewhere. And my constable took you at your word. Because you're my brother. And now he's dead. Dead. Never coming home to his daughters or his wife.'

'Kate. I'm sorry, I never—'

'No. You don't get to... You don't get to say sorry...' She glared at him. 'This is on you. Do you understand? This is on you.'

She flung the words in his face like a missile and turned away, suddenly exhausted. Pushing against her father as he tried to reach for her.

37

She drove straight home from Terranora. Geoff was waiting up for her on the couch. He didn't say a word, just folded her into his arms.

Kate breathed him in. The day-old deodorant musk, overlaid with the remnants of the pasta sauce he had made for the kids' dinner and a hint of red wine on his breath. He was crumpled and warm and smelled like home.

This. This simple act of comfort was no longer an option for Vanessa. The thought stirred in her mind and stayed there, burning a hole inside her skull. Vanessa's face came back to her now, from earlier that evening. How she had looked when she had opened the front door to Kate and Esposito. Nothing had needed to be said. She had guessed it all from their expressions. The desperate sadness and guilt for having to be the ones to break the news, for turning up at her doorstep very much alive to confirm that it was her husband who had not made it. They were the line in the sand, showing up to divide her life into *before* and *after*.

But of course, Vanessa had known already. She had seen the incident unfolding in the news. Had anticipated the worst when her repeated texts and calls to her husband's mobile had gone unanswered. They all knew to send a quick text when something was happening that would make them late, when they were involved in an incident that would be making the news, so their loved ones wouldn't worry. Kate had sent her own to Geoff. *I'm safe. I'll call you soon.*

Still, Vanessa's ingrained good manners had prevailed. She had held out the door for them, leading them into the lounge room and offering them refreshments. The mask had held, hardening into stone, even as they went through the motions and platitudes. *Did she have someone she could call? Did she have someone to stay with tonight? Did she need them to get in contact with her daughters? There were counselling services they could refer her to. Yes, the body was being held for autopsy but would be released in a few days. A police welfare rep would be in contact to help with the arrangements. They were here for her if there was anything she needed.*

Kate had seen her flinch when Esposito had spoken those words. The smallest flare of emotion. A tightening of skin across her cheekbones. She needed her dead husband to be alive again, that's what she needed. Not offers of counselling and assistance. Not for the rest of her life to stretch out in front of her, hogtied to grief, without an end in sight. She needed the last several hours of her husband's life to play out differently. For him to get in his car and drive home, rather than pursue one last job at a house in East Esserton.

'What was he doing there?'

The question Kate had been dreading. How could she answer without blurting out all the weight of her guilt? But Esposito had spoken before she had time to formulate any words.

'He was following a lead. Trying to speak with a person residing at that property. No one could have anticipated what he was walking into.'

Vanessa nodded like she understood, even though it was incomprehensible. Complete gibberish. Nothing would make sense ever again. Watching her, Kate had felt like she was in the presence of two versions of Vanessa. An outer shell of control maintained by sheer willpower, and another sitting just under the surface that could break out at any second, annihilating them with the force of her despair. She was like a ticking bomb, just waiting for them to get the fuck out of her house so she could trash the joint in peace. After leaving Vanessa, Kate had driven out to Caleb's place without thinking. She had needed to vent her anguish on someone.

She shuddered into Geoff's chest, the tears coming hot and hard. The emotion she had been holding onto for the last few hours finally allowed release.

'He's gone.'

'I know, Katie, I know,' he whispered into her hair as he held her, comforting her like she was a child.

38

Saturday

The next day was a blur, stacked with press conferences convened by a grim-faced Esposito and paperwork that would eventually make its way up the line to the offices of the commissioner and minister. Kate had offered to cut short her leave and Esposito had not argued the point.

Throughout the day, her furious, determined busyness had been punctuated by sudden gut punches of loss when she'd caught stray pieces of Darnley scattered around the station. His reusable cup on the drying rack in the kitchenette. A photo of his daughters smiling up from their shiny silver frame on his desk. His jacket, permanently slung across the back of his chair, invariably forgotten, rain, hail or shine. Someone would have to pack up his things and return them to Vanessa. Kate swallowed her cooling tea and turned back to her computer.

Outside the station, a mound of flowers had begun to grow as the news of a local officer's death spread through the town, and national media crews had started to descend. Dazed townsfolk placed bouquets and offered stuffed teddies at the entrance to the station to assuage their shock. By the afternoon, the small pile had grown into a sizable hill.

'Can someone move the fucking teddies so people can get in and out?' Esposito's grief and exhaustion had spilled out on the duty officer. Constable Grant had scurried to move some of the offerings away from the entrance.

The TV news had the story playing on high rotation: any available footage of yesterday's siege and every scrap of information on the original Nowra story. The police operation gone wrong; the death of Alexis Fincher and his teenage son, Raff; the coronial findings and the subsequent compensation claim against the police. Much was being made of the court's findings in favour of the police and their likely psychological effects on Leon Fincher. The armchair analysts were having a field day. All the focus on the Finchers meant that Darnley's death was in danger of getting buried in the noise.

Late in the afternoon, Leon Fincher's mobile records had come through. It turned out that for large chunks of the siege, Fincher had been on the phone with his mother, Ariana, a woman in her late seventies who was suffering from dementia and living in a nursing home. Kate recalled the numerous times that Demetriou had attempted to dial Fincher's number only to get a notification that it was engaged.

Kate had been in touch with the nursing home to learn that the staff often called on Leon to calm Ariana's agitation and confusion, which had worsened in the years since the Nowra shooting. Before that time, the visitor she had most looked forward to was Raff, her adored grandson. Her room was apparently packed with photographs of him. Her dementia meant that she didn't understand or recall why Raff no longer came around. She was often despondent and even aggressive with staff, who had learned to never mention the death of her grandchild.

Only the phone calls with Leon soothed her. The nursing home's policy was to allow any calls between mother and son to run for as long as Ariana wanted. She often fell asleep with her son's words in her ears. The staff had had no idea that yesterday's calls had been anything more than the regular chat between mother and son as Ariana had seemed the same as usual throughout the conversation.

Kate didn't know how to process the information. To reconcile these two sides of Leon Fincher. Had Leon been navigating another difficult conversation about Raff with his mother that day? What chance did he have of ever letting go of his anger if every day he had to rehash the sorrow with his mother? A part of her didn't want to know anything that would humanise Fincher. It was easier to wallow in the anger that still burned through her veins. It felt like a betrayal of Darnley and of Logan Casey. Whatever the provocation, neither Darnley nor Logan had deserved what had occurred.

She gave up in frustration on the report she had been writing. It could wait till the morning. Passing through the office, she saw Josh slumped at his desk, looking even more exhausted than she felt.

'You okay?'

'All good here. Putting in the hours so your brother stays out of prison.'

She felt the vitriol of the barb but didn't react. This was how it would be from now on. Josh wouldn't be the only one thinking it; holding Luke, and in turn her, responsible for how Darnley had met his end. Hell, she was thinking it, the guilt scouring her insides like acid. She continued out of the office to the carpark.

–

At home, she played with the kids while Geoff went to pick up their takeaway pizza – an easy dinner. She alternately spooned mushy pumpkin risoni into Amy's waiting mouth, while helping Archie decipher the instructions of a Lego build, the familiar chatter of *Play School* in the background on TV.

'Grandpa called before,' Archie offered as he waited for her to prise apart two tiny Lego tiles with her fingernail. She had just pressed them together when Archie had informed her that, according to the instructions, the two didn't go together. The black tile went with the thin grey tile, not the thin white tile. Of course.

'Did he, bud?' she said, wondering if she could use her teeth to pull the bricks apart.

'Yep, I answered. ''Cause Daddy was in the bathroom.'

'What did Grandpa want?' *Bloody thing.* She was definitely going to break a nail trying to separate these two bricks.

'He wanted to know if Uncle Luke was here… Muuum, no, don't use your teeth, you're going to put marks on the bricks.'

'Got it. Here you go.' She held out the separated bricks.

'Yuck, you got spit on them.'

'It's all good. I'll give it a quick wash.' She returned from the kitchen, having rinsed the Lego and got Amy some pureed fruit from the freezer. A cool treat after her dinner. She wiped the dregs of pasta from her daughter's face, her high chair and the floor, all the while wondering about her father's call. Where had her brother disappeared to now? Should she call Gray back or just leave it?

'Pizza's here.' She heard Geoff come in through the back door.

'Ham and cheese pizza for you, my good sir. And your cloudy apple. An excellent choice.' Geoff materialised a few minutes later from the kitchen and placed Archie's kids' pizza and juice popper in front of him with a flourish. Archie giggled and Amy squealed with delight at seeing her father.

'And for you, madam, a rocket and prosciutto with basil and cashew-nut pesto.'

'Ooh, fancy,' Kate said, accepting her plate and a glass of ice-cold white wine.

He squeezed her shoulder lightly. 'I tried that new place on the main street. I thought we could all do with something to take our minds off things. They do homemade tiramisu, as well,' he said, wiggling his eyebrows.

Kate smiled and took a sip of her wine. She waited for Geoff to join her on the couch before trying the pizza. 'Oh, yum. That's good.'

'It's the cashew pesto, baby.'

'Must be,' she said, laughing. As she shook her head at her husband, she felt something click into place in her brain. A wraith of an idea that she had been chasing for days, which now seemed to step into the light fully formed. But she made herself wait. To eat the pizza and drink her wine. To chat and laugh with the kids, knowing that Geoff had made an effort to create a moment of lightness. Afterwards, she tidied the kitchen and convinced Archie to brush his teeth and get into his PJs, while Geoff organised Amy's bath. Only after Amy was tucked into her sleep suit, her eyelids drooping, and Archie was splayed on the couch streaming one last episode of *Bluey*, did she escape to the study.

Kate searched for the plastic bag that held the coroner's report on Ant Reed. Finding it, she pored over the pages, which she'd only leafed through the other day. She read it in more detail, turning to the autopsy findings, searching for the words she thought she had seen. And there it was: the stomach contents.

But did it mean anything? It could be completely innocent. A meal between friends. But if so, why all the secrecy?

She reached for her phone and scrolled through her contacts for David O'Connell. It was a stretch, but she had to at least try. Ant had lived in a modern block of units. Surely, there would be CCTV footage from the building entrance or the lifts. She just had to hope that the footage still existed a month on and that Constable O'Connell would be willing to go on that particular goose chase. Text sent, she hesitated on the cusp of calling the station. She normally would have delegated a task like this to Darnley, who would have her back and wouldn't ask too many questions. Swallowing down a surge of bile, she dialled, reaching Harris. She explained what she needed – a request to the Australian Border Force for a passport check. She provided the details and hung up.

Almost immediately, her phone rang with an incoming call. It was her father.

'Have you heard from Luke?' Not even a hello.

'Not today.' Her short tone matched his own. She knew her father thought she probably owed Luke some sort of apology for her outburst. But the anger that bubbled in her chest every time she thought of her brother told her that she wasn't yet ready for that conversation.

'He called a taxi to visit Aunty Iris this afternoon, but isn't back yet. The staff at Scottsdale House think he left a while ago.'

Fuck, not this again.

'Have you tried his dope dealer?' she asked, thinking of the last time they had gone through this.

Her father inhaled, trying not to lose his patience. 'I don't have those numbers. I was hoping you could help look.'

She sighed. 'Let me call you back.'

39

> Hey, Sarah, it's Luke here. Is it okay if I visit Iris later this arvo? Need to get out of the house. What are the visiting hours?

> All good. Afternoon is fine. I'm on shift till five. If you feel like food afterwards, let me know. I know it's been a rough few days.

> Yeah, that would be great, actually. Thanks, Sarah.

> Takeaway it is!

Iris was asleep when Luke arrived. A passing nurse had informed him that Iris had just taken her medication and could be out for a while.

'Let me know if she does wake up and I'll bring in a tea tray,' she said, before leaving him alone with Iris.

He was glad in a way. It meant he could hide in her room without any pressure to converse. He curled himself into a chair, watching her tiny bird-like chest rise and fall.

Luke had called a taxi, unable to stand another minute watching the wall-to-wall coverage of the shooting. Another mistake to add to his conscience. Of course, the garrulous taxi driver had other ideas, insisting on a quick detour through Esserton (*no charge!*), even though it was in the opposite direction to Scottsdale House (*no trouble!*). The sight apparently too important to be missed. They had driven past the brick exterior of Esserton Police Station, its entrance portico awash with flowers, both a memorial and a kind of morbid tourist attraction. What would they do with all the flowers, he wondered. Would it all end up in landfill? In one big mound of rotting petals trapped in cellophane and ribbon.

Luke thought of Kate and the words she had screamed at him. He knew she'd been emotional and probably hadn't meant what she'd said – *I don't believe you* – but it hadn't been easy to hear. He'd been so focused on the Payton disaster that he hadn't really given his full attention to the whole Marcus situation. He understood that he was a person of interest in the case, but the gravity of the situation hadn't properly sunk in. Of course he hadn't killed his friend. It was so patently obvious, it went without saying. Did Kate truly not believe him? And did the rest of her team feel the same way? If no other suspects were found, *he* would be left holding the bag. Just like with Payton. He was the last person to have seen Marcus alive and he had been the last person with the video on his phone. The truth didn't matter, only how the facts could be interpreted.

He swore softly. What *had* he seen that night when he left Marcus's place? Had he really seen the bloody car? He was sure he had. But had he seen it turn into Marcus's property, or had it been a neighbour's driveway? Could he swear to it in court? Because if he couldn't, that meant Kate was right. His statement had led to that police officer's death. *Fuck.*

The sun had dipped behind Scottsdale House, and outside Iris's window, long fingers of shadow were swallowing the side garden. Luke closed his eyes, feeling his attention drift. The events of the past twenty-four hours pinwheeling through his mind, never quite settling.

He recalled the two Sydney police officers who had interviewed him, separated by a computer screen and yet so solidly present. The formality of their words, the deliberate, patient bureaucracy of the whole procedure; everything designed to low-key intimidate. Had they believed him? He honestly couldn't tell. The experience had left him limp with exhaustion, small sunbursts of pain sparking behind his eyelids from the strain of being hyper-alert all day.

He had returned home to find Gray waiting, a cold beer at the ready. There had been no questions. His father had simply kept him company in the cool of Caleb's shaded deck, sitting in a wicker chair beside him. He recalled how Gray's age spots had seemed to stand out in the afternoon light, his hair more sprinkled with silver than Luke could remember. While he had been holed away in Sydney, his father had become an old man. And Gray was doing his best, he realised. He was standing by Luke, without censure.

That afternoon, Luke had finally pushed through his misgivings and unburdened himself to Gray, an experience that had been just as excruciating as he had imagined. Gray had stayed silent throughout, as Luke had stumbled through his ordeal, only pressing a hand to his shoulder at the end and squeezing it lightly. Gray had left him alone, making an excuse to head inside for a few minutes, to allow Luke time to decompress after his disclosure. His father had been tactful and sensitive, something Luke had not expected.

When he had returned, Gray's words had been gentle. 'Whatever happens, mate, we'll get through it. We're not going anywhere.'

Luke had nodded, unexpected tears pricking his eyes. 'I loved her, Dad. I really did.'

'I know, mate. I know.' He'd reached for his son and clasped his hand.

'You can't be sleeping in here.'

Luke's eyes snapped open to find Sarah Osborne in her navy-blue staff uniform, smiling at him. He stretched and rose to his feet, rubbing his eyes with the heel of his palms.

'You right to go?' she asked.

'Yeah, let's do it.' He kissed the still-sleeping Iris on her cheek, breathing in her talcum scent. He glanced back at Sarah, who was holding the door open for him. 'Do you need to check on her or anything?'

'The orderlies will be doing their rounds soon,' she said.

For a moment he hesitated, and then followed her out of the room.

40

Kate hung up the phone to Mitch Cosgrove. No, he had not seen or heard from Luke today. She was inclined to believe him. While he had no problem relieving Luke of his money when he was after a score, Mitch had learned his lesson from the last time he had provided Luke a place to hide out. He wasn't eager to repeat that particular mistake in a hurry. In truth, Kate wasn't really worried about her brother. His previous stint had proven that he could look after himself. She was mainly going through the motions for her father.

Though she was meant to be focusing on Luke, her attention kept drifting elsewhere. She drummed her fingers, indecision pinging inside her. She had rung Scottsdale House before calling Mitch Cosgrove, trying to locate her brother, yes, but also trying to reach her friend. She needed to speak with Sarah. No, she wasn't on shift today. She wasn't rostered on this weekend. Kate had tried Sarah's mobile a couple of times now, but it kept going to voicemail. Was she overreacting? Looking for a problem where there wasn't one?

She glanced at the phone still in her hand and suddenly remembered the text that she had received yesterday from Jacob, Ant's friend and colleague. The events of the past 24 hours had wiped the message clean from her mind, but she opened it now, clicking through to the linked article. It appeared to be a draft word document. Some sort of research article with annotated notes, edits in Track Changes, and feedback comments, which weren't easy to decipher on her phone screen. She scrolled quickly down the text and then went back to the start, taking in the article title – 'Teen Suicide Ideation: What You Should Know' – and clocking the author's name, *Anthony Reed, Youth Welfare Officer.* A shiver of foreboding spiked through her. Staring at the name, she returned to Jacob's message and rang the number.

–

When she had told Geoff that she needed to head out for an hour or so, using Luke as the excuse for the impromptu excursion, Kate had seen the familiar resignation settle onto her husband's face. The lines of worry had become a permanent fixture, as much a part of his face as the stubble and softness around his chin. He barely raised an objection, which spoke volumes. As she left, she had momentarily imagined a nine-to-five job that didn't have this pull, or place these expectations on her. A quieter life, where she and Geoff had more time. With a quick brush of her lips to his, she had made for the door, mobile and keys in hand.

By the time she reached the entrance to Sarah's property, the sun was sinking low into the horizon and the evening beginning to blur into shadow. She expected to see Boof as she ran lightly up the steps of the front verandah, but no dog appeared and she couldn't hear the sound of laboured breathing. Kate tapped at the front door, and when there was no answer, she pushed it open. It was unlocked and swung wide to reveal an empty lounge room. Perfectly arranged, neat and cosy as usual.

'Hello? Sarah?'

She entered the spotless kitchen, which smelled of a lemony cleaning product and otherwise looked unused. Did Sarah eat at all? She pushed the back screen door and ventured outside. On the rear deck, facing the scraggly back paddock that divided Sarah's home from the bushland beyond, she spotted Sarah sunken into one of the cane chairs in half-darkness. Boof, who was slumped on the floor, struggled to her feet to greet Kate as she approached.

'Kate, hey.' Sarah seemed to emerge out of a reverie. 'What are you doing here? Are you all right? God, you must be exhausted after yesterday.'

'I'm all right,' she answered shortly, not wanting to get into it. She bent down to scratch Boof behind the ears. 'I'm looking for Luke, actually. You haven't seen him, have you? He went to visit Iris this arvo and apparently hasn't turned up home yet and Dad's in a flap.'

'Luke, no. Sorry, I don't know where he is.'

Kate heard the slight slurring in Sarah's voice, and noticed the wineglass she was nursing on her lap and the empty bottle of red on the floor next to her.

'I remember you mentioning you might have him over for dinner on the weekend.'

'No, sorry. We didn't end up organising anything.'

'And what about you? Have you eaten anything tonight?'

'Oh, I might get something later. There's soup in the freezer, I think.'

'I thought you hated soup?' Kate said, pulling the remaining cane chair over and taking a seat.

'No one hates soup, Kate. It's not a thing.'

Boof had settled down at her feet and Kate threaded her fingers through the dog's fur. Luke wasn't the reason she was here. Her brother was a big boy. She had no doubt he'd find his way home. She hesitated, misgiving sticking in her throat, thick like honey. She knew that once the words had tipped out, there was no turning back.

'Sarah, were you with Ant when he died?'

'What? Where's this coming from?' Sarah's answer was a beat too slow, watchfulness disguised as surprise.

'I went through Ant Reed's autopsy findings today. It's in the coroner's report that Frank passed on to me and I found something I missed previously. Among Ant's stomach contents were pieces of cashew nut, green pistachio, dried apricot and cranberries...' Kate waited, but Sarah made no move to speak.

'It didn't hit me before today, but I suddenly recalled you saying you still made a rocky road slice for Nadine's birthday this year.'

Kate thought she saw a slight tightening of Sarah's jawline at this mention of her slip. 'It made me remember that they were Nadine's favourite fillings. I'm a bit annoyed it took me so long to realise, actually. I've helped you two chop up those ingredients so many times.'

For a moment, the shared memories from their child-hood shimmered between them. The two sisters and Kate, apron-clad in Mrs Osmond's kitchen, sorting out the fillings for two separate batches of rocky road, one for each sister. Sarah's ingredients had run to the standard sweet side: biscuits, marshmallows and white chocolate chips, while Nadine – the younger, yet more sophisticated palate – had favoured the tangy crunch of dried fruit and nuts. As they had got older, Mrs Osborne had trusted Sarah and Kate with the knives to carefully cut up Nadine's ingredients for her.

'You were there that night, weren't you? Ant's body was found on the nineteenth of November. One day after Nadine's birthday. Did you visit him with a batch of her rocky road?'

Sarah remained still. She seemed to have retracted inwards, unwilling to move a muscle in case she should betray herself.

'I've asked a contact at Boondall Police Station to check CCTV surrounding Ant's apartment. So if you were there, chances are you were caught on camera. It's going to come out either way.'

Sarah met her gaze, holding it for what seemed like ages, until finally she seemed to make up her mind.

'I helped him.'

'Okay,' Kate replied.

'He begged me. He'd been begging me for weeks. Even though I tried and tried to talk him out of it, he wouldn't listen. He'd made up his mind.'

'You were with him when he died?' Kate asked.

Sarah nodded, a look on her face almost like anger. 'The survival instinct is so strong, even when you've made a decision to die. Especially the method Ant chose. Sleeping tablets and a bag over his head. If your timing is off, and the tablets don't work in time, you could still be conscious when you start running out of oxygen. And you can panic and rip off the bag, even if that's not actually what you want. He asked me to be with him to make sure he went through with it.'

Sarah grimaced like she was tamping down something painful. 'He wanted someone there that he could trust. Someone who'd seen death before and could stay calm. He knew what I had gone through with Mum, and what I deal with at work. He asked me to sit with him until he was drowsy enough, to let him know it was time. He did it all himself. The bag and the elastic to seal the opening around his neck. He just didn't want to be alone at the end.'

Kate didn't say a word, not daring to break the spell.

'He told me he couldn't stand what happened with Nadine. That he blamed himself for not being able to make her better. He said she was like a disease that he just couldn't get out of his system. That he'd tried. To go out with other girls and move on. But he just kept coming back to her. He said one way or another, this was his chosen path. And I did try, Kate. Trust me, I tried.'

Again the silence stretched, and again Kate felt that strange reluctance to keep going. For the first time in her career, she was afraid of what she might find out.

'That's a great story, Sarah. But I need you to tell me what really happened.'

'That is what happened. Ant killed himself and I helped him.'

'I know Nadine's back in the country, Sarah. I've got a request in with customs checking her arrival dates. So, you might as well just tell me.'

41

The sky was a diffuse blaze of amber, and long angles of shadow preceded him as Luke made his way along the landscaped pathway. At the gravel-and-grass layaway adjacent, he found a handful of vehicles, but no Sarah.

She had asked him to meet her at the carpark after he had signed out at the front desk. Not the Scottsdale House one, but the informal overflow lot next door. She had told him that the staff carpark had been too full that morning to get a spot. But now, looking around, it occurred to him that this lot also didn't have CCTV.

In that moment, a long, lean woman with a cropped head of blonde hair, wearing jeans and a baggy Triple-J T-shirt stepped out of a dark-coloured sedan. As he watched her walk towards him, smiling broadly, he felt a shiver run down his spine. Not quite fear, but something close.

'What do you think? Do I do a good Sarah?'

'Nadine?' Luke didn't know whether to laugh or run. Both reactions seemed to apply just as well.

'The one and only.'

'But aren't you meant to be in Bali or wherever?'

'Chiang Mai, Thailand. Yeah, drug rehab. I was there for almost three months. Top-of-the-range treatment in luxury accommodation for a fraction of the cost. Thank God for the exchange rate, hey?'

'Yeah, right, so how are you doing? How did the treatment go?'

'Good, yeah. I'm all cured.' She laughed, a slightly off-kilter sound that did nothing to reassure Luke. 'I had to. Sarah took a loan just to pay for the whole thing. I had no option but to get better.'

'You look well. You look great, in fact.' It was true. He could understand why Ant had been so obsessed with her.

'Yeah, I scrub up good when I'm not mainlining meth, ha.'

Luke laughed, not knowing what to say. She wasn't doing or saying anything that could be interpreted as threatening. She wasn't blocking his way. And though she was a tall woman, he didn't think she posed a physical threat. And yet, there was something not quite right about the situation. Something was off.

'I fooled you, hey?'

'Yeah, you did actually. I thought you were Sarah for sure.' But had he? Even in Iris's room, he'd felt a premonition of something. A sliver of doubt about the version of Sarah who had not cared enough to check on Iris. And yet, he'd walked out with her, obeying her suggestion to go out through the front doors while she used the staff exit, because in the dimly lit room, she had looked like her sister. Now that he thought about it, apart from their hairstyles and clothes, the sisters looked the same down to their body type and height.

'Yeah, I used to impersonate her quite a bit, actually, when I was a teen, pretending to be older than I was. It was pretty easy as long as I had the right hair.' She grinned. 'Straight blonde locks, the easiest wig to buy. Sarah can't stand her curls. Always with the hair straightener, that one. Me, I embraced my frizz. Well, I did anyway, before I went short,' she said, running a hand across her almost clean-shaven scalp.

'Have you done that in there before?' Luke asked. 'Impersonated Sarah at Scottsdale?'

Her lips twitched. 'Ah, no. First time borrowing Sarah's uniform. I wasn't a hundred per cent sure it would work, to be honest. I had to use one of the old wigs I found at home, though Sarah's gone much lighter in colour now. But no one noticed, thank God. It's a good racket, though. You can swipe all sorts of meds when you're in there. The old dears are all gaga and have no idea.'

Luke frowned. He remembered Iris seemingly in pain two days ago, asking after her pills and insisting she had seen Sarah that day.

'Kidding, I'm kidding.' Nadine laughed. 'I would never steal from the old biddies. Told you, I'm cured now.'

He stared at her. 'So, it was you messaging me today?'

'Yeah, that was me. Sarah was having a nap and I saw your messages pop up on her screen. I know her password, you see.' She smiled and brought her finger to her lips in a shushing *don't tell* motion.

'And… you wanted to see me?'

'I did, you're a hard man to get alone. Forever with your lawyer or your family.' She winked. 'But hey, I owe you a takeaway, don't I? Let's talk in the car.'

She motioned for him to follow her, and Luke complied, though something inside was telling him he should back the hell away. There was a volatile edge to her and he didn't know how she would react if he were to refuse. Whatever this was, he would just need to see it through. Have a meal, listen to what she had to say, and then extract himself.

She was still talking as they moved towards her car. 'Thai okay? Not as good as the real thing in Chiang Mai, of course, but I need a noodle fix. Schnitzel just doesn't cut it anymore.' She turned to him and laughed. 'Look at me, I've become one of those annoying people who go overseas for two seconds and now I'm the expert.'

But Luke wasn't smiling. His gaze was on the midnight-blue Mitsubishi Lancer, so dark that it could almost be black, that stood behind her, neatly parked rear to kerb. His eyes took in the front metal bumper, the left side of which was slightly crumpled. And suddenly, he was back in his hire car, driving away from Marcus's property, watching a dark-coloured sedan with a bent bumper in his rear-view mirror turning into the driveway he had just left. He'd forgotten this small detail with all the shit that had been going on. But now it came back to him. The thought that had popped into his head for the couple of seconds in which his brain had paid attention to the vehicle; that the wonky bumper made the car look like it was frowning. And here it was, the frowning, dark-coloured car that Kate's cop friend had died trying to find. The tiny pebbles of unease that had been floating around in his stomach seemed to coalesce into a giant fucking rock.

'You okay?' Nadine asked.

Luke cleared his throat. 'Yeah, just admiring your ride.'

'It's all right. The aircon's fucked, but hey, you can't expect much for a couple of grand. I just needed some wheels to get around in while I'm back at home.' She unlocked the door and indicated for him to enter.

Every cell in his body screamed no, but he made himself get in, breathing in the used-car smell of the previous owners, a background ozone of cigarette smoke, wet dog and takeaway, overlain by Nadine's strong, musky, floral perfume. Luke knew that scent: Chanel No. 5. One of his old girlfriends had worn it. He wasn't a fan. He noticed a beach bag in the back seat with the blonde wig and Sarah's uniform, stuffed inside.

Nadine climbed in and put the car into drive, heading north-east, away from Esserton. Sitting beside her, Luke could feel her jitteriness as she alternately adjusted something on the console – the radio, the air vents – or tapped her fingers on the steering wheel, as if her skin itself was vibrating. Was she on something? Had the rehab actually worked, he wondered. A few times he noticed her wince as she turned the wheel. Was her baggy clothing hiding some sort of injury to her shoulder?

His thoughts were in freefall. *The car… This car… If this was Nadine's… But didn't that mean…?*

'So, how long are you in town for?' he blurted. His mind flew to Ant. Had Nadine been in Esserton during her ex's funeral, but had not bothered to attend?

'Not long. I think I'm almost finished what I came back to do.'

'Right,' he said, as if he understood, though he didn't. Outside, sprays of green and shadow flew past their windows. He had to keep her talking until he could figure some way out of this. Too late, his father's words to Kate and Luke as kids came back to him, safety briefings about stranger danger and unfamiliar vehicles. *Never, ever get into the car.* Maybe he could text Kate or his dad from the Thai takeaway, assuming they were, in fact, heading there.

'I probably wouldn't have hung around for as long as I have, if it wasn't for you.'

'Me?' He turned to her, the note of disquiet that had been thrumming inside him now snapping to a full-blown roar.

'You're my wild card, Luke. You're the only one I haven't been able to figure out. The other two are obvious, easy to pin down. One an apologist, weak as piss and wanting me to do all the hard work for him. And number two, a misogynist, plain and simple. But you...' She cocked her head, observing him. 'I had you pegged as one of the good guys. You got out of Esserton. Cut ties with your old mates. You weren't even on the list. But then, I see all this stuff in the papers. About how much of a player you really are. And Sarah mentioned something about a sex tape. I mean, come on, really? So, I start thinking, maybe I've misjudged the third musketeer. Maybe he deserves a bit more attention, after all.'

Luke blanched. How the hell had Sarah heard about Payton's case? And even as he thought it, he realised, *Of course, Kate.* Shit, he couldn't believe that Kate would discuss a sensitive police matter like that with one of her friends. So much for fucking confidentiality. He tried to focus on what Nadine had said.

'What do you mean, your list? What list?'

'When I first arrived at the treatment centre,' she said, not answering his question, 'I was disappointed because it was all the same shit. The psychologists there wanted me to do the same things as the psychologists here. Write it all down. Leach the poison. Put it all in a letter that you never have to mail. And I thought, fuck, this isn't going to work. Sarah has spent all this money, and I'm going to blow it. It's not going to stick.'

She looked at him then, holding his gaze for a moment. 'It's not easy, you know. Having to face the fact that you might never get better.'

Luke broke the gaze first and Nadine continued, her eyes back on the road. 'But then I met someone there, a fellow addict. From France, actually – a port town in Normandy. And when I heard her story, I realised that we're the same in more ways than one. What happened to me, also happened to her – in a slightly different way and in a slightly different town, but in the end, the exact same thing. And for years we've been trying to survive, to move on, to escape, without making waves. Thinking of all the things we should have done to prevent it happening. To not have worn those clothes, to not have drunk so much, to not have been so forward, to not have agreed to stay the night. When, in fact, the only decision that really mattered was the one he made. To rape or not to rape, that is the question.'

Luke could feel his throat go dry. Holy fuck.

Nadine saw the look on his face and laughed. 'Yeah, I did go a bit heavy there, didn't I? Sorry about that, didn't mean to get all preachy so early in the piece. What I meant to say was, Marie – that's my French friend – she showed me that there's another way. You can lean into the rage. She had a term for it, actually – *anger as therapy*. Turns out that was something I could really get behind. A proper incentive to get better. It's what allowed me to turn the corner, my side therapy with her.'

Nadine smiled sweetly. 'The idea that I could make a list and plan my revenge.'

42

Kate had clearly stumped her. For the moment, Sarah could only stare.

'It's the perfume.' Kate answered her unspoken question. 'You hate Chanel. You only wore it because your mum bought it for you, and you stopped as soon as she passed away. But it's been Nadine's favourite since I can remember. I didn't understand why you'd suddenly started wearing it again, unless you were trying to mask the fact that someone else in the house was wearing the scent.'

Sarah erupted into laughter, a full-throated howl that seemed to ring into the night. Disturbed by the noise, Boof shuffled to her feet and ambled over to Sarah, her tail moving in a slow, tentative wag. Sarah buried her face in Boof's neck, cry-laughing into her fur. She finally subsided, wiping tears from her eyes.

'Only you. Only you would pick a fucking scent. You are unbelievable.'

'I also saw her at the Cresty,' Kate added. 'I think she spotted me, too, because she hurried off away from the bar.' She saw a trace of surprise and something close to annoyance cross Sarah's face, the laughter fading. Nadine had obviously not informed her of that near miss.

'I even smelled the same perfume as she walked past. But it didn't click then that it was her. I saw her from behind and the shaved hair threw me.'

Kate had only made the connection later. Remembering the conversation she'd had with the mother at Uki who had momentarily mistaken her two sons, because the younger had grown out his hair to match his older brother. It had struck Kate how programmed people were to recognise their peers by their hairstyles. At the Cresty, she'd dismissed the momentary feeling that the woman resembled Nadine because of her unfamiliar hairdo.

She met Sarah's gaze now. 'I never doubted that she was still in Chiang Mai. It was a genius touch asking Frank Reed to set up the funeral as a zoom-cast, so Nadine could watch it from overseas. We all believed you.'

Sarah tipped her head back and swallowed the last of her wine.

'Was Nadine with you that night with Ant?'

Sarah shook her head, a brief, annoyed movement. 'I told you already. It was just me. I assisted Ant with his preparations to end his life.'

'The problem is I don't know if I believe you, Sarah. I had a chat with one of Ant's friends from Brisbane. Do you remember Jacob, the guy who spoke at the funeral?' When Sarah didn't reply, Kate went on. 'I had a chat with him today. Actually, just before I drove out here. He's been trying to get in touch for a while. Got my details through Frank. I should have called him back before now, but, well...' Kate broke off, not needing to explain the events that had absorbed her attention. 'Didn't you just say Ant was desperate, begging you to help him end things? Well, this Jacob had a very different take on Ant's mental health in the weeks leading up to his death.'

Kate waited to see if Sarah would interject, but she remained still, her face impassive, the levity from a few minutes ago entirely forgotten.

'Jacob was actually very insistent that Ant didn't seem particularly depressed or unlike his normal self in the weeks prior. He says Ant socialised with his workmates right up to the weekend of his death. Apparently, none of his colleagues noticed anything unusual in his behaviour, either. You see,

Jacob's been asking around, and he gave me a bunch of people's names to check with. He says he didn't question the police verdict at the time, but in the weeks since, it's become harder and harder to accept. I was interested in Jacob's take as a fellow welfare worker. Because they're trained, aren't they, to catch those small signs that the rest of us tend to miss or ignore.'

Kate paused, her eyes never leaving Sarah. 'But you know the most interesting fact, I discovered? It turns out that Ant was writing an article for a health magazine on youth suicide, researching rates and methods. Jacob shared the article with me. Apparently, Ant had forwarded him a draft for feedback. The police thought that Ant's search history reflected his suicide ideation, but having read the document, I'm not so sure anymore. It was very detailed with lots of footnotes linking to his research. I'm willing to bet the citings will match up with his web history. So… can we start again about what actually happened that night?'

Sarah rose from her chair, a tad unsteady. She walked inside without a word and returned with an empty glass and a new bottle of wine. She handed it to Kate, pouring out a generous portion of shiraz. Sitting back down on her chair, she topped up her own glass.

'I'm going to need your phone.'

'Excuse me?'

'Kate, if we're going to do this Miss Marple bullshit, you sniffing the air and telling me what day I murdered the butler, I need to know you're not recording. For the next hour, I need you to be my friend. Nothing more. And I'll tell you what happened to Ant, but more importantly, to Nadine.'

Kate handed over her phone without another word. Sarah checked it and tucked it in the seat beside her.

'You know that stupid party, Marcus's eighteenth in the Gold Coast? Put on by his dad that every idiot in Esserton was killing themselves to attend? Nadine was in her first year at Griffith Uni. Just finished her end-of-year exams and blowing off steam with friends in the Goldie. She ended up at that party and hooked up with Marcus. Except... well, he raped her.' The words were choked out of her.

Something ugly twisted within Kate thinking of the two sisters suspended in time, smiling and carefree in the framed photo in the Osmonds' lounge room.

'She never told me,' Sarah continued. 'I guess it was all so close to Mum dying at the end of that year that she felt she couldn't. And no doubt she blamed herself. Mum had spent years shoving that female modesty crap down our throats all through high school. Of course, Nadine internalised it all as being her fault. It only got harder for her to talk about as time went on.' Her voice dipped for a second before continuing. 'It's not like it's something you can just drop into conversation, is it? Instead, she folded all that trauma and shame into herself and tried to forget it all by escaping. God, no wonder she fell apart. She was so bloody young. And I thought it was all because of Mum dying.'

'Sarah, that's awful. I had no idea. I'm so sorry.'

'Yeah, so am I. Mainly that it took me so long to find out. No wonder she hated visiting Esserton from Brisbane. I thought it was because the house held too many memories of Mum. But, well...' She gave a sad shrug of her shoulders.

Kate understood. Of course it wasn't the house; it was the town itself that Nadine couldn't stand. It was where her rapist had lived and thrived with a job and family, for all the world a good bloke, a famous actor's son, no less, and part of the community. She recalled how Sarah had used to complain about Nadine not wanting to go out for a counter meal or a drink at the pub. Kate wondered how often Sarah had unknowingly forced her sister to share the same room as her abuser. Because, of course, Marcus would have been there. He practically lived at the pub.

'When she started going out with Ant in Brisbane, I honestly thought she got better for a while. For a few years at least, their

266

little Brisbane bubble worked, and I think she could disconnect Esserton Nadine from Brisbane Nadine. But then Frank got sick and Ant began visiting more, which meant that he was hanging out with Marcus again. And then Marcus and Fi got serious, so I was talking about them, too, and she wasn't able to keep everything separate. Esserton had started to seep back in. And still she couldn't bring herself to talk about it, because the connections had only got more intertwined, not less. Marcus and Fi got married and had kids, and suddenly there were so many more lives that her revelations could affect. And she began to spiral anew.'

Kate knew what Sarah was referring to. Almost from the time Nadine had left university in the middle of her second year, she had struggled with addiction, coming good for a while before relapsing. She had experienced stints of homelessness and unemployment, and had been in and out of rehab programs. Through it all, she and Ant had cobbled together an on-again off-again relationship that had never quite died, regardless of the fresh shit they had put each other through. The longest track of continuous sobriety she'd managed was twenty-one months. She'd survived several overdoses, the last of which had been serious enough to trigger one final desperate treatment option: a drug rehab centre in Thailand that Sarah had managed to scrape together the money for.

'How did you find all this out?'

'Two months ago. I started receiving letters from her in Chiang Mai. She laid out everything that had happened.' Sarah closed her eyes as if she could shut out the details. 'She told me about Ant, too. How she'd tried to talk to him, but he hadn't wanted to believe that of his childhood friend. He didn't know what to do with that knowledge, so he pushed Nadine away. His guilt didn't allow him to abandon Nadine entirely. That's why he kept hanging around us. Because as long as he was looking out for Nadine, Ant could still believe that he was a good bloke.'

Sarah stiffened, as if physically controlling a tide of emotion. Her voice had sharpened, taking on an acid edge. 'He was the only person she'd trusted with the information and he let her down. If he had just believed her and taken her side, maybe she could have started to heal. Maybe he could have spared her another couple of years of pain and unravelling. He didn't bother to tell me, but worse, he kept up the front that he was being a good friend to her. I trusted him to look after Nadine, but he was gaslighting both me and her this whole time.'

Kate could see the betrayal of trust etched across her friend's face. Something feral rippling under that statue-still mask. She recalled the photo reel of images at Ant's funeral. A carefree child who had grown into a flawed man. She felt a trickle of fear, a sudden urge to stop her friend from speaking, but she refrained.

'Ant made it almost too easy. You're right. He was researching his bloody article and he'd been asking for days if I'd like to help him with his little experiment,' she said. 'That's what he called it. The stupid git wanted to experience the bag over his face and the feeling of air loss so he could write about it more *authentically*.' Sarah used air quotes to express her disdain.

'So I did,' Sarah said, the ghost of a grin playing on her lips. 'I went over that night and it was simple. I just got him drinking and talking about himself. He had no idea I'd added the sleeping pills into his whisky. And yes, I took a batch of Nadine's rocky road with me. We ate a slice together to salute her birthday. I wanted her to be there with me at the end. And for him to remember.' Her voice had gone quiet now, almost a whisper.

Darkness had stolen over them as they sat together on the unlit deck. Only the light from the kitchen filtering through the screen door allowed Kate to catch the lines on her friend's face: hard and set. A ruthless, uncompromising version of the features she thought she knew.

'When I could tell he was beginning to drift off in his armchair,' Sarah went on, 'I asked him to show me what the whole bag setup would look like. He didn't want to by that point, but I managed to convince him. I helped him get it over his head wearing disposable gloves, so there was no trace of my fingerprints on the bag. He noticed, of course, and when I grabbed the rubber band, he started to struggle. But I clamped down on his wrists and brought my mouth right up close to his face and whispered in his ears everything Nadine had put into her letters. All the fear and ugliness and self-loathing. And after a while, he just stopped struggling. He seemed to understand. I watched him die. I made him look me in the eyes until his very last gagging breath.'

'Sarah...' Kate's voice trailed off. She didn't know what to say. A cavernous space seemed to have bloomed between them, one Kate knew would never again be bridged. Her friend had crossed an invisible line, leaving her forever marooned on the other side.

Sarah looked her square in the face. 'I've never been afraid of death, Kate. It's been a constant companion, my whole life. I know when it's the right time.'

Kate's eyes rested on the black onyx ring that Sarah had worn since her mother's death, an idea blooming in the back of her mind, so monstrous that she pushed it away. *No. There's no way. That couldn't be right.* But then, why not? Mrs Osborne had insisted on spending the last weeks of her life at home, not in hospital. She had wanted to pass away in her own room surrounded by the things and people she loved. Could Sarah have helped her mother along? There were ways and means. Drugs, maybe, or possibly a pillow pressed down. *No!* There had been a palliative nurse who had looked after Mrs Osborne right till the end. All Sarah had meant was that she was no stranger to death, in her work as a nurse and with her mother dying young. Kate forced away the alternate thought.

Catching the direction of her gaze, Sarah folded her ring finger out of view.

Kate blinked and made herself speak the words. 'And what about Marcus, Sarah? What happened there?'

Sarah seemed to start to life. Her previous mask slipping off like liquid to reveal the familiar flesh and bones of Kate's childhood friend.

'That was me, too,' she said. 'I confronted him. He had the rifle leaning against the ute and I grabbed it and shot him. And then I arranged his body so it looked like it could have been an accident. He'd already driven the ute to the back paddock in preparation for one of his sessions taking aim at the rabbits. So, it made things easy for me. Nadine wasn't there, but I did drive her car. It's a dark-blue Mitsubishi Lancer. She bought it second-hand when she returned home and she's been using it to get around in.'

The dark-coloured sedan, Kate thought with a pang. Another small mystery solved. She thought back to the afternoon Marcus's body had been found when she had walked through his empty house. She remembered the scent she'd noticed inside the boy's room. The smell of citrus and flowers mixed with Marcus's sandalwood aftershave. Even if what Sarah said was true, and Nadine had not taken part in the shooting, Kate was almost positive that Nadine had been in the house.

'Did you do anything else to the body after you arranged it?' Kate asked, thinking of the postmortem contusions that Barlow had identified along the side of Marcus's hip and buttocks.

Sarah gazed at her, knowing it was a test and yet unable to provide the correct answer. 'No, I don't think so. I just left him there by the fence line.'

Kate nodded, not bothering to pursue it.

Sarah chewed on her lip, looking suddenly agitated. For an instant, she hesitated and then seemed to make up her mind.

'There's something else I need to tell you. I know I've put you in a difficult position, Kate. I know in the end, your morality or whatever it is won't let you keep this a secret. You'll feel compelled to turn me in.' She held up her hand as Kate went to speak. 'That's why I'm going to tell you. So you can do what you need to with a clear conscience. Nobody else knows, not even Nadine. Well, nobody but the doctors.'

Something jagged at Kate's chest, but she didn't interrupt.

'I'm dying, Katie,' she said, holding Kate's gaze. 'I found out a couple of days after Nadine left for Thailand. Ovarian cancer, the same as Mum. Can you believe it? How's that for a shit sandwich?' She laughed without humour, the sound like a bark.

'I don't have much time. Six months. Maybe eight. I've refused treatment… didn't want to stretch it out. It's spread everywhere, anyway. It can't be stopped. That's why I needed to do this. For Nadine. I couldn't leave her without at least trying to make it right for her. I'll be confessing to both deaths. So, you don't have to look for anyone else.'

A loud ringing pierced the air, making them both jump.

'It's yours,' Sarah said, feeling by her side for Kate's phone. She glanced at the screen as she handed it over. 'It's Luke.'

THEN

'How much, do you reckon?'

Ant tipped a giant glug of coconut rum into the blender, which already contained ice and pineapple juice.

'Yeah, I think you've got enough.' Nadine laughed.

Ant turned on the machine and it whirred, blending the mixture into a snowy, tropical, ice cocktail. Ant poured the blend into two waiting cocktail glasses, and added a wedge of lime to each. 'For you, my lady.'

'Cheers,' she said and they clinked glasses. 'Oh, bloody hell, that's good. Dangerous.'

'I'm a dangerous kind of guy, baby.'

She laughed and followed him to the balcony, where Brisbane had laid out one of its perfect balmy autumn evenings, discarding its daytime humidity and slowly sinking into the night. She settled into the outdoor lounge chair beside him, sipping on the cocktail and letting the familiar chorus of the busy street below wash over her. Nadine had got used to the sounds of traffic when she had slept rough in the past. She'd often fallen asleep to it. Its tempo, peaks and troughs giving her an almost exact gauge of the time of day in the city.

You need to tell him, her counsellor's voice pulsed in her ear. She had been trying to find the right time for weeks now; well, for years, really. But she was in a good place at the moment. Clean for over six months, vibing with this new psychologist, and having scored her first job in months – waitressing at a nearby café. And she and Ant were doing well. If she didn't take the plunge now, she never would. *Just tell him. He needs to know.*

'Hey, so, Amanda, you know, the new counsellor I've been seeing. Well, she and I have been discussing a number of things... from my past and she believes that it would be helpful if I talk some of it over with you.'

He was immediately alert, his attention focused entirely on her. With what she called in her head 'his welfare face' on. 'Yeah, of course. Anything you need. If you're ready to talk, you know I'm here.'

'Yeah, so, um, this isn't easy for me. This'll be like the second time I've said the words out loud, the first being to Amanda. If you could just listen and not interrupt until I get it all out, I think that would help.'

She sipped her drink, letting the ice slowly melt on her tongue to put off the moment for as long as she could. And finally, she took the plunge. 'You remember Marcus's eighteenth in the Gold Coast...'

When she finished, he remained silent for a long time. Too long.

'Let me get us some top-ups.' He rose without another word and headed back inside.

Whatever she had expected, this was not it. Ant was her rock, her no-questions-asked support. She had expected comfort. A hug, at least. To be enveloped in his arms and be told that it would all be okay. That he would be there for her, whatever happened.

She found him in the kitchen, leaning against the counter, a lost look on his face. 'I can't find the other juice tin,' he said when he saw her, gesturing vaguely to the pantry.

'Ant, are you all right?'

He looked at her then, a kind of desperation on his face. 'He's my best friend, Nadine. I've known him since primary school. I was best man at his wedding, I'm the godparent to his fucking sons. He and Fi have been so good about Dad, ferrying him to and from appointments when I was stuck up here. I can't just... I don't know what you want me to do with this information.'

'You can believe me,' she said quietly.

He shook his head, as if flicking her words away. 'He told me, you know... that you two had hooked up. When we first started going out, he told me straightaway. He wanted me to know, so there was no misunderstanding. He said it had been nothing, a drunken fumble. You'd both been half asleep, and he could barely remember what happened.'

Again, he pinned her with that look. Like he needed her to come up with the solution. To make it so that he wouldn't have to choose. So he wouldn't need to get his hands dirty and he could remain the good guy in both of their stories.

She placed her cocktail glass carefully on the counter. 'I'm going to take off. I might stay over at a friend's tonight.'

'Nadine... come on. Don't be like that. I just need a bit of time to process it all. Stay, all right. Don't go off and do anything stupid.'

She didn't reply. All the stupid had already been done to her. All she was doing was trying to survive it. She made for the door, the familiar fizz scrabbling in her blood, impatient for the next hit to find her veins.

—

Nadine lay on the bottom bunk, gazing at the timber slats above. She recognised the tiny hearts framing the initials of movie stars, stabbed with sideways arrows that she had scribbled on the boards using her coloured markers years ago. Some of the hearts had been crossed out and covered over with stickers by Marcus's boys, evidently unhappy with the glitter-filled embellishments. She noticed one heart in the far corner of one of the beams that had survived: N.O. + K.R. Nadine Osborne plus Keanu Reeves. She smiled.

She knew she should get going. It was stupid and tempting fate to hang around here lying in bed, dreaming of Ant. It was funny, here she was in Marcus's house, having done what she had come to do, and all she could think of was her ex. She hadn't expected Ant to haunt her thoughts the way he did. To pop into her head at the oddest occasions. Not that she blamed Sarah or disagreed with what she had done. It was her big sister who had set the ball in motion, dislodging her own inertia.

When Nadine had arrived home from Thailand on the evening of her thirty-sixth birthday, she had meant it as a surprise for her sister. She had checked herself out of the facility early. It had done everything it could for her. Apart from Boof's painful sounding barks, the house had been silent when she had been dropped off by the Uber from the airport. Inside, she had found the expected batch of homemade rocky road in the pantry – it was inconceivable that her sister would forget – but no Sarah.

Her sister had only returned late that night. Nadine had found her in the kitchen discarding a pair of disposal gloves, and washing out what looked like a Tupperware container. Sarah had been shocked to see her, and a tad flustered. But she had recollected herself, greeting Nadine and taking her in her arms.

The sun had barely risen the next morning, when Sarah had entered her room, shaking Nadine gently awake with a mug of hot coffee, and launching into the story of where she had been the night before. Between sips of Nescafe, Sarah had calmly confessed to all that had happened in Ant's apartment.

Nadine had listened speechless, as if submerged in a dream, as Sarah had laid everything out, explaining that they would need to keep her arrival back in Esserton a secret, at least for the time being. *We need to do something about your hair.*

For all Nadine's 'anger as therapy' bravado in Thailand, she had only succeeded in enacting her vengeful fantasies in long, rambling letters to her sister, and later in tearful rages over the phone. She had been playacting, she realised, but Sarah… Sarah had been willing to take the next step. With cool, steely resolve, she had stepped up to lance that source of pain from Nadine's life. As an ultimate act of sisterly love and solidarity, to make up for all the years when she hadn't known, and hadn't been able to provide comfort.

And though she hadn't said it outright, her meaning had been clear. *If you have unfinished business with Marcus, I'll support you through it.* And it had instilled her with the courage she had needed. An instant surge of powerful confidence that had burned purpose in her veins and carried her through. She had thought it was Marie who had started her down this path, but she realised with a start that it had been Sarah all along. Her sister who had always been there in the background, supporting her when she had fallen, picking up the bills, pouring her love into those goddamn baked goods that she forced on Nadine, because she didn't know how else to help.

Again, she told herself it was not a good idea to be here. She would be leaving traces in each of the rooms. All the things Sarah had told her not to do. Her sister would not be pleased. But then, she wouldn't be telling Sarah about this little detour inside Marcus's house.

The empty house had been too tempting. She couldn't leave without stepping inside. To walk around and see how he lived. And then she had seen the bunk beds. The ones she had once slept in with her sister. Slipping onto the lower mattress, it had felt like she was sixteen again, dreaming and planning. Her whole future ahead of her. She didn't feel bad for Marcus's boys. She had heard from Sarah how Marcus was treating his young sons and his wife, Fiona her old babysitter. It was yet another reason that confirmed this was the right thing. Not just for her, but for everyone.

She had been surprised at how easy it had all been. Sidling up to him at the Cresty and starting up a conversation. The fact that he had no compunction about trying to pick up the ex-girlfriend of his best friend, who had been buried less than a day – a woman he had assaulted in the past, no less – told Nadine exactly what she needed to know. He had not changed. If anything, he had got worse with age. Entirely self-absorbed, and thinking with his dick at all times.

She had fed him a line about rabbit shooting. How Ant had never been much of a shooter and how for so long she'd wanted to give it a try. He had jumped at the idea. Sarah had briefed her well.

When she arrived, he'd been easier to manage than she had imagined. He was already two sheets to the wind, having spent the whole afternoon on the beers. There was plenty of evidence scattered about on his front deck. He insisted on getting the ute out and running it the short distance to the back paddock, so they had the benefit of his spotlight for their shooting session. In the cab, he was legless and slopped most of the contents of his beer down the front of his singlet as he tried to slurp and drive at the same time. She almost fell out of the ute in her haste to get out when he lurched to a stop.

'Meet you at the fence,' she called out, trying not to visibly shudder as she walked ahead. In the car, Marcus removed his beer-stained top entirely before stepping out, leaving it scrunched in a ball in the driver's seat.

'A bit wet.' He winked at her.

He turned on the floodlights and followed her, stumbling slightly, rifle in one hand and a new can of beer in the other. A half-dozen bright eyes shone from the empty paddock. Sarah was right, his land was overrun with the creatures. Marcus joined her at the fence line.

'Here. Show me what you've got,' he said, holding out the rifle.

The physical closeness of him, his bare chest slicked with sweat and beer, and the sheer bulk of him made her freeze for a moment. Just like all those years back.

'You know how to handle a gun, right?' Marcus smirked. And she could tell he was laughing at her. Playing with her.

'I can manage,' she said flatly. Accepting the gun, she felt a shiver run through her at the weight of it and the feel of the smooth, worn surface of the stock.

'Just hold it steady. It's easy as.' Marcus smiled again, mistaking her reaction for nerves. But that wasn't the reason she had shivered. He had handed the weapon straight to her and it was all on her now.

She positioned the stock firmly to her shoulder. A practice shot. She wasn't aiming for anything in particular. Just getting a feel for the rifle.

She fired, missing by several feet, a rabbit diving easily out of the way.

Marcus laughed. A loud, raucous sound. 'Oh, babe, you're fucking terrible.'

She stood stock-still at that word. He had called her that once before.

'Give it here. I'll show you how it's done,' Marcus slurred, his hands grazing her shoulder.

'No.' She recoiled from his touch, stepping back and creating a space between them. 'Don't fucking touch me.'

'Hey, now, little girl. Let's not do anything stupid,' he said, placing his beer can on top of the fencepost and beckoning for her to return the gun.

'Do you remember what you did?'

'What?' He was thrown by her change of tone.

'At your eighteenth birthday. The last time you called me that – *babe*.'

'You want me to remember something from that long ago? All right, darling. I'll play your game. What don't I remember? You tell me.'

'I kept your fucking secret all this time. I could have destroyed you. And your fucking father. Do you think anybody would want to know you, or be your mate, or give you a job, if they knew? Do you think your Hollywood dad would want to know you if he knew the truth?'

'What truth? What the fuck are you talking about, you stupid mole? We had sex. What do you want, a fucking present?'

'It wasn't just sex and you know it.'

'Fuck off with this shit. It was a bit of fun. You wanted it, and don't pretend you didn't. Otherwise, why'd you come home with me? Why'd you lie down on my bed?'

'I said no. I asked you to stop.'

'Right, I'm over this shit. You're out. Give me back my gun and fuck off home, little girl.'

He stepped towards her but stopped short when she swung the gun barrel to face him.

'Admit what you did and I'll walk away. You need to understand what that night did to me. What it did to my life.'

'Are you for real? You need to take responsibility for your own life, girlie. You can't hang all your fucked-up druggie shit on me.'

She fired. A whip-like sound scissored the air as the rifle butt snapped back against her shoulder.

Marcus was thrown to the ground by the shot, falling half on his back and half on his side. Red bloomed across his chest, the look of stunned surprise on his face changing to a half-strangled cry of pain. His leg jerked, the frayed cuff of his gym shorts getting hooked on the barb of the fence wire.

She watched, frozen to the spot, half fascinated and half horror-filled, unable to move or make a sound. She could only stare as Marcus slowly gurgled his last breaths, his eyes turning from wet fear to glassy stillness.

She didn't know how long she stood there until her brain snapped back to life. She needed to make this look like something other than it was. Just like she had discussed with Sarah. She moved quickly to the ute, and standing by the open driver-side door, she faced the paddock beyond and fired one… two… three rounds into the empty pasture. If Marcus had been shooting rabbits alone at night, he probably would have done it from the comfort of his ute, where he could manoeuvre the spotlight. But he had obviously gone near the fence line for something, maybe to relieve himself? He was drunk and not concentrating. Maybe he had tripped on the rutted, uneven ground or had tried to climb through the fence while carrying his loaded gun, accidentally discharging it. It was plausible. Rural firearm accidents happened all the time.

She quickly wiped the rifle stock, barrel and trigger with the front of her T-shirt, and placed it on the ground between Marcus's body and the fence line. She paused, chewing her lip, thinking. She tried manoeuvring his right hand to press his fingerprints on the trigger. But it was too awkward and her hands were trembling too much. It would have to do.

At the ute, she wiped the doorhandle inside and out on the passenger side. She and Sarah had discussed this at length. If the police did happen to find some unknown prints in the car or on the gun, the chances were low that they'd be able to link them back to her. No one else knew of her connection to Marcus or about her plans tonight.

Nadine rose from her childhood bunkbed, a strange lethargy marking her movements. She felt a twinge on her shoulder where the rifle recoil had struck her. She knew she would find a bruise there tomorrow. She needed to get back. Sarah would start to worry if she was away too long. She wandered back out of the house and onto the front landing. Rather than making for her car, she walked around the side of the dwelling towards the rear paddock. A sudden compulsion to make sure that he was, in fact, dead. That it hadn't all been a dream.

At the fence line, she looked down at his face. Even in death his expression had settled into a sneer. She kicked him. A hard, satisfying thwack into his buttocks. Again and again and again. This wasn't part of the plan and she wouldn't be telling Sarah, but God it felt good. With one final hit, she turned and walked back to her car.

43

'Do you remember this song?'

The nostalgic bittersweet strains of 'These Days' by Powderfinger rose from the car's CD player. Nadine had got sick of the radio and reached into the glove compartment to pull out an old compact disc.

'It was one of Ant's favourites, remember?'

Luke did remember. All three of them – Ant, Luke and Marcus – had listened to the band on repeat. They had saved up and travelled to the Gold Coast to catch the band at Big Day Out, singing and swaying inside the massive beast of a crowd, loving every minute of it. At sixteen, they had been as tight as any three friends could be who knew jack shit about the world and about themselves.

'It's one of his old playlists. A burnt disc. Remember when that was a thing? God, I feel old. Sarah swiped it for me from one of the packing boxes in Frank's house that's got all of Ant's stuff.' Luke didn't reply. He loved this song, but listening to it now in this car with Nadine, the lyrics felt almost portentous. Like Nadine somehow was playing her swansong. Declaring to the world that her life hadn't panned out the way she had expected, so why should everybody else's.

A foreboding, keen and sharp, was building inside him with every kilometre they travelled. Try as he might, he couldn't get a proper reading on her. Was it all a bluff, a puff of bravado designed to scare the shit out of him, in which case it was working, or had she already unravelled too far to pull back now?

The evening had dipped into dusky twilight. The car sped along the endless bitumen of Tweed Valley Way, the speedometer climbing. Apparently, they were heading to Kingscliff, where Sarah had found a restaurant that served excellent khao soi, the Northern Thai noodle soup she had discovered in Chiang Mai. Outside, the Tweed River flew past his window, hugging the road in a grey-brown blur, only a thin strip of green and a spindly metal safety barrier separating the water from the asphalt.

Nadine sang along to the words with her eyes closed, oblivious to his discomfort or maybe entirely aware.

A truck zoomed past on the opposite side of the road and Nadine's eyes sprang open just in time. She turned the steering wheel, quickly correcting their path, and winked at him.

'Enjoying yourself, Lukey? This is nice, isn't it, getting to spend time together like this? Just two old friends shooting the breeze.'

'What exactly do you want from me, Nadine?'

'I want you to prove to me that you're not an arsehole. It turns out, I have a finely honed fuckwit gauge, through years of practice. Marcus, unfortunately, didn't make the grade, although that shouldn't be a surprise to anyone.'

'So, it was you that night. You killed Marcus.'

'And what if I did, Luke? People kill for such stupid reasons. Rash, spur-of-the-moment impulses. But Marcus? He had years to become a better human, to learn from his mistakes. And he chose to use that time to keep hurting his wife and his kids. Marcus had his chance.'

Luke's thoughts raced, one eye on the road but mainly trying to figure out what the hell he was supposed to have done, and how to talk her down. Marcus... well, Marcus had clearly done something unforgivable. He had assaulted Nadine. That much was clear. He didn't want to believe it of his old school friend, but the fact that it didn't surprise him said it all. When had it occurred, he wondered, and what did it all have to do with him?

As if he had said the words out loud, Nadine spoke. 'I remember you at Marcus's eighteenth. You and Ant. You were both off your faces with your tongues down a couple of chicks' throats. You both looked like you were trying to eat their faces off.' She cackled. 'At the time, Marcus appeared the most self-controlled of the three of you. Ha! How fucked up is that?' Again she laughed, a hollow sound. 'You know what happened, don't you?'

He blanched, and she turned on him, taking her eyes off the road so that his feet reached in vain for an invisible brake. 'Don't give me that face,' she shouted. 'It took me ages to remember. But it was you on the couch when I left the apartment. You were just outside his room. You must have heard. And yet, you did nothing. Nothing at all.'

And all at once, Luke was back there. Seventeen years stripped away in an instant. His awkward fumbling with the girl he had met at Marcus's party. What was her name? He couldn't even remember. Being firmly but gently rebuffed; her breath warm on his skin as she had giggled goodbye outside the venue. He had staggered back to the unit Eric Rowntree had rented for them, alone. Marcus had been crouched by the kitchenette raiding the mini-bar when Luke had stumbled in. He remembered blurting out to his friend that his date had not wanted to come home with him. Marcus had commiserated, berating the girl as a prick tease, and tossing Luke a miniature bottle of tequila. Luke had skolled it in one and collapsed onto the couch, not even making it to his bedroom.

The next thing he knew it was morning and Ant was shaking him awake bearing the gift of a McDonald's breakfast. He remembered Marcus emerging from his room and bragging about scoring with a girl. He'd thought at the time that his friend had just been lying, unable to stand the fact that of the three of them, only Ant had got lucky. But now it seemed that there had been a girl in Marcus's room that night: Nadine.

'Is it all coming back to you?' Nadine asked, an edge to her voice. 'You know, for ages I didn't blame you. I excused your behaviour. I told myself that you hadn't known. That you had been asleep on that couch. That you probably hadn't heard anything of what was happening, right next door—'

'It's true. I didn't know. I was passed out on the couch. I swear, I didn't hear anything—'

'But would you have done anything even if you had?' she snarled. 'That's what I ask myself now. Would you have interrupted your best friend's fun? Would you have stepped in to check what was actually happening. Or would you have told yourself that it was probably nothing. That it was none of your business? That it was just a bit of rough play.' Again she faced him, unheeding of the road. 'I've learned so much about you these last few days, Lukey. Here I was thinking you were different from the other two. Imagine my disappointment when I realised that you're just the same. Just one of the boys.'

He stared at her, spluttering out half-words that were no more than sounds.

'I... I... what?' She mocked him. 'C'mon, then, Lukey. Spit it out.'

Luke swallowed. 'Nadine, I swear to you. I didn't hear what was going on that night between you and Marcus. I didn't even know he had someone in his room.' He hesitated, trying to find the words that would defuse the situation. 'You're right, I don't know how I would have reacted or if I would have done anything. I was young and stupid. I was—'

Nadine held up her hand to silence him.

'Shh, this is my favourite bit.'

She threw her head back and sang over the top of Bernard Fanning's reedy, melancholic voice about life and control slipping away.

'Nadine, you have to stop,' he blurted as the car drifted dangerously to the left. 'What about Sarah? She wouldn't want you doing this.' It was a stab in the dark. A desperate plea.

Her eyes snapped open. 'Not everything I do has to be okayed by Sarah,' she said, something flaring in her expression. Irritation and a hint of defiance.

Luke didn't have time to figure out what she meant because in that instant his eyes caught movement on the road. A man in a pushie was riding along the metal safety barrier with no night light or helmet, and Nadine's attention was still focused on Luke.

'Look out!' Luke reached over and jerked the steering wheel so the car swung away from the cyclist, straying into the opposite side of the road.

'What the fuck are you doing?' Nadine shoved Luke's hand from the wheel just as the headlights of a ute reared up in front of them. The oncoming vehicle screamed its horn, and Nadine snapped the wheel back. The Lancer overcorrected left and clipped the safety barrier. The car's undercarriage seemed to catch on the end of the metal barrier, causing it to spin wildly, screeching several metres up the road and slamming into a power pole on the driver's side.

It was as if the world was suspended, a slow ticking of seconds as though time itself was mired in treacle. And then, without warning, it surged back into life like someone had turned on the volume from mute to max in an instant. All Luke felt was pain. His right side screamed like it was on fire and it hurt to move in any direction.

He turned with difficulty to check on Nadine. She was motionless, knocked out and trapped by the crushed front portion of the car, which had caved in on impact and a partially deployed airbag.

'Nadine, are you okay?' There was no answer. His right arm was too painful to move. Luke twisted his body so he could reach her with his left hand. He thought he could feel her breathing, the faint exhalation of air. *She was alive.*

Outside, he could hear shouts and the sound of people running. Passing motorists who had stopped to assist.

'Here,' he called out. 'We're in here.'

Someone wrenched open the passenger door, which was stuck shut, and he stumbled out, rolling onto the hard bitumen.

In the distance, he could hear the wail of an ambulance on its way, or maybe it was the police. Pulling himself up into a sitting position on the kerbside, the first person he thought of was Kate. He took out his mobile and dialled his sister's number.

44

Saturday – three days before Christmas

The air felt thick and weighed down by smoke as Kate, along with Geoff, joined the mass of mourners gathered around an internment site at the Casino Lawn Cemetery. Bushfires were raging to the south near Busbys Flat and in the west at Tenterfield, and the skies were tinged with a grey patina. It felt like the whole world was about to explode into flames, in anger or sadness or a bit of both.

A temporary gazebo had been erected above the gravesite where Darnley's coffin stood adorned with flowers. Discreet green curtains covered the casket-lowering apparatus, so that its metal frame and the freshly dug soil below remained shielded from the mourners. A framed photo that showed Darnley smiling in full police uniform stood atop the casket, like some sick joke. Kate rubbed the top of her sternum, a habit she had picked up in the last few days, trying to loosen the hard ball of grief that seemed to have got stuck there since she had found out about Darnley. Geoff reached for her hand and stilled her involuntary movement.

A few minutes ago, the air had rung with bagpipes as six pall-bearers had borne the casket from the hearse to the graveside: Darnley's two younger brothers, his brother-in-law, his best friend from his academy days, Esposito and Josh Ellis. The cemetery was a mass of blue. Police colleagues who Darnley had worked with across his career had turned out to pay their respects, alongside fellow officers from Esserton: Harris, Grant and Roby. The latter having returned from leave in time for the funeral.

Kate understood that the commissioner and other police representatives had offered to speak at the service, but that these offers had been refused politely by the family. There would be time for public tributes at the police memorial to be held at Tweed Heads in the new year, to commemorate the life and service of the man. This graveside service was a private affair specifically requested by Darnley's parents to allow close friends and family and their son's police colleagues, *the extended family*, to grieve away from the media spotlight.

Darnley's body had been brought back to rest in his home town of Casino, where he had been born and raised, and where he had first met Vanessa and convinced her to go out with him on a date. The service was being overseen by the family priest, the same soul who had baptised Darnley some forty-eight years ago. Kate wondered how much involvement Vanessa had had in the arrangements. Had she been too grief stricken to care about the minutiae, or had she given way to Darnley's parents out of love for her husband's family? Did it even matter in the end?

The aging and diminutive priest, with wisps of threadbare hair that fringed an otherwise perfectly bald scalp, spoke into the microphone, the strength of his voice belying his age. He spoke of Darnley, of the boy he had been and the man he had become. Of youthful football matches, skiving off school in his teenage years, of finding his feet in the police force, and later meeting his match and a safe harbour in Vanessa and his two girls. Amplified by the microphone, his voice carried through the crowd, strangely melodic and calming. A voice of comfort and reason.

Kate searched for Vanessa among the people seated in fold-out chairs set out for family and elderly mourners at the front. Vanessa was sitting very still in an elegant grey shift, her face half shielded by oversized sunglasses. She looked brittle enough to shatter at any moment. Her two adult daughters sat on either side of her, both in simple maxi skirts and dark blouses. They each held onto one of their mother's hands, as if they could physically imbue her with the strength to get through this. Their faces were locked in grief, both trying to hold it together for their mother. Kate remembered that feeling well. For this family, Christmases would forever more be marked by this loss.

Darnley's parents – Ken and Elsbeth – sat to the right of Vanessa and her daughters. They seemed much like Vanessa, utterly depleted, with the look of people for whom every tiny movement – sitting, smiling, breathing – was an effort. The row behind was taken up by Greg's three younger siblings, their spouses and children. Kate, along with other mourners, formed an untidy semicircle in the grass around the family. People fanned themselves with their printed orders of service, chasing away flies and trying to cool down damp brows and necks. A woman in heels tried to discreetly extricate herself from a soft patch of grass that she had sunk into. At the back of the crowd, a handful of uniformed officers from the local station stood guard, keeping out the media as a mark of respect for the family.

The priest finished his address not with a passage from the bible but with the lines from a poem – 'Most Importantly Love' by the Canadian-Indian poet Rupi Kaur. As the haunting lines of the poem reached the mourners, unadorned by religious symbology or empty words of comfort, speaking only the simple truth that in the end nothing mattered but the love you left behind, beyond wealth or possessions or status, Kate suddenly appreciated why Darnley's family had requested this man of God to be their son, husband and father's final caretaker. He had known Darnley, and had understood instinctively what Vanessa and the family needed at this moment.

A sob broke from her and she shook with grief as Geoff held her close.

The priest stepped away from the lectern, a sign that it was time for mourners to pay their last respects to the deceased.

One by one, Darnley's family stood and walked up to the coffin, placing something on the casket to say goodbye, a small memento or spray of flowers. Vanessa didn't make any offering, only resting her head against the coffin for a few seconds, and reaching out to retrieve her husband's photo. She waited for her daughters, who both placed folded notes on their father's casket, before walking away as a group. They stood to the side, watching as each of the mourners took their turn. Kate stood up to place a small envelope of her own. She had visited Darnley's favourite café in town and asked for a few beans of his favourite blend, tucking it into the envelope with a note. Wherever he was, at least he would have his favourite brew with him.

'I'll see you, buddy,' she said softly, placing a gentle hand against the timber.

She tried to catch Vanessa's eye, but she didn't look her way. A wave of sadness washed over Kate. Did Vanessa also blame her and Luke for what had happened to her husband? Kate wasn't surprised, but it didn't stop it hurting any less.

The line of mourners had come to an end. The priest recited the familiar lines of committal, invoking ashes and dust, and making the sign of the cross over the casket. The funeral director pressed a button on the platform, and the casket began its slow descent as 'Hallelujah' by Leonard Cohen, one of Darnley's favourite musicians, played in the background.

In the end, they didn't stay long. Vanessa and her daughters were immediately surrounded by a circle of friends and well-wishers, and it was obvious when Kate got close enough to say goodbye that the ease that had existed previously between them had vanished. Vanessa was grieving and there was no space in that darkness for logic or explanations. Greg's daughters at least returned her hugs, the eldest, Lillian, with a fierce warmth.

'Mum just needs some time,' she whispered into Kate's cheek.

Kate was grateful for small mercies.

They stopped to speak with Esposito and Josh on their way out. Kate caught Esposito's quick scrutiny of her husband, taking his measure as he shook Geoff's hand. Geoff was oblivious and Kate concentrated on greeting Josh.

'You all right?'

Josh shrugged, his face tight. The service hadn't been easy on any of them.

'When will you be heading back to Byron?'

'Not for a few weeks yet, I don't think.' He glanced at Esposito as he replied.

Kate nodded. She knew there was still a mountain of tasks ahead of them. Luke was no longer a person of interest in the investigation; however, the case had morphed into a complex inter-jurisdictional enquiry involving the NSW State Crime Command and the Queensland Police. No doubt, Esposito would want Josh to remain on the team for as long as possible to assist with the workload.

Sarah Osborne had confessed to the murders of both Ant Reed and Marcus Rowntree. Kate was surprised that Sarah had rolled the dice of admitting to Ant's death. The circumstances of that case still pointed overwhelmingly to suicide, and she had to know that without a confession a murder charge would be difficult to prove. However, Nadine being in the country at the time of Ant's death and the revelation that she often impersonated her sister with the aid of a wig, had likely swayed Sarah's decision.

So far, only a single set of CCTV footage from the night of Ant's death had been uncovered by Boondall Police – unsurprising, given the elapsed time. It showed a fair-haired woman entering Ant's apartment building, but the poor resolution meant that it was impossible to determine definitively which of the sisters had been captured by the footage. Sarah had clearly made a preemptive play to get the focus off her sister, even though the police had barely begun questioning Nadine.

Nadine remained in hospital, recovering from the multiple injuries she had sustained from the car accident with Luke. It was a miracle that neither had suffered worse effects, given the speed at which they had been travelling. She still felt a rush of fear when she contemplated how things could have ended for Luke. The front driver's side of Nadine's Mitsubishi had borne most of the damage as a result of the vehicle spinning and colliding into the electricity pylon on its right side. The collision force and dashboard crumpling inwards had resulted in fractures to Nadine's cheekbone, forearm and a crushed knee cap, as well as severe concussion, and contusions to various parts of her body. While less serious, Luke also sported a cavalcade of trauma from whiplash to broken ribs and multiple fractures to his right wrist.

Nevertheless, Luke had been well enough after a few days to hobble into the station to provide a statement. The joint statements by Luke and Kate of their respective encounters with the Osborne sisters had allowed for warrants to be granted to examine Sarah Osborne's property, various articles of the sisters' clothing and shoes, as well as their vehicles. The forensic searches so far had uncovered traces of blood on the toe cap of one of Nadine's joggers, as well as inside the centre-console storage compartment of Nadine's Mitsubishi, which had remained mostly intact in the crash. Esposito had pulled some strings at the labs, and the preliminary results on both samples had come up as matching Marcus's blood type. Two sets of fingerprints lifted from inside Marcus's kids' bedroom had also come back as a positive match to Nadine's prints.

The bedclothes from the bunk beds, including the rust-coloured stain found on the pillow in the bottom bunk, had been removed for further analysis. The running theory was that it was Marcus's blood, possibly transferred onto the bedclothes by Nadine. They were yet to ascertain what she had been doing in the boys' bedroom. DNA tests were in train and a warrant had been granted to medically examine and photograph Nadine's right shoulder and forearm for any existing injuries from before the car crash, such as old bruising consistent with the recoil of a rifle butt. Luke's hire car, meanwhile, had been cleared by forensic services. While his clothing remained in the queue for examination by the labs for elimination purposes, the focus of the investigation had moved on.

Kate understood that Sarah was claiming ownership of Nadine's blood-stained trainers as the sisters shared the same shoe size, and was insisting that she had driven Nadine's Mitsubishi to Marcus's on the night of his death. Kate knew that once Nadine was well enough to be questioned, the investigating team would be pitting the two sisters against each other to gain convictions against both women. However, if Nadine held her nerve, there was a good chance that Sarah would get her wish and save her sister from imprisonment as a final act of love before she passed away.

Seeing her childhood friend being taken into custody had cost Kate dearly. She had done exactly what Sarah had expected her to, but she had never had less appetite for the process.

'Are you both heading to the wake?' Esposito asked.

Darnley's family had organised a reception at the local club. Kate knew it would be packed, and it wasn't something she was up for today.

'No, I think we're going to head,' she said, nodding her farewells to her boss and Josh. Suddenly, she wanted nothing more than to be away from her police colleagues.

'See you on Monday, Kate. Good to meet you, Geoff.'

Geoff grinned on the way to the car, bumping her gently on her side. 'I think your boss has a crush on you.'

Kate rolled her eyes. 'Don't be silly. He does not.'

'Why is that silly? You're sexy as. Why shouldn't he have a crush on you?'

She bumped him back in response.

'Just as long as you don't have any feelings back,' he said lightly.

'Of course not. Why would I when I have you?'

'A very good point.' He kissed her, a soft caress on her lips.

'C'mon, you.' She grinned at her husband. 'We better get back before the kids get the better of the boys.'

'It's literally *Three Men and a Baby.*' He laughed, clicking the key fob to unlock their car.

'Plus Archie,' Kate said, getting in.

Gray, Caleb and Luke were on babysitting duty, so God knew what they would be coming home to. Of all of them, she trusted Caleb the most to keep the kids safe and the house still standing. Luke had decided to stay on for another couple of weeks, until his injuries were on the mend. The whole ordeal had seemed to heal something between Kate and her brother, or at least to plaster enough Band-Aids on the wound to afford them a place to begin again. Things were far from perfect, but they were talking. About Nadine and Marcus and about Payton Cavanaugh.

According to Luke's lawyer, there had been some recent promising developments with her brother's image-abuse case. Sydney digital forensics had uncovered a whole stockpile of unsavouriness while digging into Tristan Gill's digital history, from hardcore pornography to other apparent instances of online abuse involving intimate images with women he had befriended on social media. After speaking with Gill's lawyers, Ramsay was quietly confident that Tristan was close to cutting a deal with Sydney City PAC. Admitting to his real role in forwarding on the recording from Luke's phone and in sharing the video, in exchange for a plea bargain and the downgrading of his charges.

Only time would tell, but for now, Luke hadn't made any firm plans for the future. It felt good to have him home in Esserton, and Archie in particular was enjoying more uncle–nephew time. And it would be good to have the whole family under one roof for Christmas. She had already spoken to Scottsdale about the possibility of Aunty Iris visiting for a few hours on Christmas Day, if she was feeling up to it.

In the car, they travelled in silence, each busy with their own thoughts.

Seeing Vanessa and her daughters today, their lives destroyed in an instant, had crystallised something in Kate. Something that had been growing within her for months.

'Hey, what would you say if I took some extended leave? Maybe even take the time to explore other options.'

Geoff looked at her. 'What do you mean, other options? Like another job?'

'Would that be so bad? I could look at other roles within the police. Retrain as a police instructor, or maybe study in a related field.'

Geoff took a deep breath, his eyes returning to the road. 'Actually, I've been trying to find the right time to tell you. I heard back about that position.'

'Oh my God. What did they say?'

'That the job's mine if I want it. They made an offer. The only thing is, it's right down south. Like, Sydney south.'

Their eyes met and she grinned at him. 'Right, I guess we have some decisions to make.'

Author's Note

The events and characters in this novel are fictional. Whilst some real-life localities are referred to, the township of Esserton, set in the Northern Rivers of New South Wales on Bundjalung Country, is a fictional place that exists only in the author's imagination. This novel was written on Dharawal Country.

Acknowledgements

To Alex Adsett for your enthusiasm, friendship and unending support. Thank you especially for all your behind-the-scenes magic in finding a home for Kate Miles in the UK.

To my publisher, Anna Valdinger, for your trust. There were some very sketchy moments in the evolution of this manuscript and you never stopped believing in it. Thanks for being so patient as I worked through this one.

Forever grateful to the team at HarperCollins Australia for taking such good care of me. Thanks especially to Alexandra Nahlous, Lachlan McLaine, Abigail Nathan, Lucy Inglis, Kimberley Allsopp, Hannah Lynch and Stuart Henshall, and to the incredible marketing and sales teams. A very special thanks to the HarperCollins design studio for this stunning cover, which I love!

A huge thank you to Siân Heap of Canelo Crime and Bill Goodall of Bill Goodall Literary Agency for embracing the Kate Miles series and taking it to audiences in the UK. It honestly is a dream come true.

To the wonderful Australian writing community for your support and encouragement. This manuscript was by far, the hardest writing project I have embarked on to date. For the longest time it refused to do what I wanted it to. Two writing friends, Hayley Scrivenor and Alayne Campbell, took on the brunt of my anxiety, and this book would not be a thing if not for their generous feedback, patience and support. To Ashley Kalagian Blunt for being my go-to for anything industry related. Thank you for your always excellent advice. And to Vanessa

McCausland for a deep-dive conversation on writing at Ali Lowe's book launch, which was exactly what I needed to hear at the time as I struggled to find my way through this project. A huge shout out to the #debutbookgang who are still together and still cheering each other on through the highs and lows, and everything in between.

I relied heavily on the generous advice and feedback of Andrew Dante of the New South Wales police force and barrister Les Nicholls for police procedural matters, and Rexson Tse for information relating to autopsy, pathology and forensics. All errors and bending of facts to fit the story are entirely my own.

To all the readers, booksellers, librarians, podcasters, bookstagrammers, and reviewers who have made space for Kate Miles on your bookshelves and cheered her on – thank you!

As always to the McKenzie, Vitelli and Wijesekera/Wickramasinghe clans for all your love and support. To my sister-in-law who has been bugging me since the very first draft of manuscript one to include a dog in the series, you finally got your wish! And finally, to my personal cheer squad and support team, Scott, Harvey and Edie, thank you, always.